THE
SISTER'S CURSE

Also by Nicola Solvinic

The Hunter's Daughter

THE
SISTER'S CURSE

Nicola Solvinic

BERKLEY
NEW YORK

BERKLEY
An imprint of Penguin Random House LLC
1745 Broadway, New York, NY 10019
penguinrandomhouse.com

BERKLEY and the BERKLEY & B colophon are
registered trademarks of Penguin Random House LLC.

Title page art by Alex Stemmer / Shutterstock

Library of Congress Cataloging-in-Publication Data

Names: Solvinic, Nicola, author.
Title: The sister's curse / Nicola Solvinic.
Description: New York : Berkley, 2025.
Identifiers: LCCN 2024059085 (print) | LCCN 2024059086 (ebook) |
ISBN 9780593639757 (hardcover) | ISBN 9780593639771 (ebook)
Subjects: LCGFT: Detective and mystery fiction. | Novels.
Classification: LCC PS3619.O4396 S57 2025 (print) | LCC PS3619.O4396 (ebook) |
DDC 813/.6--dc23/eng/20241216
LC record available at https://lccn.loc.gov/2024059085
LC ebook record available at https://lccn.loc.gov/2024059086

Printed in the United States of America
1st Printing

The authorized representative in the EU for product safety and compliance
is Penguin Random House Ireland, Morrison Chambers, 32 Nassau Street,
Dublin D02 YH68, Ireland, https://eu-contact.penguin.ie.

To Jason, the keeper of the cats.

THE
SISTER'S CURSE

1

HANDFISHING FOR MONSTERS

"You can't keep running!"

No one really could. Truth always slithered to the light. It could wait underground for years—decades, even—exulting in darkness. But truth inevitably lifted its head and flicked its tongue at the sun. It was sometimes beautiful, often terrifying, and usually poisonous.

And painful as hell when it bit.

"It's all over, Rod!" I shouted as I ran into the gloom. The sun had set, the last golden light fading from the tassels of summer grasses.

The man I chased was just ahead of me, a stringy dude in a camo T-shirt and jorts. He looked back over his shoulder, fearful. If he had any sense, he would've gone to ground and crawled through tall grass and purple ironweed. But Rod Matthews hadn't thought straight in many years. Decades of bad decisions had led him to today, to being chased by the Bayern County Sheriff's Office, on charges of meth production. A whole nest of meth heads had been disturbed, scattering to the four winds, and Rod was my chosen quarry for the evening.

"I ain't goin' back to prison!" he shouted.

Rod put his head down and pumped his scrawny fists, running for what was left of his life. I hadn't judged Rod to be in great shape, but adrenaline was a helluva drug. I'd eventually wear him down and he'd collapse. Eventually.

I toyed with the idea of taking my time, of hunting him. Sometimes . . . I wanted to enjoy circling my prey, feeling the space of air in my lungs, and the tightness of my muscles ready to spring.

But I didn't take that slow luxury. I increased my pace. I'd take him down quickly, haul him back to his meth lab. Clean. Like the good cop I once was, and was trying to be again.

In my peripheral vision something rippled the grass, as if an invisible shark swam beside me. It moved parallel to me, surged past me.

My heart lurched into my mouth, shattering my single-pointed concentration. *No* . . .

Rod screamed and collapsed, disappearing from sight.

"Fuck. Fuck. Stop it!"

I rushed to the place where Rod had fallen. He was lying on the ground, whimpering. A large, spotted pit bull was sitting on Rod's chest, chewing his T-shirt and growling like thunder.

"Gibby! Gibby, get off!" I reached for my dog's collar.

Gibby huffed at me. He drew his lips back into what I interpreted to be a smile, but Rod took as an expression of utter bloodthirstiness. I pulled Gibby back. Gibby liked hunting, too, but his methods were more direct. I couldn't really fault him for that.

I turned Rod over, shoved him face down in the grass, and cuffed him. To my relief, I noticed no blood on either Rod or the dog—just lots of slobber.

I glanced at Gibby, who smiled and thumped his tail on the ground. "You were supposed to wait in the car with Monica."

I swore he laughed at me. I had no idea how he'd gotten out of the SUV; I'd closed the doors and left the AC running. Gibby was a rescue dog with a very questionable reputation. A year ago he was on death row with animal control for mauling a cop; I'd pulled some strings to get him released into my custody.

"You're under arrest for the manufacture, possession, and distribution of a Schedule II substance," I told Rod, rolling him over to search him for drugs and weapons. His pockets were full of foil-wrapped pills—likely pseudoephedrine—and a pop bottle half-full of liquid. I squinted at it. It was the wrong color for cola or piss. Likely, it was one of the precursor chemicals for meth production—acetone or ether. I stuffed the evidence into my pockets and hauled Rod to his feet. I read him his rights as we crossed back through the field, toward a distant barn. He'd lost a flip-flop somewhere in his attempt to escape, so I took it slow for his benefit.

Above us, starlings flew west to their nests, chattering to themselves. They clotted together in a murmuration, twisting and turning in a cloud of seething, chirping shadow. It never failed to amaze me how they could become something so much more than the sum of their feathered parts, and I wondered what invisible current drove them.

Rod hung his head and plodded along, ignoring the show in the sky. "I'm going back to prison."

"Probably," I agreed, one eye still on the sky.

"Can I cut a deal? What if I roll over on my brother, Timmy?"

"Depends on what you've got to say about Timmy. Is he in town?" Rod's brother was a well-known drug runner. He was well-known because he wasn't very good, and got caught with some frequency.

3

"He's back from Florida, with a trunk full of ketamine."

"A whole trunk full?" I was skeptical.

"He picked it up at the airport, with some dudes from Germany . . ."

We reached the barn, and uniformed officers took Rod from me. A row of Rod's buddies were sitting on the ground, their hands zip-tied behind their backs.

Captain Monica Wozniak grinned at me. "I see you found him."

"Rod or the dog?"

She winced in regret. "Sorry. I opened the door to grab my gear, and he was gone like a flash before I could get his harness on. He doesn't like being apart from you."

I stared down at Gibby, who was gazing upon me with enough adoration to cause even the stoniest heart to explode.

"What am I going to do with you and your separation anxiety?" I murmured.

I grabbed an evidence bag for the manufacturing paraphernalia from Rod's pockets. "Rod made off with some precursor ingredients."

"Great," Monica said. "Forensics will love to try to figure out what they're using to cook up smoky quartz."

A new permutation of meth had crept into Bayern County. Tweakers called it "smoky quartz," because it looked like little gray crystals. They would've been pretty in a rock collection but were a hazard out on the streets.

In the distance, I heard music, a woman singing. Probably a radio. Patrol cars were clustered around the old barn that Rod and his pals had been squatting in. But the music was coming from another direction, off to the east.

"Do you hear that?" I asked Monica.

"Hear what?" She frowned.

"Never mind." Maybe there were campers with a radio out there. "I'll be back . . . Gonna check to make sure Rod didn't drop any more evidence."

I waded back through the grass, toward the music trickling into my pulse and tightening my throat. I felt it then, the exact moment when the sun vanished and the light changed. Sunset. I turned west, to where the sun had dipped below the trees, gold melting into leaves and fading out. A brief flash of lurid green lit up the horizon. I held my breath as it flared and vanished, leaving the land in soft twilight.

The fabled green flash, a rare meteorological phenomenon. I hadn't seen it since I was a child.

———

"Don't make me go down there," I whispered.

I was maybe eleven years old, judging by the Wonder Woman Underoos I wore as swimwear. I sat on the edge of the three-foot-wide well, next to the still pump, feet dangling into the darkness. I could see something moving below me—could be water, could be snakes. My toes curled in fear.

"Quit whining and go down there," Mom snapped. She was standing in the grass in the fading light, one hand on her hip and the other holding the ember of a cigarette. "You're the only one small enough to get down there and see what's clogging the pump."

I flinched. This was my dad's domain, fixing things. But he and my mom had had an argument yesterday, and he'd taken off. "Can't we just wait for Dad?"

"No," she said quietly, a vicious smile on her lips. "We can't wait for him anymore. What if he never comes back?"

Fear trilled through me. I couldn't imagine my dad leaving forever. For a few days or weeks, sure . . . he did that sort of thing when he and Mom got into it. But I couldn't imagine him leaving me with . . . with her . . . forever.

She shoved at my shoulder with her espadrille-clad foot. I teetered, then fell in with a shriek.

I landed, sputtering, in black water up to my chin. My fingers brushed the muddy walls of the well. Evening light streamed in, in a circle above me, a diffuse light that did little to show me the PVC pipe reaching into the water beside me. My mom glowered at me.

I turned to the pipe, reaching down. I couldn't feel the end of it.

"It's too deep!" I called.

"You're not coming up until you find it."

I took a breath, closed my eyes, and went underwater. My hands followed the pipe down, down to where the debris trap had to be, somewhere . . . My fingers closed around mud and sticks clotting the end of the pipe. I flung the crud away . . .

Something brushed against my leg in the dark.

I screamed, my cry muffled in bubbles, and I clawed my way back up to the surface.

"Let me up! Let me up!" I blubbered. "There's something down there. There's—"

Mom reached for my arm and hauled me out. I didn't think she was that strong, but she tugged me up to the grass with little effort. I curled up in a ball and wrapped my arms around my knees.

Mom gazed into the well, the way she did when staring into her teacup, still and contemplative.

"Was it a snake?" I gasped.

"No," she said.

I felt it then, that moment when the sun disappeared. I'd always been able to feel that exact moment, even when I was indoors or under cloudy skies. The light changed that much. I gazed out at the fading sunset and spied the green flash.

I pointed to it excitedly. "Did you see that?"

Mom nodded, but her face was lined with tension. "I saw."

"What is it?"

She exhaled. "The green flash means that something woke up. Something bad. Something we don't wanna mess with."

"But what is it?" I had read entirely too many fairy tales. "Is it fairies?"

She gripped my arm and pulled me to my feet. "No. It's time for bed."

I frowned. It was barely dark, but Mom usually made me go to bed early. But this time I was ready to go, to get away from that claustrophobic well and that look in my mom's eyes.

———

My mom told many lies.

She had to, I think. She was married to a serial killer, the legendary Forest Strangler, who left a trail of deceit and bodies throughout Bayern County. While he lied about his whereabouts, who he'd seen, what he'd been doing. Pretty much everything.

But she'd lied to herself about what kind of evil slept under our roof, and she'd lied to the police about wanting to take care of me. She'd given me up for adoption as soon as my father had been charged and had disappeared into the night.

I'd worshipped my father when I was a little girl. I always thought of myself as my father's daughter in so many ways, even after I learned who he was and what he'd done. The forest spoke to me the way it spoke to him, and I felt its pull, that beckoning darkness. He'd lied to me the whole time. And I hated that.

And I was slowly beginning to hate him, for both what he did and the lies he told me.

I didn't know if my mom lied to me about the green flash. There was nothing in it for her to lie to me about it . . . so why would she?

As an adult, I saw a television meteorologist talk about how the green flash was a rare phenomenon that occurred when a clear sky acted as a prism under just the right conditions. The meteorologist showed some grainy cell phone footage of such a flash. When I was a child, the flash had been magic. As an adult, I was relieved to know that it was just a freak meteorological event, perfectly scientific and perfectly safe.

I supposed my mom was a liar about that, too.

Swallowing the lump of a memory, I turned to Monica, now fifty yards distant, to see if she saw, but her back was turned.

I inhaled, a whispering breeze stirring the grass in a circular pattern. It felt like something was on the move, like on those full-moon fall nights when the deer traveled miles.

At my side, Gibby whined.

I lowered my hand to his head. "We should go back." Some things in the world were not to be fucked with. This was probably one of them.

A woman screamed in the distance.

Instinct overrode my hesitation, and I burst into a sprint toward the scream. Grasses made *zip-zip* slashes against my jeans, and Gibby panted beside me. We raced across the field toward the distant cry.

"Help!"

The land was darkening by the time we burst out onto freshly mown grass, a full yellow moon rising in the east. A grand two-story brick house with a slate roof stood in the center of the lawn.

Old money, not new money. The slate was streaked from decades of acid rain, and wavy glass windows gazed down with black eyes.

A young woman, no more than sixteen, raced toward us. A brunette braid flopped over the shoulder of her T-shirt. She was wearing sandals and a long denim skirt.

"Are you the police?" Her fingers were knotted around her cell phone. "I just called 911."

I held up my badge. "I'm Anna. What's going on?"

"I'm Leah. The babysitter. I was watching Mason, and I . . . I can't find him. I . . ." Her face crumpled.

I took her by the shoulders. "It's okay. We'll find him. How old is he?"

"He's four. He's got blond hair, brown eyes. He's wearing a blue T-shirt with the Superman logo, and red shorts. Oh my God."

"Where did you last see him?"

"He was in the living room when . . . when I went to the bathroom. When I got out, he was just . . . gone."

"Show me." As we approached the house, I scanned the scene. I saw no cars whose drivers might have abducted him, heard no engines.

I spoke into the radio microphone pinned to my shoulder. "This is L4 at County Road 12. Report of a missing child."

"Roger that," Dispatch answered. "More units en route."

Leah covered her mouth with her hand. "My dad's gonna kill me."

Gibby gazed up at her sympathetically, doggie eyebrows working up and down.

As we reached the house, I saw that the back patio door was open.

"Leah, did you come out the front door or the back door?"

"The front door."

My gaze swept the manicured grass, punctured by severely pruned arborvitae and hydrangeas. Fireflies seeped up from the ground, casting fairy light over the scene. Bullfrogs twanged. Bullfrogs . . .

I froze. "Leah, is there water near here?"

"Um. Yeah. There's a stock pond." She pointed to the west.

Dread and intuition bubbled up in me. I sprinted toward the frog song, down an artificial slope to a pond reflecting the first stars prickling out of the night sky. Bullfrogs plopped into the water at my approach.

Something was floating on the surface. I could barely make it out underneath a sheen of algae.

Unthinking, I dived into the pond.

Cold water closed over me, shocking in the summer heat. I'd dived some in college, but I'd long forgotten the shock of cold water in an emergency. I pulled myself forward in the water, toward the middle of the pond. As I moved, algae covered me like a cloak, heavy on my shoulders, sliding through my fingers. It dragged at me, and I struggled to move.

I reached for a doll-like figure dressed in a blue T-shirt . . .

. . . but it was sucked beneath the water with a slurping splash, splattering my face with algae.

I kicked below the skin of algae, into the cold depths. My pulse beat like a drum in my ears. The sky above was a lighter darkness than the blackness below me. I flailed, searching for the child. I swept my arms before me, stirring up soft silt. I could see nothing, but I searched, hoping to hell that the child was close.

My fingers brushed against something fleshy, a limb. I wrapped my hand around it . . . a child's arm. It was heavy in my grip, and I pulled, swimming toward the surface.

But I couldn't pull the boy with me. It was as if he were caught in a steel trap. I pulled with all my might, lungs burning. My heel landed in the silt at the bottom of the pond, and I braced myself to tug him free of whatever held him fast.

I would not let this child go, I vowed.

I wasn't gentle. I ripped with all I had, heedless of dislocating or breaking limbs—those could be repaired; oxygen deprivation could be fatal.

Someone was laughing . . . but no sound could carry like that down here. Hypoxia must be causing me to dissociate.

Suddenly, the child's body was released, tumbling back on me. I reached for the dimness above and launched myself skyward.

My head broke the water's surface. I gasped, sucking in lungfuls of air, lifting the child with me. His body was limp and his eyes were closed, mouth slack. I shoved him into the crook of my arm, face up, and swam to the nearest shore.

Gibby barked frantically. He plunged into the pond and grabbed the sleeve of my shirt in his jaws, trying to drag me to safety.

I hauled the boy's heavy body through cattails to the bank. In the background, Leah screamed. I placed him face up on the grass and pressed my ear to his mouth, his chest. Nothing. He was cold and slack and unmoving.

But I did what I was trained to do. I laced my hands over his chest and pressed. Water poured from his mouth. I did it until the water stopped. I listened again. Nothing.

I continued chest compressions, knowing I could break ribs. Chest compressions, done correctly on an adult, let alone a child, could cause fractures, but I forced myself not to be squeamish. I counted, getting as close to a hundred beats per minute as I could. My CPR instructor had told me to compress to the beat of the Bee Gees' "Stayin' Alive," and I hummed as I exhaled.

The boy lay there. Algae dripped from his lip, and his eyes were closed and his fingers slack. Nothing. Nothing.

I don't know how long I did chest compressions. I worked until paramedics arrived to take over. I sat back on my ass in the grass, blinking stupidly.

Monica sat down beside me. "What happened?"

"I saw him . . . in the pond . . . His name is Mason." I looked back to where deputies were questioning Leah on the hill. She sat with her head on her knees.

The paramedics fitted a mask and bag over Mason's mouth to start breathing for him, then scooped him onto a stretcher. Mason looked incredibly tiny on the adult-sized stretcher as they ran him up the hill toward a parked ambulance.

I gazed at the pond, now still as a mirror. My skin crawled, and I shivered violently.

That child was in a bad way, and I needed to know why.

2

WARSAW CREEK

Waterlogged and stunned, I trudged up to the house as a black SUV pulled into the driveway, blocking the ambulance.

Car doors slammed, and a man shouted. These must be the parents. The father was wearing a sport coat and the woman was in a dress, but their clothes read more "business" than "date night." Leah must have called them.

"Where's my son?" The woman's fists were clenched, and I could see terror on her face.

I made my way past the flagstone walkway, past uplights casting shadows of Japanese maple branches on white-painted brick.

"You need to let the ambulance pass," I told the man.

The man turned his glare on me. His breath reeked of alcohol, but I wasn't about to try to pop him for a DUI tonight. "Do you have any idea who I am? I'm Jeff Sumner!"

The name didn't ring any bells. "There was an accident, in the pond—" I began.

The mother shouted at Sumner. "That stupid fucking pond! I told you that we didn't need that stupid fucking pond to impress your idiot fishing buddies!"

The husband wheeled on me. "Where's Leah? How in the hell did she let this happen? She was supposed to watch him!"

"Where's Mason?" the wife roared. Her terror was palpable. It took me aback. Maybe because my own mother never reacted that way when I got hurt as a child. Mom would've lit a cigarette and patted me vaguely before turning on the television.

A paramedic at the back of the ambulance shouted: "In here! One person can ride with us. Now, get that car out of the way!"

Sumner didn't budge. "What are you doing to him?"

"He needs a hospital!" the paramedic barked. "He's going to die if he doesn't get help."

Sumner shook his head. "We can't—"

His wife shoved him, hard. "Fuck that stupid church and its stupid rules! Our son is going to die if we don't get him help."

I stepped forward. "You can't obstruct an emergency vehicle."

Sumner growled, "I get to make the medical decisions for my son, and I don't believe in Western medicine to—"

"He's my son," the woman hissed. "He's my son and I'm giving permission for him to be given medical care. Get out of the way."

I grabbed the man's elbow. I was ready to arrest him if need be. "Sir, you have to let the ambulance pass."

Sumner shook my hand off and went to start up the car.

The mother scrambled into the back of the ambulance, breaking the heel of her shoe. She leaned over Mason, tearfully stroking his hand as the paramedics finished intubating him.

This display of emotion over a child was foreign to me. I wrapped my arms around myself. My father had loved me, in his way, but he was a monster. My mother . . . She never had.

My gaze fell on the child's foot, illuminated by the harsh ambulance lights. Scratches curled around his ankle, terminating at the sole of the foot. The blood there was red, fresh. If I hadn't felt something pulling on him in the water, I would've wondered if the boy had cut himself running into the pond.

I recalled the resistance I'd felt as I'd tried to haul him out of the pond. What had held him down? What—.

The doors slammed shut, and the ambulance, with full lights and sirens, howled up the driveway to the road.

The father lunged out of his SUV. "What the hell happened?"

I took a deep breath. "Mason was found in the pond, and he wasn't breathing. They managed to get his breathing going, but he needs the hospital. You should be there with them."

"How in the hell did this happen? Where's Leah?"

I lifted my hands in a calming gesture. "Leah is safe."

From the corner of my eye, I saw Monica escorting Leah inside the house. Sumner saw her, too, and barreled toward her.

"You were supposed to watch him!"

I got between Sumner and the babysitter, putting my hands on his chest. "Whoa. Take a deep breath, now."

He flung my hands aside and tried to shove past me. "I want to know what the hell she was doing if she wasn't watching my kid!"

I grabbed his wrist. "Mr. Sumner, I cannot allow you to talk with her right now."

That didn't stop him. He lurched forward, and I turned his arm behind his back. I hated having to do it; he was out of his mind with grief. Deputies converged and pushed him back.

Sumner bellowed: "Get out of here, all of you! This is my house. I pay for it and I'm in charge here."

"Mr. Sumner, I'm afraid that this is an active crime scene—"

He snarled at me, "Get the fuck out."

"That's not going to happen," I told him. "You need to calm down and go to the hospital to be with your son."

He struggled against me, then stopped.

"All right?" I said.

I released him and he shrugged away, casting off my hands in a sullen fit. He stomped off to his car, cranked the engine, and disappeared down the driveway.

I exhaled, relieved that he was gone.

I felt something leaning against my thigh. Gibby gazed up at me and whined. I absently rubbed his ears. In that moment, I felt leaden and cold, covered in algae.

Lights and motion blazed around me, and I felt myself receding from the churn and voices. I needed a moment to gather myself. Tonight had rattled me, and I felt myself mentally pulling away from the scene.

Gibby took my hand gently in his teeth and led me away to the quiet dark.

———

I drank coffee, sitting on the back patio of the house, with Gibby at my feet. Crickets sang, but the bullfrogs were silent. Gibby's ears were pressed forward, and he stared at the pond. I couldn't look away from it, either. My eyes followed each rill as if I expected the boy to climb out of it, whole and unharmed. Only a full moon danced on the surface. The morning news had reported that the summer solstice was tonight, the shortest night of the year. It felt far too long already.

I was scared. I was afraid of that green flash I'd seen, and of the memory of my mother that had come bubbling up from my subconscious. Here, in the dark, I felt as if I was in that liminal space that belonged to dreams and visions of my father: his mutterings of dark gods, his prolific murders, and the terror I felt when trying to make sense of it all.

I wasn't going back there, I vowed. I wouldn't.

"Lt. Koray."

I looked up. Deputy Detwiler, a fresh-faced guy who looked to be all of twelve, handed me another coffee. I took it gratefully.

"They're questioning Leah." He hooked a thumb through the French doors to the kitchen.

I nodded. I'd changed clothes, and I had dried off enough that my hair wouldn't drip on the travertine floors. I followed him into the kitchen, gleaming with stainless steel appliances and with a chandelier hanging over a granite island larger than a dining table. The house was at least a century old, but the interior had been gutted for modern amenities, the ceilings lifted with stylish beams. But there was still original plaster in places, and I could feel spots in the floor that weren't perfectly level. My initial impression was that the Sumners were the type who would build new, all-custom designs and bear none of the headaches of old construction blistering through copper pipes and horsehair plaster. I wondered what had drawn them to this place. Sentimentality?

Leah sat at a bar stool before the island, hands clasped in front of her. She twisted a small pearl ring on her left hand. Her tears dripped onto the granite. A bit of eyeliner had smudged beneath her eye. Poor kid.

Monica sat beside her, patting her back. "Deep breath. Just tell me what happened." She wasn't going to tell the girl that everything was okay, because there was no way it was ever going to be.

"Mason was playing with his Spider-Man in the living room." Leah sniffled, gesturing to the living room, where a whole bucket of large blocks had been dumped on the hardwood floor. A Spider-Man action figure lay in the center of the explosion of blocks. "I had to go to the bathroom, so I went down the hall . . ."

Light streamed from a half bath beside the kitchen. I peered into the bathroom. Water speckled the bottom of the glass vessel sink, and the hand towel was damp. That checked.

"I was only in there for maybe five minutes, tops."

"Did you have your phone with you?" Monica asked. Time flew if you were texting.

"Um. The family has a no-phones-except-for-emergencies rule."

"What if you need to call for help?"

"I did. They just tell me to put the phone on top of the refrigerator."

I made a mental note to check phone records to verify.

"What happened then? You were in the bathroom?"

"Yeah. I was washing my hands, and I thought . . ." She shook her head. "Never mind."

"You thought what?"

"It's stupid."

"Nothing is ever stupid."

Leah's brows drew together. "I thought . . . I heard someone calling my name. From outside."

"From the driveway?"

"No. I don't think so. I heard it through the window."

I ducked into the bathroom to inspect the window. It was too high for a young child to reach, but it was slightly open at the bottom. It hadn't rained recently, but the sill was wet. Not soaking wet, like after a storm, but there were droplets on the outside sill, and on the screen. Beyond the window was the pond.

"I got kinda creeped out and went to check on Mason. I came

out to the living room and didn't see him. I called his name, thinking he was playing hide-and-seek."

"Where did you look?"

"He likes to hide under his bed. I checked there first. Then the playroom . . ." She recited a list of places she'd looked.

"Did you think he could get outside?"

"No? I mean, I always make sure the doors are locked and the alarm is set when I'm here."

I crossed the kitchen to the door to the garage, where there was an alarm panel. I noticed that the readout said FAULT ZONE 16. I flipped open the panel and saw that zone 16 was labeled KITCHEN DOOR. That door had been open when I arrived.

"Did you have any trouble arming the system?" I asked.

"No. I always do it right when his parents leave."

Monica continued. "When did you call for help?"

"When I didn't find him, I called 911, and then his parents. I thought someone might have taken him." Her voice hitched.

Not an unreasonable thought. The Sumners were clearly wealthy. Someone could've abducted their child for ransom. Maybe someone tried to take him, he kicked up too much of a fuss, and his abductor threw him into the pond.

"How much time passed from when you realized he was missing and when you called 911?" Monica asked.

"Maybe . . . ten minutes? I don't . . . I don't know."

"What did you do after you called?"

"I went outside to wait for help."

"Did you go out the front door, or the back door, or . . . ?"

"Front door. I wanted to be able to flag them down in case they got lost. Then I saw the lady . . . the police lady coming through the field."

"Did Mason seem sick? Was he injured?"

"No, no . . . he was fine. He was playing with his toys."

I drifted into the living room. A massive leather sectional dominated the area before a stone fireplace. Family pictures were arranged on the cherrywood mantel. There were professionally taken pictures of Mason holding dinosaur plushies, candids of him at the zoo, and portraits of him with his family. His father was in his early forties, in a polo shirt and with an artificially white smile. Now that I saw him when he wasn't raging, he did look vaguely familiar, like I might've seen his picture on television. Mason's mother was fashionably dressed, with a very heavy ring set on her left hand. There were no siblings, but some extended family appeared in wedding pictures: grandparents and some aunts and uncles, it looked like. I counted ten groomsmen and ten bridesmaids arranged before an altar with a clergyman. It must've been a winter wedding, since the women all wore high-necked dresses with sleeves, but the bridal bouquet was full of summer flowers: lilies and dahlias.

I scanned the vacuum cleaner marks in the carpet. I imagined the Sumners had a cleaner, as there wasn't a speck of dust anywhere. I paused before the massive front door, frowning at something on the lintel above the door.

I donned gloves and reached for it. It was heavy, cold, and rough to the touch. I realized it was a rusted railroad spike, the kind used to keep tracks pinned to railroad ties.

In the distance behind the house, toward the pond, I glimpsed photography flashes. Though this was likely a tragic accident, there was still evidence to be recorded.

Just in case things were not as they seemed.

Monica led Leah to the door. "I'm going to take her to the station. I've called her father, and we'll meet him there."

"I've got this," I assured her.

It was weird that Leah hadn't called her father. She'd called 911. She'd called the Sumners, to tell them their son was hurt. But she hadn't called her parents. Hmm.

I watched from the living room window as Monica pulled away. I took pictures of my own . . . of the alarm-panel fault, toys on the floor, the railroad spike above the door. I directed evidence techs to dust the wet bathroom windowsill, the alarm panels, and the door latches.

I did a quick sweep of the house to make sure Leah hadn't left behind any evidence of alcohol or drugs, and that there wasn't an abductor hiding in a walk-in closet. The Sumners could afford to be minimalist. Their closets were empty of everything but well-chosen designer clothing, and there was no clutter. Trash cans were empty. The rest of the doors and windows were locked. I didn't see any way the boy could've exited the house except through the kitchen door. The garage was locked, and there were no other ways in or out. With the doors closed, the house smelled odd, like incense in a church. I found a bit of fragrant ash in a coffee cup in the kitchen sink. I smelled sandalwood in the cup, and it had a tiny burn mark inside it.

Slowly, law enforcement filtered away until I was left alone with Gibby. Gibby sat on the back patio, his ears twitching, staring at the pond, growling.

"Yeah," I said, "I felt it, too."

And I wasn't sure what to think about that uneasiness. Something wasn't right. Maybe my imagination had been sparked by the green flash that had opened a memory from my childhood. Maybe.

I walked down to the pond to convince myself that it was just an ordinary pond, the site of a tragic accident. It sure looked like it, full of cattails and algae. The frogs had found their voices again.

I looked past the pond, at the forest, orienting myself. Beyond, there was marshland, dried out from the drought we'd been having this summer, and there was a little creek, Warsaw Creek, which was a tributary of the Copperhead River. Evidently it wasn't picturesque enough on its own, necessitating a pond. This place was only a half mile down the road from the meth bust. That's the way it was in rural places: there were strict socioeconomic divisions via property lines. But the dark forest and the creek connected the upper crust and those who lived in the shadows of society.

I turned back toward the house. Something moved behind the trash cans, barely illuminated by the patio light.

What the hell was that?

I advanced on it. It twisted in the breeze, like a trash bag.

I captured it before it loosened free of the trash cans and skidded across the yard. It was fabric. It was some kind of a costume—a black hooded cape. The material was the kind I'd expect for a Halloween costume: cheap, filmy velvet. As I examined it, I saw a strand of long brunette hair inside.

It was probably nothing, blown in from the road. But I bagged it anyway, because it was weird and it had creeped me the fuck out.

On the way out, I paused at the end of the driveway. The rural mailbox was embedded in a stone pedestal—certain to keep mailbox smashers at bay. The mailbox's door was slightly open, and I squinted at it. The letter carrier would close it from force of habit. So would most homeowners—no one wanted rain to seep in and make an electric bill soggy.

With a pen, I opened the box all the way and shone my flashlight inside.

A skull stared back at me.

It wasn't human. Looked like a white-tailed deer skull. A doe's—no nubbins of antlers that wouldn't fit in the mailbox.

On its bleached forehead was the number ten. And a symbol.

I leaned close, peering at the symbol roughly drawn in black paint.

It was round, the outline looking like a snake. The snake's jaws clutched its tail in a perfect circle.

I wasn't sure what it was. But it sure looked like a threat.

3

FAMILIAR SPIRITS

It was almost three a.m. by the time I'd bagged the skull for evidence and left for home. I'd lifted from the mailbox some messy fingerprints that I wanted to preserve before weather got to them. I wasn't expecting much, but I'd compare those prints to the mail carrier's and the Sumners'. I had higher hopes for the skull itself, and would happily surrender it to Forensics to thoroughly comb over. The deer skull sat in a plastic bag on the back seat behind me, staring at me with missing eyes. Every so often, I'd glance in my rearview mirror to meet her black gaze. Gibby wouldn't look at her at all.

The crickets had quieted, and I drove with the windows down, relishing the cool darkness. The moon was setting, tangled in tree branches. I kept the radio on at low volume on a top-forty station, mostly because I didn't want to be alone with my thoughts. Gibby leaned his head out the window, eyes closed in bliss. I wondered if he imagined he was flying.

As I dipped into a valley on the two-lane road, I lost the station for a moment. Static crackled, and then a woman sang, eerily distant.

As I ascended the next rise, the radio station stabilized, and I was listening to a weather report on the drought afflicting Bayern County. No rain in sight.

I frowned. I was tired. I should go home, to bed.

Gravel crunched under my SUV's tires as I wound down my driveway to my house in the woods. No lights were on inside the bungalow or on the porch. The house was small by most standards—only one story, and one bedroom—but it was my little piece of silence away from the rest of the world.

I shut off the engine, listening to it tick in the dark. I didn't like how things had gone down this evening. I hadn't heard anything more about Mason. I pressed my head to the steering wheel. I wasn't the praying type, but I sure hoped the boy was going to be okay.

I opened the door, and Gibby scrambled over me and out to do his business beside a maple tree.

I drifted around the small area of grass that I bothered to mow. Behind the house, my boyfriend, Nick, had started a garden. He intended gardening to be an outdoorsy activity we could do together, growing orderly rows of potatoes, lettuce, tomatoes, and peppers. They looked wilted, so I turned on the hose to give them a splash.

In one corner of the garden, where he'd planted marigolds, he'd placed a flat, vaguely heart-shaped stone he'd found in the woods. I asked him about it. He said that this little spot was in memory of his mother. I watered the flowers dutifully, but I did my damnedest not to look at the stone, and to swallow the lump in my throat that rose when I did.

When I was satisfied that the garden wasn't going to die, I went back to the car, grabbed the skull, trudged up the squeaky wooden porch steps, and unlocked the front door. I didn't bother to turn the lights on for myself, but I'd been trying to remember to do so for Gibby's benefit, and for Nick's.

My house always smelled a bit mossy. Maybe I just really needed to clean the gutters, but it was a pleasant smell. It mingled with lemon-scented polish on secondhand furniture and the bowl of foraged black raspberries on the kitchen counter. I crossed scarred wooden floors through the kitchen to the living room, dropping my bags on the green velvet couch. Found treasures surrounded me, stones and feathers captured in jars and vases. The mantel was full of commendations and pictures of me in uniform—reminders of who I really was. Overseeing it all was a mounted deer head I'd picked up at a garage sale. Gazing serenely at my little kingdom, he cast his antlered shadow over me, thick and silent. He was different from the skull I'd found tonight. He was peaceful, protective. She was . . . dark. Chaotic. I put her on top of the refrigerator, away from Gibby's sight.

Gibby trotted inside, trailing a couple of moths, and buried his muzzle in his water dish. I opened a can of dog food, which he devoured greedily. He was still very food insecure—he'd eat anything put in front of him, and try to steal more. But his ribs were now encased in a nice layer of fat, and his speckled fur was glossy. Progress.

Gibby stayed with me, not with Nick. Nick enjoyed having a dog, but his shiny bachelor-pad condo wasn't exactly conducive to having one. Here, Gibby's nails could scratch up the floor; he could dig for stinky things in the yard and get bathed in my cast-iron bathtub. There was little fragile enough for him to break here, though, if I left him alone, I could anticipate the loss of a pair of shoes.

I showered off the scummy pond water. My fingers hesitated on scars crossing my ribs. I'd been shot once upon a time. The guy who shot me survived to see prison. My hand slipped up to soap my arms, where tiny scars from bird shot speckled my skin. Shot twice upon a time. That guy was dead; I had killed him outright. I'd gone back to work after the first time, the second time. I wondered if that was enough, if there would be a third.

Gibby poked his head around the shower curtain. I invited him in, dumped some shampoo on him, lathered, then rinsed. I toweled us both off, though Gibby shook himself all over the bathroom.

I dressed in a tank top and yoga pants, then climbed into bed. I glanced at Nick's vacant spot beside me. I thought of myself as someone who could keep her own company, but I missed him this evening.

Missing someone was strange for me. I'd let Nick into my life fully, into my present and my past. He'd accepted both. And with that, there was a kind of yearning that felt foreign, a worry. I'd let my guard down to reach for him, and I hoped he wouldn't disappear. I feared losing him, feared that he'd pull away. That he would get into an accident on the way home from work. It felt . . . anxious. Unfamiliar.

I checked my texts, finding one of his classically terse missives:

Bad case. Be there when I can.

I knew Mason was in the best hands.

Nick had a key. He would come when he could.

I rolled over in bed, shoving my pillow under my neck. Gibby crawled into bed, sighing deeply. I didn't care about a wet dog in bed. I reached down to stroke his back. Gibby and I were alike in a way, killers who'd been redeemed. Hopefully.

When I closed my eyes, I saw the symbol carved on the skull's forehead, the snake eating its own tail. I had seen that somewhere before . . .

I reached for my cell phone. A few minutes of googling yielded the answer. The snake eating its own tail was the ouroboros, a symbol of infinity; of life, death, and rebirth; of the transmigration of souls.

I drifted into a muzzy sleep, my mind chewing at the case. Someone had been at the Sumner house. Someone was threatening that family. And maybe they'd made good on that threat.

The darkness on the top of the refrigerator was still. Some part of me wondered what malevolence I'd invited into my house.

———

A green flash washed over my vision, then receded, leaving me steeped in memory.

My mom had rinsed me off and sent me to bed. She'd closed my bedroom door, then turned the lights off in the rest of the house. I could hear her moving around in the kitchen, the touch of her bare feet on the linoleum and the clink of a spoon against a cup. I had no idea what she was doing, but I certainly wasn't going to get out of bed to ask.

I slept. Then woke.

I didn't know what time it was, but I saw the gray predawn light. I crept out of bed, pushed open my door, and padded to the bathroom to get a glass of water.

I didn't turn on the lights. I felt for the tap and my plastic cup. Water flowed out, and it smelled sweet—artificially sweet, like something I might find in the candy aisle at the store. I wrinkled my nose.

I smelled sweetness, but also something warm and coppery . . . blood.

"Don't drink that. It's poisoned."

I started, stumbling back against the wall and fumbling for the light switch.

Mom, wrapped in towels, sat in the avocado green bathtub. The towels were bloody. She was pale, with circles under her eyes. There was an ashtray on the edge of the tub, and her shaking fingers reached for a cigarette.

I stood frozen. "Mom, are you okay?"

She lit the cigarette and inhaled. "I'll be okay."

"What . . . what happened?" I squeaked.

"I lost the baby." She said it quietly.

I didn't know there was a baby. I had no idea that she'd been pregnant at all.

"It was a girl. Your sister."

My brain boggled at the idea of having a sibling . . . a sister. How could she tell it was a girl, with all that blood?

I took a step toward her. "I can call the doctor . . ."

"No." She shook her head and blew out a plume of smoke. "It's done."

I struggled with question after question, and settled on: "How?"

She grimaced. "It's that water. We've been drinking it for weeks."

"What? The water . . . the water killed your baby?"

She stared straight ahead, unemotional. "There's orange juice in the fridge. Drink that instead. And turn out the light."

"What happened to the water?" I asked quietly, turning the light off and retreating to the doorway.

"I don't know." I couldn't see her eyes in the dark, just her long, pale fingers spread by her nearly empty pack of cigarettes. "But I mean to find out."

———

I awoke to a key scraping in the lock. I sat upright in bed, and turned on the bedside light. Gibby rushed to the door. I glanced at the clock. Almost five.

Nick let himself into the kitchen, and negotiated with the dog about the amount of slobber that was appropriate for a greeting. His keys jingled on the countertop, and I heard the rattle of a treat bag, then crunching.

Nick came into the bedroom to sit on the edge of the bed. His scrubs bore mysterious stains, his dark hair was tousled, and his stubble had grown in.

I didn't dare ask if he'd lost the boy. I waited, and silence stretched between us as the entanglement between our cases thickened like spiderwebs. We came from opposite realms. He was a scientist, believing in the things he could see and quantify. I was steeped in dreams, memory, and bizarre flashes of intuition held at arm's length. Our worlds usually remained separate. We both knew it was trouble when they intersected.

"The boy who almost drowned . . . he's in a coma. I don't know how—if—he'll wake up. If he survives, he's going to have a long road to recovery." His voice thickened. Nick brimmed with compassion for other people. He hurt when they did. He understood their pain. I didn't . . . not always. I thought I understood Nick's pain most of the time. I really tried to. But for everyone else . . . I hoped I did a good job of acting like I did.

"I'm glad to hear he's got a chance," I said at last.

"He was really lucky that you were there, and that the volunteer fire department was only a mile down the road," he observed quietly. He ran his fingers through his brown hair, a gesture he made when he was disturbed about something.

"Are you okay?"

"Something's not right about what happened." When he said this, I trusted him. Nick was an exemplary ER physician. He noticed all the small details.

"What did you see? The scratches?"

"Yeah. He had fresh scratches on his body, lower legs and ribs. And I suctioned mud out of his lungs."

"I pulled him from a pond, tried to get the water out."

"Right. He should've had water in his lungs, but not mud. For him to have mud, he would have had to be pressed into the mud and trying to breathe it." He looked at me with clear hazel eyes. "A kid that small can't dive that far down on his own."

My instincts were correct. Something was wrong about the case. "So, you're saying this was attempted murder."

Nick nodded.

I closed my eyes. I didn't want it to be true.

"Hey. What's going on?"

An injured child was bad, but Nick knew me well enough to know there was something else bothering me.

I took his hand in both of mine and opened a sliver of my world to him. I told him about the weird feelings I had about the pond, about the green flash. I told him about the thing I perceived in the water, how it felt as if Mason had been held down.

"And I dreamed about my mom." I told him about the memories of my mother and the well bubbling to the surface.

"When was the last time you dreamed about your parents?" He was wary. His pupils dilated just a bit. Could be concern. Could be fear.

"Not since last year." I stared up at the ceiling. "I haven't had any new memories about my father come up since then, either."

"I thought your psychiatrist had locked those away. Then they came back all at once when someone was copying your father's killings."

"That's what I thought, too. I thought that was it, and that when the case was solved, he and the Forest God just . . . went away. That we would live happily ever after."

"And that's been true," Nick said.

I drummed my fingers in irritation. "But now it's my mom. Just stupid, fragmentary stuff."

"I mean . . . that could be normal, you know? It's not your dad, and it's not the Forest God. You had a whole childhood locked away, and it's probably not unusual that more benign stuff is coming up." He was trying to understand. Nick didn't dream at all. But he was trying to grasp the internal importance of my dreams.

"No. It's not either one. I just . . ." I screwed up my face. I could never call my mother exactly benign. "It's just . . . disconcerting."

I could be honest with him. I hadn't always been able to. Nick's mother had been one of my father's victims. We had more baggage than a thousand relationships. But we'd resolved to be honest with each other. I felt vulnerable. I reflexively hunched my shoulders around my ears.

"I wish I could . . ." He trailed off.

"What?" I prompted.

"Nothing."

I leaned into his side.

He slipped his hand over his mouth. "I wish I could remember more about my own mom, you know?"

I slipped my hand around his and squeezed. "I'm sorry."

"I know."

I hated my father. I hated him for the pain he had caused my beloved. I wished I could erase my father from Nick's life, and the lives of so many others. I had been able to forget him for so long, but others couldn't.

Nick cupped my head in his hand and pressed it against his shoulder. "It's just a dream. Let's decide that it's just a dream for now, until proven otherwise."

That was a reasonable thing for a scientist to say. *Stay calm and gather evidence.*

There really wasn't anything else I could do . . . about the dream.

But there were things I could do about the investigation into the near drowning of Mason Sumner.

4

COLD CASE

I returned to the pond, this time in daylight.

The pond mirrored blue sky. The surface was still except for small ripples pushed by the breeze, and breaks in the surface tension where dragonflies touched the water. The pond was perfectly round, in a way natural ponds rarely were, maybe two hundred feet across. There were no ducks or geese here—odd for this time of year. This year's hatchlings should be clumsy and teenage by now, but there wasn't so much as a sentry goose left behind.

A man in a wet suit sat on the bank, fiddling with a dive tank. The grass was still damp with dew as I approached, showing his footprints as well as my own. I sat down in the crushed grass beside him, where I'd tried to revive Mason. "Sorry to call you so early this morning, Lieutenant."

Lt. Fred Jasper nodded. "Thanks, Koray, but it's no bother. This is Dive Team work."

The Bayern County Dive Team was down to one member. The

other diver, Sgt. Ramirez from the volunteer fire department, was out on maternity leave. Out here, in our rural county, people wore many hats. "Thanks for coming."

I genuinely liked Jasper. He was in his forties, with graying hair, and crow's-feet that deepened when he smiled. His face was sunburned from his time in the water and from umpiring for the interdepartmental softball team. He was the deputy who raised the most funds in the annual charity drive, and he donated the cash to the local animal shelter. Like Ramirez, he served on the county's volunteer fire department. When I joined the force, he was kind to me. When I was almost ready to cry after I'd gotten into my first altercation as a new deputy, he had bandaged my bloody knuckles up and given me a pep talk. I would've lost that fight if he hadn't stepped in. He never mentioned it to anyone, and I didn't forget that. Jasper was a private guy. He never invited anyone to his house, and the rumor was that he lived in a total shack and was embarrassed to have anyone over.

Jasper pulled on his flippers. "So, you don't think this was an accident?"

I lifted a shoulder. "ER says he had mud in his lungs. Seemed like he was hung up on something in the pond. I had a hard time hauling him to the surface. Maybe snapping turtles?" I wasn't going to say anything more than that. Nobody needed to think I was crazy. But I felt like I owed him some kind of warning, at least.

"Weird," he agreed. "But let's see what's down there. If there's a monster turtle in that pond, I'll find it."

Jasper stood, and I helped with his tank. I walked with him as he waddled to the pond's edge and dropped in with a controlled splash. There were no shallows here, just a sharp drop-off.

Jasper's back and the tank were visible as he floated around the perimeter, taking pictures. Gradually, he disappeared from view. The light of a flashlight swept under the surface, like a spotlight among clouds.

Here, in daytime, it was hard to believe something monstrous lurked below the surface. I wanted to believe that last night had been just a terrible accident. Something tragic had happened, certainly, but perhaps Jasper would return with evidence of a freakishly large catfish or snapping turtle. No matter what, there would be a logical explanation.

Was it too much to expect that I would never dream of my parents again? I wasn't sure. No one besides Nick knew that Stephen Theron, the Forest Strangler, was my father. Once upon a time, my psychiatrist knew, but she was dead. I wished she were still alive, so I could ask her about my dreams. I'd assumed I'd done all the psychological processing I needed to do last year, when I began to recover my childhood memories . . . I thought my memories were complete, and I had moved on, establishing that my father and I were separate entities. My father's Forest God, that antlered shadow in the forest who had exhorted him to kill, had gone silent.

My father was dead. I didn't feel his presence, the weight of his crimes and love and expectations, any longer. Now I thought of him only when I watched Nick sleeping at night, and bile rose in my throat at the pain he'd caused the man I loved.

I wanted to be free of him, to feel nothing. But all I felt was the hate. He had died a free man, but he'd deserved so much less than that.

My hands curled into fists. I refused to fall into those murky depths of fear and darkness once again. I would stay on this side of it. What I'd felt last night was a fluke, a blip. There was a rational explanation for all this, one that would be revealed with enough persistence and clearheadedness.

I couldn't fall into the realm of monsters. Not again.

I waited at the edge of the water while strings of bubbles rose to the surface. At last, Jasper emerged, gave me the thumbs-up, and then plodded toward the bank. I helped him climb awkwardly through the cattails with his massive flippers. He sat down on the shore, and I unbuckled his harness.

"What did you see down there?"

He rubbed his eyes. "Not much at first. Low visibility. But then I saw something weird."

"Yeah?"

He extended a closed hand to me and opened his fingers. In his palm was something slimy and irregularly shaped.

I picked it up with gloved fingers. It was wing shaped, with a luster graduating from gray to brown.

"It's a pearl," he said.

I blinked at him. "But that's a pond."

"Right. So, this is the cool thing . . . there are a few species of bivalve mussel that live in fresh water in Ohio. Rarely, they can produce pearls. I've never actually seen any outside of a museum, or when I was younger . . ." he trailed off.

"Do you think it might have come from someone's jewelry?"

He shook his head. "I think it's a natural anomaly unrelated to the case, but interesting."

I agreed, but still bagged it as evidence, just in case. "Did you find anything else?"

"Not much. The bottom of the pond is very soft. I was able to plunge my arm up to here in it, and it was difficult to remove." He tapped his shoulder, and mud glistened in the seams of his suit's sleeve. "The bottom terrain is dish shaped, with a lot of debris . . . looks like someone's been dumping their old Christmas trees there. Lots of carp and bluegill. Nothing that's good to eat."

"Anything that could hurt a child?"

"No. I didn't see anything that big." He sat with his elbows on his knees, staring at the pond.

"Do you think the debris could catch a child?"

"With bad luck and in darkness? Potentially." His gaze drifted to the house, and he frowned.

"What?" I prodded him. Jasper had excellent instincts; if he saw something wrong, I wanted to know about it.

"Nothing concrete. I just don't like this whole situation. It's possible for a kid to get hung up on some debris, sure. Unlucky drownings happen all the time. But people who live in a house like that are lucky."

"Maybe not." I told him about the skull in the mailbox.

Jasper shook his head. "That's creepy as hell. Makes me think the people in that fancy house have enemies you should look into. They think they own the world, rich people."

"You're not wrong. And the father certainly has that kind of air about him."

He wiggled his bare toes to dry them. "While I'm thinking about it—are you free to sub out to third base in the next game? Ramirez is taking more time with the baby, and we're down an outfielder."

"Are you asking on behalf of the cops or the firefighters?" I teased, knowing his loyalties were divided.

"For the cops, of course."

"Will there be brats and beer?"

He lifted up three fingers. "Scout's honor."

"I'll be there."

Jasper gave me a fist bump and packed his gear, then left me alone at the pond. I chewed my lip. If Jasper thought there was something hinky going on here, then I was certain there was.

Forensics hadn't gotten back to me about that skull, which I'd dropped off earlier this morning, but I didn't need their input to start poking around the idea of foul play.

I went back to the sheriff's office to run checks on Jeff and Drema Sumner.

Drema had filed a complaint when she'd found dozens of dead fish scattered on her driveway six months ago. The investigating officer had chalked it up to a benign teenage prank, but I wasn't so sure now.

A search for Drema Sumner on social media yielded no results, which was interesting for a woman of her age and income bracket. I expected to find a public profile full of pictures of her family, vacation scenery, and what she was eating, but there was nothing. The only people I'd really seen that from were women who lived off the grid and women who were hiding from something.

When I dived more deeply, I found a mention of Drema under her maiden name, Sindley, in the nearby college paper. She was a photographer whose work was at a gallery opening, and it . . . was breathtaking. She worked in brilliant colors, photographing women tangled in sheets and lounging on cushions, with something of a Pre-Raphaelite feeling. The photos conjured a lush, fleshy sensuality, earthy and vibrant. Alive. And evidently very much appreciated by critics, too. The paper noted that her prints had sold out. I found no other mention of her art, no matter how deeply I searched.

I turned my attention to Jeff. His personal social media showed him golfing, and fishing somewhere in the mountains. His was surface level, just like one would expect for any well-known local figure, not locked down. A search showed that he was the president of Copperhead Valley Solvents, a chemical company perched beside the Copperhead River, that had been running for decades.

I made a mental note to see if the company had had any financial woes or sour business dealings.

But Jeff had a past. To my excitement, his fingerprints were already on file; he was questioned about the disappearance of a young woman almost twenty-five years ago, but no charges were filed. Could be nothing, but I was always suspicious when rich kids got questioned and no charges came of it.

I drummed my fingers on the desk. My boss, the chief of the Detective Bureau, had a long memory. Maybe if I shook that particular tree, it would drop some useful fruit. I headed over to Administration, on the second floor of the county jail. The vending machine had just been refilled, and I snagged a pack of Chief's favorite, animal crackers.

I checked in with the chief's secretary. "Hey, Judy. Is Chief busy?"

She winced. "You may want to wait a few minutes."

Shouts rattled behind the closed door. Judy beckoned to me, and I slid into the guest chair beside her desk.

I heard the sheriff's voice, sharp in anger. I couldn't quite make out what they were saying, but it sounded bad.

Judy rubbed her temple. "They've been at it all morning."

"What about?"

Before she could answer, the door slammed open, and the sheriff stomped out. He was a tall man in his seventies, with a barrel chest, who looked something like Johnny Cash. He did a good job of presenting himself as a benign lawman who liked to kiss babies around election time, but he knew where all the bodies in Bayern County were buried. He had a long list of people who owed him favors.

He didn't glance at Judy's desk, and I thought I'd escaped his notice. The door creaked back, almost closing.

I flicked a glance at the door and whispered, "I can come back later."

Judy looked at the animal crackers in my hand. "You're okay. You come bearing gifts."

I peeked through the partially open doorway. Chief's office was shaped like a bowling alley, with a seating area at one far end and his imposing desk at the other. His desk was littered with a myriad of electronics parts. He was holding a handheld radio, twisting the channel-selection knob and smiling darkly to himself. Maybe he was distracting himself from the conflict with the sheriff.

I knocked on the doorframe, and Chief gestured for me to come and sit down in a club chair opposite his desk.

"New radios?" I chose not to mention the sheriff or their argument.

"New radios. They even have Bluetooth and do texts," he muttered. I could see he was trying to refocus after the fight with the sheriff. He fiddled with the controls, and my cell phone chirped.

I fished my phone out of my pocket and stared at the number that appeared on the screen. It was Chief's. A text message announced: This is some Star Trek level stuff.

"Pretty slick," I agreed. Clearly, he didn't want to talk about whatever was happening with the sheriff. And it was clearly none of my business.

He punched some buttons on his radio, and my phone rang.

I answered it.

It beeped a sharp electronic tone when I picked it up, and Chief spoke into the radio. "See? We can even make phone calls."

"Nice." I handed Chief the animal crackers.

Chief thanked me and tore into the bag. "I heard you had a tough call last night."

I nodded. "Yeah. I almost lost that kid. If I had been a few minutes faster . . ." *Maybe he wouldn't be in a coma.*

"You did everything you could. It was just shitty circumstances, kiddo."

"Except . . . I'm not so sure." I told him about Mason's lungs being full of mud, about how difficult it had been to pull him from the pond.

Chief leaned back in his chair, lacing his fingers over his chest, and listened. "And you think someone put that kid in the pond? Held him or weighted him down?"

"I think it's possible. I'm not sure where I fall on the babysitter. Her clothes were dry, and she didn't seem to register that Mason was in the pond. I got some warning bells when I looked into the father, Jeff Sumner. He's a big business honcho, maybe one with enemies, and he was seriously looked at when a girl went missing in the past."

"Mm. I remember that guy." Chief's eyes narrowed. "Sumner and some of his buddies were suspects in the disappearance of a high school girl, Dana Carson. We suspected Dana was dead, but her body was never found."

"Did you work that case?"

"Well, I tried. Jeff and his cohorts were classmates with Dana. They lawyered up immediately, and we got stonewalled pretty much out of the gate."

I leaned forward. "What made you suspect them?"

"They called themselves 'the Kings of Warsaw Creek.' They were trouble from the start. History of petty crimes and vandalism, the kinds of things that property owners can easily be paid off to drop charges."

"Sounds like you knew them pretty well." Warsaw Creek was a

tributary of the Copperhead River, one that wound, snakelike, through many acres of private land. "Why Warsaw Creek?"

"They set fire to the creek when they were kids. Almost caused a forest fire. They dumped a whole lot of chemicals from Jeff's dad's plant into the water and set it on fire for shits and giggles on Halloween."

"That is . . . spectacularly dumb."

"And typical for them. There was a three-hundred-year-old oak that stood in the park across from the courthouse. They poisoned that tree and killed it, just for kicks."

"What the hell?" I sucked in my breath. I was pretty sure that if they'd crossed paths with my father, he would've destroyed them for their affronts to his forest.

"They were minors and got off with a fine."

"What was their connection to Dana?"

"Dana was last seen at a gas station, with those guys. They were all each other's alibi, saying they left her there and went to the bowling alley that was owned by one of their fathers."

"Mm. Shady."

"Definitely. But there wasn't enough evidence to charge any of them. No body, no evidence, and we were stuck."

"But you liked these guys for the crime."

"Yeah. I did." He stared up at the ceiling. I could see from the set of his jaw that he hadn't liked leaving the case alone. Every cop had cases like that. "The girl, Dana, had no reason to take off. Popular girl. She'd never been in trouble."

"And the boys?"

"They were such arrogant little shits, honestly. My theory was that they picked her up, maybe she saw them doing something they weren't supposed to, and then they killed her to keep her from talking. Dana didn't come from a rich family, and they didn't think they would fight back."

I frowned. "Jeff has an alibi for Mason's drowning. He was out with his wife. And the guy may be a total shit, but it's rare for even a total shit to drown his own kid."

"Well, maybe someone had it in for Jeff," Chief suggested. "Like you said, he's a big fish in a small fishbowl. Maybe other fish don't like him. And you might get some ideas looking at the file for Dana Carson's disappearance."

"Will do."

"I mean, this drowning might just be an accident, but I'm all for giving it the scrutiny it deserves. Look into it until you're satisfied."

I took his advice and headed to the departmental archives. To my disappointment, I found that the archives had been moved to provide space for one of the sheriff's remodeling projects: a new conference room.

Gritting my teeth in irritation, I found myself in a dank subbasement, with boxes stacked haphazardly. After two hours of climbing ladders and sneezing dust, I located a banker's box with Dana Carson's name on it.

It always broke my heart a little to see a box from an unsolved case. It felt like failure, like grief that wasn't given closure. It was an open wound, festering in the dark. But I believed that Chief was eager to have me follow up and try to close that wound.

I put the box on a beat-up metal table and opened it.

It was like excavating the history of a life, an archaeological dig. Dana had been reported missing by her mother on the evening of the Fourth of July almost twenty-five years ago. She was seen on camera at the gas station, but then she seemed to evaporate into thin air.

I found a picture of Dana Carson, a high school yearbook photo. She had long, dark hair and dark eyes. I learned from the yearbook, with curled Post-it notes stuck in the pages, that she was an artist and hoped to go to art school. In her candid pictures in the yearbook, she had a goth look—she dressed in black, with silver jewelry—but her smile was brilliant.

I scanned the yearbook photos of the suspects. A younger version of Jeff Sumner bore more hair and less weight. His friend Quentin Sims appeared in a high school journalism photo, looking academic and pensive. They were often shown with a third guy: Mark Lister, an athletic-looking teen who ran track.

I sat back and chewed on my lip. It was almost twenty-five years since Dana vanished. Why would anyone hold a grudge for twenty-five years and not act on it sooner? It seemed implausible to me . . . until I thought of the skull, with the number ten scrawled on it. There were nine days until July fourth . . . ten days since I found the skull . . .

What was that? A countdown? What would happen on the Fourth of July?

I gathered my notes, then put the lid on the box. I carried the paper files out to my car, for further examination later.

I met Monica in the parking lot and filled her in.

Monica nodded and narrowed her eyes. "I took a spin past the hospital. Drema was there with Mason. I mentioned the skull to her. Turns out, she had a stalker in college, a Mike Renfelter. The cops weren't much help, but when she met Jeff, Jeff apparently beat the shit out of the guy."

"Yikes. I guess that explains her lack of social media."

"Jeff's persuasion apparently worked, because Mike backed off. Drema suspected he was back when fish were dumped in their driveway, but there wasn't any clear evidence."

"Did she say anything about the scratches on Mason?"

"She claims the scratches and bruises weren't there when they left. Initially, the intensivist at the hospital thought about snapping turtles. Concerned about having to treat the kid for salmonella, he called a herpetologist friend at the university. The herpetologist thinks the scratches on the kid's body aren't consistent with snapping turtle beaks. There would've been severed fingers and blood in the water."

"Damn. Sounds like someone really intended that kid harm." Statistically, when someone hurt a kid, it was most likely to be someone in the same household. Leah hadn't mentioned that Mason had been hurt when she was sitting for him, but . . .

Monica continued. "The hospital intensivist raised the possibility of child abuse, and Drema's really beside herself. I don't think she's faking that. Drema said she and Jeff got married because she got pregnant. She lost that baby, and she seems super protective of Mason now."

I exhaled. "She seemed genuinely upset last night. That tracks. But I still have a feeling someone isn't being honest with us."

"I was headed out to interview Leah again. Wanna follow me over?"

"Yeah." I wanted to see Leah in the clear light of day. I suspected there was more to her story than we got last night.

5

PEARLS

"We pray for God's will to be carried out, for us to be vessels of his will. May God use us as his submissive instruments in bringing heaven to earth . . ."

Monica and I stood on the doorstep of Leah's house, the parsonage for the Greenwood Kingdom Church.

The church itself sat on the outskirts of Bayern County, on a two-lane county road tracking the snaking path of the Copperhead River. It was a new-build megachurch, resembling a warehouse more than a traditional church, surrounded by a massive parking lot and a few limp attempts at landscaping. The parking lot was empty at this time of day.

The parsonage was tucked back on the property behind the church. A newly constructed home stood overlooking the river. Having a parsonage so close wasn't common in modern times. Centuries ago, priests and parsons would live on church grounds.

There was a car in the driveway, a mid-eighties Mercedes, glossy and black. It seemed out of place next to the new build.

The front door, painted red, was closed. We could hear a male voice leading prayer within, punctuated by female voices announcing: "Amen."

I rapped on the door. The voices within died, and a girl answered. She was maybe fifteen, dressed in a long-sleeved floral dress, with her blond hair tied back in braids. No makeup. "Yes?"

"I'm Lt. Anna Koray, with the Bayern County Sheriff's Office. This is Captain Monica Wozniak. We wanted to come by to see how Leah was doing."

Something flitted across her face as I spoke. Wordlessly, she opened the door wide and ushered us inside.

The interior was decorated in gray and white, looking like a doctor's office. Well, except for the framed Bible quotes and the crosses decorating the walls.

I stared at the cross made of railroad spikes above one of the doors. That looked familiar.

Beyond that, the place was sterile. I glanced into the kitchen, with white quartz countertops. The living room had white couches and a wall-mounted television.

Leah Sims sat on a couch. Her gaze was focused on the clock twitching on the opposite wall. Her eyes were red, and she was dressed in a denim jumper dress brushing her ankles. I noticed that, unlike last night, there was no smear of makeup on her face now. Her arms were covered by a long-sleeved T-shirt. Her hair was braided away from her face, and her hands were clasped before her. A pearl ring gleamed on her finger. Two teenage girls sat on either side of her on the couch, similar in dress to the girl who'd answered the door.

A reedy man with round glasses stood up from a recliner at the head of the room. He was holding a Bible.

"I'm Pastor Quentin Sims." He reached out with a cool hand to shake mine. "Leah's father."

I forced the neutral expression on my face to remain unruffled. I recognized him from the high school yearbook photos of Jeff Sumner's accused accomplices in the disappearance of Dana Carson, and from the Sumners' wedding pictures. I bit my tongue and introduced myself and Monica.

"I'm very sorry to hear about what happened to Mason. It's truly a tragedy. I've been praying with Jeff."

"He's a member of your church?" I asked.

"Yes. He and Drema have been members for years. Jeff and I go way back."

Interesting. While Monica made small talk, my gaze drifted to the girls. Leah sat, unmoving, on the couch. Her gaze was vacant, staring into space. One of the girls smoothed her hair behind her ears. She and the other girl were wearing pearl rings that matched Leah's. The girl who had answered the door sat on the floor at Leah's feet. She also had a ring.

"Hi, Leah," I began, but she didn't answer me.

"She's been like this since last night," the blond girl whispered, holding Leah's hand. "She won't eat. She won't sleep. She cried for hours."

I exhaled. Leah had been chatty enough last night. What had shut her down? I didn't see any lawyers in the room.

Just the father.

"I'm Anna." I extended my hand to the girls, who shyly introduced themselves: Rebecca, Sarah, and Elizabeth. Rebecca had answered the door, Sarah was the blond girl, and Elizabeth sat on Leah's left. Her long brown hair had been styled into space buns, and I detected the sheen of lip gloss on her mouth. She looked the part, perfunctorily, but I detected a hint of rebellion.

Monica and I sat on a love seat across from the girls. The clock ticked loudly above us. There was a statue of a pair of praying hands on the mantel. No family pictures of the pastor or Leah, I observed. There was one portrait, of a woman holding a baby.

Pastor Sims followed my gaze. "That's my late wife, Nora. I lost her to cancer several years ago."

"I'm so sorry for your loss," I said.

Leah's face twisted, and she blurted: "She should have lived."

"It was God's will that she be taken from us to a better place—" Pastor Sims began.

Leah's lip curled. "It wasn't God's will that she didn't go to the doctor."

Sims crossed the room to put his hand on his daughter's shoulder. "Leah. Stop."

Leah hissed, "He told me God would cure her, that she didn't need chemo."

Sims lifted his Bible, and Leah flinched. "God tells us to trust him. Leah, this willfulness does not serve God."

Leah's fingers, laced together, were white. "Was it God's will for Mason to drown?"

"We are unable to understand the fullness of God's plan, Leah. You know that."

Leah's friend whispered something into her ear, and she lapsed into silence. *Ah.* So religion had gotten in her ear . . . That was what silenced her.

Monica exhaled. "We have some questions about last night. Maybe it would be better if I spoke to the adults and Lt. Koray speaks to Leah?"

Sims shook his head. "I think anything that needs to be said can be said here, out in the open."

I didn't like that. Not one bit.

"How did Leah get the babysitting job?" Monica forged forward. "You said you were acquainted with the Sumners . . . ?"

"Leah babysits for the Sumners, and other families at our church." Sims settled back into his chair.

"We all look after the children in the cry room at church," Rebecca said.

Leah remained silent, and I turned my attention to Rebecca. "You girls know each other from church?"

She nodded. "We're all in the same homeschool pod."

I noted this, though I wasn't sure what to think. Was there real education going on here? Or was homeschooling an effort to keep the girls away from the secular nature of the world?

"How many boys and girls are in your pod?" I asked.

Sarah shook her head. "No boys. They go to public school."

"It's important to shield the girls from the temptations of the world," Sims said.

I was biting my tongue so hard at the ridiculous sexism of this that it nearly bled, but Monica was on to the next question.

"So, Leah's an experienced babysitter, then?" Monica asked.

"Oh yes. She's been babysitting since she was thirteen, for three families. They've always said great things about her," Sims confirmed.

I leaned forward and extracted my sharp tongue from the roof of my mouth. "Leah, do you know how to swim?"

Leah looked down at the floor. Whatever Rebecca had whispered to her had shut her up entirely. I was conscious of the pastor's weighty gaze upon her, too, and I was convinced we were going to get very little from this interview. I had seen Leah's genuine grief at Mason's near drowning last night, then the flash of anger at her father today. And now . . . silence.

Sims shook his head. "Women in our church are prohibited from swimming. It's an immodest activity. The waters of the womb are enough for our women and girls. Leah doesn't know how to swim."

What did that even mean? I tried to wrap my brain around it. Maybe Leah hadn't tried to drown Mason, but negligence wasn't off the table. And there were still the bruises to explain.

I turned my attention to Leah, trying to make eye contact. "Leah? When Mason arrived at the hospital, he had some bruises and scratches. Did he have any injuries when you came to the house? Or did he hurt himself while you were there?"

She didn't speak, just stared straight ahead. She shook her head.

"Leah loves children," Sims said. "She would never ever hurt anyone."

"I understand." I leaned forward, closer to Leah. "Leah, were you aware of anyone else around the house last night? Cars that might have pulled off the road or into the driveway?"

Leah shook her head again.

I looked at Sims. "Pastor Sims, we'll be asking for Leah's cell phone records, to establish a timeline of what happened . . ."

"I'm not so sure about that . . ." he began.

Leah stood up abruptly, reached into her pocket, came up with a phone in a glittery case, and handed it to me. I was surprised by her cooperation, honestly. Most teens would rather die than give their phone to an adult.

"I didn't hurt him," she hissed. Her cheeks bore bright spots of anger. "I would never."

I glanced at Sims. His gaze had narrowed behind his glasses. I thought he was on the verge of objecting, but it would be bad form not to cooperate with the police. Right?

"There. You have it," he said.

"Thank you. We appreciate your help. When we're further along in the investigation, we'd like to come back." *And get Sims out of the room*, I mentally added.

"Of course. But I want you to know . . . Leah really loves children. She wants to be a teacher. Before she gets married and devotes her life to God." Sims smiled pleasantly.

I cocked my head. "Leah isn't going to be a career educator?"

"No. She's embracing her natural role as a mother. But those things take time."

I bit my tongue hard. Leah looked away and dug her fingernails into the couch cushion beside her. I didn't think a woman's natural role was motherhood. I didn't subscribe to the idea that biology was destiny.

But I had to remind myself to be objective, to focus on the case, on all the ripples affecting this community.

I didn't want Mason's near drowning to be attempted murder.

But for Leah's sake, I didn't want it to be an accident. I wanted someone else to be at fault, and for her to have a future.

Preferably one of her own choosing.

———

"What do you think? Do you think she's to blame?"

Monica's voice cut through my mental haze. I was standing beside my car at the far end of the church parking lot, where we'd retreated to regroup. I dug through Leah's phone, scrolling through her apps, pictures, and texts. I found several casual games, tons of pictures of Leah and her friends. Most of the recent texts had been about a group homework project. I didn't see any texts or calls from last night, except for her call to 911. She had a private messaging app, but the chat log was empty. I wasn't confident that I could get much from forensic examination, even with a warrant.

"Dunno. But so far, the phone looks incredibly . . . wholesome. No nudes or mentions of weed or booze."

Monica nodded. "She didn't mind handing it over. Sounds like she wants to prove she didn't do anything to Mason."

"Yeah. I don't think she intentionally did anything to hurt him, but there's a world of unintentional harm out there."

Monica cracked her gum. "I did a quick search on Sims. His church is about five years old. Before that, Sims was doing the pastor thing with Brooks Fellowship, across town, but there was some sort of falling-out, and he started his own church. There were some charges having to do with him and a pastor at Brooks having a fistfight on the front lawn of the church, but those got dropped."

"Not what I think of when I think of clergy."

"Well, it's unlikely that any established conference would put up with that horseshit, but Sims created his own church, and here we are."

Leah Sims's social media was squeaky-clean. Weirdly squeaky. Her social media showed her singing in the church choir and teaching at vacation Bible school. I expected to see the normal teen-girl stuff—friends and sports and hobbies and clothes. She seemed to have only friends who were girls, no boys. All the young women dressed very conservatively—long skirts, sleeves, and hair. I zoomed in on the girls' hands. They wore identical rings on their left ring fingers—petite gold bands with tiny, perfect white pearls in them. A quick image search showed that they were sold as purity rings.

"You think maybe Sims scrubbed the phone before she handed it over?"

"Maybe, but we'll know for sure when we get her cell phone records."

"Eh. That phone has seen some secrets. No teenager is squeaky-clean. Not even church kids." Monica popped her gum again. "I sure as hell wasn't when I was her age."

I feigned shock, fluttering my fingers over my chest to mime a heart attack. "Monica Wozniak was not class valedictorian?"

"Salutatorian. But I sure did my share of sneaking out, and underage drinking. It's a miracle I became a cop with as much time as I spent at house parties, trying to avoid the fuzz."

I laughed. "How the tables have turned."

"I bet you were a little bit like Leah, though. I can see teenage Koray being super responsible—babysitting, and staying up late to do her homework. You've probably been a straight arrow since you passed the terrible twos." She rolled her eyes. "Though I can't picture you sitting around in prim dresses."

"No way."

I sure as hell wasn't going to tell her how much I was like my father. I hated that when I looked into the mirror I saw his gray eyes, the shape of his nose, the blond of his hair. It was like I couldn't escape him. He had cursed me with his blood, and with all the crimes he'd committed. He was poison, destroying everything he touched. And I felt like poison by extension, aware that I had the same power he had to destroy. I had to keep it in check. I had to keep that contamination to myself, away from those I loved.

I couldn't tell Monica. Sometimes I wanted to. Monica was the closest thing I had to a best friend, beyond Nick. But I couldn't be honest with her about who I was. I tried to be a good cop, and to do what I thought friends did: swapping snacks, gossiping, and keeping confidences. But there were some things I just couldn't say.

I knew Monica didn't hold back with me. She talked freely about bad dates and how much her ex–mother-in-law annoyed her when she ran into her at the grocery store. She vented about her shitty experiences with her doctor not listening to her about her endometriosis, and about how much debt her ex-husband stuck her with. She could talk to me about her life, the entirety of it. History.

And I . . . I couldn't. I wondered if she could sense that sometimes, my holding back. A couple of years ago I didn't hold back.

I honestly didn't remember my father and what he'd done. I was free and genuine with her then.

Now I was different. My fury at him burned deep in my gut, and it poisoned all of my relationships. Maybe she chalked it up to my having had brushes with death last year. I didn't know what she read into our long silences now.

I missed her. But I didn't know how to say it without opening up some wound I couldn't close.

6

ONE SLIP

Monica's phone rang, and I watched her face become wooden as she answered. "Yes. Yes. Yes, of course. We can be there. Absolutely."

I lifted my eyebrows. "Who was that?"

"Jeff Sumner," Monica said. "He wants an update."

"Is he at the hospital?"

"No. He's at work and wants us to come down."

I made a face. This early in the investigation, I didn't want to share any of my preliminary suspicions. Being summoned to give an update didn't sit well with me, either. But would I have done any different than Sumner if I had a child in the hospital?

"You'd think he'd be with his wife and kid," Monica muttered.

"Maybe he's married to his work."

Monica looked at me.

"I'm trying really hard to be charitable here," I said. "I mean, he did say he was opposed to medical care last night. Sounds like a church thing to have a phobia of hospitals."

"Maybe. Still shitty. Meet you at the plant."

—

I drove down the winding two-lane road. Tree leaves flashed above me, and I continued south for a few miles, the river burbling beyond my right shoulder.

I agreed with Monica: those girls were not being well served by that church. But I had to tread carefully. There were a thousand perfectly legal ways to be a shitty parent, but there was something about the situation that didn't sit right with me.

I thought back to the picture on the mantel, of the happy woman holding a baby. I truly thought most parents wanted the best for their children, however they defined it.

That kind of motherly love felt foreign to me. My own mother had viewed me only as an extension of my father. She never once asked me what I wanted to be when I grew up. I think she assumed I'd simply evaporate when I turned eighteen, that I'd disappear into the woods after my father.

And I came so close to that, to following the call of his Forest God, to relishing the feeling of death settling in the air around me. I had declared myself not to belong to the Forest God, had torn myself away from those obsessions and those voices in my head. I wouldn't be a vessel for evil like my father.

I don't think my mother cared about that, not really. Just as long as I was gone. She couldn't wait to be free of me when she'd dumped me at the institution and fled.

I thought of Leah, glassy-eyed and silent until she dared to defy her father in that flash point of rage. She clearly blamed her father for her mother's death. Her mother had gone along with it, and it had cost her her life.

Maybe having the full attention of a misguided mother was worse.

The road eventually led to a warehouse-like building surrounded by a concrete parking lot. In the background stood a one-story office building, and assorted chemical tanks connected by catwalks. By the gatehouse, trucks moved over scales, hauling materials in and out. The river stretched behind the gatehouse, at the end of a field of grass and scrub trees—the same river slicing through the backyard of the church just a few miles downriver . . .

Small world. It was like that sometimes, working in small towns. Everybody knew everyone. Sometimes it made investigations easier, because everyone was all up in everyone else's business. Other times, they closed ranks and no one talked. I wasn't sure which would be the case in this investigation.

I parked and rolled down the window, waiting for Monica, figuring she'd probably stopped for snacks at a gas station. The air here had a faint, artificially sweet odor. The site was very orderly—concrete and metal and glass. No weeds grew in the pavement cracks. The cars were late models with thin layers of dust obscuring their shine.

I stared out at a nearby dumpster. Just beyond it, something dark twitched and turned on the sizzling pavement. An animal?

I frowned, got out of my car to check. I couldn't leave an animal in trouble. I advanced on the dumpster. Beside it, a snake lay. A banded water snake. Harmless.

But it was in distress. Its jaws opened and closed, and its sides heaved. Its tongue dangled from its mouth, and it flipped and seized. It was about three feet long, with no wounds I could discern. The eyes were a peculiar milky color. And the scales weren't right.

I reached out to pick it up, to move it to the cooler grass. Its scales didn't feel soft and supple, the way snake scales should. These were brittle and curling. Didn't look like the snake was shedding.

I placed the snake on the grass. It seemed to sink into the green, as if it exhaled in relief. It lifted its head toward me, unseeing, then lowered its face to the ground. It stilled, and I was certain it was dead. Maybe it had waited to feel the coolness of something more natural than concrete on its belly.

I looked south, toward the river. This was a long way for a water snake to be from water. Water snakes ate fish and frogs. I wondered how it had come to be here. Did it find something in the trash that hurt it? But that made no sense. It wouldn't eat anything from there.

I gently picked up the snake again. I sniffed at it like Gibby would. I got a scent of something sweet, like the early stages of decomposition. It had been sick for a long time. I tucked its limp body under my arm. I popped open the hatchback of my SUV and gently put it inside. It deserved a burial, not to be left to rot with the trash.

When I closed the back, Monica rolled up into a spot next to me. Her hand stuck out, and a fancy iced coffee with whipped cream appeared before me.

"Ooh, thanks." I grabbed the drink and slurped down the icy goodness. Dealing with death always made me hungry, even when I was a child. Maybe it was some effort to assert to the universe at large that I was still alive in the most primal way I could, with sugar. "I wondered where you went."

"Needed caffeine." She crinkled a plastic bag. "Chips?"

"Yeah." I reached in for the chips.

When we'd drained our drinks, we hiked over to the gatehouse, in which a uniformed security guard looked upon us with suspicion until we flashed our badges and said we had an appointment with Jeff Sumner.

"Just making sure you're who you say you are," he said.

"How long has the plant been operational?" I asked, trying to make light conversation.

"Since 1963. Jeff's grandfather built it. Back then, production was high and the plant employed over a thousand people. There's a lot less demand today, though. We're down to five hundred. Too much competition from imports."

A door to the gatehouse opened, and a young woman in a hard hat approached us. "Detectives? I'm Mr. Sumner's assistant, Miri."

She extended her hand as we introduced ourselves. Miri was in her mid-twenties, conventionally attractive, and wore a tailored blouse and trousers with her steel-toed shoes.

"Pick a hat and come right this way, please."

Monica and I grabbed from a shelf blue hard hats with VISITOR printed on them, then followed her through the door and down a concrete pathway to a low building. Summer heat radiated from the concrete path. There was some traditional landscaping here, a weed-free carpet of grass and severely clipped hedges. The holly was browning on the top. Drought had reached even this artificial scenery.

Miri led us into an air-conditioned lobby. She removed her hat, and we did the same. We went down a corridor and turned right, into a plush office with carpeting and mahogany trim. A floor-to-ceiling window showed the plant in the background, and a massive desk with three computer monitors stood before it.

Jeff Sumner stood to shake our hands. "Thank you for coming. Please have a seat."

Monica and I seated ourselves in chairs across from his desk. The leather squeaked uncomfortably.

"Would you like coffee? Water?" Miri asked.

We declined, and Sumner shook his head. Miri left us and

closed the door. I noticed she left it open a crack. Eavesdropping, perhaps?

Monica clasped her hands in front of her. "We're very sorry about this situation. Clearly, this would be difficult for anyone in your position."

"It's all wrong." His eyes were red.

"How's Mason?" I asked. I knew full well, but I wanted to hear his explanation for not being at the hospital.

"I spoke with the doctor this morning. He's in a coma." Jeff looked away. "My wife won't let me stay there, at the hospital. She blames me, and she probably should."

I lifted a brow. "Pardon?"

"I had that pond put in over her objections. I insisted Mason would get swimming lessons, that he'd be too smart to drown, but . . ." He rubbed his stubble. "I screwed up, and now Mason's paying for it."

"No one ever really expects the worst to happen," Monica said.

"I should have." He exhaled.

"May I assume you have . . . religious objections to medical treatment?"

His mouth twisted. "It's complicated. But Drema made the right call last night. I just . . . It's hard submitting to God's will in the trenches."

I flipped open my notebook. "It's very early in the investigation, and we're still working on establishing a timeline for last night. I understand you and your wife left Mason with Leah to go out?"

"Yeah. We had reservations at Preston's Chophouse for a business dinner with the officers at Heartland Community Bank. We left during the dessert course."

"When were you supposed to return?"

"We told Leah we'd be back by eleven."

"I wanted to check and see if there was any video available at your house . . . I noticed a doorbell camera." I suspected there were other cameras, too.

He nodded. "I'll have video sent over to you from the security company."

"Excellent. Thank you. I noticed there was a fault on the alarm panel when we entered the house?"

He leaned back in his chair. "The panel's been acting wonky. Low battery in a couple of sectors. The company was supposed to come out and replace them on Tuesday."

"Were any windows or doors habitually left open?"

"No."

"Who else might have had your access code?"

He screwed up his face. "My wife, of course. The housekeeper, my in-laws, and the landscaper."

"I'd like to have a list of their names, please."

His brow furrowed. "I don't get it. Why do you want to talk to the housekeeper?"

"When a child is hurt, we want to make sure all the i's are dotted and the t's are crossed."

"Sure." He wrote down a list of names on a legal pad. "But we've been using those services for years, and trust them totally."

"We found something in your mailbox." Monica showed Sumner the picture of the skull.

He leaned forward, staring intently. "What the hell is that?"

"We don't know. Do you have any enemies? We're aware that Drema reported a stalker in her past."

His eyes narrowed, but they remained fixed on the picture. "No enemies that I know of. Other than that guy who followed Drema around in college. Um . . . what was his name?"

"Mike Renfelter."

"Yeah. That guy. I haven't seen him since college. I thought he'd fallen off the map. Do you think he might have had something to do with this?"

"We're not sure, but it's clear someone with hostile intent went by your house last night."

I inhaled, knowing I'd have to probe delicately now. "Mr. Sumner, have you ever been around any kind of violent crime?"

He tore his gaze away from the photo to stare at me. "Are you saying that something violent happened to him?"

"There were some marks on Mason's body that are troubling. We need to determine if this happened to him in the pond or—"

He froze behind his desk. "What are you getting at?"

Before I could continue, the door swung open. A man in a suit and tie and carrying a briefcase swept into the room. I knew this guy—Steve Cortland was the most expensive defense attorney in the county, one of the three sibling attorneys from Cortland, Cortland, and Cortland. Their firm logo was a stylized Cerberus, Hades's three-headed guard dog.

Cortland nodded to us. "There will be no further interrogation of my client. You've got my number."

We certainly did. Monica and I climbed to our feet and left. I glanced at Miri, who studiously avoided my gaze. She must have had Cortland waiting in the wings, protecting her boss like any good right-hand woman would.

"I suppose we'll show ourselves out."

She nodded curtly.

Monica and I headed back down the hallway, and the security guard approached at a swift clip.

"I don't think we're going to get invited back," I said. I was used to pissing people off, but this felt particularly gross.

"Well, we tend to let all the air out of the room," Monica acknowledged.

———

I cruised down the two-lane road, chewing on that disastrous meeting with Sumner. I had some sympathy for him, being exiled from the hospital by his wife. He seemed truly upset about his son's condition, but I couldn't forget that he had been a suspect in the disappearance of a young woman many years ago. I didn't think people changed that much over time.

I slowed as I pulled up behind a car being driven erratically. The late-model Civic crossed the center line, then entered the shoulder. I couldn't see more than the silhouette of the driver.

I frowned and radioed in the plates. They came back to meth-cooker Rod Matthews's brother, Timmy.

The car lurched off the road and onto a gravel side road without warning. I swept past, pulled a U-turn at the nearest stand of rural mailboxes, and crept down the gravel road. This road led to an out-of-the-way state park, Flint Rock Park. This place wasn't friendly to newbie hikers, so it tended to be sparsely visited. Might be a great place for drug deals, and if I could snag Timmy behaving badly, then Vice would be pleased, and they'd owe me a favor.

I wound up a hill to park in a small gravel parking lot at the trailhead. The car registered to Timmy was parked there, but there were no other cars.

I popped my door and advanced on the car. It was empty but locked. I saw no drug paraphernalia on the seats.

I frowned. Maybe he was here to meet someone. Rod and Timmy didn't strike me as the kind of guys who went into the woods to find inner peace and marvel at nature.

I turned my attention to the trail. A dirt track descended, crowded by wild dog roses and trillium. Mosquitoes were thick here. The temperature dropped by a good ten degrees as I wound my way to the bottom of a ravine. Sandstone walls rose around me, worn smooth by centuries of rain and river water. Layers of rock, like annual rings in a tree, were eroded and open to the air now.

By the time I reached the bowl-shaped depression in the bottom, I could hear water. The Copperhead River took a detour here, one that curved around in an oxbow, leaving an island covered by cedar trees at its center. In the distance, I could make out geese in their nests moving their black, snaky necks as one to watch me.

An outcropping of flint loomed above—a structure that geologists called a "geological anomaly." If one gazed straight north, one saw a gray striated stone that resembled the profile of a woman. The locals called her the Hag Stone.

The local legend was that, long ago, a witch saved a young man from drowning here. They fell in love, and made plans to run away and get married at this spot at midnight on Midsummer Eve. But the man never showed up. The witch's body was found drowned. The rock took on her countenance, gazing out upon the land for her love, her murderer, or whoever else crossed her path.

Predictably, teenagers loved to sneak off to this place. Bits of spray paint defaced the stone below the unreachable profile. I scanned the graffiti, seeing the usual artistic expressions, initials, and vows of anarchy. The witch seemed above it, glowering down. Among the graffiti, I spied an old, faded mark that looked familiar—a black ouroboros. It wasn't fresh, buried beneath a declaration of love in green spray paint. Maybe this place was sacred to someone else, someone connected to my case.

I gazed up at the Hag, feeling the coolness of her shadow.

Green light eroded my vision.

Mom was taking in the wash. She stood before the line, her hands on her hips. An hour before, she'd put the whites out to dry in the sunshine, but something had happened to them.

The sheets were strung up, streaked with rusty stains that looked like dried blood.

She growled and ripped the laundry off the line.

"Get your shoes on," she snapped.

"Where are we going?"

"To find out what's going on with this water."

Mom stuffed the laundry into the kitchen, collected her shoes, and led me from the house. At first, I thought she meant to climb into the car to go to the grocery store for bleach, but she grabbed a shovel and stalked off toward the well. I followed her to the low land behind it, where water sometimes accumulated during hard rains. This summer was brittle with drought, and the clay earth was cracked.

She stalked away into the woods, following the lowest part of the land.

I scrambled in her wake. My mom hated the forest. She never ever went there. I had never seen her camp, hunt, or fish. I rarely saw her go barefoot. She preferred the olive-colored shag carpet of our living room to any grass.

But she cut sticks from a willow tree, stripped off the leaves, and broke them down into Y shapes. She showed me how to hold the ends of a Y with the stick's main stem pointing ahead of me.

"Like that. If you relax and focus, you can find water."

She said it like it was simple, like turning on a sink faucet. I bit my lip and closed my eyes, straining to comply.

In my mind's eye, I saw the water behind me, this cool, shining vein like a river in Hades's underworld. It shimmered in the dark, far below my feet, then split away. I chased it, imagining it writhing beneath me like a snake. I traced the undulations in its spine as it moved in its sidewinder way through the cold clay, and deeper, past glittering sandstone and pale limestone.

The water snake in my mind came up, up, close to the surface. I knelt there, pressing my hand to the ground. I imagined that the snake licked my palm.

I opened my eyes. My mom was just behind me, leaning on her shovel. For once, she wasn't scowling at me.

"There?" she said.

"I think so." I sweated as Mom set her shovel to the ground.

She dug a hole, the sharp shovel chewing into thick yellow clay. As she did so, pieces of it sloughed away like snake scales lifting. I examined one of those pieces. It was a murkier brown on the inside, moist.

She dug until the ground shattered and pieces of clay fell down, down into the ground, rattling into the dark.

My mom and I crouched over the hole. About two feet below us, water blistered up.

My mom smiled at me . . . actually smiled at me. "You're a natural."

I beamed. I hadn't imagined it.

"You're like me. You can sense the water's pull." She looked at me as if she had never actually seen me before.

My heart lurched into my mouth.

"I'm proud of you."

I blinked back tears. "What . . . what is this? A well?"

"It's an underground aquifer."

I stared down into that hole. It smelled green, though there was no way the sun could reach it to grow algae. The water was almost at the lip of the hole now, radiating cold.

Dead fish, white and as long as my hand, dozens of them, floated up on their sides.

Tears stung my eyes. "How are there fish here?"

"There are underground aquifers all around here. Every body of water here is interconnected underground—the river, the ponds, the creeks. They're all interconnected in the limestone underneath, giant vaults and galleries."

I reached out for a fish, but my mom caught my hand. "Don't touch them."

"Why not?"

"They're poisoned. It's not just our well."

I leaned forward and inhaled. The water smelled sweet, artificial, like something I might smell in the detergent aisle at the grocery store. Like something that was made to smell sweet but would taste awful.

"What do we do?" I asked.

"We cover this up for now."

"And then . . . ?" It didn't feel like enough.

"We look for the source."

Mom and I followed dry creek beds and unseen veins of water. We walked for miles, from morning until dark, always in the lowest, most shaded parts of the forest. I drifted in my mom's wake as she was guided by the twitching of a stick.

When night fell, we found ourselves at the river, at a spot where it curled in on itself beneath a stone with the profile of a woman.

I gawked up at it, exhausted, and feeling her chilly shadow permeating me. I took my shoes off and let my bloody blisters air. Blood trickled into the cool sand.

"That's good," my mom said. "She likes blood."

"Who is she?"

"She's a spirit who lives in the rivers and streams in this place. The water is special here, you see. It flows up from deep, deep underground, from places light has never seen."

"Like the underworld?" I'd been reading Greek mythology.

"Like the underworld. She brings all that power up in the water. She rules the water. And it's polluted now. It killed your sister. And now we have to stop this poison before anyone else gets hurt like your baby sister."

I squished my toes into the sand. This was the first time I remembered my mom actually telling me a story. I wondered why my dad never took me here. This place was special. It felt sacred, in a way the forest didn't. I could feel the water, swirling in its cauldron, around my mom and myself.

For that moment, I felt like her daughter.

———

Sand crunched behind me, farther back on the trail. I ducked behind the cattails.

More distant steps.

I stayed low, watching. I peered above the cattails, spying a figure above me. Not a guy I recognized. He was wearing cargo shorts, a camo T-shirt, and hiking boots. A ball cap was low on his brow, covering a scruffy ponytail. He was skinny, too skinny, and his arms and face were speckled by sores he absently scratched. He was a young man, but missing a few teeth.

Was this the guy Timmy was meeting? He must have arrived after me.

I dropped to my belly, feeling cool mud under my fingers and soaking through the knees of my pants. My heart slowed to a steady, reptilian beat as he drifted away from my sight.

I crept forward soundlessly. I slithered through the under-growth, watching the edge of his camo T-shirt moving against the background.

I pursued him as he swept down the trail, casting right and left. He crept down the path, still making noise, looking clumsily for footprints in the dirt. Was he looking for Timmy, or . . . ?

He was following me. He must've seen my car in the lot, maybe followed me from the plant . . . or even farther back.

I almost laughed aloud, and I clapped a muddy hand over my mouth. The thought was ridiculous. Here, in my element.

I decided to hunt him back. Just for fun.

7

HUNTING

The man pursuing me descended to the floor of the grotto, search-ing the shadows and clefts in the sandstone, taking time to smack the mosquitoes from his arms. He passed within only a few feet of my hiding place, but when his back was turned I slithered away, ducking into a copse of fallen trees.

For kicks, I threw a stone at him. My father wouldn't have approved—he took hunting seriously. But I was not his daughter, not always.

My pursuer spun around, his face creased in anger. He had no idea where I was. He turned a full 360 degrees, doubtless unsure if some squirrel was fucking with him.

I chucked another stone, into the river. This one, I made sure to skip. Critters can't skip stones.

He crouched and whirled, trying to find me.

I circled him, wading through poison ivy. I was immune to it, and no sane person who wasn't would approach my position.

He climbed to an outcropping to try his cell phone, grunting in frustration when it didn't connect. There wasn't any signal here.

I wondered why he was here. I'd gotten close to something, to be certain.

I lay down in the poison ivy, listening. Ascending the hill, the guy walked right past me, so close . . . He was breathing heavily.

Feeling bored with my little game, I thought I should maybe start acting like a cop. I stood up in the poison ivy and aimed my gun at him. "Freeze."

He whirled, panicked.

And he ran.

I rolled my eyes. Of course, I wasn't going to shoot him. I took three steps toward him, but he lurched, then tumbled all the way down the trail to the very bottom, yelping as he went.

I peered down to find him in the gravel below, prone. There wasn't an easy way to get to him from where I was. I got as close as I could, squatted, and called out: "Hey, man. Are you okay?"

"*Ugggghhhh.*" His response was pretty robust. Didn't sound like he was hurt bad. His right leg was oozing blood onto the sand, but it didn't look serious. Still, there was no way I could carry him out.

"What's your name?"

He shook his head, not giving anything up. He looked young, too young to look as worn-out as he did. I felt a twinge of guilt about hunting him, about his winding up hurt as a result of my game.

"Why are you here?"

He stared up at me, unflinching.

"Are you here to meet Timmy?"

He was being completely uncommunicative. *Stellar.*

I sighed. "I'll get a squad for you. Don't move."

I supposed that climbing to the rim to call for help was the right thing to do. I'd get the fire department to fish him out of the bottom of the ravine.

Above, the Hag Stone seemed to look upon me approvingly in the dusk. I'd given her blood, after all.

I climbed up to the trailhead, taking long, smooth strides. My legs burned, but I moved unerringly in the shadows. I watched for Timmy, but saw no sign of him.

When I came upon the trailhead, only my car was parked in the lot. *Hell.* Timmy was gone. But where had the tweaker I'd met come from? Had he arrived on foot?

I paused before my car, sensing that something was off. My ancient SUV was sitting too low. I walked up to it with a narrowed gaze, scanning the car. No one was inside, and the windows were intact. No one was underneath it, lying in wait, either . . .

. . . but my tires were slashed. All four of them.

Message received.

I ground my teeth and radioed for backup, for a tow, and for Vice to bring me a loaner from their stash of undercover cars. I sat on the bumper of my SUV, with my gun unholstered, staring at the trailhead. If that tweaker kid climbed out, I'd cuff him, though I had the urge to smack him in the back of the head. My car was old, but it was my baby. It pissed me off that some fucker was trying to put me off the case.

Deputy Detwiler rolled up first. Didn't surprise me that he was Johnny-on-the-spot. But it must have been a slow night for Patrol, because two other cars showed up, too. I filled them in, minus my fucking with my pursuer. I told them that I had taken a walk to clear my head and I'd realized someone was following me. Detwiler and the patrolmen headed down to the ravine to search for my pursuer. They came up with bupkes. The tweaker must have been ambulatory enough to slink away downriver. I was pissed, pissed at myself. If I hadn't played with my quarry, I could have marched him up here and had a healthy subject to question.

I asked a patrol deputy to rustle me up a battery-operated trail cam from the local feed store. I took it down into the ravine with me.

I couldn't access it remotely—there was no cell service—but what it saw would be saved on an SD card. I found an unobtrusive spot on a tree to affix it to, aiming it at the graffitied wall beneath the witch's profile. I wasn't sure I'd catch anything, but I hoped I'd be able to see who was leaving these ourobouros symbols.

As far as loaner rides went, all that was available was a dusty brown El Camino from the seventies that looked like it was entirely glued together with Bondo. Sykes from Vice dropped it off for me with a great deal of ceremony, extending the keys to me as if he were presenting Excalibur. He was dressed in a band T-shirt and skinny jeans that looked spray-painted on, and he was rocking a pair of hiking boots that looked like they were solid clods of mud.

"Thanks, man. Dare I ask what you're working on right now?"

"It's more fun than you're having." He frowned at my tires. "Interestingly enough, we're looking for Timmy, too. Heard some rumors he was back in town."

I filled him in on what I'd seen, and on the guy in the ravine.

"Hmm. Sounds like a guy I busted for possession last year. Give me a minute." Sykes pulled out a cell phone in a sparkly case and summoned some mug shots to show me. "Is this your dude?"

"Yeah. That's him. But he's got fewer teeth now."

"Zach Draper. This is weird for him. Dude is strictly small-time. I just popped him for possession of a small amount. Didn't resist arrest or anything."

"Sounds like he may have upgraded his talents."

"I'll put out the word that we're looking for him. He won't get too far. All the meth heads in the surrounding counties seem to be converging here, and I don't like it."

"Usually a big bust like last night's drives them away, right?" I asked.

"Yeah. It was deeply, deeply weird." Sykes rubbed his stubble. "I saw shit in that barn I'd never seen before. The cookers weren't using the usual components. There weren't any pool chemicals or lighter fluid, you know? But the end product was definitely meth. That worries me."

"New recipe?"

"Seems like it. I sent samples off to the state crime lab for ID, to see if they've seen anything like this before."

"Keep me posted. I'm curious." I leaned forward to squint at Sykes's collar. "Is that a puka shell necklace? You know what year this is?"

Sykes's face fell, and he lifted the necklace with his thumb. "Not cool?"

"Not cool. You don't have any temporary tribal tattoos going on?" I teased.

"No comment."

I opened the El Camino's door and wrinkled my nose. A forest of tree-shaped air fresheners danced from the rearview mirror, but they were powerless against the onslaught of decades' worth of cheap stogies. I couldn't complain. Beggars, choosers, and all. I moved all my stuff from the SUV to the El Camino.

A flatbed truck arrived to load up my SUV, looking forlorn on the bed.

"Where to?" the driver asked.

I was going to make this worth my while, to interrogate as

many of the Kings of Warsaw Creek as I could. There was one King I hadn't spoken to, and he owned a car dealership.

"Lister Automotive, please."

———

Lister Automotive was just off the freeway exit, so motorists could marvel at its selection of late-model cars and trucks. A red, white, and blue sign announced our arrival at **LISTER AUTOMOTIVE—ASK MISTER LISTER FOR THE BEST DEALS!**

As I tooled down the access road behind the flatbed truck, I surveyed the cars. The lot was sparse, cars parked with plenty of space between them. Off to the right were the used cars, with a classic red Corvette on a pedestal.

We circled around to the back, to the shop. While the truck driver dropped my car in an empty spot, I went inside the shop to drop off the keys.

"Can I help you?"

A salesman approached. His over-whitened smile looked positively painful, and it didn't falter as he took in my grubby appearance.

"Hi. Is Mark Lister in?"

He blinked. "Mr. Lister's a busy man, but I can help you."

I flashed him my badge. "I'd rather speak to Mr. Lister."

"Of course. Let me check to see if he's still in."

The salesman retreated down a hallway. I studied Mark Lister's picture in the showroom, above a family tree of ten salespeople. I got an impression of a middle-aged guy with not a hair out of place and with the same bleached teeth his sales force sported. I noticed the wall paint had faded in spots that suggested there had once been fifteen salespeople. Business might not be good.

The salesman returned. "I'm sorry, but Mr. Lister's in a meeting. Could I please have your card, and I'll have him call you?"

I handed over my card. "Please tell him I'd like to speak with him."

"Of course. But how about I show you this lovely blue coupe?"

I demurred, then headed out back, to the El Camino.

As I tooled around the lot, I could see through the glass of the sales area, and my gaze fixed on a man in the largest office. His tie was loose and he looked rumpled, with sweat stains under his arms. I squinted. Yes, he looked like an unretouched version of Mister Lister, King of the Midwest Dealerships. He was talking on the phone, holding a business card that might have been mine.

His gaze met mine, and he froze. He turned out the light, plunging his office into darkness.

I was just disappointed I was unable to shake his hand. My hands were soaked in poison ivy oil, after all.

———

I got home late, late enough that Gibby gave me only a perfunctory huff before bolting out into the yard to do his business and then racing back to perform his nightly routine of eating, then snuggling in bed. Nick must've given him a bath; his fur was fluffy, and he smelled like my citrus volumizing shampoo. Snuggling would have to wait until I'd scrubbed the poison ivy off my body and put my clothes in the washer. I might be immune to the poison ivy, but I wasn't wanting to share with Gibby and Nick.

But I had something to do first.

I headed to the back of the El Camino and took out the snake. Its body was warm from the heat but stiffened by death. I cradled it in my arm and grabbed a small shovel.

I circled back to the garden, to Nick's plot of civilized vegetables. At the edge of it, I dug into the earth, making a little grave for the snake. I dug the snake's grave beside Nick's memorial for his mother, maybe to keep the grief contained.

I placed the snake in the grave. It had curled in on itself in a circle. When I'd tucked it into that round hole, it looked like the ouroboros, the serpent without beginning or end.

I kissed my fingers and pressed them to its brow. "Sleep well."

I filled the hole, and it was as if it had never existed. But it had, and it felt like a needless death to me.

I went inside to rinse the dirt off, but couldn't shake the feeling of loss. Loss of the snake, and the knowledge that I'd fucked up and lost a suspect. I'd gone hunting . . . like my father had. If I'd kept things cool and professional, I'd have a suspect to question, unharmed and maybe cooperative. I had nothing now, and it was my fault. I needed to toe the line, follow the rules. Flouting the rules was supposed to be behind me. Each time I dipped into my father's power, I risked having his memory overtake me, and I couldn't allow that.

I put the misshapen pearl Jasper had found on my nightstand, beside a mason jar full of feathers. My eye kept straying to the pearl as I dressed for bed and climbed in. In the darkness, I swore I could sense its presence humming beside me.

I'd been stupid to bring it home. I considered taking it outside and locking it in my car.

But that seemed silly. Who was afraid of something so small?

It wasn't usable evidence.

But it felt important in a way I couldn't articulate.

Gibby grumbled and rolled over, pinning my arm to my pillow. When Nick was working, Gibby slept in Nick's spot. I found that to be incredibly charming, and I rubbed his back.

"You're taking being man of the house very seriously."

He licked his chops and snored.

I reached over him for the pearl, then tucked it under my pillow. Maybe I'd dream of what my subconscious was fixating upon, about oxbow rivers and tweakers running wild.

Or maybe my mother.

I just hoped my subconscious would shake loose a clue.

———

A woman was singing, distantly.

I opened my eyes in the dark. I heard her, just, through my open window. The frogs had long since gone to sleep, but ghostly singing echoed. Soft rain tapped against the window.

I slipped out of bed and let myself out the front door. Damp grass was cool on the soles of my feet, and soggy moss squished between my toes. I told myself we were in a drought . . . and all the moss on the property had withered. As I walked, I sank into mud, and my footprints filled with water. I followed the voice among the shadows of trees to the old creek meandering through my land.

"Who are you?" I called into the rain-spangled darkness.

Water rose up over my ankles, up to my knees, and spilled out into the forest. It lapped around the trunks of birch and cedar trees. It swelled, and I felt the creek pull at me, the current causing me to stumble.

The head and shoulders of a woman emerged in the dark. Black hair pooled on the surface of the water. I couldn't make out the details of her face, only that it had the greenish tinge of the underbellies of certain fishes, the color of ripe corpses.

She reached out, and sharp claws clamped around my ankle.

"You're meant to be mine. My sister," she murmured, her voice low and melodious as wind chimes.

Something distant barked.

8

MEMORY OF DARKNESS

"Anna."

I jolted awake, shaking a hand off my shoulder. My heart thundered in the darkness, and my hair hung over my face. Hands pushed the curtain of my hair away, and I saw Nick clearly.

"I . . . What are you doing here?" I registered that we were in the forest. We stood in the creek, water up to my ankles. I couldn't feel my feet. It wasn't raining here; the nearly dry creek slithered around us.

"Gibby was going crazy when I got back. When I opened the door, he ran out into the forest. I was barely able to follow him."

Gibby paced in the water, barking to the east, then to the west, as if he were trying to ward off some awful predator. The fur on his spine stood up.

"What are you doing out here, Anna?" His voice was full of concern and dread.

"I was . . . dreaming." I rubbed my eye with the palm of my hand. Oh God. This wasn't happening again. Not again.

"C'mon. Let's go back."

We walked to the house, and Gibby followed, though he occasionally looked over his shoulder and growled at the creek.

I went inside to rinse my muddy feet off in the bathtub while Nick leaned against the bathroom wall, arms crossed.

His gaze was heavy on me. I wanted to reassure him that I was okay, but I couldn't offer that. Not really.

"You haven't walked in your sleep since last year."

When I'd worked the Forest Strangler case. When I'd remembered my father, and my own demons had awoken. But I wasn't dreaming of him now. Why was this happening again?

I closed my eyes. "I don't know what happened. I'm working the case on that boy in the pond." I told Nick what I'd learned so far, what I remembered, what I dreamed . . . the singing, the thing underwater. The dreams and memories were different, distinguished by that green flash.

I paused when I got to the pearl tucked beneath my pillow. I thought that might change how he saw me. Maybe he wouldn't understand. He believed in what he could see and touch, and where I came from . . . may as well have been the far side of the moon.

And I didn't want him to leave me. I was afraid I'd scare him again, that he would flee. I'd never opened up to someone like this, and I was so very afraid of losing him.

I swallowed the lump in my throat. I'd promised to tell him the truth, and I did. I told him about the pearl.

Nick exhaled and rubbed the back of his neck. "You know I'm here for you no matter what, right?"

I nodded. We'd promised each other that. I wasn't sure I totally believed that we would, but I believed we would try.

He came to sit beside me on the edge of the tub. "I'm worried about you. I've been thinking, since last fall . . . maybe we should move."

I blinked at him. "What?"

"Maybe we should move. Get away from here. Go west or something."

"What brought this on?" I reached out to take his hand. "What's wrong?"

He slid his other hand over his mouth. "I haven't wanted to bother you about work stuff, but it's not getting better. We've got a new guy over the ER. Dr. Floyd. It's a bad situation."

I frowned. Nick had mentioned problems at work in the past few weeks. I hadn't pressed to find out more, and guilt bubbled up in my throat. "Is this about him?"

"Partially. He's fired my best nurse for taking a too-long break to pick her kid up from school. The guy's a fucking tyrant. And I don't think he's going anywhere. He's tight with the board."

"But . . ." My mind latched onto all the impossibilities. "Your licensure . . ."

"I can apply to the medical boards of other states to transfer it."

"Is it that bad?"

"It might get that bad." The circles under his eyes were deepening. I'd never known Nick to run away from a fight. That was one of the things I loved most about him: his tenacity. Things had to be bad for him to consider leaving. And I hadn't noticed. I'd been too wrapped up in my own issues to pay attention to his.

"I've built a life here." At least, I'd built a career. A career built on lies about who and what I was, but a successful one. I couldn't imagine working without Chief or Monica. And I had this house, perfectly private and owned outright.

Nick pulled his hand away and laced his fingers together. His thumbs warred with each other. "Maybe it's not you or me or your father that's so wrong . . . Maybe it's this place. Maybe Bayern County is just cursed."

I stared at him.

"I mean, there are all those stories about haunted places that drive people batshit. I've seen some weird stuff in the ER that I haven't been able to explain. And you have, too. What if . . . it's just this place that drove your father crazy? What if there's just weird shit here, and we need to stop trying to fix it and get the hell outta Dodge?"

My mouth opened and closed like a fish's. I was shocked that Nick was willing to entertain mad theories of the unseen in spite of his worldview. He was changing . . . for me.

But I couldn't explain to him then how I felt so rooted in this place. He may as well have suggested moving to Mars.

"Bayern County has too much history, for you and for me," he said. I wondered if he was thinking of his mother then. I wondered if this was more the reason he wanted to leave than the tyrannical ER doctor was. If it was ghosts, not the living, that were driving him out.

"I understand." I thought I did.

He leaned against my shoulder. "Just think about it, okay?"

I couldn't imagine it. I couldn't imagine being anyplace other than here, with its twisted roads and its singing frogs and its little brown snakes sleeping under my porch. I couldn't imagine going somewhere I couldn't identify the trees, where I wouldn't be able to find a salamander in a creek.

I was entwined with this land. Wasn't I?

And if I was . . . what did that mean for our future?

———

I couldn't imagine leaving this place, not really.

I'd lived away from Bayern County when I was adopted, and

when I was gone for college. But when I'd applied for jobs, Bayern County hooked me back in. Maybe it was the familiar whisper of the water maples or the cicada song in summer that drew me back. Maybe it was the way the land curved around itself in hills and valleys, hiding secrets in shady crevices and around winding roads. Maybe it was the people. Nick had come from here, after all.

I sat on the beach of Sandpiper Run, a man-made beach along the Copperhead River with truckloads of shipped-in sand strewn along the cleared river's edge. The beach was pretty crowded, full of shrieks and sunburns. Teens checked one another out while small children played with sand toys. Many adults lay on beach towels and fiddled with radios, sinking into the sand.

A quarter mile down the beach, a knot of people sat conspicuously not dressed in swimsuits. Curious, I held up my phone and zoomed in on them. About a dozen women in dresses sat on a blanket with a picnic spread. Their attire looked very similar to the style of dresses I'd come to associate with the Greenwood Kingdom Church. I scanned the river. Boys in swimsuits ran back and forth from the water to the blanket, while the girls sat next to the picnic basket. Leah and her friends were among the girls, with the familiar pearl rings on their hands.

I would've liked to spy on the church picnic, but I had a job to do. I focused on the Girl Scout troop I was volunteering with. I was one of six den mothers watching over the troop today. The troop leader was on sunscreen duty, chasing after ten-year-old girls with lotion and bug spray. Monica was the snack fairy, hanging out under a beach umbrella with a cooler full of water and bags full of granola bars and fruit. Others tutored the girls for their swim badges.

I was unused to kids when I first started volunteering. Monica's niece was in the troop, and she'd pulled me in. I'd taken it on as something of a science experiment. I had a pretty good idea of how adults thought and how they viewed the world. I expected the perspective of children to be utterly alien to me, and I was curious to learn.

But when they spoke, I understood. The girls had a sense of wonder about the natural world that had been dimmed out of most adults I knew. They could watch a praying mantis eat its mate with the same delight as they watched sparrow eggs hatch in a nest. The girls were surprisingly unburdened by the guilt and fear most adults were saddled with, and I'd been that way, too.

"Feral," Monica would say, lovingly, rolling her eyes and pulling the girls away from trying to convince a reticent blacksnake to emerge from a hollow in a log.

Feral. I understood that. I hoped they'd carry some of that with them into adulthood.

I think I was a pretty good den mother. I liked spending time with the girls, but I could never envision myself with children of my own. The idea of being wholly responsible for a small human was, frankly, terrifying. Children were feral *and fragile.* I could easily destroy one, as my father had nearly destroyed me.

I never had been able to confront him about what he'd done. I wished I could demand answers. I wished he could tell me what he'd been thinking. I wanted to be able to scream at him. But I couldn't. He was gone. And I was alone with my rage.

From a distance, maybe I could do some good. Today, I was the lifeguard. I sat in a folding chair at the edge of the beach, scanning. I counted the girls' heads over and over. *One, two, three, four, five, six, seven, eight, nine, ten, eleven, twelve, thirteen.* I'd made each girl wear a dayglow pink hair clip so I could distinguish them from other swimmers.

One, two, three . . .

I felt a little self-conscious wearing a swimsuit in public. I hadn't worn one since I'd been shot last year. My black tankini covered the scars on my chest but did nothing to hide the hundreds of tiny bird-shot scars peppering my arms and right leg. They'd faded a lot, but as I tanned they remained stubbornly white. The girls stared, and asked about them. I told them I'd gotten hurt at work but was all healed up now. One of the other den moms distracted the girls with snacks, which I was thankful for. I wasn't sure how much to tell them. These girls were inquisitive, but they weren't as close to life and death as I had been at their age.

Four, five, six . . .

I was lucky to be alive. I kept coming back to Bayern County. I wasn't sure why. Maybe Nick was right. Maybe it meant to chew me up and eat me alive. Maybe I'd just gotten lucky those times I'd brushed up against death.

Seven, eight, nine . . .

At what point should I move forward, create a life with Nick? I'd discovered my father's secret grave, and I'd put his copycat in prison. I had redeemed myself. Maybe I'd done all I was supposed to do here, and it was time to move on. I mean, maybe I *could* move on . . . I wasn't feeling the heartbreak Nick had felt with his mother being taken from him. I just felt a low, simmering rage without an outlet.

Ten, eleven, twelve . . .

If I was honest, I wasn't sure who I would be without this place. My adoptive parents had created a life for me far away from here. I just hadn't fully taken on that identity the way I could've. Maybe it wasn't too late to do that. Maybe I could choose to wake up from the spell that held me fascinated here.

. . . Where the fuck is thirteen?

I rocketed to my feet. Thirteen was Charlotte. Charlotte was a strong swimmer, but that didn't mean much against water hazards.

I rushed toward the river, calling her name and blowing my whistle.

In my peripheral vision, Charlotte's head popped above the surface. She grinned under her goggles. I exhaled shakily. She'd just been underwater for a moment.

"Miss Koray!" a girl shrieked.

I spun to my left. Tisha, Monica's niece, was screaming and waving her arms, rushing out of the river, toward me.

"What's wrong?" I demanded.

She pointed behind her. "That boy . . . he's drowning."

I saw no boy, only turbulence and bubbles in the brown water.

I blew my whistle again and bellowed for everyone to get out of the water. I plunged into the murky depths, pulling myself toward the thrashing. Hands flailed, and the head of a teenage boy struggled to rise above the waterline.

I grabbed the boy's arm and slung it over my shoulders. But he turned and struggled in the river, and something else stirred. Something sharp sliced into my calf, dragged the two of us under.

I couldn't see anything underwater but bubbles and gritty sediment. The boy screamed, muffled by the water. I kept my grip on his arm, kicking with all the force I could muster at whatever it was that grabbed me from below. I struck once, twice, three times with the ball of my foot.

Suddenly, the grip slackened, and I kicked away. I cast about for the boy.

He was windmilling yards from me, and a man shouted: "Stop fighting, and lie still!"

At that familiar voice, a sense of calm settled over me. Fred

Jasper was here. Jasper was rescuing him. He immediately towed the boy to shore, and I followed.

Jasper placed the boy on the beach. His chest was bleeding. He was pale, and twitching like a fish caught on a line and flung up onshore. *A good sign,* I thought distantly. He turned over on his stomach to throw up water. Jasper rolled him onto his side to make sure he wouldn't choke.

"Miss Koray!" A Girl Scout grabbed me by the hand. "You're bleeding!"

I looked down at my leg. Blood dripped from my calf into a puddle in the sand.

Tisha wrapped a towel tightly around my leg and ordered me to sit down. She elevated my leg on a cooler.

"Aunt Monica called an ambulance," she said, very seriously, offering me bottled water.

I put my hand on her shoulder. A kid who could keep it together in an emergency was going to be a helluva doctor or soldier someday. "You just earned your first aid merit badge, kiddo."

Tisha beamed, and I grinned back at her.

Maybe it was moments like this that kept me in Bayern County.

———

The paramedics insisted on taking the boy and me to the hospital. I refused initially, but Tisha insisted that I go in the ambulance, so I did. Trying to be a good example and all. The other troop volunteers told me they had all the girls accounted for and would call their parents. Monica barked orders for the sheriff's office and the Department of Natural Resources to gain control of the scene and make sure no one was allowed back in the water.

"It's a good thing you were here," I told Jasper. "You saved that boy's life."

Jasper sat next to me on the beach. He was unnerved by the near drowning; his hand shook a bit. "Just lucky timing. I was checking the buoys cordoning off the swimming area. Got to make sure everything's ready for the Fourth."

I nodded. "What happened out there?"

"I don't know. I just saw him splashing, saw his head going under. I knew it wasn't horseplay. We need to mark off where the deep water begins better, to keep things like this from happening." His gaze fell on my bleeding leg. "And we need to do a sweep for debris. That looks nasty."

I frowned. "It didn't feel like debris. It felt like an animal of some kind—sharp . . ."

"Let me see that leg."

I showed it to him, still oozing blood.

"Yeah, that looks like a tooth or something. Maybe a snapping turtle? Water snakes don't attack like that."

"I can't help but think about the wounds on that other kid who almost drowned, Mason."

Jasper nodded. "I see it, too. I think we should broaden our horizons. I'll talk to DNR and see if they have any reports of invasive species going on here. I mean, Maryland has found snakehead fish, and those buggers have teeth."

I made a face. "There's something creepy about fish with teeth."

"Right? If I'm honest, I gotta say I'm creeped out, too." He stared out at the water. "I know what's usually down there, but if there's something new, we need to know, to protect the public. Especially with the Fourth coming up."

"Let me know what you find out," I told him. Maybe the monsters here were invasive fish, an ecological disaster. There was something about a fish invasion that made it more comforting than the alternatives.

When the ambulance arrived, the paramedics strapped the boy down on a backboard and carried him up to the road. A group of teen boys followed him, carrying his personal effects, muttering quietly among themselves. I was last, limping along. I didn't like to admit it, but that cut began to smart once the adrenaline wore off.

I sat in the ambulance, propping my foot up on the gurney while the paramedics got an IV line started on the kid and a medic stared at his eyeballs with a flashlight.

"What's your name?" the medic with the flashlight asked.

"Boba," the boy said distantly. "Boba Fett."

"Your name is Boba Fett?"

"Yeah." He sounded very unsteady.

"How many fingers am I holding up?" the paramedic asked.

"Three, I think."

The paramedic put his index finger in front of Boba Fett's face. "I want you to follow my finger with your eyes . . . Good."

I scooched closer to Fett as the paramedics applied pressure to the wounds on his chest. Nothing looked life-threatening, but even small amounts of blood could be serious.

"Am I gonna die?" he squeaked, staring down at the blood.

"No. Just look at the ceiling," the paramedic ordered.

I seized the opportunity to ask questions. "What happened out there?"

He gazed at me with glassy eyes. "There was a girl."

"What girl?" I hoped to hell someone hadn't drowned without my noticing.

"I heard a girl singing. She sounded hot," he mumbled. "So I swam over there."

"Did you see this girl?"

"Yeah. She was smokin' . . . Goth girl."

"What did she look like?"

"Pretty."

I figured I wasn't going to get a better description. "Was she in trouble?"

"Nuh-uh. She was singing, calling me . . . I thought I might get her number . . ."

"Then what happened?"

Fett glared up at the ambulance ceiling. "She . . . she grabbed me. At first, I thought she was playing. She grabbed me by the shoulders and pushed me down."

I inhaled sharply. "And then . . . ?"

"That's . . . that's all I remember . . . her pulling me down."

9

SMALL-TOWN SECRETS

The ambulance swerved on backcountry roads. Boba Fett turned his head and puked. A paramedic caught the vomit in a bucket, and I leaned back against the wall.

A girl. A girl had tried to drown Boba Fett. Well, the kid was pretty out of it. Probably hypoxic. That might be total bullshit, but I dug in my bag for my cell phone and called Dispatch.

"This is Lt. Koray. I've got a message for the deputies on the scene at Sandpiper Run."

"Let me patch you through Bluetooth," Dispatch said.

I didn't know they could do that. Must have something to do with Chief's new radios. After a moment of static, I heard a *BEEP*, and then Deputy Detwiler's voice: "This is D6."

"This is L4. Victim reports there was a girl at the scene who tried to drown him. Don't know if she's at risk of drowning herself, but please be advised. Victim is pretty out of it, and the info may be sketchy."

"Affirmative, L4. We'll be on the lookout and will also relay to DNR."

The line clicked dead, and I heard a few notes of a distantly hummed song, as if from a radio station.

"Dispatch? Is this a secure channel?" I demanded.

The line lapsed into silence.

I hung up, chewing my lip. It wasn't unheard-of for drowning people to grab at others and take them down with them. I didn't think that was what had happened here, but I couldn't rule it out. From the kid's description, it seemed like an attempted drowning. He wasn't exactly a reliable witness, but he wasn't with it enough to be deliberately misleading, either.

We hit a bump in the road, and a backpack rolled open at my feet. It must have belonged to Boba Fett and have been chucked into the ambulance by his friends. A Nintendo Switch, an energy drink, and a wallet rolled out. I chased the energy drink can across the floor and scraped it back into the bag with the Switch. I grabbed the wallet and opened it.

According to his school ID, Boba Fett was really Ross Lister, age fifteen, a student at St. Michael's Prep School.

Lister. Ross was Mark Lister's son.

First Jeff Sumner's son nearly drowned.

Then Mark Lister's.

Totally different scenarios, but this was still a helluva coincidence.

I scrubbed my tongue on the roof of my mouth. It tasted metallic, sharply sweet, not like the soft siltiness of river water. I asked for a bottle of water to rinse my mouth as Ross babbled about a Sith Lord borrowing his Switch and not returning it.

Not the most reliable narrator, that one.

The ambulance roared up to the hospital, and I limped out and got the hell out of the way of the paramedics. They took Ross into the ER, and I trailed behind. I'd only taken my flip-flops and purse with me, and it was awkward, dripping in my clammy swimsuit and clutching my bag. I made squeaking noises and dripped everywhere as I walked, scars and cellulite on full display.

I got taken to the back right away, because I had bled through my towel. I sat on a bed with a paper cover on it, soaking it. It tore anytime I moved. And it was cold as fuck. I poked around the room for something to wear. I would've taken the world's ugliest hospital gown at this point, but there wasn't anything in the staging area.

A fabric curtain separated me from the rest of the emergency room, and from Nick's voice as he worked on Ross in the area beside me. Ross sounded all right, but seemed unable to remember his parents' phone number and what day it was. He also announced that he was the leader of a cult of death-metal robots that fed on cheeseburgers. I guess that was a step up from believing himself to be Boba Fett, bounty hunter.

Nick told one of the nurses: "He's hypoxic, delirious. Let's get him on oxygen, get the bleeding stopped, and then get a chest X-ray. I want to see his lungs, make sure they're clear."

I twiddled my thumbs until the curtain got pulled aside and Nick frowned at me.

"It's just a scratch," I said.

He peeled back the towel. "That's more than a scratch. That's about ten stitches."

"Awesome." I shivered.

Nick opened a drawer and handed me a hospital gown. He leaned close to me, kissed my temple, and whispered: "Stop scaring me."

I sure wished I could. I was doing a pretty good job of scaring myself.

I waited behind the curtain for a PA to come by and sew me up, continuing to eavesdrop through the curtain. Maybe Ross had hallucinated the girl in the river, just as he was now hallucinating that he was the king of a gang of robots. That was certainly the most rational explanation.

"Where's Ross?" a male voice demanded. I sat up a little straighter.

A nurse told him: "He's in X-ray right now. He'll be back soon."

"Is he all right?"

"He's awake and talking. You're his father?"

"Yes."

"You can wait here. I'll send the doctor in when he gets test results."

Rustling sounded in the bay beside me, as if someone sat heavily in a chair. Then the voice began again: "Jeff, this is Mark. There's been an accident at the river."

I leaned forward. The elusive Mark Lister. He had to be on the phone.

"Ross almost drowned. Yeah . . . yeah. I don't know."

There was a pause, and I assumed this was Jeff Sumner's side of the conversation.

Mark's voice sharpened. "No. Let me tell you. My son better be okay. No, I'm going to say what I want. Yeah . . . go fuck off."

There was an exhalation, then the tapping of a shoe on tile.

I stared up at a fluorescent light. Mark didn't seem to think the two near drownings were a coincidence. Maybe someone had it in for those guys and was taking it out on their kids?

Mark sounded angry. Perhaps there was a fracture in the brotherhood of the Kings of Warsaw Creek. Maybe Mark would talk.

The PA arrived to rinse out my wound, and seemed determined to chat to distract me from the pain, but I was more interested in eavesdropping on next door. I caught fragments of a tearful reunion between Ross and Mark, and a few snatches of Nick talking.

"What about . . . infection?" Mark asked hesitantly.

"We'll make sure he gets a course of antibiotics to counteract any waterborne bacteria he might have inhaled," Nick said.

"But . . . I keep reading about parasites and brain worms. Could something like that hurt him?"

"We don't get brain worms in this climate. But if he starts showing any kind of unusual symptoms, I'll have you follow up with his PCP."

I struggled not to hiss as the PA sewed my wound together. I stared down at the angry red weal in my calf, about eight inches long.

"This is a bad spot," she murmured. "Take it easy, and don't flex that muscle much. No marathon running."

"No danger of that." Running a marathon sounded like a really bad time to me on a good day.

In the next bay, Mark whisper-yelled at Ross: "I told you not to go into the water."

"But my friends and I were just—"

"Don't go into the water!"

The rest of the conversation was unintelligible. I wondered what Mark knew that I didn't.

———

Later that night I was cleared to go home, with a bottle of antibiotics and a heavy dose of my boyfriend's worry. Monica came by to pick me up. Thankfully, she brought me the rest of my clothes from the beach.

I hopped on one foot, trying to jam my swollen leg into my jeans, wincing.

"Luckily, there were no other injuries," Monica was telling me as she scrolled on her phone. She was wearing her swimsuit, with a pair of cargo pants, and a pink sweatshirt jacket with *Girl Power* emblazoned on the back. "Jasper's liaising with DNR. They're going to comb through their records, try to figure out if there have been any similar injuries recently."

"Anyone see anything at the beach?" I kept my voice low to prevent anyone from eavesdropping. "Any sign of the girl Ross talked about?"

Monica shook her head. "No one saw her. I interviewed Ross's friends. They said they lost sight of him but didn't see a girl."

I rubbed my forehead. "I hope to hell we don't find another body."

My swollen leg wound up not fitting into my jeans. Monica was kind enough to use the PA's funny bent safety scissors to cut a slit in the side.

"Fashionable," she observed. "Kick flares are back in."

"You should talk," I retorted with a grin. "Y2K called and wanted their cargo pants back."

She stuck her tongue out at me. "I'll go get the car. See you in the pickup area."

"I can walk," I insisted.

"Shut it." Her hand made a puppetlike mouth that opened and snapped closed, and then she disappeared behind the curtain.

I sighed. I probably couldn't catch up to her. I limped out from behind the curtain, headed past the nurses' station, and went down to the elevator banks.

An elevator's door was open, so I called out: "Hold the door, please."

A hand shot out to hold the door open, and I shuffled inside . . . to find myself face-to-face with an older version of Ross, tall and thin, with brown hair. A bit more realistic than the portrait at the car dealership.

I stuck out my hand. "Anna Koray. Nice to meet you, Mr. Lister."

Lister swallowed and shook my hand. "Thank you for helping my boy."

I nodded. "It's part of the job."

He looked at me quizzically, and his brows drew together, as if he were trying to connect my name with my visit to the dealership.

"I work for the sheriff's office."

"Ah." His hand froze around mine, and then he withdrew it. "We were lucky you were there."

I had him here, trapped. I hadn't punched a floor button. "I have to be honest with you, Mark. There's something weird about Ross's accident. He said he saw a girl who tried to drown him, but there's no sign of the girl."

"A girl?" He seemed to pale beneath his spray tan.

"Yeah. Ross described her as a goth girl. Does he have any friends, or maybe a girlfriend, who might match that description? I'm worried about her."

Mark's hand slid to his mouth. "No. I don't remember him talking about a girl. I thought . . . maybe he was just involved in some horseplay."

"Why do you think he might say something like that?"

He looked away. "Don't know. He seems really out of it."

"This isn't the only near drowning I've seen lately." I pressed onward. "You likely saw on the news that Jeff Sumner's child nearly drowned."

He stared into the cup of coffee he was holding. "Jeff told me."

"From an outsider's perspective, this is a really odd coincidence."

"How so?"

"Well, as I'm investigating that case, I look at the backgrounds of the adults to see if there's anything significant. And I saw in our records that you and Jeff and Quentin Sims were accused in the disappearance of a girl twenty-five years ago."

Mark squeezed the coffee cup so tightly that liquid sloshed through the plastic lid. "That was nuts. I don't want to think about that."

"I have to wonder if someone else, someone connected to that girl, harbors a grudge. And that person—or people—is directing some anger at you."

He closed his eyes. "It's bad. It's really bad."

The elevator, summoned from a lower floor, began to move down.

"What happened, Mark?"

He seemed just about ready to confess something to me. He'd licked his lips and opened his mouth when the doors slid apart.

A very irritated-looking man in scrubs stared at me. He was in his fifties, with graying hair and a harsh line of a mouth. The badge on his lanyard read: ER DEPARTMENT DR. FLOYD.

Shit. Nick's boss.

Floyd glowered at us and elbowed his way into the elevator. "Excuse me."

Lister shook his head, his confession trance broken. "I'm sorry. I can't help you."

He exited the elevator, and I stumped after him. "But there's—"

He turned on me in a flash of anger. "Leave me alone. This is police harassment."

I paused, taken aback by his sudden change of mood.

He stabbed a finger at me. "You were at both drownings. How do I know that you didn't have something to do with them?"

I blinked. "That's not—"

"Stay away from me."

Lister slipped away, into the lobby, practically at a run. Definitely faster than I could pursue him.

Mark Lister knew things. Jeff Sumner knew things. But neither one of them was saying anything. Jeff seemed angry. But Lister seemed scared.

But scared of what?

I found Monica's car in the pickup area and eased into the passenger seat.

"I saw Lister flying out of there like a bat outta hell. Was that your doing?" I noticed that she'd raided the vending machines. She handed me a candy bar, and I took it gratefully.

"Almost had him spilling his guts. He knows something. He might be easier to get to than Jeff."

"Well, we got a nice letter from Jeff's attorney, threatening to charge us with harassment."

"Not surprising."

"Well, he doesn't have a leg to stand on. CPS is involved in Mason's case now. The social worker assigned to the case wants to know everything we find out."

"If we're investigating a crime, he can't claim harassment."

We bumped fists.

"You know what's weird?" I said. "It will be twenty-five years since Dana disappeared this Fourth of July. And now, all of a sudden, the children of the principal suspects in that case have been harmed. It makes me think that's not a fluke, especially given that number on the skull."

"You think it's a countdown?"

"Could be. I mean . . . what if a kid like Leah is next? Even if the girls aren't allowed to swim, I feel like we've got to warn the parents."

"Agreed."

I called Pastor Sims. He picked up on the second ring. "Hello?"

"Pastor Sims, this is Lt. Anna Koray from the Bayern County Sheriff's Office."

"Hello, Lieutenant." His voice echoed peculiarly. Maybe he was in the bathroom, which I didn't want to imagine. "What can I do for you?"

"There's been another near drowning in your social circle recently."

There was a pause. "I heard about Ross."

"Yes. I wanted to call because I'm worried about your daughter—"

"Did she do something?" He seemed awfully quick to jump to that.

"No, no. She's done nothing wrong. It seems like a pattern is emerging, that there are peculiar near drownings associated with the children in your church. I'm concerned for Leah."

"Leah isn't allowed in the water. Too much temptation there. Water awakens lasciviousness in women."

I closed my eyes and pinched the bridge of my nose. "I mean to say that I think you should keep an eye on her, just in case something happens."

"I always do, Lieutenant, as a concerned parent. Now, if you'll excuse me, it's late."

"I—"

The line went dead before I could begin to ask him about the disappearance of Dana Carson. I made a face at the phone.

"Let's assume for a moment that these guys were indeed responsible for the disappearance of Dana Carson, and that they killed her. What doesn't make sense to me is that they still seem to be buddies," Monica said.

"Yeah, that's strange," I agreed.

"Right? Usually, when a group is involved in a homicide, they break up. One turns on the rest. Or at the very least, they disperse. It's very odd that they're still friends. Some strange fraternity."

"You'd think they'd want to start fresh at a new location. Have a clean slate, start over." As soon as the words left my mouth, I thought of Nick, and his wanting to leave this place.

Damn. Maybe Bayern County had some weird hold over all of us.

10

SALT

I didn't want to dream again.

I meant to stay awake as late as I could.

The supernatural was trying to creep into my head again. That madness. I didn't want it. I didn't want to go back to that place again, where I couldn't distinguish reality from fantasy. I needed to stay on this side of the line, grounded. In control.

I hobbled into my house, where I was immediately bowled over by Gibby, who was in a rush to fall all over Monica. She knelt to receive the full magnitude of dog slobber that Gibby had been saving up for her.

"Who's a good boy?" she cooed at him. "Does my good boy want a piece of jerky?"

He grinned in adoration and slapped his tail on the floor.

"How about I walk him and give him a treat?" she suggested.

"Thanks." I wasn't relishing stomping around in the dark while Gibby sniffed every tree stump and toadstool from here to the creek.

She headed out, Gibby bounding behind her.

"Watch out for skunks!" I called. Gibby, God bless him, didn't have the sense to leave other animals alone. He truly believed every animal he met was either a friend or potential lunch. He'd gotten sprayed earlier this spring, and Nick had had a miserable time washing him in vinegar and tomato sauce.

I changed into yoga pants and a T-shirt. I stared at my angry red leg. I'd had worse injuries before—much worse. It would heal, and it was better the less I thought about it. I poured myself some water and took my first dose of antibiotics, with ibuprofen.

Monica returned with Gibby and threw an empty bag of beef jerky into the kitchen trash. She was holding her phone. "He peed four times, and pooped at the edge of the woods."

"Awesome. Thanks."

"Also got a background check back on Drema's college stalker." She put her phone into her pocket.

I sucked in my breath. "Maybe he's our guy?"

"Michael Allan Renfelter went to the local college twenty years ago, which was about the right time for Drema and Jeff to be there. Never graduated. He worked in information technology for a handful of years, then wound up in federal prison on RICO charges."

"Interesting. What did he do?"

"Looks like electronic money laundering for some drug lords. He's been cooling his heels at Edgefield, South Carolina, this whole time. No furloughs, either."

"Damn. I was so hoping for a slam dunk. Writing him off the list of suspects means that the Sumners have more enemies than we thought."

Monica shook her head. "More money, more problems, I guess. Do you need me to take the trash up to the road or anything?"

"No. I really appreciate you doing this for me." I had a lump in my throat. Monica had always been a good friend and mentor to me. I could really count on her in a pinch.

"No worries, girl." She cracked her gum and gave me a hug. "Let's touch base in the morning."

I watched from the window as she drove up the driveway out onto the main road. I locked the door. I'd installed double-keyed dead bolts at every place I'd lived in that had glass in the front doors. I'd seen too many cases where burglars just broke the windows in the doors, flipped the dead bolt latch, and let themselves in. When I was home, I normally left the key in the inside face of the lock in case I needed to get out quickly.

But I didn't tonight. If I went sleepwalking again, I wanted to stay home. Walking barefoot in the dirt sounded like an excellent way to get an infection in my leg, and I was not wanting to tempt fate . . . or whatever the hell might be out there.

No, I told myself. This was just my own mind churning, wobbling out of orbit once more. I had to get control.

After I locked the door, I put the key on top of the fridge.

I opened a can of dog food for Gibby, who devoured it in two bites. He launched himself onto Nick's side of the bed and glanced over his shoulder at me with a come-hither look.

I hauled the case file for the Dana Carson disappearance to my nightstand and began reading. I flipped to the picture of Dana from her yearbook. It was always strange for me that someone tangible enough to appear in a photograph could disappear without a trace. I hoped to gain some insight into who she was, who she might be if she was still alive. I got the impression that she was outgoing and confident, searching for something.

My gaze fell on her necklace, the crescent moon resting on her collarbone. I squinted at it. That necklace looked as if it had a stone in it. A pearl.

I looked at the river pearl on my nightstand, compared it to Dana's. Dana's pearl and the pearl from the pond were different shapes, but they looked pretty similar in sheen and color.

Coincidence, right? Maybe Dana was wearing some kind of freshwater pearl she'd bought on a vacation.

Maybe.

I stayed up reading the file. The original investigators' frustration was palpable. They had a witness who'd seen Dana with three boys at the gas station on the Fourth of July. The witness was an upperclassman working a summer job as a clerk, and she recognized them. Before Dana's arrival, the boys were trying to convince the clerk to close early and go watch fireworks with them, but she refused. When Dana arrived to buy a Coke, the boys invited Dana to go with them. Dana declined; she was supposed to meet her sister. The boys said they would go with her, and crowded her out the door.

Dana's older sister, Vivian, reported that she was waiting for Dana to meet her at the burger joint down the street. I knew that place well; it overlooked the river and had an ancient burial mound in the parking lot. The parking lot had been entirely paved except for the mound, on which was planted a tulip tree with a picnic bench perched beneath it. Vivian waited at the picnic bench until the sun went down, and Dana never showed. As the fireworks started, she went into the restaurant to call their mother, who hadn't seen Dana, either.

Records showed that the girls' mother contacted the sheriff's office. The office sent a car, but didn't have any luck finding her that night. The hope was that Dana would return of her own accord in the morning.

But she never did.

An APB was put out, and Dana's face was televised on the news channels for weeks afterward. No trace of her was ever found.

Detectives did the rounds, eyeballing the three boys who had seen her last. The boys' wealthy parents refused to allow their sons to be interrogated, and lawyered up. The statements given through lawyers all corroborated one another: the boys had walked Dana down to the beach, where a crowd was assembled to watch the fireworks. Dana voluntarily left with a man none of them knew. A sketch of the man was included: a generic-looking guy in his twenties, with brown hair and blue eyes. He was reported to be five feet eleven inches, wearing shorts and a white T-shirt.

The case stalled. The sketch was circulated, and a number of men who met that description attended the fireworks. The boys pointed the finger at a college guy who was back home, visiting his girlfriend. But the girlfriend and her family gave him an alibi—he was seen grilling for an extended family of fourteen people—and that went nowhere.

The detectives had shaken the tree of people in Dana's life who might've had motive. Her estranged dad was in prison for forgery; her mom wasn't dating anyone currently. Dana had an ex-boyfriend, though, a Rick Smitz. They'd broken up three weeks before she went missing, but he was a hundred miles away at the time of the disappearance. Smitz had a bulletproof alibi: he'd gotten a speeding ticket on the way to a concert.

Dana had dated several guys. If she were a boy, she would've been called "popular"; the lawyers for the Kings of Warsaw Creek called her a slut. In addition to Rick Smitz's, there were three boyfriends' names in the file: Jason Williams, Luke Peterson, and Wally Westerville. Jason had been grounded for bad grades and was home with his parents. Luke was out riding motorcycles with some other boys. And Wally claimed to have been at the library. A librarian vouched for him.

I exhaled.

Nothing.

It was a whole lot of nothing that I had to find something in.

A green flash moved slowly over my vision, from left to right, like headlights washing across my face.

My mom liked to sleep in. Today was no exception.

I stared at my mom's closed bedroom door for many minutes. I put a T-shirt on over my Underoos, found my sneakers, and then slipped outside.

I plunged into the cool shade of the forest. Confusion roiled in my head. I was at home in the woods; my dad had called me his heir, a princess of the forest. I adored him and shadowed his footsteps, looking upon my mom as the villain, the one who made me put on shoes and comb my hair and go to school. Mom was boring, all about limits and telling me what to do. Dad was about freedom and following tracks in the forest. My dad had magic, showing me where salamanders slept beneath rocks and which fiddleheads were edible.

But he was gone, and Mom had surprised me. Without my dad's presence, I felt hers, serious and watchful. And it wasn't as awful as it had been in the past. My mom had her own way of doing things, her own magic unfolding in the dark. And despite all her coldness toward me over time, I still wanted to please her. Some hope that she could love me had been ignited in me.

But it felt like I was betraying Dad. He'd been gone only a few days. He was coming back. And how would he react if he saw me closer to my mom? Would he cast me aside, too?

I never knew what brought the two of them together. I knew only that they hated each other. And I didn't want both of them to hate me.

Wading among the cattails, I descended to the muddy river. I bent and sniffed the water. It smelled all right.

I walked in, then let the cool water soothe my sunburned skin.

I floated on my back, looking up at the sun. Suspended between water and sky, I felt the river moving at my back, a great vein of energy unfurling below me. It was different than when I was on land, listening to birds and observing deer. Water swished over me, slowing my pulse and supporting me as if I weighed nothing.

I drifted downstream in the river's intangible grip, my eyes closed, until I became aware of something sliding against me. I thought it might be a log or some other kind of debris. I opened my eyes and saw something brown floating beside me.

It turned in the river's current, and I screamed.

I stared a deer in the face, his antlers reaching out like claws and his eyes white and milky, his disintegrating tongue trailing in the river.

I scrambled out of the water. Mom had been right—it was poisoned, all of it. I jammed my feet into my shoes and ran home.

I let myself into the bathroom and turned on the shower, hoping to rinse the poisoned water away. But the sickly sweet smell hit me, and I knew it was still poisoned, too.

I backed away from it, bumping into Mom.

She looked down at me, wet and disheveled. I was certain she was going to scream at me. My shoulders went up around my ears.

Instead of screaming, she went to the shower and turned it off. She put the stopper in the tub and turned the faucet on.

She left me staring at the tub, then returned with a glass mason jar. She poured its contents into the bathwater, then ordered me to strip.

"What's that?" I asked meekly.

"Salt. Baking soda. Epsom salt." She tugged my T-shirt over

my head and herded me into the bath. The sweet smell of the water had faded.

I pulled my knees up to my chin, feeling weird about being nude in front of my mom. As the tub filled, she poured shampoo on my hair and began to wash it. Not roughly, like that time a kid had put gum in my hair. She was gentle.

I'd begun to wonder if this was what it would be like if Dad stayed gone. Part of me wanted it to be like this with her.

"Do you think Dad is coming back?" I asked her quietly, and then immediately regretted spitting out the question.

"Do you want him to come back?" She paused in lathering my scalp. "He left us, you know."

I swallowed the lump in my throat that rose at that abandonment. Mom could be mean, but she was always there. She always was. If I got sick, she was the one to pick me up at school. She signed all my notes for my teachers. She paid the bills neatly every month. She was boring to my mind. But maybe she was something else, too, something steady.

Did I want him to come back?

I shook my head, knowing this was the answer she wanted, and not trusting that my voice would hold steady if I spoke. Maybe he'd left because of me. Maybe it had been my fault.

"Good girl. We'll be fine, just the two of us. You'll see."

"Did he leave because of me?" I whispered.

"No. Not because of you. Lie back in the water."

I lay back to rinse my hair, looking up at the tiled ceiling. I had never feared my dad, not in the way I feared my mom.

But I didn't fear her at all in that moment, as she wiped soap from my eyes and I slid under the surface of the water.

11

THE WICKED WITCH OF BAYERN COUNTY

It took three cups of coffee to clear my head the next morning.

I walked down the beach at Sandpiper Run, dragonflies zinging around me. The beach had been cleared, and yellow police tape was woven among the trees. Dark leaves whispered overhead, and I smelled cloying honeysuckle. As people drove by the parking lot, I could feel eyes boring into my back. There would be pressure to open the beach soon.

I limped down the beach. The only shoe I'd been able to jam my swollen foot into was one of Nick's tennis shoes, and I minded my footing. I'd put three pairs of socks on my healthy foot to wear the other shoe properly. I sure as hell wasn't going to be involved in any foot chases today.

Someone had been here despite the lines of crime scene tape strung along the trees. Designs had been carved in the sand of the beach, unintelligible, over and over: The snake eating its own tail. The ouroboros. And the number seven. Seven days until the Fourth of July . . .

I took pictures. Likely, sneaky teenagers had crossed into the scene overnight and had been unnoticed by the deputy who was supposed to be guarding the scene. He was on the beach now, but he likely parked by the road. I'd have a word with him. This meant any evidence we gathered from the scene from here on out would be contaminated and inadmissible.

A splash sounded, and I turned to see Jasper wading out of the river. He waddled to the shore with his fins, then sat down heavily beside a pile of gear. He began stripping off his fins.

"Hey." I sat down beside him. "What's it look like down there?"

"Silty." He showed me the camera he'd been using to take pictures. I saw very little on its screen, just dirt and fuzzy water.

"Any snakeheads or other creatures with teeth?"

He shook his head. "I've been searching since yesterday for the girl who was reported by the near-drowning victim. No sign of her. Nothing weird underwater, either. Saw a very nice water snake, though."

He clicked the pictures forward and showed me one of a dark gray snake creating tiny ripples as it swam. It had a round head and a slightly derpy expression. Nothing that could kill a human.

"That's a pretty snake," I said.

"It was. My contact at DNR says they've had a few reports of what they call 'suspicious aquatic encounters.'" Jasper made air quotes around the words. "She's skeptical, because most of the calls she gets about being bitten by something underwater wind up being about dumb stuff people have done, like messing with snakes."

"So it's okay to just take pictures?" I teased him.

"Look, but don't touch." He lifted a brow. "You know, there's a study an ER doctor conducted several years ago. The vast majority of ER admissions for snakebites are teen boys and men. Small children and women don't get bit nearly as often."

"Why is that?"

"Small kids and women have the sense to get away and leave snakes alone. Dudes gotta mess with wildlife and reap the consequences." He grinned, and I grinned back.

"Makes sense." I gestured to the beach, to the symbols carved in the sand. "What do you make of those? They're the same as the symbol on the skull in the Sumners' mailbox."

He lifted a shoulder. "Looks kind of occult to me, honestly. Wouldn't surprise me. The summer solstice was a couple days ago. Longest day of the year, and it's a big deal at places where pagan folk gather, like Stonehenge. They have a live feed and everything when the sun rises and sets."

"Sounds like you know about that stuff."

"Not so much. But timing is important in the natural world. I just keep track of the summer solstice because the river tides are higher. Something about the angle of the sun. It happens every year, even this far inland."

I sighed. "Forensics came up with nothing about that skull. No prints. A total dead end."

"Ah, that sucks."

"It just makes me think the cases are connected. And I've been researching the Dana Carson disappearance case. The numbers on the skull and the sand . . . It's now seven days until the Fourth of July, the anniversary of her disappearance."

"Think about the timing," he said. "Somebody might have sat on this for twenty-five years, waiting for justice, and decided they were gonna take it into their own hands when it didn't come."

I rested my chin on my knees. "That makes more sense than any theory I've got right now. But why now, after so long?"

"When you think an injustice has been committed, there's no time limit on anger," Jasper said.

I looked at him.

"We all have cases like that." He shrugged.

"Chief remembers," I said. "I guess it's not a stretch to think that Dana's alive in someone else's memory, too."

"Chief's a good man. Listen to him."

I nodded.

"You'll get it worked out, Koray. I know you will."

He packed up his gear and left me on the beach. Jasper had confidence in me, but I wasn't so sure I was any closer to figuring out who the perpetrator was than I was the night Mason drowned.

I heard a car engine above me, on the road. Near the caution tape, a black SUV idled. Jeff Sumner was staring down at the beach, his expression cold and unreadable behind his sunglasses.

Our gazes met, and he drove off.

I didn't know why he was there. Concern? Curiosity? An attempt to control? It was hard to guess.

Water lapped at the edges of my sneakers. I frowned as I saw something shiny at my feet.

I reached down, into the silt, picked up something green. I stared at its iridescent surface.

A river pearl.

My gaze narrowed. I'd gone my whole life without finding a river pearl . . . and I'd seen two in three days.

I sifted through the sand, finding nothing else.

I stared at the palm of my hand. In defiance of the gathering summer heat, it felt like an ice cube.

In spite of myself, I shuddered.

———

I needed to get closer to Dana.

Her sister, Vivian, still lived in Bayern County, at their childhood address. I coasted over ribbons of two-lane roads. I found the address on a dented rural mailbox and followed a dirt driveway into a forest. After a quarter mile, the drive ended in a clearing where a farmhouse stood. The house likely dated back a century, but it was in pretty decent repair—slate shingles were stained from acid rain, and the windows were still intact, but it looked as if there hadn't been any updates in decades. Gardens surrounded the house, a cottage riot of orange ditch lilies, catnip, and purple bee balm. A garden studded with tomatoes and sunflowers sprawled out back.

A woman with jet-black hair sat on a porch swing. She was pale, with silver rings flashing on her fingers as she smoked a cigarette and watched me with narrowed eyes.

I climbed up onto the porch. "Hello. I'm Lt. Anna Koray with the Bayern County Sheriff's Office. Are you Vivian Carson?"

She looked me up and down. "I'm Viv. And I've been expecting you."

Viv leaned forward and gestured to a wicker chair and coffee table between us. There were two glasses of iced tea there, with fresh ice crackling in the heat.

"You were expecting me?" I blurted.

Vivian looked down at a potted plant on the porch. It looked like an ordinary Boston fern, but I saw something moving underneath it, the undulating scales of a black rat snake. A tongue flickered out in my direction.

"Is he a pet?" I'd spent a lot of time around snakes, and I knew this one wasn't venomous.

"No. He's an employee. Pest control."

I eased myself into the chair and thanked her for the tea. Despite the smoking, her face was remarkably unlined. Probably a benefit of being goth, and shunning the sun. She had to be in her forties by now, and she wore her age well, with no gray hair. She was dressed in a black tank top and jeans, and she was barefoot. Her arms were scarred up. Didn't look like self-harm, though. They looked like animal scratches.

"I'm here to talk about your sister. Is this a good time?"

Vivian stubbed out her cigarette in a glass ashtray. "Always. Has the case been reopened?"

"It was never closed, and I'm looking into it now. You're the only relative I could find an address for, and I wanted to ask what you remember."

Her mouth turned down. "Yes. I would be the only one you could find."

"Is your mom local?"

Her gaze flicked away. "Mom tried to kill herself six months after Dana vanished. She was institutionalized."

"I'm so very sorry." I leaned forward, pressing my elbows to my knees and clasping my hands before me.

Viv exhaled. "It was just the three of us after Dad left, when I was five. She couldn't imagine living in a world in which her daughters didn't outlive her."

"She thought Dana was dead?"

"Yeah. There was no way Dana would've been gone from us that long if she were alive."

"How did it happen?" I asked gently.

"I came home from school and found Mom in the bathtub." Viv took a sip of iced tea. "My mom never wanted to make a mess, so she slit her wrists in the tub."

"That had to be beyond terrible."

"It was. I sat beside the bathtub, waiting for the paramedics. I didn't know if she was alive or not. I just stared at that red water, hoping they could fix her." Her gaze was unfocused, and then she looked up at me. "Would you like to see some pictures of her and Dana?"

"Yes, please."

Viv stood and beckoned me into the house, opening the wooden screen door. Inside, the lights were out and a fan hummed. The place probably hadn't changed much since Viv's sister went missing. There was yellowing blue and white wallpaper, and a stopped clock on the wall.

Viv followed my gaze. "That clock stopped after Dana vanished. I never had the heart to change the batteries."

I understood then. This place was a monument to Viv's grief.

She led me to a sitting room containing a threadbare couch and overstuffed chairs. The place smelled like dust.

Two large dog crates stood against the fireplace. I peered inside the first, at a knot of gray fur snuggled down in a box. "Baby opossums?"

"This is the time of year when some fall off their mom and need help."

Her watch beeped. "Speaking of which . . . I need to do a feeding."

"Don't mind me," I said.

I glanced at the second dog crate. A fluffy gray raccoon the size of a cantaloupe stared at me from a nest of towels. He yawned, showing sharp little teeth.

She slipped away to the kitchen, and I took in the rest of the room. On an upright piano, photographs stood. I looked at them, one by one. There were two dark-haired girls, the sisters, and their mother. The mother looked barely old enough to be the girls' parent, and might be mistaken for another sister.

Vivian returned with a bottle, opened the first cage, and picked up two baby opossums. She snuggled them in her shirt and began bottle-feeding the tiny blobs of fur. The first one that took the bottle moved its black ears as it nursed. When he was full, Viv turned her attention to the second, which was fussier about the bottle but eventually got the hang of it.

I looked at a picture of a girl in a dark red prom dress standing beside a young man in a suit. Her dress plunged low, and she had the sauciness of a silent-screen vamp. Her date looked thrilled to have her on his arm.

"This is your sister?"

"Yes. That's her prom picture. Her date was Rick Smitz. Nice guy."

I looked at the fresh-faced, smiling young man. "They had been together awhile, sort of. Broke up Rick's senior year before he went to college."

"Was it amicable?"

"Oh sure. Neither one of them wanted to be tied down, especially with him going to college. Dana was a free spirit. She dated a lot, and she and Rick weren't exactly exclusive."

"Do you remember any of the other boyfriends?"

She put the opossums back in the box and closed the cage door. "Um. There was Jason Williams. A guy named Luke—I don't remember his last name. And Wally—we used to call him 'Wally the Wunderkind.' I think he became an astronaut or something. Dana was catnip to guys. Everyone who saw her fell a little in love with her. But she was always fair. She made no promises."

I nodded. That tracked with what I'd seen in her file. I knew young men might take things more seriously than she did, and I mentally added to my suspect list. Maybe one of them had fallen in love with her. I made a note to make background checks on these men to see if there were any red flags that might have come up in their adult lives.

Viv opened the second cage and began to feed Cheerios to the raccoon. He took the bits of cereal with dexterous fingers, scarfing them quickly.

"Rick came by a lot after Dana was gone, and after my mom got sent away. I think he felt guilty, somehow, though none of it was his fault."

I looked closer at the picture of Dana. She was wearing the moon necklace with the pearl in it, settled in her creamy cleavage. "Can you tell me about that necklace?"

"It was her prized possession. She was learning to make jewelry. Dana had this uncanny knack for finding these freshwater pearls. She'd be down at Sandpiper Run and sometimes find three in an afternoon." Viv smiled sadly. "I've never found one myself."

I stifled a shudder. I felt as if I were walking through cobwebs.

I turned my attention to a picture of Viv, a candid of her in a short black skirt and waffle-soled platform boots.

"How old were you when your mom tried to kill herself?"

"I was eighteen. Just old enough to be able to get the deed to the house signed over to me. Not old enough to know what the hell to do with it, but I got it figured out. I got a job as a waitress, and ends somehow met." She shook her head sheepishly. "I won about twenty thousand dollars on scratch-off tickets that year, so I was able to get by. The animals are taken care of mostly through donations."

I didn't comment on her luck. I picked up a picture of the mom and the girls as little ones, wearing matching purple dresses, likely at a Sears portrait studio. "What did your mom do?"

"She was a secretary. Worked for Jeff Sumner's father, at Copperhead Valley Solvents."

Small world. "She quit?"

"She stopped going in. When the company sent flowers to the house, she set them on fire and cursed them."

"Cursed them?" I echoed.

She shrugged. "As one does. I cursed those little bastard Kings of Warsaw Creek, too."

I blinked. Most people at least tried to disguise their hate in front of the cops.

She looked at me and laughed. "You know curses."

"Um . . . when you say you cursed them, what does that mean, exactly?"

"I wished them all dead in the most awful, shittiest of ways. Mom was a witch, and I just followed in her footsteps. Don't pretend you don't know." Viv turned away and sat on the couch.

My gaze roved around the room, and I saw things I hadn't noticed before: a jar of dried chicken feet, a handmade willow broom in the corner, a deck of ornately patterned cards on the coffee table that looked too big to be playing cards. Little crystals were tucked on top of picture frames, scattered on the coffee table, and above the mirror that spread over the back of the couch.

"You mean, because I'm an investigator and I'm drawing conclusions based on your eclectic décor."

"Nope." Viv leaned forward. Her eyes glistened. "Because you reek of darkness, of some evil spirit that's worked its way under your skin. You don't talk about it, no. It's your secret, how intimate you and the dark are."

I went still, though my heart beat evenly, as I assessed how big a threat she was. She was playing head games, and I wouldn't fall victim to them. "What makes you so sure of that?"

"There are dark things in Bayern County, things that crawl under rocks and slither through the river. Mom taught me about them. Unseen spirits. Things that were never human, things that gather here."

My throat was dry. "Why would that be?"

She lifted a shoulder. "Some folks say Bayern County is at the center of a bunch of spirit roads, and many spirits come here and stay. Or maybe they can't leave. Maybe it's because of all that underground water. Mom said this place is like a big piece of fly tape, where we all get stuck and wriggle around until we die."

A fly zoomed past me in the room—or something I thought was a fly.

On my phone I pulled up pictures of the symbols on the beach and the skull in the mailbox. "Did you do these?"

She shook her head. "That wasn't me."

I didn't think I believed her. "Do you know what they are?"

She leaned forward and squinted at the photos. "Looks like an ouroboros, a snake eating its own tail. It's about the cycle of decay and rebirth. What goes around comes around."

"Do you know why someone would put that here?"

She shrugged. "I don't have any insight into another witch's casting."

"Another witch?" I echoed. There were witches . . . plural . . . in Bayern County? "Who might have done this?"

"Like I said, this is a place where powers converge. Lots of people tap into that. Could have been anyone. But if I knew, I wouldn't tell you." A smile played on her lips.

My attention was snagged by the familiar sound of claws clicking on hardwood. I turned to the hallway to see a red fox trotting into the room. It looked at me and yawned with a squeak before going to sit beside Vivian. The fox glanced into the opossum cage, then slipped under Viv's hand.

"This is Sinoe," Viv said.

"She's gorgeous." I extended my hand to the fox. She sniffed my hand and stared at me with brown eyes.

"She's been with me since she was a pup."

"Another bottle baby?"

"Sort of. She never really domesticated herself. She comes and goes as she pleases."

I turned my attention back to the investigation. "I'm working Dana's case. I want to know what you know, if there's anything you can tell me that might jog something loose."

Viv leaned back and draped her arm across the spine of the couch. "Of course."

"Did you have any contact with these . . . Kings of Warsaw Creek before or after Dana's disappearance that made you think they were responsible?"

Viv sipped her tea. "The police said those fuckers weren't allowed to talk to me and I wasn't allowed to talk to them. But we went to the same school, so of course that didn't last long. When I walked by them in the hallways, they'd bang their lockers to make me jump, and flick their lighters at me."

"Ugh." It slipped out before I could stop it.

"Yeah. I wanted to fuck them up, destroy those sons of bitches who were going to get away with everything because they're dudes and they're rich." Viv drummed her fingers on the back of the couch. "Mom told me to let her handle it, that justice would prevail. And if it didn't, her curse would.

"But then my mom went insane, got locked away, and I was alone to make my own curses."

"How did you curse them?" I ventured.

"Many ways. So many ways." Her dark eyes glittered. "I poured my blood into the ground and the creeks, asking for them to get their just deserts. I stuffed jars with sulfur and nails and piss and buried them all over the county. I carved their names into candles and burned them down at every black moon ever since. It's taken such a long time . . . Those motherfuckers must be seriously magically fortified."

"Viv, how . . . open are you about doing all this hexing?" There was nothing illegal about what she admitted to doing, but . . . fuck. The honesty was a bit terrifying, no matter how deluded she was. Maybe it was hereditary. Maybe she'd just lost her mind. Maybe she could keep it together, refocus her trauma to help wild animals. But I wasn't sure.

She laughed. "I make no secrets about how much I hate those assholes. I want them to suffer. But I'm not about to get arrested."

"I'm confused about why you're telling me this."

"Because," she answered matter-of-factly, "you're a sister in these things. In things that creep around the dark."

I shook my head sharply, swallowed, and shifted tactics. I asked her where she was yesterday and the night before that.

"I was at work, at the Grey Door bar. My boss will have my time cards." She didn't seem offended at all that I was asking. "Why?"

I didn't see a television here, but I figured she would hear about it eventually. "There were near drownings . . . involving children of those men."

She was still, very still, and I couldn't read her. "I see."

"Viv, did you do something to those kids? Did you visit the sins of the fathers on the children?"

She shook her head. "I spat in jars and poked holes in poppets with pins. I did not, in any way, shape, or form, touch *anyone*."

The hair on the back of my neck lifted. I thought she was telling the truth. But damn. She had motive. Such powerful motive.

When I left, I glanced up at the lintel. There was a railroad spike on it.

I asked Viv, "What's the railroad spike for?"

She patted the cold metal. "That's to keep evil out. It works most of the time."

I walked back to the car, remembering when I'd seen a railroad spike above a door . . . at Jeff Sumner's house. And again, at Sims's parsonage.

Maybe the Kings of Warsaw Creek believed in the occult, too. Small world.

12

TRUST

"Get a grip, Anna. Get a grip."

I repeated this over and over to myself like a mantra, clutching the El Camino's sticky steering wheel as I drove back to familiar ground. Viv was playing me, and she was likely unhinged from the trauma in her family, existing in a fantasy world she'd created. She just happened to be really good at reading people, like so-called psychics who fleeced folks at festivals.

Right?

I didn't like how she'd decided I was some kind of dark entity creeping around the margins of Bayern County. I was a Girl Scout den mother. I always turned my library books in on time. I had commendation medals from work. There was no fucking way this woman could peer into my soul and decide I was tooling around the county's occult underbelly. There was no way she could tell I was my father's daughter.

Right.

I headed by the Grey Door bar, tucked away on a side street near the Copperhead River. It was the kind of place I had no interest in, having broken up more than my share of fights there during my Patrol days. It was a one-story building with no windows and with a scuffed door painted gunmetal gray.

As I opened the door, a bell jingled. My eyes adjusted to the dim light, my gaze sweeping over the bar, the sticky floor, the booths, and the cracked jukebox playing vintage hair band music. There were only three patrons, including a couple of guys in a booth who seemed to be deep in conversation. When I walked by, they glanced up at me and shut up. Probably for the best.

A familiar figure sat at the end of the bar. Rod Matthews looked at me like a deer caught in headlights.

I nodded at him. "I'm surprised you made bail this early, Rod."

He looked down at his drink and mumbled something.

"I'm sorry?"

He cleared his throat. "My mom bailed me out."

"Ah. You gonna show up for your hearing?"

"Yes, ma'am." He hiked up his pant leg to show a GPS tracker fastened around his ankle.

Well, at least I'd know where to go looking for him next.

"Is your brother, Timmy, back in town? I thought I saw his car."

He shook his head. "I haven't heard from Timmy."

"I ran into one of your friends the other day." I described the man who'd followed me into the gorge at the Hag Stone. "Does that sound like a guy you know?"

He stared down at his shoes. "No, ma'am."

He was lying; he wouldn't meet my gaze.

"Would this be someone who might be involved in a certain criminal enterprise with you?"

"It doesn't sound like it." His voice was a whisper.

"I'd very much like to find out what this guy is up to, and what your brother's doing back in town."

He lifted a shoulder. "I dunno. I hear a lot of guys are getting work from some rich guy. Side jobs, like scrapping and construction and stuff."

"A rich guy? Do any of these people look familiar?" On my phone I summoned pictures of the Kings of Warsaw Creek.

Rod looked away. "I dunno. I don't hang out with guys like that anymore."

"You wouldn't happen to know where the supplies you guys were getting for meth manufacture came from, would you?"

"No, ma'am. My mom told me to behave myself."

"Mm. Well, you'd let me know if you hear anything, wouldn't you, Rod?"

He nodded vigorously. "Yes, ma'am."

Rod wasn't breaking the law at this exact instant (that I knew of, anyway), so I left him alone. But he'd pretty much confirmed my suspicion that my pursuer had been hired. And that led me back to the Kings of Warsaw Creek. But which one had hired him?

I sat down at the opposite end of the bar and waited for the bartender. I knew him to also be the owner, Owen Destin. Owen kept a shotgun under the bar, and I didn't comment on it. Wasn't what I was here for.

Owen was bald, clad in a flannel shirt, and had a tattoo of a snake peeping out above his collar, where it seemed to lick his jaw. "Can I help you, Lt. Koray?"

"Yeah. Could I get a Coke and a few minutes of your time?"

"Coming up." He poured a drink for me and stood behind the bar. "What's up?"

"Does Vivian Carson work for you?"

He nodded. "Viv's been working here since high school. Good girl. Never misses a shift."

"Could you tell me if she was here the past few days?"

"Yeah. She worked two p.m. to close every night this week. I was here." He frowned. "Is Viv in some kind of trouble?"

"No. I'm just checking on some things, and her name came up," I said vaguely. "Do you happen to have her time cards?"

"Sure. Let me go get 'em." He disappeared into the back.

Rod scooted toward me and lowered his voice. "Did she hex somebody?"

"What?"

Rod whispered: "Viv's my favorite server. I saw on the news that Jeff Sumner's kid nearly drowned. She's been pretty open about hexing his ass. Him and his other little rich bitch buddies. I told her to shut up about that, but she just laughed at me and told me she's not afraid of them. I told her not to be going on about that kind of thing at work."

"You think Viv can hex people?" Viv had denied touching the children of the Kings of Warsaw Creek. She'd hexed their fathers . . . did she hex the children, too?

"I seen it." Rod looked right and left. "There was a customer here last year who backed into her car and busted her taillight. She said she cursed him. Dude wrapped his car around a tree a week later and was in the hospital for a month."

My mouth turned down. "That sounds like a natural conse-quence of drinking and driving."

"Maybe. But I do not fuck with that."

I slid Rod a fifty-dollar bill with my card. His eyes lit up, and he snatched up the bill and card.

"There's more where that came from if you remember other

stuff." I was skeptical about what he'd told me, but I felt uneasy enough to keep lines of communication with Rod open.

Owen returned with the time cards, which looked legit. I thanked him and paid for the drink. By then, Rod had retreated to the men's room and was offering no further commentary on the magical powers of the staff.

The door banged open, and I squinted at the sudden light. A familiar figure darkened the doorway in a rumpled dress shirt, a loosened tie, and a bad attitude: Jeff Sumner.

Sumner stomped over to the bar.

"Where the hell is Vivian Carson?" he demanded. His cheeks were red, and he looked drunk. He slammed something down on the bar, and it took me a moment to figure out what it was. It was a skeleton of a snake, curled in a perfect circle, with its tail tied into its mouth with baling wire. "I found this on my car."

The bartender's fingers surreptitiously slipped under the bar, toward the shotgun, but he replied evenly. "No idea."

"She's supposed to work here," Sumner growled. "I need to talk to her."

I slid off my stool and approached the other side of the bar. "Mr. Sumner, I have to ask you what you're wanting with Vivian Carson."

Sumner wheeled on me, eyes narrowing. "None of your fucking business."

The bartender remained with one hand on his hidden shotgun. "I think you should leave."

Sumner turned back to him. "You can't kick me out."

"I reserve the right to refuse service to anyone. You can leave of your own accord, or the lady and I can make you." The bartender nodded at me.

Sumner swept his arm across the bar, sending glasses sliding across it and shattering on the floor.

"All right, that's enough." I reached for his arm. He shrugged my arm away and stomped to the door.

I glanced at the bartender, then at the glass on the floor. "You want to press charges for destruction of property?" I was hoping to hell that he'd say yes, but Owen shook his head. "Not worth the headache."

I reached the parking lot in enough time to see Sumner's SUV peeling out of the dusty lot in a cloud of irritation.

By now, the sun was beginning to lower on the horizon. There was still a good five hours of daylight left. Somehow, standing in the sunshine in a crumbling parking lot with crabgrass growing out of cracks in the sizzling asphalt felt safe. Like everything was normal and fine with the world as long as the sun was shining. After dark, though . . .

Fuck. I didn't really want to expand my personal cosmology to include curses if I could help it. Since there was nothing illegal about cursing someone . . . I wasn't sure what the hell I was supposed to do about this.

Maybe Viv's hexes and the misfortune of the Kings of Warsaw Creek were just coincidence.

But I'd seen enough strange shit that I couldn't rule it out.

My attention was snagged by a flyer stapled to a telephone pole. I approached it, my eyebrows crawling up into my hairline. Tucked between a lost dog poster and an ad for a mattress sale was a neon pink flyer reading, in Gothic script letters:

"There shall not be found among you any . . . that useth divination, or an observer of times, or an enchanter, or a witch, or a charmer, or a consulter with familiar spirits, or a wizard, or a necromancer." (Deuteronomy 18:10–11)

Our community is under assault by the occult. Find God and be placed under his loving umbrella of protection.

I frowned at the word "witch." I noticed that there was church information at the bottom: Greenwood Kingdom Church's.

My phone rang, and I picked it up, wincing at the *BEEP* that greeted me before Detwiler's voice: "El-Tee, this is D6. Dispatch received an anonymous call about a girl screaming at Greenwood Kingdom Church. I'm en route, but I thought this might relate to your case."

"Yes. Yes, it might."

———

I headed out to Greenwood Kingdom Church. Despite it being a weekday, the massive parking lot contained maybe a dozen late-model cars, and Sims's vintage black Mercedes. A billboard out front encouraged congregants to **GIVE YOUR SOULS TO GOD AND PROSPER.**

I wrinkled my nose. I had little use for organized religion, and prosperity gospel, in particular, rubbed me the wrong way. But it looked like the people whose cars were in the parking lot could afford to lay down some cash for Christ, and who was I to say what they should do with their money?

But I sure as hell was gonna judge them for how they treated their young women—especially if one of them was in trouble.

Detwiler pulled in after me. We nodded at each other, and approached the church.

We crossed the parking lot to open the heavy front door, and were immediately hit with a wall of frosty air-conditioning. We walked down a hallway that reminded me more of a school than of a church, then turned right where a sign listed today's worship times. The door to an auditorium was propped open.

A scream sounded.

Detwiler and I swept into the auditorium, calling for backup.

The auditorium was dark like a movie theater. There were a dozen people up front, circling a stage lit by nothing more than a ring of guttering candles. In the center of the ring was a girl on her knees before a large washtub. Her face was buried in her hands. Her head and shoulders were soaking wet. Quentin Sims stood before her, shaking a Bible.

"Repent of this evil!" he bellowed at her. "I cast out the devil in you!"

He grabbed her neck and plunged her head into the tub. The girl struggled against him, her fingers clawing at the tub's edge. They were trying to drown her.

"Police! Let her go!" Detwiler and I shouted in unison.

Sims turned toward us, his face twisted in wrath at the interruption. But he didn't let her go.

Detwiler and I stormed the stage, scattering candles and shoving aside people in the circle. Detwiler grabbed Sims and dragged him off the girl. I pulled the girl from the water. She was gasping, her hair stuck to her cheek.

"Breathe." I pushed her hair back. I recognized her as Rebecca, one of Leah's friends from Sims's house. "Deep breaths."

Her face crumpled, and she sobbed against my shoulder.

Detwiler had Sims down on the stage, his arm behind his back. The surrounding people, who I assumed were parishioners, had begun to back away, turning toward the exit.

"No, you don't!" I shouted. "Everyone freeze."

The exit was darkened by deputies sweeping in, Monica's horrified face among them.

I looked down at the girl. "What happened?"

She couldn't be more than fourteen. She was capable only of sobbing.

A man elbowed forward, one I'd seen in the surrounding circle, not intervening. "That's my daughter. She's fine."

I turned on him. "She's *not* fine. What's the matter with you?"

"She needs to submit to authority—"

"The only one who's going to be submitting to authority around here is you," I snarled, rising from the girl. "Sit down and put your hands behind your back."

Soft laughter hissed behind me. I wheeled to see Quentin Sims chortling under Deputy Detwiler's knee in his spine.

"What's so funny?" I demanded.

His glasses had slipped down his nose. He said it loudly, loudly enough for his followers to hear and murmur in agreement: "It's just a baptism. You've interrupted a baptism."

"It sure looked like child abuse to me," I growled at him.

Sims smiled at me beatifically. "The Lord's work is invisible to the evil of the world."

I wanted to throat-punch him.

Instead, I called EMS and CPS. EMS determined that the girl's vitals were stable, and swept her away to the hospital.

Detwiler and I began questioning the participants, who were all members of the congregation. To a man (and I noticed that they were all men), they said that Rebecca was being rebaptized with holy water to cleanse her soul after some disobedience. When the nature of the disobedience was exposed, it turned out that the offense was the high crime of sneaking out to go swimming when the air-conditioning at her house went out.

My colleague Kara, from CPS, called from the hospital as I was pacing the parking lot. "She's not talking. She's too afraid."

"You can't bring her back to her parents," I said.

"I know. I can stall for maybe seventy-two hours. But I'm going to need something more after that, or she's going to have to be returned to her parents."

My grip on the phone was white. "I'll get back to you."

I turned to the doors as the parishioners were walking out. Not in handcuffs.

I wheeled to Monica. "I'm going to charge them with attempted murder—"

"I know. I know." Her jaw had hardened. "I read them their rights. But then I got told to stand down."

"By who—?"

I followed her gaze as it landed over my shoulder.

At the end of the parking lot sat the sheriff in an unmarked car. He was smoking a cigarette, watching the cars leave.

I took two steps toward the unmarked car, but Monica caught my elbow.

"Don't. I already tried."

"But that girl—"

"We gotta find some other way to help her." Her expression smoldered in wrath. "Nobody who does that to little girls gets to walk free in Bayern County."

The sheriff beckoned to me with the lit end of his cigarette.

I stalked toward his car.

"Sheriff, those people—"

He made a slicing motion with the ember in his hand. "Don't you go bothering these people anymore, Koray."

"They were trying to drown that girl!"

"That was a baptism."

I peeled my lips back into a smile. "Shall I tell Child Protective Services to let her go?" I knew full well that the sheriff had no jurisdiction over CPS.

"Koray, one more word from you, and I'll have you demoted to the secretarial pool."

He started his engine and pulled away, smiling as I fumed.

I exhaled and walked back to the church. Above the open doors that had just belched out their contents of human trash, I glimpsed something I hadn't before: a cross formed with two railroad spikes tied together, perched above the doors.

My eyes narrowed. That was too much of a coincidence.

Witchcraft for me, but not for thee?

———

I'd been told to leave this investigation alone.

I sure as fuck wasn't going to. But if I didn't have the support of my chain of command, I was screwed. I didn't have any designs to be promoted to a public role, like chief of the Detective Bureau or elected sheriff, one day, but I wanted to continue to work. And the sheriff could make that very hard for me.

I went back to the office, to the Dispatch pool, to listen to the recording of the anonymous call. I couldn't use it as evidence of anything, but I wanted to know if I recognized the voice.

The voice was female, whispering: *"Hi. I'm, um . . . calling to report a girl in trouble."*

"What's the address?"

The female whispered the address of the Greenwood Kingdom Church. *"There's screaming. Please send someone."*

"Do you know who—"

Before the dispatcher could get more information, the line went dead.

I frowned. I listened to the recording three times. I couldn't be one hundred percent certain, but the voice sounded a lot like Leah's.

When I returned to the Detective Bureau to file my report—which I intended to do in excruciatingly correct detail, minus my suspicions that Leah had dropped a dime on her father—Chief was leaning in the doorway of his office. He must've heard about my confrontation with the sheriff. He gestured for me to follow him into his office.

I did so, and Chief closed the door.

"Chief, I—" I began.

"Don't you dare apologize for stepping on the toes of some privileged rich fuckers." Chief's eyes narrowed, and he looked pissed. "You don't worry about the sheriff. I'm your commanding officer, and I tell you what to do."

"Yes, Chief."

He paced up and down the length of his office floor. "You run that investigation how you see fit—the current investigations and the cold case."

I told him what I'd found so far, which felt like precious little.

"You keep on asking questions." He finally settled in his chair behind his desk. "I have my own biases about this case, and I'm not going to burden you with them. You just go wherever the evidence leads. Understood?"

"Understood."

He nodded sharply, and I took that to mean I was dismissed.

I turned to leave, and heard him call out after me. "Koray."

He wrote something down on a Post-it note. "Judge Jorene Chamberlain is on vacation, but this is her personal cell number. If you need warrants, feel free to contact her."

I thanked Chief and took the note. Judge Chamberlain was narrowly elected last November. She was most decidedly not part of the old boys' club, and I admired her for the way she spoke out in the press about police violence in the national news. I'd never asked her for a warrant before.

"Chief, you think the Kings of Warsaw Creek are involved in some kind of criminal conspiracy?"

"My opinions on this don't matter." He leaned forward, with his elbows on the desk, and steepled his fingers. "But I will say the old boys' club has run this county for far too long."

I sucked in my breath, thoughts whirling. "If I'm out of line, I'm sure you'll say so, but it sounds like you might be wanting to run for sheriff next year."

Chief smiled under his moustache. "And go to war with Sheriff Wilson? I'd do no such thing."

Nobody sane would. Sheriffs here handpicked their successors from the chiefs of the Detective Bureau, Patrol, and Jail Administration. The favorite was known well in advance, as he would shadow the sheriff for a time, and the sheriff would retire quietly. That was the way it had worked as long as I'd been here.

"You would," I said brazenly.

He grinned and sat back in his chair. He put his finger to his lips like he was Santa. "Go work your case, Koray."

I left then, my head spinning. Was Chief planning a coup, or an all-out war? Or was he waiting for the torch to be passed gracefully? When the sheriff was out for his cancer treatments, Chief stood in for him, so he was the presumptive favorite.

I really couldn't ask him. And I was damn well gonna keep my lips zipped. Chief was playing three-dimensional chess when I existed only on a two-dimensional plane. Chief had been splashed all over the national news in the Forest Strangler investigation. He was the man whose detectives put an FBI agent behind bars. That was "fuck you" credibility in any arena.

I would continue my investigation . . . quietly. I pocketed the note with the judge's phone number on it.

I didn't like the idea of the sheriff gunning for me if I made things difficult for the Kings of Warsaw Creek, but at least Chief had my back. I wouldn't put him in the line of fire unless I had to.

Loyalties being what they were and all. It was damn sure a good thing to have some of my own, people I could trust.

13

RUSALKA

I received a text that my car was ready. I had to admit, I'd gotten pretty used to the spotty El Camino, but I was eager to have my own car back. I got Detwiler to take me to Lister's dealership.

Detwiler's brow was furrowed. "El-Tee, can I ask you something?"

"Sure."

"What the hell happened back there?" His voice shook in anger, something I'd never seen in the guy before. "They were gonna kill that girl."

"I know," I sighed. Detwiler was a good egg, and I decided I could trust him. "That's how I see it, too. Hopefully, CPS will be able to help that girl, keep her away from this."

"What can we do to help?"

I exhaled. "I'm gonna give a copy of my report to CPS. And I'm not gonna let this go."

He nodded sharply. "I'll give mine, too."

"But we have to be careful," I told him. "Watch your back. The sheriff commands a lot of loyalty, and he can sink your career."

Detwiler shook his head. "I'm not worried about my career. I didn't become a cop for this."

"Good man. Keep your eyes and ears open."

As we pulled into the dealership, I could tell something was off. Most of the expensive cars and trucks from the front row of the carefully arranged display had been removed. Even the candy apple red Corvette was missing from its platform.

I wasn't buying the idea that business was good enough for Lister to have sold them all. As Detwiler and I circled around back, I saw that the service area was full of cars under tarps and car covers.

"Wonder what happened here," Detwiler mused.

He parked the patrol car and we got out. Nobody was immediately around, so I pulled up a car cover.

I stared at the gorgeous red Corvette. On its hood, someone had spray-painted in black a snake eating its own tail.

"Detwiler," I said.

He'd pulled a tarp aside on a truck. The whole side of it had been painted similarly. The paint was fresh—still tacky. Maybe even from tonight.

I looked at all the cars, counting them under my breath, expecting that they'd all been similarly vandalized. "Do you know if this was called in?"

Detwiler had a quick conversation with Dispatch on his radio, punctuated by those irritating beeps I'd come to associate with the new system. "No reports, El-Tee."

A man in service coveralls approached. "Hey!"

Detwiler turned to the man. "I see you've got some trouble here, sir."

The service technician flushed. "We've got that under control."

"You don't want to make a report? For your insurance?"

The man shook his head. "Boss said there's no point in getting stupid kids in trouble. We'll try to buff it out."

"You've got cameras up." I pointed to the lights overhead, where dome-shaped cameras were mounted.

He frowned. "The cameras got nothing. It was like the power cut out."

Detwiler and I looked at each other. There wasn't anything we could do if they weren't making a report.

But it looked weird as hell.

Predictably, I got stonewalled from talking to Lister. He wouldn't even talk to Detwiler. But I was able to pick up my car. I didn't trust Lister, but getting work done at the dealership had given me a plausible reason to keep trying to talk to him. And that had come to nothing. I figured he'd overcharged me for tires by at least a couple hundred bucks.

I had Detwiler follow me to the next exit on the freeway and scan my car for bugs with a new gadget Patrol had acquired. While he did so, I crawled under the car to check the brake lines. Everything looked good, and Detwiler came up with nothing. Maybe I was just paranoid. Maybe the dealership had their hands full dealing with that vandalism. Whoever was at the beach at Sandpiper Run was at the dealership, too, and I chewed on what Viv had said about . . . witches.

I wasn't sure what I thought about witches. I knew there were weird things in Bayern County, like preachers performing apparent exorcisms by candlelight. Belief in the supernatural was a powerful thing, and certainly some people in the county believed. But I resisted expanding my personal cosmology to include witches handing out curses. I needed to think of mundane explanations for the crimes I investigated first . . . and the most mundane explanation was that someone like Viv believed they were a witch, and purchased a few cans of spray paint. It was the law that driver's licenses had to be given over to buy spray paint, to deter vandalism, and I could theoretically run down recent sales in the county. I wasn't sure that would yield anything. People kept cans of spray paint in their garages for years. Even if I could investigate the vandalism at Lister's dealership, I didn't have access to perform a paint match. And if I could prove that Viv bought black spray paint at the local hardware store last night and didn't have an alibi, I would be no closer to finding the truth without evidence.

Nick's SUV was in the driveway when I got home. As he always did when he got home first, he'd left the porch light on for me. I let myself inside the house. He'd left the light over the stove on for me, too, and snoring echoed from the bedroom.

I locked up and left my keys in the bowl on top of the refrigerator. I took some ibuprofen and antibiotics for my leg and got into my pajamas.

I slid into bed, between Nick and Gibby. Gibby was awake, giving an aggrieved huff when I climbed in. He closed his eyes and was soon snoring heavily.

I'd grown accustomed to this, the warmth I felt sandwiched between the two of them. I loved them, and I could trust them entirely, with everything I was.

It wasn't like there weren't other people I trusted with my life. I trusted Monica, and the chief, and probably also deputies, like Detwiler and Jasper. But trusting someone with my life was a very different matter than trusting a person with who I was.

Maybe I would always be on the outside, looking in on relationships. But what I had here, in bed with me . . . that could be enough. The snores and the dog hair and the late nights.

That was enough, and I wouldn't let it go.

———

A green flash seared my vision, then faded, leaving me in the dark.

I was eleven years old then, creeping through the yard at night, toward the well. I hadn't forgotten the feeling of something brushing against my leg in the dark. I was afraid an animal was trapped in there, in the poisoned water, one that needed my help.

I crouched by the edge of the well. The pump hummed a low pulse, and I felt like I was sitting next to a hive of bees.

"Hello?" I whispered. I stared into the dark, searching for ripples in the water. I reached down with a stick and stirred. If there was a snake there, I could catch it and pull it to safety.

Something grabbed the stick and tore it away. I flung myself back and landed on my backside.

Slowly, I crept to the edge again.

Below the buzz of the pump, I heard a musical hum, the hum of a woman, echoing off the well's earthen walls, then the distant cry of a baby.

I called out to it. "What's down there?"

Water churned, and something pale roiled beneath. The moon's reflection fractured in the black, and I glimpsed the profile of a woman below the water.

I leaned forward, toward that musical humming.

"Who are you?" I needed to know.

I jumped as someone grabbed the back of my neck, drew me away. My mom.

Her eyes were as black as the pool.

"Mom," I gasped. "What is it?"

She closed her eyes as the thing in the well cried with the sound of a baby.

"There's a spirit in this place," she said. "A spirit with many voices, many stories of pain and suffering. She takes on the suffering of the dead, takes their voices and their faces and visits her wrath upon men who abuse and kill women and girls. She's a vengeful spirit, summoned by grief."

I heard the baby cry again and strained away from Mom to look into the black water. "Is . . . is my sister down there?"

"She is your sister. She's a hundred murdered women and girls. She is Rusalka."

I lurched upright in bed, gasping.

Gibby yelped at my feet. I must've kicked him.

I forced myself to steady my breathing. I was soaked in sweat; it dripped down my chin in rivulets and my T-shirt was stuck to my chest. Morning trickled gray light beneath the curtains.

I jumped when Nick began to rub my back. "Hey, you okay?" he asked, his voice slurred by sleep.

I pushed my hair out of my face. It felt cold and slimy as algae. "Yeah . . . yeah, I think so."

Nick was sitting up beside me now. "Another dream?"

I nodded. "I dreamed about a thing . . . a thing in the bottom of the well at the house I grew up in." The thing called *Rusalka*. It conjured up half-remembered fairy tales about wronged women who lay in wait at the bottoms of rivers to drown men who passed by.

And I didn't want this thing to be part of my world. I wanted my world to be rational. Orderly. Unhaunted.

Nick exhaled, waiting for me to continue. "Do you want to talk about it?"

"I'm not sure." It was still too fresh in my panicked brain to put into words.

He took my hand. "I'm worried about you."

"I know." I leaned over to kiss his temple. "I'm okay."

I pulled the covers back and swung my legs out of bed. I wanted nothing more than to take a shower and make sure I was thoroughly and truly awake.

Pain lanced through my leg, and I hissed.

Nick rolled out of bed. He turned on the bedside lamp to scrutinize my injury. The stitches still held, but my calf had continued to swell. The wound was greening and mottling around the edges.

"That doesn't look good," I observed.

"No. It doesn't." He probed it gently with his fingers. "I'm going to call you in some stronger antibiotics. If they don't kick in, we may have to do a debridement."

Reflexively, I pulled my leg away from him. "That doesn't sound like fun."

"It's not. But you don't want to get gangrene."

Gangrene. I didn't think people got gangrene anymore. I climbed to my feet, headed to the bathroom, and stood in the shower, washing the wound with antibacterial soap. I smeared it with antibacterial ointment, using close to a quarter of a tube. I didn't want to be slowed down by a medical procedure. Nick wrapped my calf up in a bandage while Gibby watched and tried to nip the ends of the gauze.

"How's Mason?" I asked, trying to change the subject.

"I checked in with ICU. Still in a coma, and the pulmonologist isn't happy with the state of his lungs. Some kind of deterioration forming in there, likely an infection. They're hitting it with some nuclear-weapons-grade antibiotics."

"Poor kid."

"Yeah. Here's the weird thing." He leaned on the sink, crossing his arms. "I saw something like that once before."

"When?"

"A few years ago. An older lady. I first thought it was histoplasmosis, and prescribed antifungals. She turned up in the ER one night, struggling to breathe. She died a few weeks later, and I remember that her films were weird like that, a weird deterioration."

"Do you remember her name?"

"Not offhand. I'm gonna have to look through records to figure it out. This makes me wonder if there's some kind of bacteria or fungus in the water that's affecting people with compromised immune systems, or the young and elderly."

"But I'm betting your elderly lady didn't go swimming in the Sumners' pond."

"Might be a microbe transferred by birds or something." Nick's gaze was distant, and I could tell he was already running tests in his mind. "I'll go bug Mason's pulmonologist. And I'll get some samples from Ross Lister."

It made sense, like there was some kind of connection among these cases.

But I had no earthly idea what.

And no unearthly one, either . . . a witch couldn't kill through lung infections, could she?

14

DIVINATION

I couldn't sleep, so I hunched over the light of my computer, re-searching witches and water.

I confirmed some of what I already supposed—that Rusalki were Eastern European water spirits who bedeviled men. They were always female, and were considered to be the unquiet ghosts of women or girls who'd killed themselves or been murdered by drowning. They then sought revenge by drowning men besotted by their watery charms.

Some academics suggested that Rusalki were fallen fertility spir-its or corrupted genii loci. Much of the lore was rooted in blatant sexism: a woman's highest calling was to be a mother, and a woman who became a Rusalka could never be that. The best she could do would be to abduct living children, which never went over well.

As in much folklore involving supernatural feminine forces, Rusalki eventually devolved into witches and seductresses. A Rusalka was the dark feminine incarnate, uncontrollable and re-jecting the natural order of death and life.

Did they have any connection to my father's Forest God, Veles? They certainly came from the same part of Europe. I suspected that Veles, or some fragment of him, had hitchhiked with my father, from his travels. Or maybe they were universal forces, and that was just what my father called them—I didn't have enough of a background in theology or folklore to guess.

My father had killed dozens of women. Why was it so hard to believe that something wanted revenge? Someone . . . a Rusalka? As a girl, I found him easy to love. As a woman, he was an object of hate.

I struggled with believing in the Forest God, in that shadowy spirit crowned with antlers that my father had killed for. I had encountered him, and I'd been terrified. But maybe that was one anomaly, one blip in my consciousness and the consciousness of this place. Why couldn't I simply buy the idea of nymphs drifting about in rivers, searching for prey?

I probed my resistance. Maybe it was because I'd then have to admit that the world at large was stranger and more disturbing than just my father's corner of it. That I was peeling back the edges of reality, and afraid to look at what lay beneath.

And why that grubby corner of unreality wanted me.

I headed over to Viv's, rolling into her driveway just before eleven a.m. There was a car in the driveway I didn't recognize: a yellow Volkswagen Beetle with a COEXIST bumper sticker. Didn't seem like the kind of ride Jeff Sumner would take, so I relaxed.

I walked up to the front porch and knocked on the screen door, peering into the darkness beyond.

Viv came to the door. "Yes?"

"Could we talk?"

"I'm in the middle of something . . ." She looked over her shoulder, toward the kitchen. "If you want to wait out here, that's fine."

I settled into the creaky porch swing.

But I wasn't alone on the porch. The fox, Sinoe, was curled on a cushion under one of the chairs, watching me over her fluffy tail.

I extended my hand down for her to sniff. I was too far away for her to touch me without climbing out of her nest and sliding under the wicker coffee table.

She watched me, untrusting.

Sinoe was entirely different than Gibby. Gibby was domesticated, despite all his faults. He craved approval, food, and his favorite spot in bed. This one . . . was not. I could tell by the way she looked at me that she was not tame. She chose to stay with Viv and reap the benefits of that relationship. But I had no doubt, looking at her, that she could flee at a moment's notice and never come back.

I withdrew my arm. She continued to watch me.

The window beside me was open, and I could see Viv and another woman seated at the kitchen table. Viv was laying cards on the table. The cardboard whirred as she shuffled and drew.

"Don't worry," Viv said. "This relationship is gonna be good for you. See this? This is the King of Cups. He's going to be loyal to you."

I couldn't see the other woman's face beyond a curtain of dark hair. "Is he the one? Should I say yes?"

Viv put more cards on the table. "The Two of Cups shows a successful partnership. He's the man for you. He's your happily-ever-after."

Card readings. I wasn't surprised that Viv had a side hustle. What surprised me was that there were enough people who believed in such things in Bayern County to make a business of it.

I looked at the coffee table before me. Viv's mail was there. I touched the stack with the toe of my shoe. Looked like bills. Junk mail. An envelope from a medical center. And something with letterhead from the nearby university, addressed to Viv. It was open and partially crumpled. People usually only did that with bad news.

After some time of murmuring over cups and swords, the screen door opened, and a brunette woman was wiping tears from her face and smiling at Viv.

"It's going to be good," Viv told the woman, hugging her. "It's okay to believe in love."

The woman nodded and walked down the porch steps. She got into her Volkswagen and drove away.

Viv watched her go, and turned to me. "You're not here for a reading, I take it, Lt. Koray?"

"I've got some questions. Can you tell me where you were last night?"

Viv lifted a brow. Her eyes were puffy, and she looked a little hungover. She sat down in the chair Sinoe had claimed. The fox's black nose reached out to touch Viv's calf. "Well, I got some bad news, and I went to the bar for a drink."

"You mind me asking what kind of bad news?"

She looked down at the mail with the return address from the university. "I had a little dream of maybe becoming a biologist, once upon a time. Didn't pan out." I could see her jaw hardening. Being tough.

I considered probing the edges of that rejection, but decided to leave it alone.

"Any witnesses?" I asked.

"What's this about?" Viv asked, irritation creeping into her voice. Sinoe lifted her head and stared at me. Sensing movement, Viv reached under her chair to scratch her ears.

I showed her a picture of the vandalized Corvette on my phone. "Do you know who might have done this?"

Viv squinted at it. "Where's this?"

"Lister's car dealership."

Viv laughed. "Glad someone improved his car."

A shrill cackle emanated from under Viv's chair. My gaze fell on Sinoe. She'd rolled onto her back, exposing her belly to Viv, and was cackling at me. It was an eerie laugh—much like the way crow voices sounded almost human, but not quite.

I tried to stick to business. "I'm going to need the approximate time you were at the bar."

"I was there from nine until closing. My boss saw me. He actually drove me home, because I was in no shape to drive."

I frowned. I knew Owen to be a decent dude, but it sounded like he was her go-to alibi. More than I liked.

Viv shrugged. "Is there anything else?"

"I've been looking at your sister's case, and I want to make sure I'm not missing anything."

Viv picked a pack of cigarettes from her pocket, tapped out one, and lit it. Her eyes shone. "Get to the point."

Well, so much for easing into the idea. "I want to talk to your mother to see what she remembers."

It was a big ask. Depending on the mother's mental state, she might not take well to this kind of questioning.

She flicked some ash into a tray on the windowsill. "You don't need my permission for that."

"Your mother's in a mental institution. You're her next of kin."

"All right, then."

I nodded. "Thank you."

Viv smiled. "But I want something from you first."

"What is it?"

She blew smoke out. "I want to read your cards."

"Why?"

"I'm curious about you. I'm not curious about most people. I want to know what your motives are. And Sinoe likes you." She looked down at the fox, who was gazing at me with half-lidded eyes.

"My motive is to solve this case."

"Everyone has many motives, and I want to know I can trust you. Besides, you're interesting. You have a lot of old energy about you, and I like poking at things."

My knee-jerk reaction was that tarot cards were bullshit. Reading them was just some con she was running on gullible people with turbulent romantic lives. Or maybe she believed in them herself; I wasn't sure. It felt like she was trying to roll me in a scam, but I was willing to let her try, to open myself a sliver to that magical life she led and see if she could tell me the truth.

"All right." I'd play the game.

Viv set her cigarette in the ashtray and went into the house. Sinoe rolled over onto four feet and watched me with suspicion. I was just as suspicious of her mom.

Viv came back with a small parcel wrapped in a scarf. She unwrapped it, revealing a deck of cards with black-and-white designs. She handed the deck to me.

"Shuffle."

The cards were worn, their edges curling. I felt the paper whir in my fingers as I shuffled once, twice, three times. They felt a little sticky, like the paper was humid and wanted to cling to itself.

"Please cut the deck three times with your left hand."

I did as instructed, then handed the deck back to her.

Viv bent over the coffee table. "First question I've got is . . . who are you?"

She drew a card and put it on the table. She turned it over, revealing a picture of the moon rising over a mountain. A woman's face was in the moon, and it wept on the land below. A dog and a crayfish rose out of a river, the dog baying at the moon.

"You see things that others don't. If you listened to your intuition, a whole dark world would open to you, the primeval connections between things." A smile played at the corners of her lips.

I leaned back in the swing, mentally refusing to participate further.

"And what do you want?" Viv asked. I let her talk to herself. This required no input from me.

She pulled a card with a woman holding scales and a sword. "Justice, reversed—your own vision of the truth, which may or may not be fair or just." Viv gave a small shrug. "That doesn't necessarily bother me. I'm more about the end than the means."

She returned her attention to her deck. "And how will this whole thing turn out if I trust you?"

She pulled a card with the Grim Reaper riding a white horse over open graves. "Death. That's excellent." She smiled sunnily at me. "I couldn't hope for more."

"Are you satisfied?" I asked quietly, feeling uneasy to be pulled into this delusion. Especially since the delusion whispered truth back to me.

She nodded sharply. "Yes. Go ahead. Talk to my mom." She pressed forward, her elbows on her knees. "But I have to warn you: it's at your own risk."

The fox cackled from the floor.

———

I'd promised I'd take Gibby out on a proper walk, and I thought I might be able to kill two birds with one stone. I headed by the house to pick him up, then drove out toward the river, down the curvy roads into the forest, to the site where the Hag Stone kept watch. It was still somehow fresh from my dream nights ago, and I couldn't shake the hold it still had on me even in daylight. I had dreamed of it, and my subconscious felt it was important.

Besides, I wanted to see if my camera had captured any activity here.

Gibby and I descended the trail into the ravine. Birdsong echoed around us, surrounding us in a stone aviary.

I walked on, down to the water. Cattails reached into the river where it curved around the oxbow from my dream. In the center island, birds' nests had accumulated decades' worth of debris. A sentry goose peered at me, but didn't hiss. Maybe it sensed that I was also of the forest, and not a threat.

I frowned when I smelled fresh paint. I stood beneath the Hag Stone, seeing new graffiti painted on the ravine's sandstone walls: the ouroboros, once more. In the rocks below it, beside a fallen tree, there was a scorch mark in the dirt. Like something had burned here. A circle was worn in the dirt around it, trodden by many pairs of feet. They had been bare, leaving no shoe tread marks. A few of the prints belonged to women.

I exhaled. Were these Viv's witches? It was one thing to think the Wicked Witch of Bayern County was a lone woman. It was entirely different to imagine that there were more of them . . . many more.

I found my tree cam, popped out the SD card, and replaced it with a fresh one. I was excited at the prospect of catching something on camera that would bring me close to the shadowy rumors of witches. I wondered if I'd see Viv on the video, raging against the moon.

I descended to the riverbank and stood among the cattails. My mother's voice echoed in my head, the reverent way she'd uttered the word "Rusalka." An incantation.

My father never said anything about a Rusalka to me. He had spoken of poisonous mushrooms and plants, certainly. But not of a woman lying at the bottom of dark waters, drowning children.

If there were such a creature . . . how could she move from a pond to a river, unless she had legs and was human? Jasper had searched the pond and found nothing. He'd found nothing in the river, too.

But Ross had described a goth-looking girl. Maybe . . . or maybe that was Dana . . .

I dipped my fingers into the cool water. It smelled like iron, and looked curiously sterile. No crawfish or tadpoles, or insects of any kind.

"Rusalka," I whispered, "are you here?"

A breeze cast ripples on the water. No answer.

I looked east, listening to the breeze rattling in quaking aspen. Sun cascaded in a waterfall into this dark space.

I stilled, melting into the ground. Maybe it was a sort of trance, this sense of falling away from myself. My breath synchronized with the river's lapping on the shore, and my pulse slowed. Sun heated my forehead and right cheek. As my muscles loosened, my spine and neck made dozens of tiny cracks and pops that sounded like the squirrel flinging acorns to the ground across the river.

A splash sounded to my left, and I turned to see a flash of scales before they receded into the water. *Bluegill*, I thought. *Just bluegill*.

But my trance was broken. Gibby went racing into the river, snapping at the fish.

I stood, calling him back. But Gibby searched for prey, splashing in the water.

I took my shoes off and waded out to retrieve him. I trod carefully; even though the river was slow, the rocks beneath my bare feet were sharp. I waded into water up to my knees, turned toward my dog . . .

. . . and saw a dead blue heron floating in the water, wings splayed. I reached toward it, seeing its dull feathers and milky eyes. I picked it up and turned it over, finding no wound. I cradled the bird in my arms and took it to shore.

I ordered Gibby to return to the bank. He sensed the sharp alarm in my tone, and obeyed.

I reached into my pocket for an unopened bottle of water. I dumped out the contents, then filled it with river water. I capped it and climbed out of the river, my toes squishing in the muddy bank.

Gibby regarded me with twitching eyebrows, a look of concern.

"You didn't do anything wrong. You're a good boy."

The tension in his stance dissipated, and he leaned against my leg. I patted his head and put on my shoes.

I held the bottle up to the sun. It was filthy. River water was always brown, full of debris. Maybe Nick could analyze this. Maybe he could find something to help Mason.

A tremendous splash echoed behind me.

I turned, seeing only ripples in the water.

Gibby's fur stood up, and he growled.

"Hello?" I called.

The river didn't answer me. At least, not in words.

I exhaled. My mind was playing tricks on me.

Something was here, though. My skin crawled.

A gunshot sounded behind me, echoing off the stone of the ravine.

Instinctively, I crouched to cover Gibby and drew my own weapon. My first thought was that maybe a hunter was here, that the shot was a mistake.

"Bayern County Sheriff's Office!" I shouted. "Stand down!"

A second shot rang out, and splintered a nearby tree.

That was no mistake. That was almost murder.

I dragged Gibby away, behind a stand of cattails. Gibby's chest vibrated lowly, without a sound. My fingers wound in his collar.

I scanned for the shooter. The forest was silent, birds stilled by the gunshots. Even the creaking cedars seemed to be holding their breath.

The river was at our backs, and wasn't a good spot to retreat to. As near as I could determine, the source of those shots was between us and the dirt track leading to the car.

Our best chance would be to melt into the forest, to try to circle back and lose our pursuer. Get to the car, then call for help.

I tugged at Gibby's collar, and he followed me into a stand of trees. I walked soundlessly, glancing over my shoulder, trying to detect the shooter in the trees over the sight of my gun. Our pursuer might be wearing camo, which would make him harder to spot but not impossible.

A shot echoed from across the river.

My gaze narrowed. Two shooters. Alone, I knew I wouldn't have any issues locating and picking off one shooter in the woods. Maybe two, if they were separated. Part of me relished the idea of hunting these asshats, of tracking each one of them down and shooting them. It had been a long time since I had been responsible for a death, and part of me was horrified to contemplate it again. The other part, buried deep in my chest, woke and seethed and demanded blood . . .

But I had Gibby with me, and he was not a dog built for stealth. With two shooters, I couldn't risk it. I couldn't risk him.

I made eye contact with my dog, desperately hoping to communicate that he needed to follow me quietly. I placed my finger to my lips and released the collar.

He remained still, ears flattened and tail tucked between his legs. He didn't like the gunfire. Didn't blame him.

I tapped my leg.

He trotted forward, following me. Not in perfect silence, but I'd take it. I picked my path through the forest through as little leaf debris as possible, sticking to the undergrowth of black raspberries. Thorns clawed at my shirt and pants, staining the fabric black where berries burst. Gibby tried to bite the thorns, and I pushed the brambles out of his way with my shoe.

I heard rustling far behind us, at the river. The *crash-crash* of a two-legged animal.

I crept deeper into the woods, heading north, circling back around to the place where the dirt track led up. I broke into a light run parallel to it as the crashing neared. Behind us, disturbed mourning doves warbled as they took flight from the ground.

I exhaled when we reached the trailhead, but was startled to find no other cars there. That was for the best—if we were parked in, we'd have to jog to the road.

I opened the car door, shoveled Gibby in, and jumped in behind him. I cranked the ignition and reversed down the one-lane road.

I didn't see another car the whole way down, and there was no one on the main road.

I sighed when we made it out onto the pavement.

I called in the cavalry to look for those assholes, like a good girl. But part of me wanted to make sure Gibby was safe . . . and then plunge back into the forest and bring them to ground myself, in the bloodiest way possible. They had crossed me, and they could have killed my dog.

I closed my eyes. *No.* I would follow the rules.

Without the rules, I feared what I might become.

15

FLIGHT RISK

To my frustration, no one was found at the park.

To add to it, I called EPA. After some time with considerably soothing hold music, I finally reached a pleasant-sounding person, who took my report but wouldn't take my sample. She said EPA had to take their own readings, and she'd forward my request to an agent, but she warned me that they were facing a backlog of requests. Even though this request was from law enforcement, there would be a wait.

It didn't sound hopeful, at all. If I were honest with myself, the evidence I'd shared with her wasn't great . . . just some dead animals. That was pretty thin, and my dreams and hunches just weren't something I could put in a report.

I ground my teeth and called Nick to see if I could drop the sample off at the hospital lab instead. He agreed, and I dropped it off. *Fingers crossed.* If they found nothing, maybe I could convince myself that my memories meant nothing and that everything was fine.

I was on the way back to the house when an APB came out over the radio:

BEEP. ". . . missing juvenile. White female, age sixteen, five feet six inches tall, one hundred and thirty pounds. Blue eyes and brown hair. Leah Susanna Sims was last seen on County Road 13, hitchhiking . . ."

Shit. That was Pastor Sims's daughter. Her last known location was on the other side of the county, and I was sure it would be crawling with cops.

I parked, and fished Leah's phone out of my purse. I hadn't gotten anything back about her messages yet, but I could see if she had wiped her location history.

She had location services turned off. *Damn.*

I went to her pictures. Maybe there would be something here that I hadn't noticed before. I scrolled through the photos that Leah had taken of herself and her friends. They seemed like pretty ordinary photos: the girls at a playground, swinging on swings. The girls working on homework. Pictures of an herb garden, with the plants neatly labeled.

I looked at the backgrounds. Many were the living rooms of houses, judging by carpeting and couches. I recognized the park as a community park downtown, beside the courthouse. Many pictures had a stage behind the girls, where they were working on some kind of art project with costumes. The church, I supposed. Maybe getting ready for a Christmas pageant.

There were a few photos, though, that gave me pause. They were selfies of Leah, outdoors, in low light. She was gazing at the camera with a sense of knowing, with a come-hither look. The top buttons on her dress were open, and her right hand was in her hair. Her hair was undone, wild around her shoulders. I detected makeup: eyeliner, lipstick, mascara.

These pictures were meant to depict her as sexy. For herself . . . or for someone else?

I found a few more like them, her playing with her hair. Some were at the golden hour, looking across a barren parking lot.

I stared at the background: an overgrown field, a gravel lot with weeds growing through it. An abandoned place. One of the pictures showed her laughing, and behind her was a corner of a building with chipped paint. And there was a picture of her looking at a road, with the shadow of a gas pump outlined in a sunset before her.

"Gotcha," I whispered.

———

I zipped down backcountry roads. Gibby sat beside me, in the passenger seat, panting. He knew we were chasing something, and his tail thumped his excitement.

"We're going to find her," I told Gibby. But I wasn't sure what else I was going to find. I just knew I had to get to Leah first. Kids didn't run away out of fits of pique. Most of the time, they ran away from something serious . . . like what I'd seen happen at Rebecca's botched exorcism.

I drove to the outskirts of the county seat, to a closed-down gas station. As a cop, I knew where all the twenty-four-hour gas stations were in the county, and remembered when they closed down. The lights were out at this one, but I pulled into the cracked concrete parking lot. The station had been vandalized with graffiti, and trash was strewn around. Windows had been boarded up, and the place looked deserted. It had been at least two years since Monica and I had gotten our caffeine fix in the middle of the night here.

I shut off the engine and went to the door. It was locked. I regarded the graffiti on the door with narrowed eyes. The ouroboros was drawn in black paint. It was reasonably fresh, too, painted over anarchy symbols and a colorful portrait of an animated dragon. There was no number here, so I didn't get the impression that the symbology was here as a threat, necessarily. Maybe some personal sigil?

I went around to the back. Gibby followed me, tail wagging. Everything was locked up there, too, but I noticed cigarette butts beside the back door. They, too, looked reasonably fresh, the filters still intact and not disintegrated by rain or the sun.

I inspected the back door. It was locked, but the plywood covering the bottom panel was loose. I plucked at a corner of the plywood, and pulled away easily. I shone my flashlight into the station. My light picked out old metal shelves and paper on the floor.

On my hands and knees, I crawled inside and stood up. Gibby wiggled in beside me.

"Hello?" I called into the dark. "Leah?"

I smelled cigarette smoke. I followed the smell past the restrooms, to the main sales floor. It was completely trashed, with rodents scuttling in the periphery of my vision. Gibby peeled away to chase one.

I exhaled. "Leah."

She was sitting cross-legged on the old counter, behind the empty lottery machine and cigarette displays. She was wearing a T-shirt and shorts, her hair long and loose over her shoulders, and she hugged a duffel bag to her chest. Winged eyeliner adorned her eyes, and lipstick glossed her lips. She seemed much older now, almost an adult.

She froze when she saw me, ash dripping from her cigarette. "Did my dad send you?"

"No," I said. "I'm not here because of him. I'm here because I thought something might have happened to you."

She made a face. "I'm trying to get out of here. Can you . . . can you maybe pretend you never saw me?"

"How are you going to get out of here sitting in a gas station?" I asked.

Bored of mice, Gibby trotted out of the shadows and headed behind the counter. He snuffled at Leah. She rubbed his nose. "Is he a police dog or something?"

"Gibby's not a police dog. He's my pet."

"He's cute."

I waited for her to speak again. It was a tricky thing, waiting for a victim to open up. Leah had things to say. I didn't think I got the full story from her the night Mason nearly drowned—she was too focused on that, and she didn't know if she could trust me. She didn't dare say much in front of her father, angry as she was. But now . . . it was just her and me and the dark. She was in huge trouble. She knew it. And maybe she didn't have anything to lose.

She eventually sighed. "My boyfriend's supposed to pick me up here, and we're gonna run away to the city."

I pulled up a wobbly stool and sat down. "Your boyfriend?"

"Well, I thought he was my boyfriend." She stared at the ceiling, blinking back tears. "He didn't show up. And he left me on read."

"I'm sorry, Leah." She must have had a burner phone.

"Yeah, me, too." She scrubbed her arm across her face, smearing her makeup. She wasn't wearing her standard-issue pearl purity ring. "There's gonna be hell to pay when I go back, that's for sure."

"What do you mean?"

She focused on Gibby. "My dad will be furious that I tried to run away. He'll be humiliated, and if he's humiliated, he'll take it out on me. Last time I embarrassed him, he locked me in the basement."

"Leah, that's not right."

She shrugged. "Yeah, well . . . nobody's gonna stop him, you know? My mom didn't."

"How long has she been gone?"

"She died when I was eight." Leah's fist clenched, and she radiated wrath. "Dad—I mean, he's really my stepdad—wouldn't let her see a doctor. Said that God would heal her. He didn't. I stopped believing in God then."

"I can see why." I exhaled. "Where's your biological dad?"

She shrugged. "No idea. Don't remember him."

"Leah, did you call 911 yesterday, about screaming from the church?"

She looked away. "Yeah. I couldn't . . . I couldn't stand the screaming."

"Did you know what they were doing?"

She nodded. "Girls get rebaptized if they're disobedient. It's a thing. Purified."

My heart hammered. If I could get her to say this to CPS, then I could keep Rebecca safe. And Sarah and Elizabeth. And maybe more girls . . .

"Do you believe in God?" she asked me.

I was taken aback by the question. I mulled it over. "I don't believe in a god, no, not the way there's one in the Bible."

"I didn't think you did. If you were in my dad's church, you wouldn't be able to be a cop." I thought I detected a moment of longing in her voice.

"Leah. Is your father abusing you?"

She pressed her crimson lips together. "I'm supposed to do what he says, since he's a man. And God talks to him. I get sent to the basement if I misbehave. Away from God's light, he says."

"Does he hit you?"

"Sometimes. When I get mouthy." She picked at a piece of dirt on the countertop. "It's not hard, not enough to leave a bruise. People would notice."

"Does he make you uncomfortable? Touch you in a sexual way?" I hated to ask, but I had to.

She looked away, and that told me what I needed to know. Rage thudded through my temples.

"I'm so sorry, Leah."

She stared at her hands, a tear dripping down her nose. "Nobody cares. I mean, nobody but the other girls."

"Do the girls at school know?"

"My homeschool pod?" She laughed and rolled her eyes. "We don't do anything but study the Bible. Dad says that women don't need to be educated. Our highest good is to be a fertile vessel for more children, to bring God's love to the world." She spat the words with venom.

"My dad . . . My dad did some really awful things, too," I said slowly. "But not to me."

She looked at me. "Then you know. You know the lies."

I nodded. "And I know how much I loved him. And how much I hate him."

"Is your dad in prison?"

"My dad went to prison. He's dead now," I said.

"So everyone's safe."

"Yeah. It's a relief, honestly. I never confronted him. I'm not as strong as you are, Leah." I had never stood up to my father to the extent that Leah had in her living room, accusing him of killing her mother.

Leah shook her head and whispered: "I'm scared of him."

"I know. I *know.*"

I exhaled. I certainly wasn't giving her back to her father.

I leaned forward and put my elbows on my knees. "Leah, if I could take you away, to a safe place, would you go? And would you stay there, and not run away?"

Leah blinked. "What do you mean?"

"I have to contact Social Services. I have a colleague there who will take good care of you."

"Will my dad know where I am?"

"No. An investigation will need to occur, to determine if you should go back to him."

Her shoulders slumped. "They would give me back to my dad. I don't have any marks. And the basement is creepy, but I don't think—"

"That's not for you to decide. Or me to decide," I said. "I can't say for certain what would happen from here on out. But I'd like to put you in the custody of Child Protective Services. If you'll let me."

She met my gaze. "As long as they don't have a basement."

I went outside, called CPS, and explained the situation.

My colleague Kara listened. "I'm going to deem this an emergency placement. There's a nice couple who fosters kids for us who would take her. Let me give you the address."

She read off the address, and I jotted it down. "Thanks, Kara."

Kara sighed. "I'm willing to fight for her. But you have to know that you're gonna bring a shitstorm down on your head for interfering with that church."

"Sounds like you've dealt with them before."

"Let's just say they'll close ranks and not take this lying down. But this is the right thing to do."

I agreed, and went back for Leah. She was hugging Gibby and sobbing into his ruff.

"Leah," I said gently.

She looked up at me with a tear-streaked face. She seemed so very young then. "I'm ready."

We walked around the gas station, to the car. My gaze rested on the graffiti on the door.

"Do you know what that is?" I asked her, pointing to the ouroboros.

Her eyes quickly slid away. "No."

She might have been lying. Or just scared. I couldn't tell.

I opened the car door for her, and she climbed in. Gibby clambered in after her, and we headed off into the dark.

"What's going to happen to my dad?"

"I don't know," I admitted. "But that's not for you to worry about."

We pulled up before a two-story farmhouse. The lights were on. I walked Leah up to the door, which was immediately opened by a couple who looked to be in their fifties. The man was sunburned and wearing overalls, while the woman had indelible smile lines.

"Hi, Leah," the woman said. "I'm Margie, and this is Dave."

"Hi." She shifted her weight from one foot to the other.

"We promise to keep you safe." Dave stuck his calloused hand out to her.

Leah took it and shook it.

They took her inside. I had a good feeling about the two of them. They seemed . . . normal. Good. And goodness was a rare thing in this world.

I just hoped Leah could stay with them as long as she needed to, and that the Kings of Warsaw Creek didn't pull strings to get her back into Sims's basement by morning.

———

I wanted to be the one to tell Sims that his daughter was safe. Safe from him.

I drove toward the parsonage. Just as I was about to pull into the church parking lot, a black vintage Mercedes peeled out of the lot and disappeared down the road in a flare of brake lights and screech of tires.

That was Sims's car.

I gripped the steering wheel and floored the accelerator. I slapped my magnetic bubblegum light on the roof of my car and lit it up. Red and blue light flashed into the darkness, and Sims hurtled through the night.

Cool night air slid through my hair, and my lips peeled back into a smile. I had only intended to inform him that Leah had been found safely, and not to tip my hand by arresting him right away. I was going to gather bulletproof evidence and bury him. But he was going to make this easy. He wasn't pulling over, so I was going to pop him for fleeing and eluding.

As he zipped over hills and into valleys, I radioed for backup. Beside me, Gibby hung his head out the window, as thrilled by the chase as I was.

"You sorry son of a bitch," I hissed at Sims. "You're not getting away from me."

I got close to him, feet from his bumper. He was the only one in the car. My headlights flashed off his mirrors and his round glasses. He caught a little bit of air with his car on one hill, and then his ancient undercarriage slammed down on the pavement with sparks. He swerved between the lines.

"Oh God. If he's drunk, too, this is my lucky night."

We came out of the two-lane road to the Silver Bridge crossing the Copperhead River. Where the hell was he going? Out of state?

He floored it on the straightaway of the bridge, and I struggled to keep up. I heard the rev of his engine, the hiss of air in my ears, and . . . music. He must have had the radio on . . .

I heard thin notes of a woman singing, a song that sounded familiar . . .

I reflexively slowed.

Sims accelerated ahead of me, then jerked a hard left. His car sprawled across the oncoming lane.

"What the hell?" I whispered. I didn't see a deer or another animal that he might be trying to avoid.

The car launched through a guardrail with a shriek of metal and hurtled through space, disappearing into blackness. Something splashed like a bomb exploding below.

"Fuck."

I parked and erupted out of my car, sprinting to the ruined guardrail.

The bridge creaked and sighed.

I stared down at headlights receding into the blackness and disappearing. I shouted into my radio for EMS and God and everyone to show up. I swept my flashlight below me, into the rushing water, waiting for Sims to bob up from the depths, but he never came up.

A melodious giggle sounded below me, and I shivered.

Sims didn't emerge.

EMS, the fire department, and the sheriff's office closed off the bridge. The fire department sent out people in boats to search for

Sims. They couldn't pinpoint the site of the wreck exactly, and there was supposition that the strong current had shifted the small car. The river might have to be dredged. I sat on the bumper of my car, holding a cup of coffee, relating the story to the chief and Monica. I omitted the part about the singing.

The chief rarely came out into the field, but I understood that this was likely a political nightmare. "You didn't touch his car?"

"No sir."

"How fast were you going?"

"Um . . . fifty-five? He accelerated, though. Maybe sixty-five at the end."

"I think he knew Leah would talk," Monica said.

"You think suicide?" Chief asked.

"Maybe. With Koray on his tail, he might have thought the jig was up."

"There's no way he knew it was me," I said. "I had lights on, so he couldn't see my face."

Chief's expression was unreadable under his moustache. "There's no going down after that wreck tonight. Go home, Koray."

———

I did as I was told.

I took Gibby home to give him a bath. I didn't want him getting sick from any contaminants that were in the river earlier in the day. I filled the bathtub, lured him in with his rubber-ducky squeaky toy, and lathered him up. When Gibby was done, I showered and threw my clothes into the laundry.

I focused on simple household chores, deliberately trying to dissociate from this evening's events. I didn't see how Sims could've survived that accident. I didn't feel sorry about that, about him being dead. I did feel sorry for Leah. She was going to have all kinds of things to work through. But at least I could guarantee that her father wouldn't hurt anyone ever again.

I paused. I *should* be feeling other things. I should be sorry about the waste of life. I should be worrying that my actions contributed to Sims's death, that I chased him to death. I should be analyzing my performance for errors, errors the Kings of Warsaw Creek would no doubt analyze with their legal team.

Now, that bothered me. I might get desked for this. I reviewed my steps in my mind. I had followed procedure. I had radioed for backup, established that Sims was in flight. There wasn't a scratch on my car. My gun hadn't been fired. The skid marks on the bridge showed a sharp left turn, just as I said.

There was no point in worrying about that. I had been aboveboard in my actions, even if my motives had been deeply wrathful.

No one could see inside my head. As long as I kept that anger behind my eyes, no one could touch me.

I thought of the giggle I heard, the singing. Had Sims heard it, or was that all in my head, too?

Gibby crawled into bed, and I wrinkled my nose. No matter how often I washed him, he still smelled like wet dog. *Wet dog* was a reassuring, safe smell. I came back to myself and kissed his brow.

I opened up my laptop and stuck in the SD card from the trail cam at the Hag Stone. I held my breath, skimming over the footage. The motion detector caught birds during the day, then a couple of hikers. At night, deer drifted through, munching leaves near the camera. The flash of an owl's wing washed over the night vision in a flare of black and white.

As the night wore on, the wildlife disappeared. Shadowy figures moved at the edges of the camera's sight. I couldn't tell how many people there were, or who they were, only that there were more than three. A fire blazed in the sand, and they flickered before it. I had no sound on the trail cam, so I couldn't tell what they were saying. I strained to make out faces, but the footage was blurry, as if someone had put Vaseline over the camera lens.

They stayed for more than an hour, circling the fire, lifting hands to the sky. When the fire guttered out, they moved away . . .

. . . walking into the water. I froze the video and stared. Maybe they had a boat out there? There had to be one, just out of sight.

Maybe that was the way the tweakers chasing me were getting in and out of the area, by boat. This area of the river was too shallow for a speedboat, but maybe there was a rowboat.

I stared at the dark screen, at the frozen shadows. I didn't know what the hell to make of it.

I closed the laptop and dozed. Part of my mind was reluctant to sleep deeply enough to dream, but another part of me sensed that I was on the cusp of something important. There was something I needed to remember now, and I struggled with how to access it safely.

Keys scraped in the lock, and the front door opened. Nick kicked off his shoes, and Gibby lunged out of bed to greet him. Nick put down his bag and came to the bedroom to sit beside me.

"Hey." He bent down to kiss the top of my head. "How are you doing?"

"Mm . . . it's been an eventful day. I'll tell you later." I was deliberately not wanting to deal with Sims's death tonight. Lately, I had been distracted when I was dealing with Nick, and he deserved a bit of normalcy, my full attention. "And you?"

He looked tired. "Feeling a little at odds."

"Tell me. Is it Dr. Floyd again?" I was ready to deal with more mundane workplace drama.

He slid his hand over his eyes. "Mandatory overtime for every-one through the July Fourth weekend. We're down three nurses and one ER physician, and Dr. Floyd won't fill the positions. He straight up told us that he thinks we're overstaffed, but we're not. It's just not sustainable."

"Damn. I'm sorry." I squeezed his other hand.

"A friend from med school told me about an opening in the city, with the university. It's primary care." It came out in a rush. "It would be less money, but it would be regular hours. Less time on call. Weekends free."

I kept still and listened, though my heart pounded.

"I could sell the condo and get a place in town. I've got enough saved up, and I could keep paying my student loans. Might be a little tight for a while, but the numbers could work . . ."

I let him trail off. When he lapsed into silence, I asked: "Is this what you want?"

"It is." He sighed. "But it's not the only thing I want." He reached across for my other hand.

I squeezed his hands. "You should apply."

"Will you come with me?"

My tongue stuck to the roof of my mouth. I wanted to. I re-ally did.

He shook his head. "You don't have to decide now. We could do long distance for a while and see how it goes. I—"

"I don't want to lose you."

"You won't." His eyes were sincere. So sincere.

But we both knew things could change. We knew that lives could be violently torn apart in an instant.

Or dissolve quietly in a few months, with distance and good intentions.

———

Mom and I went hunting for the source of the pollution that summer.

A green flash washed over me, and I was a girl again, sitting in a low tree branch. Mom was hunting. She'd called the authorities about the poisoned water several times, left messages in hopes that something would be done.

But no one ever called back. So she hunted.

She didn't hunt the way my dad did. Dad would've followed the tracks of men in the woods, their feet and their tires. He would've been able to determine the ages of the prints in the dust and what kinds of men made them.

Mom hunted with sticks. She tracked water with her dowsing rods, searching for the root of the pollution. Her sticks led us deeper into the woods, pulled by the magnetic veins of water. I soon began to distinguish fresh from poisoned; fresh water hummed and flowed evenly, while polluted water seemed to crackle in my ears, like static.

My mom and I spoke little, but the silences weren't hostile, like before. My shoulders relaxed from being hunched around my ears, and I soaked in every bit of instruction she gave me. Now, she seemed focused on analyzing a stand of dying cattails beside the river. The cattails had yellowed, and dead fish had washed up on the beach. We buried the fish so that hungry herons wouldn't eat them. There were tire tracks here, and footprints, but little else.

The day was brutally hot, and the tracks vanished near the road. Mom scooped river water into a black coffee mug, staring into it wordlessly without drinking. I thought at first that she was staring at her reflection, but her unfocused gaze seemed too slack, staring beyond the bottom of the cup.

It reminded me of the way she looked into the mirrors in the house. She hung mirrors she collected from garage sales, reflecting light back and forth into the shadows. I used to think she was vain, looking at her reflection, but maybe she saw something more there.

She often invited me to look over her shoulder at the mug, telling me to sit and soften my gaze. I saw clouds in the water sometimes. Sometimes, a coin-sized moon. I concentrated very hard now, wanting to see my dad, but all I saw were flower petals drifting near the bottom of the mug.

The trail of my mother's quarry had gone cold. I sat with my back to the tree, paging through a library book of fairy tales.

Today I read a story called "The White Snake." It was about a servant boy who tasted the king's supper—a cooked white snake—which gave him the power to speak to animals. The boy found the queen's missing ring, which had been swallowed by a goose, and he was turned out into the world with a little money. While on his travels, he helped animals, and found his way to a kingdom with a princess whose father would sell her hand in marriage to the man who could complete a series of tasks, including retrieving a ring from the bottom of the sea, collecting spilled grain, and stealing an apple from the Tree of Life. The boy completed all the tasks and was awarded the princess. Everyone lived happily ever after.

I slammed the book shut and scowled. I jammed it back into my pack.

"What's wrong?" Mom asked, finally noticing my rage.

I rolled my eyes. "The boys always get to do the cool stuff in fairy tales. The girls are just furniture. They don't get to pick their husbands. They don't get to go anywhere. They're like dolls. They do what they're told."

Mom laughed and sat beside me on the tree branch. Her laugh

was pretty when she used it. "How about I tell you the story of some women who don't do what they're told?"

I crossed my arms over my chest, but leaned forward. I wanted to hear the story.

"In a part of the world covered by dark forests, there was once a peasant girl who caught fish for her family. She would sit by the river and whisper to the fish, and they would fling themselves onto the bank. She kept her family fed in lean times and was content in the deep woods, singing to the birds and the deer. She had a beautiful singing voice.

"One day, a boat came down the river. It belonged to a local prince who had gotten lost on the many rivers that spider-webbed over the land. He heard the girl singing and followed her voice. When the girl saw him, she was instantly lovestruck. And so was he. The girl directed the prince back to the main river, and he would sneak away to see her over that long summer. They planned to get married, envisioning a shining future together.

"When the prince told his parents, they disapproved. They forbade him to marry the peasant girl. He was meant to marry a girl of his station, a proper princess. The prince told the girl what had happened, that they must break it off.

"But the girl was steadfast. She wanted to run away to get married. The prince agreed, and told her he would meet her at midnight by the spot in the river where they first met. She waited at that spot at the appointed time and date . . . and he didn't arrive.

"In the morning, the girl's parents found her drowned among the cattails. They were furious, but had no recourse. Did the boy kill her? Did his parents? Did she drown herself in grief after he failed to show up? No one knew."

I made a face. This was starting to sound like another one of those fairy tales where the girl got the short end of the stick.

"But what they did know was that the place became haunted, haunted by the spirit of the girl who drowned. People would hear her singing or see a dark shape swimming in the river. If they had sense, they ran away. The spirit never harmed women or children, who usually had the sense to flee. It was the men who would be ensorcelled by her song, who would be invited to come into the water, where she drowned them."

I leaned forward. This sounded more like my kind of story. "What happened to the prince?"

"The prince went on to marry a respectable princess, and they had a son. One day, the prince was on a hunting trip with his son, when they heard singing. They were beckoned into the water by the spirit of the girl, who gleefully drowned them both."

I nodded. This was more satisfactory, though I felt a little sorry for the boy, who was blameless.

"This happens often in that part of the world. When a woman is murdered, or commits suicide, she can haunt the rivers and streams. She stays there for all time, seeking revenge. There are hundreds such spirits, and they are all called by the same name: Rusalka."

"Rusalka." I repeated the word, rolling it around in my mouth. It tasted exotic and powerful, so much more so than the word "princess."

She gave a sly smile. "I think you've just been reading the wrong kind of fairy story."

The sound of an engine rattled through the woods, and our heads turned. Mom's eyes narrowed, and she took off at a run.

I sprinted after her, listening to the whistle of breath in the back of my throat. I didn't know my mom could run, and definitely not so fast. I struggled to keep up with her, my backpack bouncing uncomfortably against my shoulder blades. We followed the sound to another bend in the river, where I stopped short. An iridescent sheen of oil was spreading over the water, with a sickly sweet smell that caused me to gag.

Mom's gaze was murderous. She turned and followed tire tracks through the grass. A beat-up Jeep was making a retreat, speeding up a hill. Metal drums clanked noisily in the back.

I tried to memorize the license plate number, repeating it to myself like a mantra: *ADP 1123, ADP 1123 . . .*

Mom shouted at the Jeep, but the driver floored it and lurched up onto the road. Within seconds, it was gone from sight.

I stayed by the riverbank, helpless, watching that iridescent oil spread. It would've been pretty under other circumstances, if I could tell myself that it was some kind of fairy spell. But it wasn't. It was a thing that brought death to whatever it touched.

Just downstream, a blue heron turned its head toward me. I shooed it away, and it took off in a silent flutter of wings.

"Don't come back!" I yelled tearfully, hoping it didn't have a nest nearby.

Mom returned to the bank, her gaze black, furious. That was the look of the mother I knew—stiff and scowling.

"I memorized the license plate number," I told her.

She shook her head. "It won't do any good."

I sighed in frustration, scrubbing at my red face with the back of my filthy arm.

"This is something we will take care of ourselves," she said quietly, with unfathomable malice.

16

DETHRONED

One of the Kings of Warsaw Creek had indeed been dethroned.

I pulled up to the Silver Bridge just after sunrise. Mist clung to the river below, and the metallic bridge shone pink in the morning light. It would've been pretty if not for the police cars blocking the bridge.

I rocked up with a giant jug of hot coffee and put it down on the hood of a patrol car. Monica appeared and began blearily pouring out a cup.

"You've been out here all night?" I asked.

"Not the whole night. I made Detwiler guard the scene and slept in the car for a bit. That fucking radio never shuts up." Monica walked down to the shore. The bridge was above us, and a tow truck was parked by the shore. The tow line extended far into the river while the driver leaned against his truck and watched the line draw out from the winch.

"Not a fan of the new radio system?" I noted that Monica had called me only over her cell phone lately.

Monica made a face. "I'm waiting until I can thoroughly read the manual. I'm anal like that. I want to make sure it's not scanning our brains."

"That sounds a little paranoid."

"I didn't get to be captain without a healthy dose of paranoia. Which is probably something you could use." She glanced at me sidelong.

I winced. "There's going to be hell to pay for this mess, isn't there?"

"Not saying that I would've done anything different. But yeah. Especially now."

I looked up at the bridge. From this vantage point, I could make out the broken guardrail.

"It's good you got the girl away from him." Monica sighed. "But now we gotta fish him out."

A disembodied hand far away in the river popped up and gave a thumbs-up—probably Jasper's.

When Jasper had made it to shore, the tow truck driver activated the winch. The river slowly began to churn.

"We haven't had much rain this summer," Jasper said somberly. "The wreck wasn't down very far."

"What's it look like?" I asked.

"About how you'd expect. Tons of front-end damage. Guy was strapped into the driver's seat. I didn't see any passengers."

There was a sucking sound from the river, and something large seemed to twirl in the current. Over the hum of the winch, it was slowly dragged to land. It landed wheels down, and the metal of the crushed front end chewed at the flattened tires as the car was hauled up onto the gravel.

That car was expensive and unique. I wondered if it was something Lister had procured for him from the dealership.

Monica signaled for the tow driver to stop pulling the line in, and we approached the car. Water streamed from its crevices and the broken windshield. Monica reached for the driver's-side door and opened it. Water splashed out in a wave.

The figure in the driver's seat slumped. I approached, tongue glued to the roof of my mouth.

It was Sims. He was rubbery and dressed in a T-shirt and shorts, likely dead on impact. The whole interior of the car was coated in mud. His glasses were missing.

Wordlessly, we began taking pictures. I started at the car's exterior, moving toward the interior. I clicked into business mode, moving methodically. I needed to document everything, especially if I was going to cover my own ass.

"Hey, look at this." I pointed to Sims's chest. The seat belt was partially cut, and bone glistened through tears in his shirt and skin.

"That's a weird injury." Monica bent to take a closer look. "I don't think safety glass could have done that. Maybe some metal from the engine got ejected? It's not like this car is the picture of current safety standards."

"Maybe." I looked at his left arm, the one closest to the broken driver's-side window. That arm was completely shredded, as if he'd stuck it into a garbage disposal. His head wobbled on his neck and bowed forward, exposing thick gashes.

"That's an awful lot of damage," I muttered. I thought of the scratches on Mason and on Ross. My own leg ached.

"There's suitcases in the trunk," Monica observed. "Maybe he was headed out of town and had too much to drink."

My phone beeped, so I knew someone in the sheriff's office was playing with the new radio system. I picked it up. "Koray."

"Hey, El-Tee. It's Van Wert in Forensics. I've got some info for you about the Sumner house."

"Hit me."

"So, about that costume you found: we found a few exemplars of long dark hair, but without anyone to match those with, we can't draw any strong conclusions."

"Understood." I was thinking about whether there was a way I could snag a piece of hair from Viv to compare.

"We got a lot of prints that you'd expect—family, friends, and people who worked there. And a whole bunch of unknowns that we don't have in the system. Most of them are from women, so maybe cleaning crew?"

I chewed my lip. "How can you tell?"

"Ridge density is higher for women than men. We focused on the alarm panel, and got only prints from the husband, the wife, the maid, and the babysitter. Nobody else."

"Okay. What about the back door?"

"Nothing unusual there. We found the child's prints on the door handle, and that would have been within his reach. We also found the babysitter's, but we don't really have a way to determine whose are most recent."

"Understood."

"We did find something interesting on the bathroom windowsill, prints that had been there for a very long time. There was a coating of dust that made them fairly easy to process."

"How long?" I asked.

"Can't really tell. But I'm betting a long time, given who they belonged to."

"Who?"

"Dana Carson, a missing person from twenty-five years ago. That was before my time, but I saw in the departmental records that her case remains unsolved."

"Interesting." I told her I liked Sumner and his friends for Dana's disappearance.

"I'd love to have a warrant to dig further into that house," Van Wert told me. "It's an old house, and if there was foul play there, then I'd like to poke around and see what's going on."

I agreed that sounded like a good time, and that I'd see what I could do about getting a warrant. "In the meantime, I've got a car I'm sending to you after the coroner gets done with it. My gut says it's related."

"Looking forward to it."

"Just beware . . . it's soggy."

"Ugh. Floaters? Tell me there's not a floater in there." I didn't blame her; everyone hated floaters.

"Well . . . it doesn't stink yet."

"Terrific."

I hung up, and stared at the car Monica was photographing. These cases were connected, but I couldn't prove it. Not yet.

This could have been an accident. Sims seemed to want to get out of Dodge. Or it could have been suicide, because he felt the net closing in. But neither one of those explanations truly resonated in my gut.

I gazed out at the water, remembering the singing I'd heard last night, right before Sims wrecked. A chill settled over me, and I shuddered.

Did the monster in the river call Sims to his doom?

If not . . . maybe his death was on my shoulders, and I was the only monster here.

———

I dreaded this part of the job more than any other.

My social-worker friend, Kara, and I climbed the steps to the foster house I'd left Leah in the night before. I'd met Kara here; I'd already briefed her on the situation over the phone.

"This is a mess. But it's a substantiated mess. Rebecca's starting to talk. We can at least keep her and Leah safe. Maybe more. But the death of a parent . . ." She shook her head. "It's hard, no matter how much your parent sucks."

"Yeah. I feel terrible that Leah's going through this." I knew what it was like to have a father who died, a father who was a monster. I had to be the one to tell her.

Kara knocked on the door, and Margie and Dave answered. From our brief conversation, I could tell that Kara had called them beforehand. We all knew, except for Leah.

Leah was sitting at the kitchen table, eating Froot Loops and watching television. She was dressed in a T-shirt and joggers, looking way too young for this information.

I sat down opposite her, and Kara sat at the end of the table. Margie and Dave took seats flanking Leah.

"Hi, Leah," I said.

"Hi." She set her spoon down. "You've come to take me back, haven't you?"

I shook my head. "No. I've come to tell you that something has happened. Something I'm really sorry to have to tell you."

She met my gaze. "What is it?"

"Your stepfather was in an accident late last night."

Her hand stilled on the spoon, and she stared at me.

"It was a very bad accident. He didn't make it."

One eye twitched. Margie put her hand on Leah's shoulder.

"I'm so sorry," I said.

Leah looked down at her cereal. Her lips peeled back from her teeth. "Good."

She took a bite of Froot Loops.

Kara led me away, to the porch. "That isn't an uncommon reaction," she said. "She's likely in shock, and it will hit her in a few days."

I understood that reaction, though. I understood it all too well. "I'm afraid that the abuse was worse than I thought."

"Me, too, but I won't know for some time. Her world has been turned upside down, and we have to work slowly."

"What's going to happen to her?"

"She'll stay here for now. We'll go through the usual process, see if there are kin who might be permanent-placement candidates."

I shook my head. "I hope none of those candidates belong to that church."

Kara exhaled. "She's safe for now. That's the best we can do."

I looked over her shoulder, at the house. Maybe that was all I could do.

But there was so much more I wanted to.

———

I wasn't getting anywhere with Quentin Sims's death.

But I could look into the past.

I tracked Dana and Viv's mother to a state-run mental health facility a couple of counties away. It was difficult to have someone committed to a mental health facility long term, so Cassandra Carson had been in and out of institutions since the disappearance of her daughter. Mostly in. I was able to contact the facility's director, who permitted me to visit . . . under certain conditions.

"I ask that you don't upset her too much," the director said. "Cassandra is a very fragile patient, and we don't want to see her agitated. She can become very . . . . difficult to handle."

I understood. I promised to be gentle.

I drove two hours down a freeway studded with orange barrels. Traffic should've been light, but the narrowing of the road to one lane in each direction slowed it, and there was nothing to be done about it. I stared out the window at green hills, cow pastures, and knee-high corn. It was bucolic here, in its way. Maybe therapeutic.

I was stuck in traffic when my phone rang. I took the call immediately: it was Nick. Nick never called; he only texted.

"Hey, what's up?"

"Hey." His voice sounded taut. "I wanted to tell you the hospital lab tested that water you collected."

"Yeah?"

"They found some stuff you'd expect—typical bacteria and algae. But they also found a weird viscous benzene compound that's a liquid at room temperature."

"Benzene?" I echoed.

"Yeah. It's a component of crude oil, and is used in manufacturing industrial solvents."

"Like what Copperhead Valley Solvents might be using."

"That's my guess. And it's also my guess that this is what caused the death of that patient I mentioned losing two years ago."

"Does this help at all with treating Mason or Ross? The water sample wasn't from the pond where Mason nearly drowned, but . . ."

"I brought it up to the pulmonologist. She's calling Ross back to the hospital to do a CT. She thinks Mason might be suffering the effects of having oil in his lungs—it's called lipoid pneumonia. She can increase his steroids and do a lung lavage."

"That sounds unpleasant."

"Yeah. It's a general-anesthetic procedure, essentially washing out the lungs one at a time."

That would be a lot for a little kid to handle. But it didn't sound like it was the only thing on Nick's mind.

"Hey," I said, "are you okay?"

"Yeah. I just . . . we'll talk when you get home."

We exchanged "I love yous," and hung up. I didn't like hearing stress in Nick's voice. He was the most unflappable person I knew. Maybe work was getting to him. I hoped he was going to be all right.

He had to be. He was all I had.

When I'd pulled off the road to gas up the car, I bought a sandwich and called the state EPA's enforcement division again. I left a message describing the lab sample. They probably thought I was an annoying local yokel trying to tell them how to do their job, but they were my best shot at getting to Sumner. Sumner might be bulletproof where local politics were concerned, but I severely doubted he had that much influence at the state level.

I got back on the road and wound my way through a small town, and up a hill to a facility overlooking a small college. The college had a psychology program that provided mental health professionals to this facility. I'd never been here before.

Trinity Springs's main building was from the 1930s, perched on top of a freshly mown green hill studded with mature maple trees. The gardens around the slate-roofed three-story brick building were well manicured, with purple roses of Sharon blooming near the foundation.

I checked in at the front desk, in a green-tiled atrium. The clerk sat behind plexiglass, and the doors to the facility within were locked. The reception clerk invited me to sit in a plastic chair in the waiting area. I noted that the chairs were bolted to the floor.

Eventually, a woman in a white coat was buzzed through a

door. She was tall and square-shouldered, white hair held back in a messy bun. Her skin was tan and speckled with sun freckles.

"Hello. I'm Dr. Fox. It's nice to meet you."

She extended her hand to me, and it was cool when I took it. I swallowed my discomfort at dealing with people who dug around in minds for a living; I had too much to hide in my own, and feared pieces falling out.

"I'm Lt. Koray. Thank you for seeing me on such short notice."

"I will always clear my calendar for a chance to help long-term residents. Would you like to take a walk outside to discuss the case?"

"Of course." I thought it a bit odd that she seemed not to want me to see the facility's interior, but maybe I should give her the benefit of the doubt. Likely, the presence of strangers, especially police, upset the residents.

We headed out the front doors and walked around the corner of the building. I commented on the landscaping, observing that the blooming joe-pye weed had attracted monarch butterflies.

She smiled. "It's important that our residents get to see nature, in the limited fashion that we can allow them to. We partner with our university's entomology and botany departments to ensure that our gardens are appealing to songbirds and pollinators."

"That sounds expensive."

"It would be, but the contributing departments have found grant monies to help us as part of a permaculture initiative. We're also fortunate to have received a windfall from the family of a long-term patient who found comfort in the gardens."

I generally looked upon such facilities with skepticism, but perhaps it said something that a family had been pleased enough with the treatment to leave a bequest. Indeed, the exterior didn't feel like any state institution I'd encountered before. Through a gate we entered the back gardens, where broad sweeps of lawn were crossed by crushed-gravel paths and dotted with island gardens and trees. Mature maples shaded gardens containing hardy plants: spiky blazing star, spiderworts with long fingers of leaves, and ninebark cultivars with crimson foliage.

I scanned the scene, where staff watched over people seeming to be generally elderly and in poor health. I saw a man in a wheelchair; a woman with a cane; and a woman sitting in the grass, patiently plucking petals off a purple coneflower. In the distance, a tall chain-link fence circled the entire garden, but it was painted green and blended in with the forest beyond.

I wished, for a moment, that my father could've wound up in a place like this. A place where he could have felt the shade of a tree and combed grass with his fingers.

But then anger flashed through me. He didn't deserve this place. He deserved to rot behind cold concrete for decades, withering away from the source of his power. Even when he died, he had died outdoors, in his element. He'd won.

Dr. Fox gestured for me to sit at a table. The table and chairs were set in concrete. "But you're not here to talk about flowers. You're here about Cassandra Carson."

"Yes. I'm working on her daughter's disappearance. I'm trying to get familiar with the case, but it's been twenty-five years."

Dr. Fox frowned. "That was the inciting incident for her psychotic break. Cassandra was unable to cope with her daughter's vanishing, and I'm concerned that discussing it might set her progress back."

"How's her progress? I learned from her daughter Viv that Cassandra attempted to commit suicide after Dana went missing."

Dr. Fox sighed. "Cassandra has entirely broken with reality. When she was younger, we sometimes were able to bring her back to reality. But when she returned to her everyday life, she'd fall into a depression and attempt to kill herself. The attempt immediately following her daughter's disappearance wasn't the only one. She tried to kill herself twice after that time, once by hanging and the other time by stepping out into traffic. Based on scans, we think her brain was structurally damaged by oxygen deprivation."

"I'm so sorry to hear that. I can't imagine what this was like for her." Maybe coming here was a bad idea.

"When she's here, removed from things that remind her of Dana's loss, she's able to exist in a liminal state. She believes that Dana is alive and still in high school. She remains frozen in a moment in time before Dana disappeared. When Viv comes to visit, she doesn't recognize her."

"I see." My hopes for gaining information from Cassandra were fading.

"Cassandra is also prone to a number of other delusions. She believes she's a powerful witch. She will come to the garden to gather plant matter and conduct her 'spells.'" The doctor made air quotes around "spells."

Not so different from Viv. I certainly didn't have any room to decide where the line of reality should be drawn. I wondered about the point at which a delusion became grounds to take a person's rights away, to hide them away from the world. When the delusion harmed others? When one caused harm to oneself?

I couldn't say. I only knew that I'd been very close to that boundary in the past.

"Where did that delusion come from?" I asked neutrally.

Dr. Fox exhaled in frustration. "I suspect it was reinforced by her daughter. I've suggested that Viv might benefit from therapy, but she refuses. I find that after Viv has visited, Cassandra is agitated for many days afterward."

"Would I be able to talk to her?"

"Under certain conditions. I would want this to be under my supervision. And I ask that you do not discuss Dana's disappearance. We don't know if she would survive another suicide attempt."

I frowned. "You want me to pretend that Dana is alive and well?"

17

POISON

It wasn't that I was unaccustomed to lying. I was used to telling lies to protect my own reality. This felt like more than that. It was lying to protect someone else's reality, and I didn't want to break that illusion and for Cassandra to suffer the consequences.

Dr. Fox lifted her shoulder. "Yes. I'm sorry if that's not the answer you want to hear, but my first duty is to keep my patient safe."

I nodded. "I understand. If it's possible, I'd like to see her."

Dr. Fox gave me a small smile. "I'll have her brought out." She reached under her coat for a radio and spoke quietly into it.

I scanned the parklike setting. I didn't know what would be worse, the illusion that things were fine, stuck at a fixed point in time, or the crushing knowledge of something awful. I knew what I would choose for myself—I'd consistently chosen awful knowledge over time. But I couldn't force my desires upon someone else.

I had to walk into Cassandra's world and agree to participate in her version of reality.

A side door opened, and a woman in a pink tracksuit was led by an orderly in a white uniform. Cassandra had long gray hair, and dark eyes that rested on a tree, then a shrub, then the grass. She seemed uninterested in people. Her gait was slow and shuffling, and her posture was stooped. Though she was in her early sixties, she seemed much, much older.

The orderly led Cassandra to us and helped her sit on a concrete bench that curved around the table.

"Hello, Cassandra," said Dr. Fox. "How are you today?"

Cassandra looked at a point somewhere off Dr. Fox's shoulder. "I saw a monarch. They must be migrating." Her speech was slow and deliberate.

"Yes, the monarchs are here. Aren't they pretty?"

"Yes. They travel a long way, all the way from Mexico."

Dr. Fox smiled at her. "Someone's here to see you, Cassandra. I'd like for you to meet Anna." She moved her hand to my place at the table, and Cassandra's eyes followed her hand, then looked up at my shoulder.

"Hello, Cassandra. It's nice to meet you."

"It's nice to meet you," Cassandra echoed, not sounding at all interested in my presence. Her gaze followed a dragonfly.

I took a deep breath. "I saw your daughter Viv the other day. She says hello."

Cassandra smiled, her teeth small and worn. "Viv is such a nice girl, isn't she? She writes me letters."

"What does she write you letters about?"

"She tells me what she's cooking. She likes to cook. And she got some eggs from her neighbor who keeps chickens. Not so many eggs this year as usual."

"It's been very hot," I acknowledged. "But fresh eggs are delicious."

"Yes. The neighbor has Araucanas. Good layers. I used to do a lot of things with eggs, when the girls were little."

"Like what?"

"Oh, omelets, quiches. They're also very good to clear out your energy, you know."

"What do you mean?" Out of the corner of my eye, I saw Dr. Fox frown slightly.

"Oh, they're great for that." Cassandra leaned forward. "You take a fresh egg and pass it all over your body. Every inch. And then you crack it open and empty its guts into a glass of cold water. You let it sit for a half hour before interpreting it."

"What does that do?" I played along.

"If you see spikes, people are talking bad about you. If you see an eye, someone has given you the evil eye. If you see dark spots, you've been hexed," she whispered, eyes gleaming.

"That doesn't sound good," I said.

"That's why you have to pour that down the toilet, eggshells and all, and take a bath with lots of salt. The egg takes on the darkness. You have to do it over and over, until it comes up clear . . . over and over . . ." Her gaze grew misty. "You should try it. It would help you. You've got a very dark aura, you know."

Dr. Fox gently reached out for Cassandra's hand. "We talked about this, remember? About things that aren't real?"

Cassandra rolled her eyes. "I'm not allowed to talk about that stuff."

I changed the subject. "Tell me about your daughters. I'm sure you're very proud of them."

Cassandra smiled. "My girls are so smart. Smart and beautiful. Viv wants to be a biologist when she graduates. She got accepted into college. She's going to be so good at it. That girl has the biggest heart."

I thought back to the Viv I knew, who had abandoned her dreams to work at the local bar and mutter curses in her parlor. She was trying to get back to that—I recalled the college rejection letter on the coffee table. Once upon a time, she had been someone else.

We were all someone else, once upon a time.

"She's going to be a great biologist," I said. "How about Dana? What does she want to be when she grows up?"

Cassandra blinked, as if a bug had flown into her eye. She rubbed her brow and smiled. "Dana wants to be an artist. But I'm hoping she'll choose journalism. She's really good with people."

"That's wonderful. We definitely need more journalists."

"She's got this charisma. She can put anyone at ease. Strangers will walk up to her and tell her their life stories."

"What else does Dana like to do?"

Cassandra's brow furrowed, and I realized her recall was proximate. She could remember things from twenty-five years ago as clearly as if they had happened yesterday. Maybe she was the best witness I could find. "She's really popular, and that worries me. All those boys circling her like wolves."

"I heard she has a boyfriend."

Cassandra made a dismissive gesture. "I told her not to fuss with boys. Boys come and go. She likes that boy Rick. He's a good boy, but it's not good for a girl to settle down so quick. She said they agreed to be friends."

"That makes a lot of sense. How did he take that?" I hoped Cassandra's memory was from very close to the time when Dana disappeared . . . frozen at a point just before she vanished.

I was most struck then by the softness in her eyes, the affection with which she spoke about her daughters, the details she knew about them.

"I think it was his idea. He's going off to college. She agreed that it made sense, but she's sad about it, you know? Young love's like that, always bittersweet."

"Are there any other boys who like her? I heard about Luke and Jason and Wally."

Cassandra frowned. "There are too many boys looking at her. I don't like that."

"Which boys?"

"Those rich boys from Warsaw Creek. They came to the door the other night, looking for her." Cassandra's mouth turned down.

"Who? And when was this?" Cassandra would never be acceptable as a witness in any court, but maybe she could lead me to hard evidence.

"I think it was Wednesday. Viv and Dana were both out at their part-time jobs. They both work for the milkshake shop."

"Who came to the door?"

"That boy Jeff. And his friends Quentin and Mark. Dana doesn't like those boys. They made fun of her for being poor." Cassandra's knuckles whitened on the edge of the table. "We aren't poor, but everyone looks poor to them."

Dr. Fox shot me a warning look.

"What did the boys want?" I asked.

"They heard Dana had a Ouija board. They wanted to borrow it from her. I told them no, and that they needed to leave my girls alone." Cassandra's lips pulled back on her thin teeth.

"That's a very strange thing to ask for," I said.

"Those boys have bad magic. Very bad." She shook her head. "They knew my girls were witches. I always told the girls to be quiet, to go under the radar, but they knew, they knew . . ." Her gaze grew distant, and her soft fingernails dug into the concrete table.

"I think that's enough for today," Dr. Fox said.

I leaned forward. "They wanted your girls because they were witches?"

Cassandra's gaze fell full and heavy on me. "Those boys wanted Dana's blood. They wanted power, and they took her . . ." Her face crumpled, and she covered her face with her hands. A high-pitched keening sounded, like the cry of a bobcat at dusk, and it lifted the hair on the back of my neck.

She looked at me through parted fingers. "But they'll pay. The river spirit will make sure that their bloodlines end in the bottom of the river . . ."

Dr. Fox stood abruptly and wrapped her arm around Cassandra. She nodded to the orderly, and they lifted her to her feet.

"I told him. I said: 'Frederick, you watch out for my daughter.' And he didn't!" she wailed. "He was a hundred miles away when . . . when . . ."

"This interview is over," Dr. Fox said curtly. "I hope you got what you wanted."

I watched as they took the wailing woman back to the brick building.

I didn't know if I'd gotten what I wanted, but I got . . . something.

I sat in the car. Something was prickling at me. I pulled out my laptop and continued background checks on the boys Dana dated. I knew the Kings of Warsaw Creek were assholes, but I wanted to see if I needed to broaden the field.

The first guy, Wally, was career military. A response from the DOJ said that he was in OPSEC, at an undisclosed location, right now, and that he hadn't been in the US for two years. I could cross him off the list of suspects.

The second, Luke, had died in 2004, in a motorcycle accident in Montana. He'd been startled by some bison crossing the road, ditched his bike, and unfortunately met his end bleeding out in that ditch.

The third guy, Jason, was working on a crab fishing boat in Alaska. I guessed it was possible that he held a torch for Dana and had come back to create havoc. But his parole officer said that, to her knowledge, he was on the straight and narrow after serving his time for armed robbery. She'd left a message for him, and he'd called her back from Sitka when his boat was unloading. It was high crab season, with thousands of dollars to be made, and it didn't make sense that he'd sacrifice the money to go trekking down to the mainland to cause trouble. Revenge could wait for the offseason, right?

That left the regular boyfriend, Rick. I liked him more for revenge, since he'd been more than just a casual hookup.

"Frederick." I repeated his full first name, the one that Cassandra had used. I had found his high school records before, but the trail went cold after that point. I'd sent out a request to the Social Security Administration to see if he'd changed his name and court records.

I'd gotten one hit back from the clerk of courts—Frederick Alan Smitz had taken his stepfather's last name, and had been officially adopted, at the age of eighteen.

I stared at a scanned image of his Social Security card. *Frederick Alan Jasper.*

"Holy shit." I exhaled.

Fred Jasper had been honorably discharged after two tours of duty in Iraq. He got a degree in criminology on the GI Bill, then applied to the Bayern County Sheriff's Office. He'd passed a background check. At that time, maybe the office just ran a criminal records check and a credit check. Maybe nobody connected him with Dana Carson. And even if somebody did, that wouldn't exclude him as a candidate to be a sheriff's deputy. It would truly have been nothing—if anyone had even noticed.

But now . . . now Jasper was working this case. There was a clear conflict of interest there. Why hadn't he said anything? Yes, there was literally no one else to do the work, but we could have called someone in from a neighboring county. Although it would have been days, at least, before they could get over to us.

Fuck. Fuck. Fuck.

I reached for the phone, but then my hand stilled.

I had been in his shoes. I wasn't using my real name. And I'd worked a case I had no business working. My intentions hadn't been pure, exactly, but I'd been pursuing a killer. What if Fred was doing the same thing?

I exhaled. I wasn't going to act now. I would gather information, and talk to Jasper. There was no advantage in going off half-cocked and calling hellfire down on an innocent man. Especially one I trusted.

I could detect a killer if I looked him in the eye, right?

Right?

I wasn't so sure.

———

For all her flaws, Cassandra loved her girls, and the loss of her daughter had driven her to madness. Her love for them was palpable. Pride shone in her face, even this many years later. I couldn't imagine the depths of her despair, or the depths of that love.

I felt a pang of jealousy at that. My mother had never felt that way about me. Intellectually, I knew her feelings were tangled in her hatred of my father. I was his child, and I looked at her through his eyes. And so she rejected me, had my memory swept away, and went on to live her own life.

Maybe she was the only one of us to truly move on, to be released from this curse.

I wasn't far from Carlisle, the town where my mother was living her new life over the state line. On impulse, I drove south, down the freeway, and then coasted through small-town streets. In anticipation of the Fourth of July, red, white, and blue bunting hung from streetlights. I passed a corner store, a library with windows covered in construction-paper drawings, and a school closed for summer.

I turned right on my mother's street. I parked a half block away, staring at the brick ranch house where my mother lived. Pastel balloons were tied to a sign staked to the front lawn. RAINA'S BABY SHOWER was lettered in calligraphy.

My jaw clenched so hard that it ached. Raina was my mother's daughter with her new family. I watched as the screen door opened, admitting visitors carrying packages tied with green and yellow ribbons.

I spied activity in the backyard. I slowly tooled down the street, turned left, and observed the backyard from the next block over. The yard was bounded by a chain-link fence, and picnic tables were set up in the shade of a large maple tree. The tables were covered with yellow plastic tablecloths, and flowers in vases. A young brunette woman sat in a lawn chair, cradling her pregnant belly. A balding man manned a grill. He looked like my mother's husband. He was tan and round, totally unlike the stringy sharp angles of my father. People milled around a table heaped high with presents—diaper towers, a car seat, and a hundred plastic baubles that I didn't know the purposes of. I scanned the guests, observing a man and woman, who might be the honoree's siblings, playing croquet on the grass with barefoot young children who rolled the wooden balls through wire hoops.

My lungs felt hollow. This was what my mother had replaced me with, this perfect slice of American pie, this sunshine party over the shadowed forest my father and I inhabited.

I could never do this. I could never live a conventional life. I could never bring myself to have children. What if I passed my dark legacy on to a child? I couldn't forgive myself. I was not . . . I was an observer in life. I stood back, recorded, watched. I was not a participant. I remained on the other side of the glass, then and now.

I glanced in the rearview mirror. I didn't see my face—I saw my mother's when she was younger and stalking along the river, as she had been in my dreams. I blinked, and saw myself once more, with my sun freckles and uneven mascara.

I rubbed my eyes. I was . . . imagining things. And I didn't like that.

I put my sunglasses on and turned my attention to the yard, trying to focus on what was real. I searched for my mother. She called herself Rebecca now. She had a smile that seemed to reach her eyes as she cut slices of pink cake for the guests. I watched her. Was she playing the doting grandmother-to-be? Or was she really capable of that kind of emotion?

I wasn't sure. She'd never displayed that kind of emotion to me, as far as I remembered, except in my dreams. That didn't necessarily mean that she wasn't capable of it. Maybe she was faking. It was possible, I supposed. She had the same genetic marker my father and I did, the rare Lyssa variant, that was associated with psychopathy.

My gut lurched at the thought of our bloodline continuing. It was highly unlikely that my mother could've passed the fully expressed Lyssa variant on to the children she had with her new husband. That would require that her husband also carry the fully expressed Lyssa gene. It was so improbable that it was nearly impossible.

I watched her kiss her daughter on the head and hand her a plate. Maybe she really did feel things. I knew I felt things: love, compassion, admiration. Maybe she did, too.

Her gaze drifted across the yard to land on my car. I was wearing sunglasses in an unmarked car. It was unlikely that she would think anything of me. I remained still, but I felt the weight of her gaze on me.

A challenge, maybe. Recognition? I'd come to her house a year ago, working a case. Would she remember me from that investigation? Would she finally remember who I really was—her lost daughter?

She kissed her real daughter again and moved into the house.

I started the ignition and put the car into gear. I went back around the block, saw my mother standing on the front porch step, smoking a cigarette.

She walked down the steps, toward my car.

My heart lurched into my mouth. I could just keep driving, avoid her, pretend she didn't recognize me. I'd avoided conflict with her my whole life. Why would now be any different?

But I pulled over to the curb, shut off the engine, and rolled down the window. I listened to the radiator tick and a catbird scream a warning from the crab apple tree in the front yard.

She crossed the street to the car, her arms folded, holding the cigarette close to her chin. She stopped and looked down at me with that cold expression I remembered.

We stared at each other. I waited for her to speak first.

"I thought I'd seen the last of you." She flicked ash away. That was the woman I remembered from most of my childhood—cold and calculating. Not the woman from my dreams, who really saw me. My dreams felt distant now, like yearnings conjured by my sleeping mind, not the woman she really was.

I lifted my shoulder. "I'm like a bad penny that way."

She exhaled smoke. "Why are you here?"

I wasn't going to say it out loud. "I was just in the neighborhood. Got curious."

She looked down at me, the way she did when I was small. "I'm sorry, but I'm all out of cake. You understand."

My mouth turned up. I didn't remember her ever baking a cake for me. "Enjoy your cake. Maybe some other time."

I cranked the ignition, and she stepped back. I pulled away from the curb slowly, and she returned to the house.

I waited until I got out on the main drag to start trembling, the way I'd wanted to when she approached the car.

Stalemate. We understood each other. We each knew what the other truly was: monstrous.

And neither of us could rat out the other without revealing her own monstrosity.

Wholesome family-picture stuff.

I chewed on it the whole way home. I shouldn't have gone there. Regret surged in the back of my throat. If my mother dropped the dime on me, my life would be over. There was nothing to be gained from poking that bear.

It didn't matter if she was a monster to her daughter and grandchildren. What mattered was that she was a monster to me. There was no reconciling this. I, better than anyone else, should've known that people were different people in different situations. They were chameleons. I could spend years trying to unravel my mother's psyche, but I would likely unravel only my own life.

Poison was poison, and I had to learn not to touch it.

18

CURSED

I led a charmed life.

My SUV blew a head gasket on the way back, just after sunset.

I was going seventy miles an hour when the engine started to overheat. When white smoke started rolling out from the exhaust pipe, I lost power immediately.

I let off the accelerator and coasted to a stop on the side of the road as the engine hissed. I shouldn't have trusted Lister's dealership to work on my car. My car had a hundred and fifty thousand miles on her, but she'd never left me in the lurch.

I popped the hood and looked down at the aftermath with the flashlight on my cell phone. My radiator fluid reservoir was dry. I poked around and pulled the oil dipstick, which came back milky with what I presumed was radiator fluid mixed in. Fuck. I wasn't a car-repair gal—I knew only enough to get by—but this looked expensive as fuck. Still, I was lucky that it had happened in an area with no traffic, and that nobody had gotten hurt.

I stared at my phone. There was one bar here, and that was

enough to call for a tow. I opened my door and sat in the driver's seat to wait, feeling the heat shimmering up from the pavement and smelling burning oil and radiator fluid as the engine cooked. It would be hard to prove Lister's guys had fucked up my car; it wasn't like my car had just rolled off the showroom floor. But I was sure as fuck gonna try.

I scanned the highway, seeing nothing except hayfields and distant woods drenched in twilight. This was a pretty peaceful place to break down, as far as places to break down went.

Car headlights swept down the road, slowed, then pulled in behind me. Its windows were tinted, and no front license plate was required in my state. I watched in the rearview mirror as the car just sat there, engine on. I couldn't see anything else.

My hand slid down for my sidearm. I didn't like how this was going. I felt as vulnerable as any woman with a breakdown in the middle of nowhere. The driver of the car would be able to see through the headlights that there was only one person in the car before them, and see my ponytail. I closed my door and locked it.

Was this a run-of-the-mill opportunist? Or were the Kings of Warsaw Creek following me?

The headlights went out, and darkness washed across the road.

I heard a car door open, then another. Behind me, I could make out two shadows.

I inhaled, my heart beating steadily behind my sternum. If they wanted trouble, I'd give it to them. I clicked my gun's safety off.

They were approaching from the driver's side and the passenger side. If they were both armed, I'd have the chance to shoot only one before the other shot me . . .

A new set of headlights appeared on the road behind us, and I exhaled. The people from the dark car turned tail, climbed back into their car, slammed their doors, and peeled away.

I stared at the car as it passed me and zinged down the road. I saw two heads in the glare from the headlights behind me. The license plate was obscured by a certainly illegal tinted license plate holder.

The second car pulled up behind me, and red and blue lights switched on.

I sighed in relief.

A highway patrolman with a Marine buzz cut exited the car and came to my window. "Ma'am, can I help you?"

"Yeah, you certainly can."

———

The tow truck showed up and I thumbed a ride with the highway patrol to the county line, where Monica picked me up.

"Hey, I really appreciate you riding to my rescue," I said.

"No worries," she said. "Where did you get the car towed to?"

"To Kapp's Automotive." Kapp's was a smaller dealership specializing in luxury cars the next county over. They'd laugh at my battered little SUV. "I'm pretty sure they're gonna say it's toast."

"Fuckers. Maybe they can help you build a case that Lister fucked it up?"

"I hope so. But honestly . . . book value on that car is only around three K. Even if I win a lawsuit, that's not gonna touch a down payment on a new car."

"You are, indeed, screwed."

I scrunched down in the seat and sighed. I filled Monica in on what I'd learned so far today, omitting my little detour to visit my mother, and what I'd learned about Jasper. I also told her about the car that had pulled up behind me.

"What's up with that?" Monica muttered.

"Dunno. I'm feeling like these guys are every—"

I was interrupted by Monica's radio chirping. "C1, this is D6. Requesting your presence at 1142 Devlin Road."

I lifted my eyebrow. "That's the address for Lister's dealership. Wonder if they got vandalized again."

Monica frowned and reached for the radio. "I'm en route with L4."

By the time we rolled up to the dealership, the place was lit like a Christmas parade, with patrol cars and fire trucks lining the service road entrance.

Monica rolled her window down at the roadblock, which was manned by Detwiler. "Detwiler, what's going on?"

"You gotta see this for yourself," he said, his eyebrows crawling up into his hairline. "Just don't get too close."

We tooled around, to find our path blocked by a fire truck. We parked and got out, walked around the fire truck, and were confronted by a firefighter.

"I'm sorry, ladies, but you can't go any farther."

"What's going on?" I flashed my badge.

"A whole lot of destroyed cars." He gestured to a line of caution tape.

He moved aside, and I sucked in my breath.

The parking lot had disappeared. A black pit had opened below it, swallowing dozens of cars and a corner of the building.

I wondered if the symbols spray-painted on those cars might have been a harbinger of what was to come, or if they had somehow summoned this disaster.

"What happened?" I whispered.

"Sinkhole," the firefighter said. "Freak accident."

"Anyone get hurt?"

"Fortunately, no. Just an unimaginable amount of property damage."

Honestly, I felt a sting of satisfaction that Lister had gotten some of what was coming to him. "Is Lister here?"

The firefighter pointed to the edge of an EMS wagon. Lister sat on the bumper, holding a cup of coffee, staring into space.

"Mr. Lister?" I said.

He didn't look at me. "I'm ruined. Totally ruined."

"What happened?" Monica asked.

He shook his head. "I heard this terrible, terrible sound . . . like the earth opened up . . . and all those cars just fell in, one after another. Fifty-two brand-new cars."

"Did they say why?"

He lifted a shoulder. "Insurance guy says that sometimes underground pockets form, worn away by water, and they break open . . . Of course, my policy doesn't cover this."

"That's rough," Monica offered.

"I'm cursed," he said.

"Cursed?" I echoed, hoping he'd elaborate, maybe confess to something.

He shook his head. It seemed like he'd say more, but he only looked past us, at a black sedan pulling up. I couldn't say it was the car that had pulled up behind me on the freeway, not for sure, but my skin crawled.

Jeff Sumner emerged and pushed his way through the crowd. He ignored Monica and me and went to Lister.

"It's gonna be okay, buddy. It's all gonna be okay. I swear." Sumner's eyes were hard and glinting when his gaze crossed mine.

When Monica and I retreated, I peered into the yawning pit of the car lot. From the depths, metal shifted against rock, squealing, echoing, bits of silt raining down.

And I swore that something laughed musically from the bottom of that pit, beckoning to me.

Transfixed, I slipped beneath the caution tape, listening. Water rushed from broken pipes, swirling around the bumpers of ruined cars.

Something thrummed and cracked below me. The ground shifted, pavement fracturing beneath my feet. I stumbled, and the blacktop I was standing on sheared away.

I twisted, clawed the air, grasping for a ragged edge of pavement as my feet kicked into space.

A hand grabbed mine and hauled me back, away from the pit. I was dragged back to solid ground, retreating behind the caution tape, scrambling back to safety as the firemen squawked into their radios.

"Jesus, Anna." Monica's hand was so tight around my wrist that it bruised me. "If you had gone down there, there would've been no way to bring you back."

I nodded, not trusting myself to speak. Monica would risk herself to save me, even when I was being fucking stupid and didn't deserve it. I couldn't say that about very many people in my life.

And I understood that something down there would also stop at nothing to pull me down into its depths.

———

I got home just after midnight, when the fireflies lit up the forest at the edge of the house.

"You want some coffee?" I asked Monica.

"Nah. I'm heading home to bed. Catch you in the morning."

We said our goodbyes, and I let myself into the house. Gibby came to greet me, his nails clicking on the scarred hardwood floors. Nick was in bed, snoring.

So much for that talk we were going to have.

I slipped into bed, and Gibby wriggled in between us.

I had faith that Nick would talk to me when he was ready.

I stared at the ceiling, thinking about this family I'd made. Family was a terribly fragile thing. I didn't want to let it go. If Nick wanted to move away, I didn't think I could bear being apart from him. Not in the middle of the night, when all the fears that I couldn't talk about clouded my head.

I couldn't ask him how to interact with my mother. My father had killed Nick's mother, long ago, and Nick had lived with his grandparents. I had a model of motherly love, certainly—my adoptive mother. She and my adoptive father were enjoying their retirement, traveling. They were currently on a cruise in Alaska. I vowed that when they returned, I would take time off, enjoy my adoptive mom's cooking and bring her flowers. Yes, that felt normal. Sane.

Nothing like my biological mother, who was masquerading as a member of a happy family. I knew better. She was a sociopath. She carried the Lyssa variant, the genetic mutation that I suspected drove much of my father's psychopathy. I carried it, too. I refused to believe that biology was destiny, but with her . . .

How could she have abandoned me at twelve like that? How could she have sent me away without a second thought, to create a new life? I wanted answers from her. I knew I would never get them.

The dreams I was having stung. They showed me a version of my mother that I wanted, someone who was softer, who didn't hate me for being my father's daughter. In those dreams, I felt like I was her daughter, too. That maybe she loved me, just a little bit.

But I couldn't trust those dreams. They were so different from what I knew, of her coldness and her abandonment.

There were no answers. It wasn't as if I could ask her. Even if I did, I was certain she would lie to me, just as she did decades before.

———

I awoke to my phone ringing.

"Koray," I answered muzzily. I rolled out of bed to take the call away from Nick, who was still sawing logs. Gibby snuffled at me and burrowed under the covers.

BEEP. "El-Tee, it's Detwiler. Got a crime scene here at the quarry that might be of interest to you." He sounded a little green, which didn't bode well for the nature of the crime.

"Copy that. Send me the directions?"

"Done."

It was then that I realized I didn't have a car. "Um, can you also do me a favor?"

"Shoot, El-Tee."

"Can you please get Vice to drop a car off for me?"

"Sure thing."

BEEP.

Ugh. The new comm system's beeping was like a bullet to the brain. I got dressed and headed out to the driveway, wondering what the fuck was going down at the quarry. Vice had apparently already come and gone, leaving me with the El Camino that smelled like cigars. Well, it was certainly better than nothing, but I was sure they were cracking up at the fact that they'd hung some pink fuzzy dice from the rearview mirror. *So retro.*

As I left, Kapp's Automotive called to tell me that the SUV was ruined. I asked them if they thought it could have been sabotaged. They couldn't definitively say that, but they told me that the car would cost more to fix than it was worth.

I sighed. I'd miss the SUV. I patted the El Camino's dashboard. "You and me are gonna be friends for a while longer, old girl."

Detwiler met me on the road to the quarry, a favorite local

swimming hole. Once upon a time, limestone was mined here, and it had since filled in with deep water. It wasn't the sort of place where you'd take children swimming, more the kind of place that teenagers would sneak out and drink at. It was usually littered with beer cans, and the occasional lost swimsuit. We'd also fished a couple suspicious vehicles from the depths.

Detwiler had set sawhorses up as a roadblock, and he let me in via an access road overgrown with weeds. "Nice ride, El-Tee." He nodded at the El Camino through my open window.

I made a face. "Whatcha got?"

"Two men, late twenties. Kind of old to be in the party scene, found floating on their inner tubes this morning by a couple teen girls."

"What were the girls doing here?"

"One of them left her cell phone here last night. Apparently there was a party." Detwiler lifted a shoulder.

I liked Detwiler, but he was way too square to know about parties. As a kid, he was working on his Eagle Scout badge when his classmates were toking up. "Gotcha. Are the girls still here?"

"They're with another deputy, on the far side of the quarry, out of sight of the bodies."

"Understood. Thanks, Detwiler." I cranked up the window and headed down the road.

A narrow gravel trail, wide enough for only one car, opened to a stone beach. I parked close to the gravel, not wanting to get the rear-wheel-drive El Camino stuck. The back of the quarry was cliffs, from which people often made ill-advised dives. The water level was lower than I remembered it ever being, owing to the drought. I saw a patrol car there, as well as a white sedan and a black SUV. Two girls were sitting in the air-conditioning in the back of the patrol car, looking distressed.

In the distance, I spied two orange inner tubes. I could make out two sets of feet, toes up. I wondered how Detwiler had arrived at the conclusion that these men were dead and not just hungover and passed out, but my suspicious were confirmed when the breeze pushed the inner tubes around.

Both bodies were headless.

"All right, then," I breathed.

I went to the patrol car, nodded at the deputy there. "How are the girls holding up?"

The deputy looked overwhelmed. "They're freaking out. I tried to calm them down. I took their phones away to keep them from sharing evidence, but I called their parents."

"They're minors?"

"Both seventeen, and terrified about being busted for underage drinking."

"So, they found the missing phone?"

The deputy handed me two phones. One was in a purple-glitter case, and the other one was jet-black, with a cracked screen.

"Okay. I got this. You wanna call Dive, Forensics, and the coroner's office?"

"Will do."

I popped open the back door to speak to the sobbing girls. "Hi. I'm Anna. What are your names?"

"Teresa."

"Evie."

"Teresa, Evie, I want to make it clear that you're not in trouble here, okay?"

Teresa rubbed her eyes. "My parents are gonna kill me if they think I've been drinking."

"Well," I amended, "there's not much I can do about that. What I can do is say that I'm not gonna charge either one of you with any wrongdoing if you tell me what the heck went on here last night."

The girls nodded tearfully.

"So, do you know those guys?"

Evie shook her head. "No. Not really. We went with some friends to just have some beers and relax, you know? We wanted to take some videos, since it's creepy here after dark."

"Friends your age?"

"Um, yeah."

"I'm gonna need names."

The girls exchanged glances, then coughed up a list of five high schoolers.

"Okay. You and your friends were here, drinking and hanging out. What was the deal with these guys?"

"We didn't know them. They showed up after. They were real gross, asking to take pictures of the girls." Teresa made a face. "They were old."

"How old?"

"I dunno . . . old."

"Okay. Did either of them touch you or your friends?"

"No. We bailed."

"Show me the video you took."

I handed the girls their phones, and they showed me a video of two men, who looked to be in their late twenties, leering at the young women around a campfire.

"Can you send me that?"

"Sure."

"What time did you leave?"

"I dunno. We left when it started raining."

"Understood. I need to get your contact information for further questions."

I scribbled that info down, and took the phones just in case there was more information on them than the girls had shared. I had Patrol escort the girls, in their car, out to the road to meet their parents, leaving me alone on the beach.

I took pictures of the debris there. There were dozens of beer cans, and maybe there was some DNA on the rims worth testing. I found one flip-flop, a broken bong, and a soggy sandwich covered with ants.

Next to the SUV, I found a duffel bag. With gloved hands, I opened it. Within were men's shoes, jeans, and T-shirts. I was betting these belonged to the men on the water. There were cell phones and wallets, too. I cracked open the wallets and looked at the drivers' licenses.

Amos Lister, twenty-nine.

Patrick Lister, twenty-seven.

My eyebrows lifted. There weren't that many people with that last name in the county.

A Google search coughed up a social media picture of Mark Lister standing with the two men at a family reunion. Judging by the names and the resemblances, I was pretty sure they were at least cousins, maybe half brothers. I did some poking around on social media, and identified the men as Mark's second cousins on his father's side. I radioed the car's plates in, and they came back registered to Patrick Lister.

Gravel crunched. Forensics and the coroner's van rolled in. The coroner's van stopped beside me, and the county coroner herself, Dr. Navarro, hopped out.

"Hi, Doc. I thought we kept you busy enough to keep you chained to your desk."

Dr. Navarro sighed. "Everyone's on vacation, so it's all-hands-on-deck, Koray. Though that floater you sent me was interesting."

"Anything you can share?"

She leaned against the side of the van. "Quentin Sims's cause of death was drowning, though I noted a number of wounds on the body that weren't consistent with the kind of accident he was in."

"I did see some at the scene, and I wasn't sure what to make of them."

She pulled out her phone, showing some pictures of the corpse. Deep scratches trailed along Sims's ribs and arm, long gashes in the pale flesh. "Here." She advanced to a shot of the corpse's head, revealing claw marks at the back hairline and along his neck. Bone glistened. "And here."

"Weird." I counted five stripes. "Looks almost like a hand, and those are fingers."

"Sure, but humans don't grow knives on their fingers, and there's nothing in the river that does."

"Maybe they were inflicted before the accident?"

"I don't think so. The vascular damage and blood pooling aren't consistent with that. Pragmatically, I'd be really surprised if there was a swimmer in the water with a knife at the time of drowning. Very surprised."

"No ideas what that is?" Viv was off my list of suspects for the near drownings and Sims's death. But I imagined Fred Jasper swimming with a knife in the dark and stifled a shudder.

"None. You bring me a tool, and I'll compare. I didn't find any inorganic material, like metal burrs, in the wounds, either."

I exhaled. "Weird."

"That oddity notwithstanding, cause of death is drowning. The quantities of prescription opioids in his system were sufficient to impair his driving, so I'm ruling this death as accidental."

"He had opioids in his system?"

"It's surprisingly common. According to the state's automated prescription-reporting system, he had a valid prescription for back pain. It wasn't doing him any favors while operating heavy machinery, but he probably wasn't feeling much pain at the end."

At least Sims didn't suffer much. A small, dark part of me wished he had, though. He didn't deserve an easy death.

I backed up to let Forensics do their thing. I caught up on messages. To my disappointment, EPA hadn't called me back. I called them again, and was in the process of leaving a message when Fred Jasper rolled up beside me in a sheriff's van.

I ended my call and steeled myself to talk to Jasper.

"You trying to reach EPA?" he asked, brow furrowed as he climbed out of the van.

"Yeah." I blew out my breath. "They're not responsive."

"I may have a contact there, from when I was in the military. Want me to reach out?"

"That would be great," I admitted. Now I was really feeling bad that I was going to confront him about what I'd learned. I squared my shoulders and faced him. "Fred, can we talk?"

"Sure. What's up?"

We walked a bit away from the scene, to where we couldn't be overheard.

"I've been looking into the Dana Carson disappearance."

He nodded. "I figured you would."

"You didn't tell me you were Dana Carson's boyfriend."

He stared out into the river. He wasn't hostile and didn't seem to be provoked by my discovery. His expression was just wistful. "Dana was a great girl. She was kind, smart, funny, artistic."

"Why did you break up?"

"I was going to college in the fall. She was three years younger, and it didn't seem fair to leave her behind and have her wait for me. In retrospect . . ." He sighed. "It was the biggest regret of my life."

"You must've been devastated."

Jasper's voice was quiet, barely above a whisper. "Yeah. It was what made me decide to be a cop."

I felt that. I think that, subconsciously, I'd also become one to purge my father's sins. Maybe it was a way to have the power I never had as a girl. "I get it. You think Jeff and his friends did something to her?"

He nodded. "I do. I hope that someday they get caught and stand trial."

"I could see that. Do you feel like you can still work this case?" I asked. A decision would be made, far above my head, if Jasper could remain on the case.

"I think so, but that'll be up to Chief. I'm just going to dive, and report back what I see. You and Chief get to decide what happens from there."

"What do you think happened to Dana?" I hated picking at old wounds, but I needed to know what he knew.

His gaze darkened. "The Kings of Warsaw Creek were always bad news. They had no limits, and they knew it. Still probably don't. I think they saw her, and they just . . . took her for thrills. I think they killed her and threw her away somewhere, somewhere she hasn't been found yet."

"I'm sorry, Jasper."

He exhaled. "I don't want to prejudice your investigation. I'm here to answer any questions I can, though."

I frowned. I didn't like that he hadn't been forthcoming about his involvement with Dana. It just didn't sit right with me. "Fred, I have to ask you, because I have to ask you. Where were you the last several nights?"

He didn't seem to take offense. "I was working overtime on those days, directing traffic for the Flower Festival."

I nodded. That should be easy enough to corroborate. The Flower Festival was usually a tame event, attended by gardeners, old hippies, and random guys who carried guitars in the woods. "Thanks. I appreciate it."

"No problem. I know you've gotta do what you've gotta do." He smiled at me. "You still want me to suit up and check this out? I can wait for you to run it up the flagpole."

I nodded. "I'll do that, just to cover our asses."

"Sounds good. I'll just do a check on my equipment while you're clearing it. If the boss doesn't clear it, I know three guys from the city dive team are on call this weekend."

I gave him the thumbs-up. While Jasper busied himself with his gear, I walked down the road, toward Detwiler's roadblock.

I was a big hypocrite calling Jasper out like that. I called the chief. His secretary said that he was busy, but he'd call me right back.

I paced along the gravel, feeling super weird about this thing. I didn't really believe Jasper was capable of murder. If he wanted to, he could have killed the Kings of Warsaw Creek years ago. I refused to believe that the twenty-fifth anniversary of Dana's disappearance would cause him to snap like this. Most grudge killers didn't wait that long to explode.

My phone rang, and I picked up.

"What's going on?" Chief asked.

I told him about Jasper. He was quiet, which meant that he was digesting.

"I don't like that he wasn't up-front about this," Chief said, "but he has an alibi. Watch him carefully. If he does anything weird, I'll ground him."

"Yes, sir."

We hung up. I didn't like Jasper being this close to the investigation. He had too much motive to hold a grudge against the Kings of Warsaw Creek, and people close to them were winding up dead. *Fuck.* This could be a huge conflict of interest. Or it could be murder. But Chief hadn't taken him off this investigation, so all I could really do was watch.

I couldn't help but wonder if Chief knew something I didn't know. Chief was locked in a power struggle with the sheriff. I didn't know where Jasper's loyalties lay, if he was trusted by the chief or maybe drank beers on the sheriff's boat on weekends. That was the trouble with Jasper: he was amiable to everyone, and I had no real bead on his loyalties.

I walked back down the road. "Chief says to proceed."

Jasper gave me a cheerful thumbs-up. I watched him don his gear, slowly, methodically.

"Hey," I said, unwilling to let him have access to the crime scene without supervision. "Is Ramirez's suit in there? Can I come with you?"

Jasper paused. "Have you had dive training?"

"I dived a bit in college. My certification has lapsed, though."

Jasper seemed to consider. "Well, I'm a certified instructor. It would be safe if I supervised you closely."

I nodded. We would watch each other.

I suited up in Ramirez's gear. I was a little taller than her, and the neoprene felt tight across my shoulders. Jasper helped me put the heavy tank on my back, and I waddled, in my fins, behind him to the shore.

It would be easier to drop from a boat, but we waded awkwardly in. The quarry was still, with no current, so that was in our favor.

Jasper swam out to the orange donuts, taking pictures. I was at his elbow when he grabbed the handles of the inner tubes, and we began to tow them to shore.

Once we'd gotten them within reach of the coroner's people, we turned back to the water.

"Let's see if we can find the heads," Jasper said.

I took the respirator into my mouth, dropped the goggles over my eyes, and plunged into the cool water.

It closed over my head, cutting off the birdsong echoing in the quarry. The water was clear, and I could see to the bottom, tiny pebbles disturbed by my fins. Jasper was by my side as we searched, moving deeper.

I listened to my heartbeat and my breathing, sounding like Darth Vader's, as we descended into the quarry, searching a grid from the shallows to the deeper parts of the quarry. Jasper's camera flashed as he took pictures.

The water had a bluish tinge, the further we went in. Something about the pH of the quarry water discouraged algal growth. The deeper we went, the dimmer the light. I switched on my headlamp.

And it was cold. Before, I might have thought I didn't need a wet suit, but I was thankful for it now. I felt a slight pressure against my body, squeezing my chest as we went farther down. I saw Jasper's light to my left. I was watching him; he was watching me.

I felt sort of bad for keeping Jasper under scrutiny, for doubting his motives. I was the biggest kind of hypocrite. I worked the case involving my father's copycat, and I told no one. Part of me wanted to grant Jasper some grace; part of me wanted to be better than that and follow the rules.

The floor was rocky here. I saw debris—an abandoned oar rotting, a broken piece of chain. I wondered if some debris was from the former mining operation, and how much evidence from other crimes had been chucked here, into blue water that swallowed everything.

Maybe even severed heads. Human bodies tended to float, but I remembered reading in an article about mob hits that found heads were heavy enough to sink, at least until decomposition set in. When that happened, gases would cause the heads to rise. I sure as hell didn't want any drunk teenagers finding severed heads later.

And I was concerned about this development. The previous incidents had been plausible accidents in water. Why this change in MO? Was I perhaps dealing with more than one killer, or—

Jasper tapped my elbow. He gestured to a stack of pale rocks before us.

At first, I didn't see what he was pointing to. I saw a bunch of small, shimmery boulders, the kind that weighed about fifty pounds and would fetch a pretty penny at a landscape supply store. The rocks were stacked up in a low wall where they must have fallen years ago.

. . . And then I spied the heads. Two of them, sitting beside each other, staring at me with glazed eyes and open mouths.

I exhaled a stream of bubbles.

They looked like they hadn't fallen there. They looked as if they'd been deliberately staged there, waiting for someone to find them. Jasper took pictures from every angle.

He opened a bag he'd brought with him. Gently, we coaxed the heads into the bag, disturbing as little as we could.

Jasper began to comb the area around the rock pile, taking pictures of a rusty stain that looked like blood on the limestone.

I stared at the bag. Was this Viv's curse? The creature she'd summoned?

My headlight went out, and something grabbed the back of my neck. I lurched, flailing. I turned and twisted, trying to free myself from the grip of whatever had me. My air hose was ripped free of the tank, and water rushed into my throat.

19

MISSING

Something soft brushed my face, tenderly, caressing . . . and then a bright pain dragged along my ribs.

I spat out the mouthpiece and struggled to orient myself, flailing against that grip twisting into my side. A stream of bubbles trailed to my right . . . That way must be up. I kicked hard to rise to the surface of the water.

Something snagged my right fin. I thrashed until it came free. Lopsidedly, I rushed upward, where my bubbles led me. My lungs burned, and my vision narrowed.

A hand grabbed me under my arm, hauling me up, up into the light.

I broke the surface, gasping.

Jasper's face bobbed beside me. It was his hand under my arm, not the Rusalka's. "Are you okay?"

I coughed up water and nodded, giving him the thumbs-up.

"Let's get to shore."

I flopped to shore with Jasper's help, relieved to reach the beach and feel land under my naked foot. Jasper placed the bag of heads beside me and sat on my other side.

"Take long, even breaths," he advised. He reached for my severed hose, and stared at my foot, missing a flipper. Blood was trickling down my bare foot from the wound in my calf. I'd popped some stitches. The neoprene on the right side of my suit was perforated, and there were scratches on my tanks.

"What the hell happened?" Jasper asked.

"I don't know. Something was around my throat." I unzipped the neck of my suit. I wasn't bleeding anywhere else, at least.

I didn't want to tell him about the Rusalka. "I . . . must've gotten hung up on some debris down there. You saved my bacon."

"You've gotta be careful down there, Koray. It's dangerous."

My gaze fell to a random spot on the beach, and I crouched before something shiny.

I picked up a river pearl, green and blue, and iridescent in the sunshine.

———

I drove out to the Lister house to break the news. I'd been told to leave Sumner alone, but I had not been explicitly told to keep my distance from Lister. I was hoping that since he knew me, he might be willing to open up to me about more than the cousins.

As I drove, I passed a billboard for the sheriff's reelection campaign. Sheriff Wilson grinned in his dress uniform before an American flag, exhorting voters to **KEEP LAW AND ORDER IN BAYERN COUNTY**.

I made a face as I passed. I had never had any particular feelings about the sheriff before, positive or negative, until he told me to leave Sumner alone. *Fuck that, and fuck him.*

When I glanced up at the billboard, I saw in my rearview mirror an advertisement for Mark Lister's car dealership. **CALL MISTER LISTER FOR THE BEST DEALS ON TRUCKS. MISTER LISTER!** Mark stood in a suit before three shiny trucks, giving two thumbs up to the viewer. Those trucks probably were at the bottom of the sinkhole.

Lister's house sat in a pleasant suburban development. An HOA clearly ruled: all the two-story houses had the same beige color scheme and exactly the same carpet of weed-free grass. They were apparently allowed three hostas and a single hydrangea bush, but no more vegetation.

I pulled into the Lister driveway, where a basketball hoop had been set up. I wondered how Ross was doing. I didn't see a ball or a bike in the driveway.

I knocked at the front door.

I waited, scanning the porch, not seeing any doorbell cameras, but noticing that mail was halfway stuffed into the mailbox. One envelope contained a bill and was marked PAST DUE in red.

The door eventually opened. Lister was in a rumpled T-shirt. He didn't look like he'd shaved or combed his hair in days.

"Mr. Lister, I'm sorry to bother you."

He crossed his arms and narrowed his gaze. "I thought I told you to leave me alone."

"I have some bad news, and I wanted to tell you in person."

"More bad news?" He seemed too exhausted to fight me. He looked like he hadn't slept, and maybe I could use that to my advantage.

"Is there somewhere we could sit?"

"Yeah. Come in," he said at last.

The house was painted in shades of fashionable gray, with a living room that seemed to be missing some furniture. There were blank spots on the walls, where paint had faded around absent pictures. This was décor I'd come to associate with divorced dads.

I sat on a recliner opposite a large television, and Lister sat on the couch. Neither one of us touched the gaming chairs on the floor.

"Before I begin . . . can I ask how Ross is?" I asked.

A cough echoed behind me. I turned to see Ross in the hallway, dressed in a T-shirt and basketball shorts.

"Hi, Lt. Koray," he said.

"Hi, Ross. I hope you're doing well." I was honestly surprised he remembered me, given his delirium when I last saw him.

"Getting better. Doc says I should be back to normal in a week or so." He gave a half smile.

"He's taking his horse pills on schedule," Lister confirmed.

Ross made a face. "I have to take these steroid pills, but I haven't turned into the Incredible Hulk yet."

"Give it some time," I said. It sounded like he was being treated, and he had plenty of color to his face. I was relieved.

Lister nodded at his son. "I need to talk to Lt. Koray. Would you be okay with giving us some privacy?"

"Sure." Ross gave an awkward wave and drifted off down the hallway.

I waited until I heard a door close before speaking again.

"I wanted to tell you that there's been an incident involving your cousins Amos and Patrick."

He leaned back against the couch and crossed his arms over his chest. "No, I'm not gonna bail those guys out if they're in trouble again."

I looked askance.

"My family treats me like a cash cow," he admitted. "I'm not doing it anymore. I have a son to look after."

"I understand. It's nothing like that, Mr. Lister. I'm afraid Amos and Patrick have died."

He blinked, and froze. I waited for him to speak again, watching the knowledge register on his face. "Dead? What . . . what happened?"

"We don't have the details yet, but they were found in the quarry."

He sagged forward and covered his face with his hands. "Oh no."

"I'm so sorry. Were you close?"

"No. I saw them, like, twice a year, at holidays. It . . ." He shook his head. "Do their parents know? They live out of state. I probably have an address for them, somewhere . . ."

"Our office will take care of notifying them. I just wanted to talk with you about it."

He exhaled into his hands. "How did it happen?"

"That will be for the coroner to say, but there were signs of violence. Did they have any enemies?"

He removed his hands from his face and stared at the ceiling. "No. They're party boys. Most of the trouble they get into is just for stupid pranks—drunk and disorderly, that sort of thing. Took some cars from the dealership, joyriding. They got arrested once for stealing the statue in front of the diner in town."

I remembered that diner. It had a giant sculpture of a boy in overalls holding a plate of pancakes. At some point, it disappeared in the night and reappeared in a cornfield.

"Everyone likes them," he whispered. "They never do anything really wrong, just dumb shit."

He was referring to them in the present tense, which suggested that the news of their deaths was indeed a surprise. I waited in the silence, hoping he would speak more.

When he didn't, I ventured: "There have been several suspicious incidents involving water lately. They seem to center around you and Jeff Sumner and Quentin Sims. I have to ask you if you've made any enemies I should know about, in order to protect you and your family."

He slipped his hand over his mouth and shook his head. "No. There's no one you can protect me from."

It was bad form to interrogate someone during a death-notification call, but I pressed further. "I know the three of you were accused in the disappearance of a girl twenty-five years ago. I can't help but think that someone blames you and is looking for revenge."

"I don't know anything about that. I'm sorry." He took a deep breath and stood. "Thank you for telling me, Lt. Koray. I have to go make some calls."

I stood and nodded. "Please call me if you think of anything. I'm so sorry for your losses."

He stared into the distance, looking haunted. "So am I."

———

I needed answers from Viv, answers to questions that I couldn't ask anyone else.

Was there something lurking in the depths of the water, this Rusalka? Was she real? Though it defied rationality, I couldn't deny what I felt.

I had been willing to accept that my father's Forest God was real, after a fashion. Was this another face of the same entity? Or was this something different, an adversary? The Forest God demanded women as sacrifices. The Rusalka took men. What other hungry spirits might exist in the shadows?

I rolled up her driveway, and the hair on the back of my sweaty neck stood on end.

Viv's front door was wide-open.

After radioing my location for backup, I crept up the porch quietly, then knocked on the doorframe. My right hand rested on the butt of my service pistol.

"Viv, it's Lt. Koray. Are you home?"

I sucked in my breath as a snake crawled out of the darkness of the house.

I held my breath as the four-foot-long rat snake crawled over my shoe. Its spine made nervous ripples as it moved over me and across the porch, to disappear in the lattice underneath. For that time, the only sounds were the rasp of its scales against shoe leather and wood, and the thundering of my heart.

I stepped inside, mindful not to touch anything else. "Viv?"

I stood in her dark parlor. The place had been tossed. Photographs on the walls had been dashed to the floor, and my shoes crunched on the broken glass of their frames. I frowned—no burglar would do that. This was personal.

The cages that had contained the opossum and raccoon babies were empty, and my heart leapt into my throat . . . *the animals.* There was no sign of the opossum joeys and raccoon kit, or of the fox.

The couch had been shoved over and the credenza rifled through. All the drawers in the kitchen were dumped out and cabinet doors open. A broken jar of spaghetti sauce was splashed on the floor. The place smelled like mint; there was some drying on a rack in a dark corner, untouched.

I wound up the wooden staircase. The master bedroom smelled of dust, dried flowers, and evaporated perfume. All the clothes had been torn from the closet and strewn on the floor. Another bedroom must have been Dana's once upon a time; posters covered the walls, and a dried-out paint set was on the dresser. The bedspread was a celestial print, with moons and stars on a navy background. Dana's art stood on her dresser and easels, paintings of haunted woods, and serpents coiling around crystals. Someone had torn the canvases, slashed them open.

This was so, so very personal.

I flipped through the canvases, pausing when I saw a familiar image: a black snake biting its own tail. It was painted in acrylic on a canvas with a wine-red background. The title was scrawled in the corner: *Forever.*

I inhaled. Dana knew this symbol. And Viv did, too. Despite her alibis, it looked more and more like Viv was to blame for what was happening to the Kings of Warsaw Creek. And now it seemed like they were getting their own revenge.

I peered briefly into the bathroom, at the clawfoot tub where Viv's mother had tried to kill herself. To my relief, it was empty. The bathtub faucet dripped musically over a spreading rust stain on the cast iron around the drain.

Viv's bedroom smelled like incense. The curtains were drawn, and orange afternoon light burned through. I stared at the unmade bed, not seeing blood there, but there were signs of a struggle: there was a hole in the plaster to the right of the bed, at the right height for the head of a woman of Viv's stature to land. I examined the hole for hair or blood, but nothing was visible to the naked eye.

I turned to an armoire, its doors open. Within, I saw what might have been the remains of an altar: candles and years upon years' worth of wax in layers dribbling from a shelf, curling around crystals that had become embedded in it. The candles were burned down, and the wax was long cold. In the background were framed pictures nailed to the back of the armoire: Dana and their mother. A mirror was turned down on the shelf, and a shattered mason jar, once full of garlic cloves and nails, lay on the bottom shelf of the armoire.

I poked at the jar with a pencil. There was a piece of paper inside it. I donned gloves and pulled it out and unfolded it. On the paper were the names of the Kings of Warsaw Creek circumscribed by that symbol that kept turning up—the snake eating its own tail.

It should've been warm in this room, on the second floor of a house with no central air. But this place was cool, cool as evening shade.

I returned downstairs. I heard something then, a scraping in the kitchen. The sound was coming from the sink's drain. I stared at the drain, wondering if a snake was going to crawl up from it.

Instead, I heard a giggle.

I leaned forward, holding my breath, daring the voice to say something.

It didn't. I must have imagined it.

Right?

I poked through the mail piled on the floor. Viv's rejection letter from college was rumpled on top. I found some solicitations from animal-rescue organizations and a bill from the local medical center. I opened that.

My brow creased. It was a bill for a D&C procedure. Reading in between the lines, I determined that Viv had had an abortion.

There might be a hostile boyfriend in the mix.

I paused at the front door, looking up. Viv's railroad spike was missing from the lintel. I wondered if she had removed it, or if someone else had.

An older-model Jeep with four flat tires was parked behind the house. I ran the plates, confirming that it was Viv's car. I made note of tire tracks, then went to the driveway.

I took pictures of the dirt there. I could see Viv's Jeep tracks in the clay, and my own tracks from the El Camino. But there were others here, too, from new tires that had cut sharp marks into the dirt. The tracks were likely from a larger vehicle, given the span of the marks. And there wasn't just one set; I counted at least three unknowns. Might be clients, might be the perpetrators. These marks were fragile, pressed into dust and likely to blow away in a stiff breeze.

I paced around the house, through Viv's garden, smelling lemon balm and mint and rosemary. I wondered if she found any peace here. She slept with that curse unfolding in the dark of her bedroom, surrounded by the until-now untouched bedrooms of her family.

I waded deeper into the backyard, smelling something freshly burned as I got closer to the tree line. Grass. Grass and wood. Probably applewood; I could detect that sweet note in it.

A round burn mark spread here, piled high with ashen lumber. It looked like the remnants of a bonfire. For a moment, I was afraid of finding Viv's remains in it, a body curled in the heart of it.

I circled it, touched the ash. Pieces of broken glass shone among the ashes. Maybe this was part of one of Viv's workings? Or had someone come here to destroy hers and put the remains here? I wasn't sure, but in the ash, someone had drawn the ouroboros I'd come to dread.

I retreated, examining the perimeter. The grass was worn in a circle here, as if someone—or many someones—had paced around the fire. *Witches.* I imagined Viv orbiting that fire at night, murmuring to it her plans for revenge. And maybe in the company of others, the same ones I'd caught on camera at the Hag Stone— everywhere and nowhere.

Or maybe whoever had taken Viv had burned evidence here.

Part of me wanted to believe this was Viv's work, that she was still alive. But she would never leave her animals behind, definitely not scared and hiding in shadows.

I thought of Dana. If whoever had taken Viv had also taken Dana, no one would ever know.

———

I guarded the scene until Forensics arrived. I tried to call Viv, but her cell clicked over to voicemail. I didn't hear it ringing anywhere in the house, so maybe she had it on her. I checked in with the cell company, to see if they could triangulate her whereabouts. They reported that the last ping they got from her phone was from the Grey Door just after two a.m., around the time I'd expect her shift to end.

I called Monica to tell her Viv was missing.

Monica was quiet for a moment. "Did you find any blood?"

"Not so far, but Forensics will look for traces. It sure looks like foul play to me."

"What do you think the odds are that the Kings of Warsaw Creek got tired of Viv's agitating and decided to silence her?"

"Pretty high. I just can't prove it . . . yet. I'd like just fifteen minutes in the Sumner house. It gives me the creeps."

"You're thinking about Dana Carson's fingerprint on that windowsill."

"I want to get back in there and dust every surface. That's an old house, and I bet it talks."

I checked on the Sumner house on the county auditor's website as we spoke. The house had been built in 1911. It had changed hands several times, to people with the same last name, Sumner. Jeff had grown up in that house. He'd been there when he and his chums burned Warsaw Creek, and he was there when Dana disappeared. It could be a crime scene.

Digging around in the Sumner house sounded like a good time, but all we had right now was Dana Carson's prints on the windowsill. It wasn't enough to get me a warrant. Any lawyer worth their salt would argue that Dana and Jeff were chummy, and that she visited his house for a party back in the day. I couldn't refute that perfectly reasonable explanation, even though I knew in my gut what had happened. I was hamstrung by the rules, and I had to follow them.

I ordered tails on the Kings of Warsaw Creek, hoping they would lead us to Viv. The Vice guys were bored, and they were delighted to pick up some OT. But we had to track down the men first.

I tooled by the Sumner house, but Jeff wasn't there. Nor was he at the hospital, but his wife's car was. I checked the plant next. No car.

My phone rang. The call was from Monica's number. I noticed that she was calling me direct again, not using the sheriff's office's new radio system. Maybe she was being a curmudgeon about it, and I was ready to tease her when she announced:

"Good news. I just got word that Mason Sumner woke up from his coma."

20

AWAKE

I expected that Jeff Sumner would be at the hospital.

And he was, sitting in a car with Lister's dealer plates, in the front row of the hospital parking lot, watching the door. He was scrunched down in his seat, sunglasses on, trying to be stealthy.

I parked next to him, taking it in: the new car; Sumner watching the entrance, not going inside. I was betting Drema had banned him from Mason's hospital room, and he was here to follow her.

I made eye contact with him, got out of my car, and approached his.

He put his car in gear and drove away.

Interesting.

Monica was waiting for me at the hospital elevators, holding a gift bag from the gift shop. A green plush tail poked out of the top of the bag.

"Whatcha got?"

Monica lifted the bag. "Everybody loves dinosaurs."

We headed down the hallway, and paused outside the door to Mason's room.

Mason's mom was sitting at his bedside, holding her son's hand. Mason was sitting up in bed, looking pale, hooked up to wires and tubes. He held a Spider-Man action figure in his lap.

I knocked on the doorframe. "Pardon me. Mrs. Sumner?"

Drema Sumner turned to face me. Her eyes were red and swollen from crying, but she smiled joyously. "He's awake."

"That's such great news."

She pushed his hair back from his eyes. "The doctors say his respiration and heart rate are normal. CT doesn't show any brain damage." She hiccuped a sob and pressed her fingertips to her mouth. "But he won't speak."

I ineffectually patted her shoulder. "I'm so glad he's awake."

She nodded, getting ahold of herself. Monica handed her the gift bag. Drema opened it, took a plush stegosaurus out of the bag, and gave it to Mason.

Mason stared at the toy on his lap, clutching his Spider-Man to his chest. He coughed a miserable cough that sounded like a goose's honk.

"When do they think you might be able to take him home?" I asked.

"Not sure. They want to run more tests." She combed his hair with her fingers. "I won't be bringing him back to that house, though. Not ever."

"I'm so sorry this happened," I said.

Drema rubbed her eyes, and I noticed that her wedding rings were absent. "I can't believe Jeff would try to deny medical care to his own son. I can't . . . I can't get past that."

I didn't say anything. It wasn't my place. But I was certain that if I were in her shoes, I wouldn't do anything different.

She exhaled. "This is gonna be hard, leaving Jeff. I know he's going to fight me on custody, tooth and nail. He's got money and power. He told me I wasn't going to get away with it.

"But here's the thing . . . I have my own money. I'm not from here, I get it. But I come from a family of lawyers, and I'm not going down without a fight." Her cheeks blazed red with rage.

"Mrs. Sumner . . . Drema . . ." I began, sensing an opening. Maybe I could trust this woman, just a tiny bit, so I reached out: "How much do you know about your husband's past? Before he met you?"

Her brows drew together. "Was . . . he married before or something?"

"No." I took a deep breath, glancing at Mason. "Maybe we should take this somewhere else, though?"

Drema nodded. "We can get some coffee in the waiting area."

We reassembled down the hall, in a group of chairs before windows overlooking the parking lot. I didn't know how much of our discussion Mason would understand, but I wanted to keep my aspersions on his father's character away from his ears. I knew firsthand that it was a terrible thing for a child's vision of their father to be punctured.

I plunged in. "Jeff and his friends were suspects in the disappearance of a girl many years ago. They weren't charged, but we've reopened the investigation. And there's another disappearance we're investigating, that girl's sister."

Drema had questions, and I gave answers, making certain to be factual. In other circumstances, I'd never consider telling the spouse of someone I was investigating where I was going, but I sensed that Drema was serious about kicking Jeff to the curb: she wasn't wearing her wedding rings. And I had a lot to gain by involving her.

"He never told me this. I knew about his friendship with his boys, but . . ." Drema shook her head. "I never liked how they would just disappear for days on end. To be honest, I assumed they rented out hotel rooms and called up strippers. I convinced myself that I was just being jealous, until one time, I went into Jeff's trunk to look for the diaper bag and I found . . ." She lowered her voice. "Costumes."

"What kind of costumes?" I asked.

"Like, stupid bondage stuff." She looked down at the floor. "Hoods and candle wax and stuff. I figured he hired women to do that, since I have too much self-esteem and not enough daddy issues for that bullshit."

Monica almost choked on her coffee, but I kept a straight face and continued. "Does this look familiar?"

I showed her a photo of the cape I'd found in her backyard. She nodded. "Yes. Stuff like that."

"I normally don't comment on ongoing investigations like this, but . . ." I began.

"What do you need from me to nail that bastard to the wall?"

I blinked. Most people had a hard time believing that their spouse had done something awful, especially if they weren't convicted. Drema Sumner had had enough, and she was willing to put her money where her mouth was. I could see that a mutually beneficial relationship was in the offing.

"I'd like to have access to the house," I said. "I want to look for evidence connected with the disappearance of Dana Carson, and to see if there's any evidence connected with the abduction of Vivian Carson. We would be discreet, though, and not enter at times when your husband is home, since we don't want to tip him off."

"Do it. You can toss the place to your heart's content. Let me give you the alarm codes and a key. I'll even write you a note." She got up and went to the nurses' station to get a pen and paper.

Monica and I stared at each other.

"That's a woman who knows what she wants," Monica said.

"She wants her husband in jail," I agreed.

"No, she wants him *under* the jail."

Drema returned with a legal pad and wrote out a note giving us permission to enter the house at will. "In case his lawyers give you any shit about it, we can go to the hospital notary and get this notarized."

"This is amazing, Drema," I said. "Thank you."

"No, thank you," she said fiercely. "I don't want to share custody of my child, and having Jeff in prison is the best way to accomplish that."

I admired her ferocity, her willingness to defend her child. I'd vastly underestimated her, and I felt guilty about that. Drema Sumner was a fighter, and she was a strategic one. It felt good to have one secret ally in the Kings of Warsaw Creek's circle.

We returned to Mason's room. Drema kissed him on the head. "Mommy's going to go get a paper signed and go down to the cafeteria. Would you like me to bring you something to eat?"

He looked up at her, nodded, and coughed miserably.

"What would you like?"

He stared at her blankly.

"Hamburger?"

He nodded.

"French fries?"

He nodded.

"Cookie?"

He nodded.

"Okay. Just sit tight for a little while. I'll turn on the TV for you." She sat on the bed and clicked the remote, finding cartoons.

Mason was playing with the plush dinosaur and Spider-Man.

Spider-Man had his leg in the dinosaur's mouth, and the dinosaur was trying to devour him.

He moved the blanket on the bed, and I saw the angry marks on his leg. They were red and black, like my own marks.

He smashed Spider-Man's leg into the dinosaur's mouth, and I shuddered.

"Would it be okay if I talked to Mason for a bit?" I asked tentatively. "I won't ask him anything traumatizing. I promise."

Drema paused. "I . . . Sure, if it's okay that I'm here?"

"Of course."

Drema patted Mason's shoulder. "Buddy, this nice lady has some questions to ask you. Is that okay?"

He looked at her, then at me.

"You can just nod yes or shake your head no, okay?"

He stared at me and nodded.

I sat on the other side of the bed. I was terrible at interviewing kids, but maybe he remembered me a little bit from the night he almost drowned. "Hi. My name's Anna. I'm glad you're feeling better."

He turned his attention to the epic struggle between superhero and dinosaur.

"Do you remember the night you fell into the pond?"

He nodded, not looking at me.

"Do you remember leaving the house?"

He gave a sharp nod.

"Did you go outside on your own?"

He shook his head. He walked Spider-Man down his leg.

"Was Leah with you?"

He shook his head again, and coughed miserably.

"Was someone else with you?"

He nodded. Spider-Man stopped walking at the space between his knees, which formed a little crater in the bed.

"Do you know who it was?"

He shook his head. *No.*

"Did that person call you down to the pond?"

He nodded vigorously.

"Can you show me what happened? With Spider-Man?"

I held my breath.

Spider-Man paused at that gap in the blankets, where the dinosaur lay. The dinosaur rushed up and grabbed Spider-Man's leg. Spider-Man fought and thrashed, but got pulled under by the dinosaur.

"Oh, honey." Mason's mom's eyes filled with tears.

Solemnly, Mason grabbed my hand and put it around Spider-Man. He used my hand to pull Spider-Man out of the fuzzy pond.

A lump rose in my throat. "You're a very brave boy, Mason."

Mason leaned into his mom's chest, and she enfolded him in a hug.

"I'm gonna go find that notary, and bring back some food," Monica said quietly, sensing that Mason's mom wasn't ready to leave him.

I stared at the stegosaurus on the bed. I couldn't take a child's nonverbal playacting as testimony, but my intuition was screaming at me.

Monsters. There were monsters in the water.

And they were as pissed off at Mason's dad as Mason's mom was.

———

That night, I dreamed of Rusalka.

I was sitting on the river's shore, beneath the Hag Stone. I was barefoot, and the poisoned water licked my toes.

Rusalka slithered through the cattails, peering at me. She wore Dana's face tonight.

"Haven't you done enough?" I asked.

She gave a musical giggle. "No. It's never enough. Not while those men still walk on the earth."

She reached out for my ankles. Her palms were cool when she rested them on my skin, cool like the bellies of fish. "It can't be enough for you, can it?"

I frowned. "It doesn't matter what I think."

"But you live in this world, where men oppress the women around them. How can that be acceptable to you?"

"It's not. But murder isn't the answer."

"And how would you propose to stop this, then?" Her eyes narrowed.

Words like "law" and "justice" died on my tongue.

"I thought so," she said. "It is the highest degree of arrogance to think you can change people."

"Please," I begged her, "let me try."

"You have until the anniversary of my death, my sister. Work quickly." Her fingers slipped away from my feet, and she sank below the water.

21

BASEMENTS

I opened my eyes in bed and stared at the patterns of sunlight shifting on the ceiling. Light and shadow.

I glanced over at Nick. He was a good man. He abhorred the oppression of women as much as I did, but I didn't think he'd really understand, not the way that women did.

And I didn't expect him to understand this shadowy world I was drowning in. Was I losing my grip on reality again? Was the Rusalka just a projection of my own rage at my father? I couldn't say. I could say only that she *felt* real, as real as my father's demons had.

When I'd finally climbed out of bed to start the day, I received an email from the Sumners' alarm company. Drema had granted me access to the alarm company's records and app. I downloaded the app to watch the video from the night Mason was hurt. It contained mostly ordinary stuff—Leah arriving, and Jeff and Drema leaving for their date, captured by the front-door cameras. But the front-door camera fizzled out around sunset.

I stared at the footage, over and over. Something black washed over the lens. It looked to me like spray paint—black spray paint, like the kind used to create the ouroboros symbols that kept appearing.

I listened to the audio, hearing whispered female voices. The speech was too indistinct for me to understand what they said, but it sounded as if they approached and then receded into the distance. The alarm company's log showed that the front door opened three times after the Sumners left. Once was moments after the video was killed; the second time was a half hour later; and the third was fifteen minutes after that, when, I calculated, I'd found Leah in the field.

Witches. I thought of the cape I'd found. I'd been expecting Jeff or one of his cronies to be at fault here, and disappointment flashed through me.

Leah was involved with this.

The log showed a fault in zone 16, the back door, around the time Mason must have left. *Interesting.*

I changed the view to the back cameras, and a chill settled over me. I saw the back door open, but I didn't see anyone open it. Maybe it was because of the angle, but it looked creepy as hell.

Mason walked out onto the back deck. He was holding his left arm up, the way a child does when their hand is being held by an adult. But there was no adult there.

I watched as Mason moved off the deck and out of the camera frame, still holding his arm up. It looked a helluva lot like the kid was being led by someone unseen.

I also checked the cameras for the night that Viv disappeared. I wanted to see if the Kings of Warsaw Creek were in the living room, watching the game.

But I got nothing.

I went through Leah's phone records. Thanks to a warrant issued by Judge Chamberlain, the private messaging app she was using had coughed up the user profiles and associated phone numbers she'd been texting. It took only a little time to match them up to the other girls in her homeschool pod—seven of them. The numbers matched the girls' numbers saved in Leah's contacts.

But there was one number that wasn't in her contacts.

It belonged to Viv Carson.

I exhaled, only beginning to understand the rebellion that had begun to foment beneath the nose of the church.

I got a call from Kara from CPS and picked up right away.

"Leah wants to go back to her house to get some of her clothes," she said, "but she says she's afraid to go. Would you mind accompanying us?"

"Of course I can help."

"Great. I'll meet you at the church."

I exhaled. This was my chance to poke around Sims's haunts without a warrant.

———

The church parking lot was empty except for Kara's station wagon. I parked next to it and approached Leah.

"Hey," I said awkwardly. "How are you holding up?"

Leah met my gaze and nodded. "I'm good."

I glanced at Kara, behind her. She nodded.

"I'm happy to help you, however you need," I said.

The parsonage was still, locked up, with no porch lights on. Maybe Sims had never intended to return the night he died.

"How long have you lived here?" I asked Leah.

She lifted a shoulder. "We didn't move in here until after Mom died. I hate it." Leah opened the red front door with her keys, leading us inside.

I stared at the cross made of railroad spikes above the door.

"Leah," I said, "do you know what that is?"

She gave it a passing glance. "Dad collected crosses. Even ugly ones."

Leah and Kara went down the hallway to Leah's room. I turned left, into the master bedroom.

This room didn't belong with the rest of the house, which was almost sterile. The closet had been ransacked, and I saw tracks in the carpet from the wheels of a piece of luggage. I peered into open drawers, seeing men's clothes.

I went to Leah's room. Leah was putting clothes and notebooks on her bed, and Kara carefully placed them in garbage bags. It seemed so harsh to move a child out with garbage bags, but this was the way of things.

I glanced around Leah's room. A Bible sat on the nightstand, which Leah didn't bother to pack up. She grabbed notebooks out of her closet, and framed photos of a woman with Leah, who I presumed to be her mother.

"You look like your mom," I said softly.

Leah stared down at the picture in her hands. "I miss her."

Kara put her arm around Leah. "It's gonna be okay, kiddo."

"Yeah. Yeah, it is." She nodded to herself.

My gaze fell on one of Leah's notebooks. It had fallen open, showing some of her art. There were very good pen-and-ink drawings of a cat, a lion, and a woman with angel wings. "You're a very good artist."

"Thanks. Dad thought my art was a waste of time."

I flipped the page and saw a picture of a snake eating its own tail. I kept my voice light. "What's this?"

She glanced over her shoulder. "Nothing." She closed the notebook and stuffed it into a bag.

"Leah, I have to tell you that I think this symbol is important to the case I'm working. I need you to be honest with me."

Leah looked at me, her chin lifted a notch. "It's nothing."

"It's something. It's something I keep seeing, and I don't think it's a coincidence."

Leah crossed her arms over her chest. "Why should I tell you anything?"

I sat on the edge of the bed. "I know the adults in your life have failed you in a really major way. Trust isn't something that's given freely. I get that. But there are people dying here. This is serious."

Leah looked away. "I saw it at the gas station. I traced it."

"I think you and your friends have been in contact with Viv Carson. Viv has gone missing."

Leah blinked. "She's missing?"

"Yeah. We're trying to find her. We suspect foul play. If there's anything you can tell us, it might save her life."

Leah's shoulders sagged. "She's like my mom in a lot of ways, you know? But stronger. My mom never really fought back, but Viv does."

"Viv is the leader of your coven." Saying it aloud felt like cracking a geode open, exposing to light something that hadn't been seen in many years.

She nodded. "Viv showed us that we're not just here to serve. We're here to be powerful. To be free."

"Leah, did the coven kill those people?"

She looked away.

"I can't help you unless I know what happened."

Leah's lip trembled. "I . . . I had an abortion six months ago. Viv took me."

The bill at Viv's house wasn't for Viv's procedure. I sat beside Leah and took her hand. "That's not what I—that's not killing."

She rubbed tears away from her eyes. "My dad would say it is—if he knew. But he . . ." Her shoulders shook. "It was his."

Rage flashed through me. *That piece of complete and utter shit.* If he weren't already dead, I'd want to kill him.

"I'm so, so sorry that no one protected you." I felt wrathful and helpless.

She blinked away her tears. "But someone did. Viv did."

Kara enfolded Leah in a hug. I sat beside her on the bed.

"He hurt a lot of girls. Not just me."

"You're safe now," Kara murmured.

My blood boiled, and I struggled to keep my voice soft. "Leah, I know the other girls were with you at the Sumner house when Mason almost drowned."

She stared at me. "You know?"

"I know about the coven. And I need to know what you know, to try to find Viv."

"I haven't heard from Viv. I hope nobody hurt her." She clasped her hands before her in something like prayer.

"I hope so, too, but Viv's enemies think she had something to do with what happened to Mason, Ross, your dad, and some of Ross's relatives. So I need you to tell me."

Leah stared down at her shoes. "The girls came over when I was watching Mason. It was a chance for us to get together without any adults. That's what we do—we say we're doing homework at someone else's house, and we gather whoever's free. Our parents think we're out of trouble when we're with our study pod. Since we're not in school, we've got a lot of free time, so it sort of works for us."

"Was Viv with you?"

"No. She had to work. Four other girls from the coven were,

though. Viv told us what Jeff and the other guys did to her sister, and we thought it would help if we did a revenge spell at the house."

"What did you do?"

"The girls came over around seven thirty. We went outside to burn some candles and ask for justice for Dana. One girl brought a skull she found in the woods."

"I found a black cape in the yard. Did that belong to one of the girls?"

"No. We don't dress up like trick-or-treaters. That's stupid." She scrunched her face up.

"So, you went outside, burned some candles . . . Then what?"

"We asked for justice for Dana. And justice for the rest of us." Her eyes shone dark. "We asked for freedom."

I exhaled. I wondered if that spell, fueled by the girls' rage, was enough to awaken Dana, to pull the Rusalka up from the depths. "And then . . . ?"

"They put the skull in the mailbox and they left. Mason woke up wanting a snack." She shrugged. "He was playing with his action figures, and everything else happened as I told you."

"You didn't hurt Mason?"

She looked shocked, then wounded. "No. I would never." She wrapped her arms around herself. "We asked for justice, not for . . . not for whatever this is."

She dissolved into tears, as if something had broken open in her.

Kara held her. "I think that's enough for today. Anna, could you please go into the kitchen to get us some more bags?"

I wasn't going to be allowed to go further. I nodded and went to the kitchen. I found the bags underneath the kitchen sink, and then my gaze fell on a door. A door that had to lead to the basement.

I noticed that there was a lock on this side of the door. Gritting my teeth, I turned the knob and peered down the wooden steps.

I flipped a light switch, but nothing happened. The light bulbs must have been taken out. Eyes narrowed, I descended the stairs. I took my cell phone out, turned on the flashlight, and swept it before me.

It was an unfinished basement with cinder-block walls and a concrete floor. A washer and dryer stood at one end, a furnace and water heater at the other. Unused exercise equipment was jammed in a corner. *Ordinary enough.*

The copper pipes running to the washer and dryer caught my attention. I bent to examine them.

Connected to the copper pipes were three pairs of handcuffs. And next to the washer was a plastic bucket smelling of urine.

In the dust coating the side of the dryer, someone had drawn a circle. It might have been a circle, or it might have been an ouroboros.

I exhaled and texted Kara: Need you in the basement ASAP.

I vibrated with anger as I waited for Kara, imagining those girls huddled down here in the dark.

"Jesus," she said. "There was more than one girl down here."

Fuck that guy. I was glad he was dead.

———

The girls from Greenwood Kingdom Church were the witches dancing in the dark of Bayern County.

I thought I understood. The girls, powerless, sought control over their surroundings, even if it meant chanting in the dark and putting pins in dolls. The girls channeled their rage, and Viv channeled them. But did they kill the men related to the Kings of

Warsaw Creek? I couldn't imagine Leah wanting to hurt an innocent like Mason; she seemed to truly love him.

The girls might've asked for justice in their ritual, but maybe
justice had different ideas than they did.

I headed home to let the dog out and pace in the garden. The
heat had wilted the peppers and tomatoes, and weeds reached up
from the cracked clay soil. I soaked them with the hose. They
seemed fragile and puny, though, unlike the spiky Russian this-
tles beginning to claw their way up from the earth. I pulled them
away from the heart-shaped stone for Nick's mother, and the grave
for the snake.

My phone dinged, announcing a text from the Vice guys on
Sumner's whereabouts:

Subject is at the worksite. No sign of the victim.

TY. Keep me posted, I typed awkwardly with my thumbs, around
dog slobber.

I figured Sumner would be involved with work for at least a
little while. I texted Monica:

Wanna head over to the Sumner house?

You know it. Meet you there.

If Jeff looked at the door-chime alerts on his alarm app, he would
know if someone had opened the front door. But since I had access
to his account, I could easily archive our movements, and I doubted
he'd sift through the archives to check for unwanted visitors.

Gibby was thrilled to ride shotgun, his tongue flailing from his mouth like a pink banner as he stuck his head out the window. When we arrived at the Sumner house, I put him on his leash, tied him to the open car door's handle, and put down a water dish for him.

"You gotta stay put, okay?"

He grinned his inscrutable doggie grin at me. I wasn't sure he would stay put.

Monica rolled up, carrying evidence-collection bags. "Ready to rock and roll?"

I slipped the key into the lock while Monica rushed to the alarm's panel to disarm it. I stood in the doorway, put my hands on my hips, and said:

"Well, that wasn't what I expected."

I wasn't really sure what I had expected. I'd hoped to find Viv tied up and unharmed, and bring the case crashing down around the ears of the Kings of Warsaw Creek.

Instead, I'd walked into a frat house.

Beer bottles had leaked out onto the beige carpet and were scattered across the couches and the coffee table. The television mounted above the fireplace had a crack in its screen. Something smelled vaguely of garbage. The curtains were drawn, plunging the place into semidarkness.

I walked into the kitchen, finding more bottles, and an open pizza box with crusts hardened like bones. No dishes were in the sink, at least.

Monica peered into the fridge and grimaced. "Some new civilization's in there, ready to call Sumner their leader."

I headed down the hallway, looking into the bedrooms and closets. They were a mess, but not a criminal mess. I checked the garbage. Nothing unusual there.

I clicked my UV light on and swept it down the hallway. I

didn't see anything interesting in the living room or the bedrooms.

I went to the bathroom where I'd found Dana Carson's prints.
The place had been painted in the twenty-five years since her disappearance, and the fixtures updated, so I wasn't expecting to find
much. I'd lucked out with the prints because they had been in a
protected place on the exterior windowsill, where they wouldn't be
disturbed.

"See anything?" Monica asked from the hallway.

"Not yet." I held out hope, though, that I could retrieve some
speck of evidence to blow the case wide-open. But there wasn't
anything in the bathroom.

I headed to the basement, while Monica went to check Sumner's office. When I was halfway down the steps, I was nearly
knocked over by a dark shadow.

"Gibby!" I hissed.

He thundered past me into the basement. He was the Houdini
of dogs. I had no idea how he'd slipped his lead.

I swept my UV light on the carpeted steps before me. It looked
like the carpet hadn't been replaced in a long time. At the bottom
of the stairs, I saw a couch, a television, a bar, and wood paneling
dating back to the sixties. It was weird that the Sumners hadn't
ripped it out, but basement bars had come back into vogue recently. Everything else in the house had been updated. I wondered
why the basement den hadn't been.

Gibby sniffed around the perimeter of the room, tail twitching.

"How did you get loose?" I reached for his collar, but he evaded
my grasp, nose glued to the floor, and sprinted to the other side of
the room.

I paused, seeing faint luminescent blue marks in the grooves of
the paneling. My heart skipped a beat. They could've been blood,

or any number of other bodily fluids I didn't want to think about. I spritzed them with luminol, and the glow remained. *Blood.*

I swabbed the panel, hoping to get a sample. I followed my light to a spot where the glow pooled on a baseboard, and tore out a chunk of the baseboard. Maybe Forensics could work with it.

I turned my attention to the bar. There was no actual plumbing here, and the Sumners had evidently been using the bar for wine storage.

I peered below the bar with my UV light, and frowned. I saw some stubs of burned candles. I sniffed them, detecting a whiff of carbon. They'd been lit recently. Maybe Sumner was into mood lighting. Maybe something else.

I glanced over the bar. A railroad spike had been driven there. Peering at the corners of the room, I saw three more spikes, driven into the walls. I spritzed the spikes with luminol, but they remained inert.

Gibby found a spot in the middle of the floor that he was inhaling. He pawed at the carpet.

"Gibby, stop that!"

He sat down on the floor and whined.

Monica came down the steps. "Lookit this."

She held up a black hood. "You think this is one of the kinky things Drema was talking about? Or do you think this belongs to the girls?"

"I doubt it belongs to the girls. They think costumes are for losers." I took it from her with gloved hands. "I think that belongs to Jeff. Anything in his office?"

"Just a printer. He must work on a laptop that he takes with him. There's nothing interesting in his paper files."

"I think something happened here." I showed her the luminol streaks.

Our eyes fell on the floor, on the incongruously old carpet, and on the perturbed Gibby.

"Wanna rip that carpet up?"

I shrugged. "I mean, we have the homeowner's permission."

"Cool. I'll grab a crowbar from the car. Be back in a minute."

I stared at the railroad spikes. They meant something to the Kings of Warsaw Creek, and to Viv. All I knew was that Viv had told me they were meant to keep evil out.

Monica came down with a toolbox. "Let's get doing."

We shoved the couch up against the bar, donned heavy gloves, and then started at a corner where the carpet was loose. Monica jammed the crowbar into the tack strip, and we pulled the carpet back. It was heavy as fuck, and the farther we went, rolling the dusty carpet back in an uneven roll, the heavier it got. Gibby retreated up the stairs and watched us from the steps. We sweated and shoved the carpet back to the far wall, warping it and leaving it flopping against the couch.

"Well," I said.

There was a brown stain on the concrete floor. It wasn't body shaped exactly, but there sure as hell could have been a body there. Untreated concrete sucked in a whole lot of stains. The stain was smeared, like someone might have tried to clean it up at some time. And it was right in the spot Gibby had pointed out.

I looked at him. "That's a good boy."

He thumped his tail once on the step, and whined.

I didn't know much about Gibby's background, but it disturbed me that he knew the smell of human blood.

I spritzed the stain with luminol. It glowed under my UV light. I slapped a ruler down on the concrete and snapped pictures.

Monica plucked a hammer and chisel out of the toolbox and started taking pieces of the concrete for evidence.

My phone rang.

"Hello?"

BEEP. "Hey, this is Calvert. Your boy Sumner is on the move, headed your way."

"Oh fuck. We just ripped the carpet up in the basement." My heart pounded. "Can you delay him?"

"Let me see what I can do. I'll let you know when he gets within a mile." *BEEP.*

I spun to Monica. "He's on his way."

"Shit. Shit. Shit. I mean . . . it's an option to let him walk in on us, since we have Drema's permission."

"Yeah, and if he knows we're looking this closely at this stain on the floor, he'll be on a plane to Europe within the hour."

We scrambled to roll the carpet back out, tugged it into position. I was sweating hard through my clothes, and the salt stung my leg. We got the carpet lined up with the tack strip. Monica moved the couch back into position while I hammered the carpet into place. Good thing it had been stretched out and the nails had come out mostly straight. I tacked a bit around the room's perimeter. It wasn't obvious at first glance that the floor had been ripped up, but it wouldn't pass close examination.

Monica looked at her watch. "C'mon. We gotta go."

We gathered our gear and evidence and thundered up the steps. I snatched up Gibby's leash, grabbed his water dish, and shoved him into my car.

My phone rang, and I didn't bother to pick it up. *Fuck.* Sumner was gonna be here in minutes.

Monica slammed the door of her car. With lights out, we peeled out on the gravel and lurched onto the road. We'd been on the road for only about thirty seconds when a single headlight appeared behind us.

I slowed and followed Monica to the next crossroads, where we pulled over. From this distance, we could see the house, but Sumner couldn't see us running dark.

I quickly pulled up the alarm system app and archived the evidence of us entering and exiting the house. I watched the black video, listening to him open the front door.

Another car headed down the road. It was Calvert's, and he was laughing so hard that he couldn't speak when he parked beside us.

"Dare I ask what you did to delay him?" I asked.

"I plopped my bubblegum light on." He pointed up at the magnetic red and blue light on the roof of the car. "I came out of nowhere, with lights on, like a bat outta hell. He nearly pissed himself. In his rush to pull over, he hit two mailboxes and landed in a ditch. I blew past him, like I was chasing someone else."

"Sounds satisfying," I said. That explained the single headlight.

"Very."

"Was he alone?"

"Yeah. No sign of the woman you're looking for."

I wanted to drive up to Sumner's house and arrest him. I didn't have enough evidence yet, though, for an arrest warrant. I had to have things airtight.

And more than arresting him, I wanted him to lead me to Viv.

22

SMOKE AND MIRRORS

Maybe it was time I retraced my steps.

I drove toward Viv's place, stopping at the Grey Door bar. I pulled into an open parking space out front, realizing too late that the El Camino sorta stuck out like a sore thumb among pickup trucks and motorcycles. But it also kind of belonged. I left the AC on for Gibby, and headed in.

At this time of night, things were busy. Young men in neon T-shirts sat at the bar—they were likely construction workers, as crews used brightly colored shirts to distinguish the sparkies, the plumbers, and the carpenters. Men and women in bikers' leathers crowded the booths, and sunburned men who looked like they'd just returned from fishing took up the remaining tables.

I slid up to the bar. The owner, Owen Destin, nodded at me. "I'll be right with you. Shorthanded tonight."

I glanced at the mirror behind the rows of bottles. I saw myself sitting at the bar, and the seat beside me was occupied by a woman who looked remarkably like Dana Carson, down to the moon-shaped pendant in the hollow of her throat. She stared with black eyes at me through the mirror.

I turned to my right, and found the bar stool there empty.

I knotted my hands before me and stifled a shudder. I was seeing things, and that meant I couldn't trust myself. *Fuck, fuck, fuck . . .*

The owner's shadow fell over me. I looked up at Owen. Circles tugged under his eyes, his flannel shirt was stained, and he seemed run pretty ragged.

"What can I do you for?" he asked.

"A beer, whatever you've got on tap. And a moment of your time."

He poured me a beer and leaned down to the bar. "What's up, Koray?"

"Viv Carson has gone missing. Have you seen her?"

Owen frowned. "Shit. She didn't show up for her shift today. I called, but she didn't answer. Is she okay?"

"We don't know." I told him briefly what I'd found at her house. "Have any of Viv's customers given her trouble lately? Anyone seem to have an interest in her?"

The owner shook his head. "I don't put up with that kind of nonsense in my joint. No hitting on the help."

"Did she have any close friends? People she was dating?"

Owen sighed. "Viv was pretty private that way, all business when she was here."

I asked him a few more questions, about Viv's hours, when she worked openings and closings. The owner didn't have any cameras in the establishment, but he showed me her time cards. Viv's day off had been yesterday. I couldn't be sure no one had followed her home from work.

"I sure hope Viv's all right," the owner said. "She's a little kooky, but she's a good girl. Hard worker. I shoulda known something was wrong when she didn't show up."

"I'll be in touch."

I made notes on my phone, and the owner went off to serve other patrons. He seemed genuinely concerned about Viv. I could see it in his posture, hunched over and deflated.

A man in a neon yellow shirt from a local electric company leaned on the table next to me. "You know Viv's a witch, right?"

I looked at him. He took a swig from his beer bottle.

"Hi. I'm Anna Koray."

"I'm Chris Hasterly."

We shook hands. "How do you know Viv?"

"I come here a lot. Viv is really out about being a witch. She doesn't put up with shit from nobody."

"What does she say?"

"She puts curses on people who fuck her over. Like, there was this guy a few years ago who sold her a car knowing the head gasket was bad. The gasket blew, and Viv put a curse on him. Within a week, the IRS came down on him for tax evasion and his wife served him with divorce papers." The electrician nodded solemnly. "He never said boo to Viv after that."

"So you think she's got the juice?"

"I wouldn't fuck with her. Put it this way: when the electricity goes out this way, Viv's house always has power. Makes no fucking sense whatsoever, but it's true."

Another lineman peered over at me. "I saw Viv hex a guy who smacked her ass. The owner threw him out, but he lost his dick to a pig a week later."

"You're pulling my leg." I smirked.

"Seriously. Dude got drunk, fell asleep in the barn, and a pig gnawed off his dick."

This was sounding like urban-legend material. "Either of these guys got names?"

I got names, but I was pretty sure both those guys were in prison right now. "Anyone else maybe have it out for Viv?"

"Well, she cursed the Kings of Warsaw Creek," Chris said matter-of-factly.

Viv was apparently open about that with everyone. "What did she do?"

"She thinks those guys killed her sister, so she curses them every new moon. Says that sooner or later it's gonna catch up with them."

"Do you think they know she cursed them?"

The men shrugged. "Maybe. It ain't exactly a secret."

"Do you think the curse is gonna work?"

Chris stared up at the ceiling. "I wouldn't fuck with a woman who can make a pig chew off your junk. Those men oughta get right with God, because they ain't right with Viv."

———

Forensics had left Viv's house and the door was sealed with yellow tape, but I cut it with my pocketknife and let myself in. I had a duty to follow random leads: weirdos who didn't tip at the bar; enemies in her personal life; being the wrong place at the wrong time. But every cell in my body screamed that Viv had been taken by the Kings of Warsaw Creek, and I was out of leads.

The house was eerily silent. I didn't turn on the lights. I could see well enough by ambient light—a gift from my father. *Thanks, Dad.* Gibby's toenails clicked on the hardwood floors. The heat was stifling with the windows closed; candles were melting and dripping wax in a slow tapping on the wood floors. I crossed the parlor in the dark and sat on the sofa.

I watched Gibby. I wondered if he would smell what he had at the Sumner house—if he'd sense blood.

Instead of pacing agitatedly, he gently sniffed the piano bench and the doorway to the kitchen, then came to sit on the floor beside me.

"You've seen some shit, huh?" I asked him, rubbing his ears.

He whined softly.

"I hope Viv is still alive. I hope it wasn't her you smelled in the basement."

He didn't comment, just rested his head between his paws. I hated traumatizing him. I had very little idea of his background. He knew death. Part of me wondered if he could be trained as a cadaver dog, but he didn't have the right personality. Police dogs were biddable, calm, and took orders well. Gibby was none of those things.

But he was mine, and I loved him. I stroked his back.

I stared at the deck of tarot cards on the coffee table. I didn't have the first idea of how to read them, and I didn't touch them. Beside the cards was a mirror with an ornate, tarnished handle.

I turned it over, expecting to see my reflection in it, but the glass was completely black. My silhouette was just a blacker patch of night on it as moonlight flooded in from the window at my back. The moon was a coin-sized blob in the mirror behind me.

I remembered spending time in my psychiatrist's office, staring at a candle flame in the dark until the darkness swallowed the world behind me and I fell into the labyrinth of my mind. As I focused on the moon, I felt the same. It glowed brighter, and darkness surged around me. Finally, the moon dimmed and winked out, and I was suspended in that familiar hypnotic state.

Night and I were old friends. I didn't fear the darkness of the woods, and I wouldn't fear the darkness in Viv's house, either. She might be a witch, but I was the daughter of a serial killer. I had more evil in my pinky finger than she could muster in her whole body.

The darkness rippled. Whether in my mind or in the glass, I couldn't be sure. It moved like water, undulating. I saw Dana's body, curled beside the river somewhere, in a nest of burned grasses. The water washed over her, and the nest was empty.

A figure sliced through the water with exhilarating speed, faster than any human could swim. I glimpsed Dana in profile, long dark hair a cloud streaming behind her. She turned, gazing upon me with black eyes, pale lips curled back on sharp teeth.

I felt it then, her desire for revenge, stewed in and nurtured by Viv's hate and the fear of her coven. A creature had been conjured forth, a curse, a force to be reckoned with in its element, one that would drag a man down and drown him.

An unstoppable force, with clawed hands and rot-speckled skin. She was beyond human law, beyond control. She'd have her revenge, twenty-five years after her death, under the same un-blinking moon.

"But the children," I whispered. "They don't deserve this. They're innocent."

Her musical laugh shivered over me. How could I hope to stop her?

"I was innocent, too, once upon a time," she whispered, her voice like bells. "Blood calls to blood, and I will have theirs."

I gazed on her then, in terrible understanding. I had to try to stop her, but I knew, deep in my gut, that she was beyond my power. I was only human. She was . . . not.

"Please," I said.

She reached forward to touch my face. "Daughter of darkness, let the dark do its work. Do not interfere."

I opened my mouth to object, to try to ask her to stand down, but her hand covered my mouth. She dragged me down, into the depths. My lungs filled with that cold dark, burning, then became still as I drowned and hung in the water.

I was at one with the dark, suspended in it. I rubbed my face, and my hand came away greenish and with webbed fingers. I jerked my head back. My tongue scrubbed across sharp teeth. I inhaled, feeling frigid water in my lungs, going in, pressing out . . . no pain.

"What did you do to me?" I hissed. I cast about for the Rusalka, searching for her. My body cut through the waves, powerful and sinuous. For a moment, I forgot my shock and reveled in that power.

"There have been many Rusalki." Her voice washed over me. "Dana. And now you."

And I understood this infinite lineage of women who had been wronged, who sought to continue this lineage of horror, in many times and places.

My webbed hand slid over my mouth. Was this my destiny? To become a vessel of revenge, as they had?

"I don't want this," I whispered around my fingers.

"It doesn't matter. It doesn't matter what any of us want." Her voice was distant, fading . . .

I was snapped back into my body on the couch in Viv's house by the sounds of a crash and Gibby barking.

I jerked upright on the couch and sucked in my breath, flinging my arm over my face. The front window was shattered, and fire raced across the floor in a blistering explosion.

I dropped to the floor and cast right and left. Escape through the front door was blocked by fire. Flames licked the aged wallpaper, reaching up for the broken photos of Viv's family on the piano.

I looked behind me, at the window. I jumped up to it and fumbled with the latch. Smoke rolled across the ceiling and down the wall. Distantly, I smelled something sweet in the smoke, something like the scent of artificial roses.

I forced the window open. I gathered Gibby in my arms and flung him through it. Lastly, I lurched through, landing in a shrub beside the house. My sleeve was on fire, and I rolled in the dirt and thorns, trying to knock the flames out in the dust. The fire spread over my back, and panic set in. I smelled burning hair. Gibby growled beside me.

I forced my mind to still, though my heart jackhammered in my chest. Mom had taught me how to find water. I visualized a silvery serpent of underground water in my mind. It twisted, turned, moving up to the surface . . .

I heard her voice: "You're a natural. Try again."

Operating on pure instinct, I trusted that voice of darkness. I flung my arm out, casting out, searching for those veins of water, my eyes tearing.

Something laughed in the darkness, a surreal cackle.

I followed that sound. I stumbled to the tree line, to the creek beyond, and hurled myself into cool water. I submerged myself in coldness, feeling it close over my head.

I rose up out of the creek, gasping, feeling raw and surrounded by steam. I splashed back and landed on my ass. Cold, silver water curled around me, hissing.

In the distance, a shadowy figure moved away, the silhouette of a woman. She looked like Viv, treading water in a curiously eel-like fashion.

"Wait," I implored. "Wait."

But she was gone, leaving only the glitter of water droplets in her wake as she slithered upstream.

Gibby stood in the water, barking at the trail she left behind.

My rational mind said it was just a water snake.

My irrational mind said it was the curse, the creature that lurked in the water and drowned victims who shared blood with the Kings of Warsaw Creek.

She could've killed me. But she didn't.

Gibby looked at me and growled. His fur stood on end.

"Gibby!" I gasped, before I realized he was not looking at me, but past me.

I looked over my shoulder.

A fox sat on the bank. Sinoe. She cackled once more, that sound I'd followed into the woods.

I reached a hand to her. She padded to me and sniffed, cautious.

Gibby whimpered.

"All right," I said to the two of them. "We can coexist, right?"

The fox cackled, and Gibby huffed.

I was not optimistic.

23

BRINGING THE FOX HOME

I lured Sinoe into the car with the remains of yesterday's sand-wich. I turned the AC on while she stretched out on the back seat and yawned. She didn't seem disturbed at all by the heat of the burning house or the embers drifting like fireflies.

I called an animal sanctuary, to learn that they did not take foxes. But, interestingly enough, they'd taken in two opossum joeys and a raccoon kit the day before yesterday. And Viv had been the one to drop them off.

What the hell? Did she have some premonition that she'd be abducted?

Or did she leave on her own?

Surely she didn't toss her house and set fire to it . . . That had to happen after she left.

"What happened to Viv?" I asked Sinoe.

She looked in my direction without lifting her head.

The volunteer fire department arrived in a half hour. By then, the scene was swarming with sheriff's deputies. Gibby and I sat on the El Camino's tailgate and watched the house burn. There's always something heartbreaking about watching a house fall on itself, the roof trusses breaking and everything in the house collapsing like a star.

Paramedics treated and released me on the scene. I was told I was lucky.

Funny. I didn't feel lucky.

When I got home, I opened the car door for the fox, unsure what else to do. Sinoe hopped out, stretched, and yawned. She followed me to the porch, jumped up on a chair beside Gibby's food and water dishes.

I opened the front door, and she showed no interest in following me inside. She curled up in a fluffy ball on the seat of the chair.

"If you change your mind . . ." I began, but she closed her eyes.

Gibby circled behind me into the house, tail tucked between his legs.

Nick was home. He was sitting in his scrubs on the couch, staring at the television. His posture was slumped. Gibby scrambled up to lie in his lap.

"What's wrong?" I asked.

He didn't look at me. "I've been placed on administrative leave."

I sat down beside him and took his hand. "What happened?"

"I got called in on the carpet by Dr. Floyd for a HIPAA violation."

"A HIPAA violation?"

"Yeah. For unauthorized searching, and sharing patient records."

I sucked in my breath. "The people who had benzene in their lungs. But they were your patients—"

"The EPA started nosing around. They learned about the benzene thing through you. The hospital went nuclear that I shared details of patients' files with you." His tone was flat, unemotional.

"But . . . isn't there an exception for public health hazards?" I protested. "If Copperhead Valley Solvents has been dumping shit in the river and—"

"They've targeted me. And I'm guilty."

"I'm sorry." *Fuck.* I was to blame for all of it.

We sat in silence for a moment, that useless apology ringing around us.

"What happens now?" I asked. This was beyond my ken.

"Depends on what the investigation finds. I could get fined. Sued. Lose my license."

"No." My hands balled into fists. "I'll take the blame. I'll tell them that I demanded the information at gunpoint. I won't let this stand—"

He shook his head. "You can't affect their process. They have to review it. We'll see what happens. But for now, one thing's certain. My application to the university's primary care office in the city is tanked."

I wrapped both of my hands around his cold one. I'd fucked up. I was chasing this case, and hadn't considered what this would mean for Nick—Nick and all the stupid fucking rules. "This is all my fault."

"No," he sighed. "I should've known better."

He turned his gaze to me for the first time, and his brows drew together. "What happened to you?"

I looked down. I was rumpled and wet, and I smelled like smoke. Parts of my hair and jacket were burned. "I'm okay."

"Are you?"

"Yeah."

I glanced at the black television screen. I hadn't realized he wasn't watching anything.

"I'm worried about you," he said. "You aren't invincible. One day, there will be a fire or a bullet you can't dodge, and I don't want to lose you."

"You're not going to. No matter what."

I meant it. Nick had given up so much for me . . . and now his career was in jeopardy. I couldn't help but wonder if this sudden inquiry was a way to get me to drop my investigation. I didn't know how tight Sumner and his friends were with the hospital administrators or the board. *Fuck.*

I ran a bath to wash the smell of smoke out of my hair. Thinking of my mother, I threw a handful of salt into the tub. I sank into the bathtub, hissing as water lapped at my reddened skin. First-degree burns—no more harmful than a sunburn, but I still felt them. I'd turned the lights off. I didn't want to look at my body, at all the damage it was accumulating. Nick was right. I wasn't invincible. I felt my body degrading with each new hit. It took longer and longer to bounce back.

Gibby nosed his way into the bathroom and lay down on the rug. I reached out and stroked his nose.

Maybe Nick and Gibby and I needed a fresh start, away from here. I tried to imagine what I would do if I moved away with Nick. I was older than the recruitment limit for the city police department, and I wasn't thinking they'd be much interested in a transfer. I'd developed a bit of notoriety from working the Forest Strangler copycat case last year. Maybe I could find work with the state Bureau of Criminal Investigation.

Or maybe I could take early retirement. And then what? What would I be if I wasn't a cop?

I sat with that, in the warm, stinging water on raw skin. I'd never seriously considered it before. Maybe I'd work with dogs? I wondered what it would take to become a vet tech, or to go back to school to be a veterinarian. I couldn't hope to pay back student loans before I died, but maybe it was worth considering.

What would Nick do if he wasn't a doctor?

I didn't know the answer. I don't think either of us ever saw him as anything else. He'd wanted to be one since his mother died. Since my father killed his mother.

Fuck. We just kept on fucking his life up, didn't we? My father and I were excellent at destroying everything we touched. Like poison.

Lulled by the warmth and the darkness, I dozed in the bathtub as the stinging faded. I was suspended for a moment, existing in an instant of unfeeling, unthinking nothingness.

Something giggled from the drain near my feet, burbling up near my toes. The water was red, red as it had been when my mother lost my sister, red as I imagined it had been when Viv's mother tried to kill herself. Somewhere, beyond the drain, a baby cried.

I jerked awake, and yanked my feet back with a splash. On the floor, Gibby yelped and lurched to his feet.

I steadied my thundering heart, staring at the drain. In the dimness, I could see that the plug was intact. There was nothing there.

I rubbed my wet hands on my face.

Would things like this be able to reach me in the city, or wherever we wound up after this?

I supposed that depended. Was this real, or was this in my head?

Because if this was in my head, it could follow me anywhere, and I could never escape.

———

I stared at myself calmly in the bathroom mirror. In the gray light of morning, I could see the damage to my hair much better. The ends were unevenly burned; my ponytail had been half burned off in the conflagration. I guess I was just lucky I wasn't wearing flammable hair spray yesterday. It seemed like the rest of my hair was a darker blond than I remembered. Maybe it would wash out over time, but I wasn't sure.

I ran my hands through it. I wasn't particularly vain, but I was hoping it wasn't screwed up enough to cause Monica to force me into a salon.

Nick tenderly combed my hair straight over my shoulder, then lifted his scissors and started cutting.

Blackened hair fell to the floor as he worked, beginning on my left side. The scissors made grainy slicing sounds. He moved to the right, pulling pieces under my chin to make sure they were even. He moved to the back, fingertips dusting fallen strands of hair from my shoulders. I closed my eyes and let him work.

When he was finished, my hair hung a couple of inches below my jaw. I leaned into my hair and sniffed it. It didn't smell like ash. And I didn't think it looked bad, either.

I turned around in Nick's embrace and kissed him. He put the scissors down, slipped his hand up to the bare nape of my neck, and leaned into the kiss.

He was my person. I knew this on a cellular level. I knew it when I told him my secrets, when I let him cut my hair, and when we tumbled in bed.

No matter what happened, I couldn't be without him.

I slipped out of the house afterward. Nick had finally fallen asleep, and I didn't want to disturb him. I kissed Gibby on the head, certain that he would watch over his dad.

The fox was gone. I worried that she was too domesticated, that she needed people. But maybe, also, she needed to be free.

I met Monica in the parking lot of the local waffle house. I wanted to avoid the office as much as possible, to avoid the sheriff. I arrived at the waffle house early, so I caught up on email in the car.

My attention was caught by movement to my left. I recognized Rod Matthews, sauntering across the lot with his hands in his pockets. His ankle appeared to be missing its monitoring bracelet.

I followed him into the restaurant, hung back until he was seated in a booth, and then scooted beside him.

"Hey, Rod. How's it going?"

He blinked at me like a deer in headlights. "Um."

"I see you lost your monitoring bracelet. Does your PO know about that?"

He stared down at his menu. "No."

"What's going on, Rod?"

He put his head in his hands. "I want to leave the state. Start over. I was supposed to meet a guy here about a ride to Nashville."

"And why would you want to do that?"

"I'm in trouble." He said it so low, I could barely hear him.

"This isn't about the charges you caught?"

He shook his head. "I'm trying to get out of the life, and they won't let me."

"Really? Who's 'they'?"

"My brother. He's running meth up to Michigan."

"Well, I might be able to help you out, but you're gonna have to be honest with me."

"Mm-kay."

Monica slid into the booth, opposite us. "Hey. Nice haircut."

"Thanks." I played with the ends of it.

"Looks like you already got a brunch date."

Rod groaned.

"Rod was about ready to tell me about meth production in Bayern County. And some other stuff, about the local meth heads being in the employ of the Kings of Warsaw Creek."

Rod hunched his shoulders. "Yeah, I guess."

Monica grinned at him. "How about I'll start? I just learned from the state crime lab that the stuff you're using to cook meth is a benzene compound from Copperhead Valley Solvents. Its trade name is Vapozene. Does this sound familiar?"

Rod sighed. "Yeah. We pick it up by the barrel at night, by the loading docks. It cooks so much faster."

"How much are you doing?"

"Six barrels a week."

Monica emitted a low whistle. "That's a lot of crank."

I rested my chin in my hand. "And are your friends and brother also taking orders from Jeff Sumner? Doing his dirty work by intimidating witnesses? I really didn't appreciate getting shot at the other day."

Rod stared at his menu again. "If I admit I know some stuff, can you get me out of here?"

Monica shrugged. "I think it's entirely possible that we could make your charges go away and you could go on your merry way, but you gotta produce some tangible evidence. Not just your word, 'cause tweakers don't come across as being particularly credible to judges."

Rod nodded. "Okay."

"Great!" Monica said brightly. "Let's get pancakes."

I grinned. Maybe things were finally going to go my way on this case. If I couldn't nail Sumner for murder, maybe I could nail him for drug trafficking.

Rod Matthews vomited up a surprising amount of information about the local meth trade. Monica took copious notes over the next few hours at the waffle house. I paid for a steady stream of coffee and hash browns to keep Rod singing. It was all hearsay at the moment, but if we could verify even a quarter of what he was telling us, then we had a pretty damn good case against Jeff Sumner.

Monica closed her notebook. "I'll call Judge Chamberlain, see if we can get warrants for records at Copperhead Valley Solvents."

"What about me?" Rod sighed.

"If you promise to stay put, I'll put you up in a nice hotel room with a breakfast buffet."

"That sounds better than jail."

My phone rang. "Koray."

"Hey, it's Jasper. I heard back from my contact at EPA. Can we meet?"

"Sure."

"Can you meet me at these GPS coordinates at dusk?"

I wrote down the familiar coordinates. "Did you find something?"

"I hope so. Just come."

He hung up, and I frowned. I'd been all high on the idea of getting Rod Matthews to roll on Jeff Sumner, but now a chill crawled across my spine.

I didn't trust Jasper. Not even close.

I just hoped this wasn't a trap.

24

UNSEEN ALLIES

I met Jasper at the Hag Stone at dusk. The coordinates he'd given me were for the oxbow in the river, where I'd taken my water sample. I pulled into the lot and parked behind a sheriff's office van, so this might be official business. Still, I had an uneasy feeling about this, and I brought Gibby with me.

I hadn't been keen on leaving Nick. I'd checked in on him. He'd arisen in the afternoon and had been talking with lawyers, pacing the floors and gesturing into the air. I knew to let him be when he had these kinetic bursts of action. I kissed him on the shoulder before I left, and he tangled his fingers in mine.

"Anna."

I paused, holding Gibby's leash.

"I'm going to fight this." His face flushed with anger.

"I know." He knew when to fight for others, and now for himself. "And I'll do anything to help."

He nodded. "But if I lose . . ."

"If you lose, we'll move to Alaska." I meant it to sound light, but it came out like a vow.

In that moment, I loved Nick more than my entanglement with Bayern County. And I hoped that moment would last.

I climbed out of the car at the trailhead, and Gibby came with me. I didn't turn on my flashlight. But I rested my hand on the butt of my gun as we ducked soundlessly under the chain gate and made our way to the river's edge.

The forest was thick around us, closing over our heads, blotting out the stars. We walked, noiselessly, down the path to the river. In the dimness, I spotted a familiar figure holding a flashlight at the river's edge.

I didn't go to him right away. I held Gibby's leash and scanned the dark, listening. Once satisfied that there was no one else here, I approached him.

"Jasper? What's up with the cloak-and-dagger?" I tried to sound casual, but probably failed.

"Hey." His gaze swept the woods behind me. "Did you get followed?"

"No," I said warily.

He exhaled. "I was followed earlier tonight, by a car with plates from Lister's dealership."

He glanced down to my side. "And who's this?"

"This is Gibby."

Gibby leaned against my leg, uncertain.

"So, what are we doing here?" I asked.

He knelt, showing me a bag full of a dozen glass vials. "My friend at EPA needs some convincing. I'm bringing water samples to him from nearby bodies of water, for him to test unofficially. If there's something there, that might spur his superiors to action."

"I'm excited that you were able to get someone to take you seriously," I said dourly.

"But I wanted to show you something important." Jasper took what looked like a flashlight from his bag. "This is a UV light. Gasoline, benzene, and several other aromatic compounds glow in its presence." He flashed a beam of UV light at one of the vials, and the surface glowed with an unearthly light. I suppressed a shudder. It reminded me of fox fire.

"It's an old firefighters' trick. Tells you where the accelerant is before mass spectrometry can be used to identify it in an arson case."

He gestured for me to follow him, and we walked to the water's edge. It was a curiously quiet darkness; I heard no frogs or crickets, only the rush of water in the distance. It sounded like water moving in a sink in a public restroom, echoing and cold.

Jasper swept his light ahead of us, and I saw nothing remarkable at first. But as we approached the river, soft fluorescence gleamed around us on foliage, on the ground. He turned the beam to the water, and a sheen glowed on the surface, looking like a faint oil slick.

"Is that what I think it is?"

"This is some kind of artificial compound. I'm betting it's Vapozene, one of Copperhead Valley Solvents's proprietary benzene compounds. It's a very strange one, chemically. Its viscosity and oil-like characteristics mean it can persist in the environment and doesn't evaporate straightaway, like most aromatic compounds do."

"Vice is investigating the use of one of Copperhead Valley Solvents's benzene compounds in the manufacture of meth. But . . . why dump it if it's valuable?" It didn't make sense to me.

"Copperhead Valley Solvents typically produces massive quantities of this stuff. Sales may have slowed, and they may be looking into cheap avenues for disposal."

I frowned. "I guess there might be another limiting factor in the amount of meth the local dealers can create. They can probably get only so much pseudoephedrine."

"What I'm saying is just conjecture at this point. EPA will have to make sure before pointing the finger at the company."

"And what does that mean for those involved in illegal dumping?"

"Fines, likely. If there was knowledge, EPA will probably push for any applicable civil and criminal charges. My buddy says that if he can, he'll nail them to the wall, all the way down. I sense that you're on the same page?" He looked at me hopefully.

I nodded sharply.

I seemed to be amassing unseen allies.

Jasper said he was heading to the state capital that evening to drop off his samples. Which was probably a good thing, since the Kings of Warsaw Creek had a way of creating obstacles for those against them.

Since Jasper had had the opportunity to kill me and take me off the investigation permanently and he hadn't seized it, I was willing to believe he wasn't involved in the string of near-drownings and deaths I was investigating. This situation had been sketchy as hell, and he had been on the up-and-up. I felt guilty for suspecting him of any wrongdoing.

When he'd left, I checked my trail cam. To my disappointment, someone had sprayed black paint over the lens, and the SD card was missing. The witches of Bayern County got around.

I took it down and crouched at the riverbank. I felt both at the edge of realization on this case, and the height of frustration. I had to be very, very careful to make sure my case against Sumner and

Lister stuck. But that meant I had to find Viv, and the evidence was leading me nowhere. It was all well and good to hit Sumner in the wallet, but I wanted more. I wanted him and his cronies to be held accountable for what they'd done to Dana and Viv. I wanted to remove their political capital, to shame them, to reveal them as the monsters they really were.

I reached out to the monster that lay beneath the water. I knew she was there; I could hear her breathing in the back of my head. Gibby sat still beside me, his ears alert. Maybe he heard her, too, or maybe he just heard my voice. I understood Rusalka—whether she was Dana or not, whichever face she chose to wear. I understood her desire for vengeance. I knew, deep in my heart, that Dana was dead. Dead like thousands of other girls across the country who were dead and buried in forgotten places, mourned and lost forever, for the whims of men.

At least my father never did that, for all his evilness. He put girls where they would be found.

I reached forward, stirring the water with my fingers. I tried not to think about the pollutants in it.

"Rusalka," I whispered, "I want what you want. I want these men to pay. If you kill them outright, their reputations will live on. Even now, people are likely planning Quentin Sims's funeral, canonizing him in their heads and with their words. They will admire the money and influence Sumner and Lister wielded. Help me take them down, ruin their reputations, dispel their power for all time."

The words flooded out of me like a dark incantation.

The black water burbled, and Gibby whined softly.

The moon gleamed on the water, a distant, pale coin. I reached into the river for it, jammed my fist into the mud. I lifted the mud high above my head, letting poisoned water run down over my arm.

I opened my hand.

It was full of tiny pearls. Three of them, nestled among ordinary milk quartz and rusted iron slag.

I turned to the island at the oxbow's center, where angry geese slept. Something moved underwater, undulating, toward the island. Whether it was a snake or something from my dark imagination didn't matter.

It was leading me to the island.

My heart beat, slow and steady, against my rib cage. I told Gibby to stay. I stripped off my shoes and my jacket and left them on the shore. The river was poisoned, but I needed to risk this. My gun stayed behind, too. Somehow, I sensed that it would be rude to carry a weapon into the Rusalka's domain. I waded into the water. The current swirled around my thighs, and silt pressed soft against the soles of my feet. I waded in up to my chest, feeling the warm water pushing against my sternum.

I took a deep breath to fill my lungs with air, and kicked off, letting my arms pull me through the slow current. Something brushed against me in the dark, maybe some debris or fish. Maybe *she* was testing me, making sure I was brave enough to see what lay before me, on the island.

I inhaled and exhaled in time with my pulse, slipping through the water. I reached forward for the moon, feeling the water caress my cheek, keeping the island in the distance in sight.

Water streaming from my shirt and pants, I pulled myself up through the cattails of the tiny island. It was only about fifty feet wide, a teardrop shape in the center of the oxbow, shaded by a clump of trees.

The geese in their nests regarded me silently, raising no calls of alarm. They knew I was also of the forest, and I knew they wouldn't deter me.

I closed my eyes and reached out as I had so many years ago, when I was dowsing, for water and for dead things. I visualized silvery water rushing all around me, staticky in texture. Maybe that was the Vapozene in it. It dug into the marshy center of the island with veins that thrummed and chewed into the mud. Years from now, this little island would be worn away and the river would rush straight through once more. The trees would drown, and the island would be forgotten—just like all the missing girls.

The ground was dotted with nests. But there was one place where there was no nest, no river birch tree, and where no grass grew. I walked to it, half seeing the pattern of water encroaching upon it. There was something not right about this place.

I found a flat rock about the size of my hand and used it to scrape at the sandy dirt. It was loose and glittering in the moonlight. I dug like a child hunting for shells at the beach, searching. This looked like that place in my vision, where Dana was curled in on herself in a burnt nest.

A splash sounded at the bank, and I turned, expecting Rusalka to appear. But it was only Gibby.

I scolded him. "You should've stayed at the bank." I didn't want him exposed to the toxic sludge here.

But he'd seen me digging, and he wanted to dig, too. He and I dug deeper, scraping away layers of gritty dirt streaked with black. Something had burned here, long ago, and stained the soil. Organic things that were burned tended to decompose quickly, but the crystals in the sandy soil here had been changed by fire, warped . . . fused together by unnaturally high temperatures.

I paused when my rock struck something black and hollow. Gibby snuffled it, and I brushed dirt away.

Bone. Smooth and black.

The geese watched us, every head on a silent, black, snaky neck turned to witness us.

I should've stopped and called someone, but we kept going, trapped in the spell of what we were uncovering. We scooped the sand away from the claws of ribs, from a clavicle. I swept sand away from vertebrae, from a jaw.

Human. Curled up in a fetal position, like a dead bird in a nest. Judging by what we'd excavated, it was a small human. Likely a woman.

I leaned forward to blow sand away from the clavicle. The remains of a charred necklace floated in the shallow grave. Even in this darkness, I could distinguish a moon and a river pearl.

A shudder racked through me at this discovery, this truth hidden away for so long. Moonlight flooded her bones, outlining evidence of her last moments on earth.

"Dana," I breathed.

A deep, female sigh exhaled into the air, disturbing the roosting birds in the trees above me.

———

I returned to the other shore and put on my shoes and gun like a civilized person. Gibby shook off a galaxy of stars into the night. I tied my stringy hair up. *Civilized.*

I called for backup, for Forensics and Monica, and for someone to guard the scene. I waited at the trailhead. I'd have to explain why I was here so that what I'd found would be admissible into evidence. That was easy: Jasper had invited me. He was taking samples for EPA. He had left, and I'd noticed the area where nothing grew on the island. My dog—my dog who had shown a talent for finding dead things—had swum out into the river and started digging. As a dog owner, I went after him. As one does. And there was Dana. I crammed that mystical experience into terms of rules and logic and chains of evidence . . . so I would be believed.

Forensics came, as did the coroner's office. I'd told them to bring hazmat suits, on account of the chemicals Jasper expected to be in the river. They'd brought a boat and a body bag and bright flashlights, which they swept through the forest. They wouldn't dig Dana up until daylight came, but Forensics would do what they could in the dark.

Finally, someone saw her.

Monica came to stand beside me. "That's some amazing police work, Anna."

"Thanks. I just hope we can start nailing those sons of bitches." I frowned at my phone. I'd been trying to call Jasper to tell him what I'd found, but it kept ringing into silence.

Monica took a deep breath. "Have you been listening to the scanner?"

"No." I'd been under the forest's spell.

Monica gripped my arm. "I just found out . . . Jasper was in an accident. His car went off the road on I-71. Flipped and turned into a fireball."

I sucked in my breath. "Is he okay?"

Monica shook her head. "He didn't make it."

My hands balled into fists and bile rose into my throat.

"He was a good man," I whispered. "He was just here."

Monica put her hands on my shoulders. "We're gonna get them, okay? We're gonna get them all."

25

HOWL

Jasper was dead because of me.

Through the highway patrol, I learned that the accident was suspicious as hell. Jasper's van was found flipped on its side in a ditch. The van had caught fire and burned. It had happened on one of those empty patches of road where there were only trees and highway and the moon. A truck driver had seen the fire and radioed for assistance.

There wasn't any way to determine if Jasper had died on impact or in the fire, highway patrol said. Skid marks suggested that another vehicle was involved, but that wasn't conclusive. The van had burned down to the axles. The rubber from the tires had melted into the pavement. Highway patrol suggested that an accelerant might have been used. There was precious little to examine, but they promised they would do a full investigation.

I closed my eyes. I didn't want to imagine that . . . Jasper, injured in an accident . . . and then burned alive.

I suggested that they look into Vapozene, told them Jasper had been investigating Vapozene poisoning and was en route to EPA. The patrol was very interested in this information, promising to coordinate with both me and Jasper's contact with EPA. As it stood, they'd be pulling in the state Bureau of Criminal Investigation.

It sounded like Jasper's death was going to get some scrutiny, at least.

I wasn't going to let it be for nothing.

I turned away to feel the heat of the sun on my face. Sun and wrath.

I hadn't been able to get ahold of Sykes, who was supposed to be watching Lister; or Calvert, who was babysitting Sumner. I needed to know if they had eyes on the two of them last night, or if the remaining Kings of Warsaw Creek had hired local meth heads to take down Jasper.

Monica was grilling every tweaker Rod Matthews could finger. Somebody would crack, would confess to killing Jasper—I hoped.

I pulled into the sheriff's office parking lot and made my way to my desk. I hadn't been home to change clothes or wash the dog. Gibby slipped under my desk, sighing his exhaustion. On my blotter there was a sticky note with **SEE ME** written in the chief's handwriting.

When Chief used capital letters, things weren't good.

I stopped by the chief's secretary's desk. Judy handed me a chocolate from her secret stash of candy. She did that only when shit was about to go down. She also handed me a wet wipe from her desk. "Here."

Though I was dry now, I realized I was rumpled and there was mud in my hair. I looked like I'd been out on a three-day bender.

She pointed to a streak of mud on my cheek, and I dutifully cleaned it off and tied my hair into what I thought was a neater ponytail.

She nodded at me.

I wolfed down the chocolate, thanked her, squared my shoulders, and knocked on Chief's door.

"Come in."

My heart sank. Chief was behind his desk. The sheriff was in one of the club chairs opposite Chief's desk, and Cortland, Sumner's attorney, was in the other. Calvert and Sykes from Vice were standing at attention with their hands behind their backs, which would've been fine for marines, but looked ridiculous for a couple guys in Tom Hardy T-shirts.

"Jasper's dead," I blurted quietly.

Chief closed his eyes. "I know. I just got off the phone with the FD."

"He was a good man," the sheriff rumbled. "A true public servant."

I scanned the rest of the room, lifting a brow. What the fuck were they doing here?

Chief said quietly, "Jeff Sumner discovered his tail last night and confronted Vice. He's pressing charges against the department for harassment. The estate of Quentin Sims is also alleging that you had his daughter taken from him and badgered him into suicide because of a personal vendetta."

"Chief, I—"

Chief made a slicing motion with his hand. "This investigation is suspended, effective now. Vice is going to spend some time serving subpoenas. Koray, you're suspended until further notice."

My heart plummeted into my shoes. "Chief, a man was killed—"

"Enough." Chief pointed to his desk. "Badge, radio, gun, and keys right here."

Numbly, I put my badge, radio, gun, and keys to the El Camino on his desk.

Chief turned to Cortland. "We deeply regret any inconvenience to your client."

Cortland stood, brushing imaginary lint off his jacket. "It will be up to civil court to determine how much your department deeply regrets its actions. I'll be in touch."

I looked at the sheriff. He glowered at me, then turned to Chief. "I trust you'll handle this. I want her out of my sight forever."

"Yes, Sheriff."

The sheriff nodded, climbed to his feet, and lumbered to the door. On the way out he shut it quietly, which was somehow worse than a slam.

I drew breath to speak, but Chief lifted one finger. He was shaking with anger, and I instinctively recoiled. He'd never been this pissed at me before.

"Sykes, Calvert, go check with subpoenas," he snapped.

"Yes, sir," they said in unison.

"Dismissed."

They scrambled out like chastened children, leaving me alone to face Chief's wrath.

"I told you to go about this quietly," he said. "And now a man is dead."

"Chief, I'm so sorry." It felt like it was all my fault.

"I want you to tell me why," he insisted.

I told him what I'd found, and about Jasper. And what Sims had been doing to his daughter and the other girls.

He listened, stony faced, until I lapsed into silence.

"I need for you to leave the office. I do not want to see your face around here."

My shoulders slumped. "Yes, sir."

"Tell Monica to keep looking for Viv. And you go get some ironclad evidence to bring these motherfuckers down."

I blinked at him. "But you told the sheriff—"

"I told him you were suspended. I'm telling you privately to get this case handled and nail those bastards to the wall. Take anything you find to Monica. She can file with Judge Chamberlain for warrants—she's the only judge in the county who will sign one against those fuckers. Both you girls need to keep a low profile and stay the fuck out of the sheriff's way."

I nodded sharply. "Yes, sir."

"Dismissed."

I exited the chief's office, stomach churning. I hated to have caused trouble for Chief and the Vice guys, never mind what it meant for my own career. It was very likely that I'd be out of a job entirely. If I was found to be at fault for harassing Sumner, or worse, for Sims's death, then my police career would effectively be over and I would be in disgrace. Hopefully I wouldn't be charged with a crime, but with the judges around here under Sumner's thumb, that was a crapshoot.

Chief's secretary passed another piece of chocolate to me.

"Thanks, Judy."

She nodded, stood, and took the entire bag of candy into Chief's office.

———

I slipped out to the parking lot, with Gibby trotting quietly behind me. I put on my sunglasses and jammed my hands into my pockets.

I didn't know if I wanted to scream or cry. Those fucking assholes. They were trying to destroy everyone around this case, anyway they could.

I could be a good cop and play by the rules. Go home and wait for my punishment. Accept it and go sit in a jail cell or an unemployment office.

Fuck that.

I took an Uber to the only car rental place in town and scored a silver four-door sedan smelling like air freshener. I removed the clip-on air freshener before Gibby gulped it down.

I texted Monica on my personal cell. I got suspended.

Monica called me on her personal cell. "I heard. How are you holding up?"

"Fucking bastards," I said through clenched teeth. "I'm pissed."

"Good girl. We'll get through this. I swear."

I took a deep breath. "Highway patrol said Jasper was hit by another vehicle. I'm betting EPA isn't going to send anyone else if there's a hazard to their investigators, which I get."

"That's what Sumner wants, to scare everyone off."

"Well, it's working."

"Listen, I talked with Forensics this morning. They're still going through evidence from Sims's car, but they found some stuff."

"Tell me."

"Working theory is that there was an electrical system malfunction. There was a recall on that vehicle about fifteen years ago, and the vehicle hadn't been to the dealership to get the fix. The malfunction could cause electrical surges in the system, and disrupt the cruise control. It's possible that there was a sudden increase in speed that the driver couldn't control, but we can't say that conclusively yet. It's more likely that the driver just lost control out of human error, or he may have committed suicide. But that would be weird, given the luggage in the back."

"Right." I was liking this line of thought better than the idea that Sims got so rattled by my questioning that he committed suicide.

"But this is where things get really weird. They found some hair in the trunk, near one of the wheel wells. It's long, black hair that doesn't fit with the subject. We also found bloodstains in the upholstery seams."

"Shit." I thought of Viv.

"I asked them to compare those against the body you found last night, and known exemplars for Dana Carson and Viv, and that stain in the basement of the Sumner house. If we get some correlation, then Judge Chamberlain will give us an arrest warrant."

"I'm gonna bet that Sumner will throw Sims under the bus, say he did it."

"If he knew, it's conspiracy. We aren't gonna let them get away with this. We just have to let the evidence connect the dots."

I sure didn't feel like sitting on my hands while this happened. This had become personal.

———

I headed home to change clothes and drop Gibby off. Nick was gone, but he'd left me a note saying that he was consulting with lawyers. I scrubbed Gibby and myself down thoroughly, then crowded into a closet with the UV light from my evidence kit. Nothing glowed, so I figured we were okay. Still, I was determined to watch Gibby for any effects from contaminants in the water. He was content to crawl into bed and stretch across both our pillows.

I stepped outside, into the dry, brittle forest. I walked a good distance away from the house, seething. I should get my shit to-gether, work on the case.

But I was pissed. I'd devoted my life to my career with the sher-iff's office. I had put my life in danger to do that work. I'd been shot, more than once. The fucking sheriff owed me more than a fucking suspension for flouting his stupid rules.

My hands balled into fists, and I howled into the woods. I filled my lungs with air and bellowed an uncivilized scream of fury. I'd followed the sheriff's rules, been stuffed into box after box, been forced to tiptoe around politics and sensibilities and money. Men in power made the rules; men in power protected themselves. To hell with the women who were victimized, burned, and buried. We were mere things to them.

And I was done with it. I was done with being tamed. I had worn the power of the sheriff's office for a long time. It was time I wore my own.

Birds fluttered from their nests in trees, and a squirrel fled. My voice echoed, chasing garter snakes and frogs from their dens.

I announced it. My voice roared with my pulse in my ears. Funny how I never screamed, not even when I'd been shot. I al-ways kept my voice strictly modulated and reasonable, to avoid ruffling the feathers of any colleagues or suspects.

Fuck it all.

I turned on my heel, feeling a deadly peacefulness, though my throat was sore.

The fox was sitting in Nick's garden. The garden was withered and browning, and full of freshly dug holes. She'd unearthed the marigolds near the memorial stone for Nick's mother. Sinoe watched me with narrowed eyes. She wasn't laughing. Instead, she was crunching up a mole.

I regarded her, thinking how different she was from Gibby,

who begged for tortilla chips. How she was domesticated only when it suited her.

Maybe she had things to teach me.

She swallowed, lifted her head, and yipped.

I took that as approval.

When I returned to the house, I had a message Monica had forwarded to me. It was from Owen Destin, the owner of the Grey Door.

"Look . . . I think I know where Viv is. She's in trouble. I don't like having to turn her in like this, but . . . she needs your help."

He left an address way out in the boonies.

Could be a trap. But he sounded sincere.

I had no choice but to follow.

26

FEEDING THE CURSE

I drove down a gravel road that dropped off to a dirt drive. The humidity was thick, and cloud cover obscured the stars. I pulled off before a rusted trailer. It didn't look like anyone lived there; the windows were busted out and the grass was up to my knees.

I stepped up to the front door and rapped. The sound echoed in the trailer, but I heard no movement within. I knocked again, still with no response. I looked down at Gibby. He didn't alert to anyone in the trailer, being more interested in chewing his toes.

I circled around the back of the trailer, where a meadow sloped away to forest. In the distance, I thought I heard singing.

The hair on the back of my neck prickled. My hand came to rest on the butt of my gun, but my gun was missing.

An old pickup truck pulled up, driven by Owen Destin. He jumped down and nodded at me. He was carrying a backpack and wearing hiking boots.

"Thanks for coming," he said. "She won't listen to me."

"You knew where she was this whole time?"

"Yeah." He frowned. "Viv was looking for a place to lay low for a while. She said some meth heads had come by to threaten her. I told her I would help."

I glanced back at the trailer. "Is she in there?"

"Nah. That's my granddad's old place. Nobody's lived there for many years."

"Where is she?"

"Follow me."

Destin turned toward the woods.

We waded through the meadow, into the forest. Gibby trotted merrily along beside me. Rain began to prickle against my face and shoulders.

We wound into the woods, following old deer trails, walking in silence. I knew the trails, having followed many with my father. As we walked, my leg ached, feeling hot against my wet pant leg. Gibby pressed his nose to the ground, tail wagging, thrilled at the scents of foreign woods.

Owen paused before a series of rusted tanks and a small metal shack.

I poked at a rusty pipe. "Your granddad was into moonshining?"

"Yeah. Family business," he admitted. Owen knocked on the shack door, three times, and it opened, spilling light on the muddy ground.

Viv stood in the doorway. She didn't look good. Her tank top and shorts hung loosely on her body, and her cheeks were sunken. Dark circles spread under her eyes. Her hair had a gray streak. She took a drag on her cigarette.

"You've got a visitor." Owen slipped inside with his backpack and started unzipping it. I saw bottles of water, fruit, and sandwiches inside.

Viv looked me up and down, looking a little pissed. "Come in."

She closed the door behind me. Like most old moonshiners' shacks, this one was well sealed to prevent light from leaking out and alerting the authorities. The interior had a dirt floor, and water dripped down a wall. A sleeping bag and camping lantern were tucked inside, and a stack of paperback books teetered beside the burning lantern. The place reeked of tobacco smoke, and an overflowing ashtray sat on the floor.

Viv sat down on the sleeping bag. I knelt opposite her on the floor with Gibby, the ashtray between us. Owen leaned against the wall behind me, seeming to disappear into the shadows.

"Viv," I said, "I have some things to tell you, things that aren't easy to say."

"Tell me what?" Viv demanded.

"I found Dana's body. At the island in the oxbow near the Hag Stone. I'm sorry."

She exhaled, and smoke rolled from her nose. "Finally." Her voice crackled with unshed tears. "Can you tell what happened to her?"

"Not yet. She's been taken to the coroner's office to determine the cause of death."

She nodded and swallowed. "You have other things to tell me."

"Your house was tossed, and then burned." I felt like shit telling her that her life was gone.

"Sinoe. Did they hurt my fox?" She leaned forward, her eyes glassy. "I was going to take her with me, but she didn't show up for breakfast. I figured she'd be okay on her own for a few days . . ."

"She's fine. I took her home."

Viv closed her eyes. "Thank you."

"You're welcome." It seemed like the least I could do in this awful situation.

She steadied herself and opened her eyes. "You were in that house?" She looked at me carefully, and her nostrils flared, as if she could smell scorch on me.

"Yeah."

"I'm sorry for that." She stared at the ember of her cigarette. "Truly."

"Viv, what the hell's going on?"

"The fucking Kings of Warsaw Creek are trying to get me before the curse is completed." She grinned, and I saw that one of her front teeth had chipped. "They think that if they kill me, they stop the curse."

"Well, they're trying pretty damn hard."

She shook her head. "I won't stop it. Nothing can stop it now."

"I know about you and the coven. Did you recruit those girls?" I demanded.

Viv laughed darkly. "Those girls are desperate for a sense of control over their world. I gave it to them. I just showed them their own power. I taught them to fight back."

"You can't just—"

"I can't what? Show them there's a world out there that's more just than the one they grew up in? I can't show them they're being victimized, try to help them?" Her hands had curled into fists, and she was nearly shouting. "Those men have to be stopped by any means necessary."

I dropped my voice to a whisper. "Viv, did you and the girls kill those people?"

She lifted her fingers in a Girl Scout salute. "Scout's honor. No. That was the curse's doing. The girls just helped me wake it up."

"What exactly is this curse?" I asked, impatient. "Tell me how you did it."

"It's more of a summoning." She smiled. "We called up a spirit, an old one who found our goals to be in harmony with hers. Think of her like a Rusalka."

"Rusalka . . ." I echoed, as if I were in a dream. My skin crawled.

"She's a spirit who feasts on the tears of evil men. She lies at the bottom of rivers and pools and drowns the unlucky. She's worn many faces over time, but she understands the rage of women who can't fight back."

I pinched the bridge of my nose. "Viv, innocents—children—are being hurt. A little boy almost died."

Viv shrugged. "Dana was innocent. Nobody cared about that. So was Leah, and the other girls."

"Leah could still be hurt."

"Rusalka won't touch Leah. She's a girl. The curse is going to work as intended."

I stared at her. Viv was too smart. That wasn't an admission of guilt. Casting curses wasn't against the law. I could prove she was in touch with the girls, from cell phone records and the girls' confessions. But I couldn't prove that any of them had committed murder. Besides, they all could be lying to me. They were a sisterhood, one I was not a part of.

"Viv, you need to eat." Owen rustled in his backpack and handed her a sandwich, which she picked at.

Viv shrugged. "I will." She put the sandwich down. Gibby snooted at it until I gave him a warning look.

"You don't look good," I said.

Viv grinned. "I feel it, you know." She spread her fingers out on her sharp clavicles. "All that power . . . being pulled out of me. Given to her."

I shook my head. Viv was fucking crazy. But she was in danger, too. "Viv, I have no doubt in my mind that these men are trying to kill you. They killed an investigator. I don't want you to be next. You need to be in a safe place."

Viv leaned against the shack's metal wall and gestured up to the leaky roof. "I'm in a safe place."

Owen shook his head. "Viv, you need to be someplace where you can sleep. Someplace with a lock on the door, and three squares.a day."

"Sounds like jail. Not going."

"That's not what we mean," I said. "I want to take you into protective custody until we get those guys arrested."

Viv smiled at me. "I appreciate what you're trying to do, bringing these guys to justice. Believe me, I'm glad to have someone finally on their asses. But I'm not interested in being babysat by the cops."

Owen reached out and touched her arm. "Viv, this isn't good for you. I mean . . . your sleeping bag's wet. There's no clean water. At least go someplace where you can rest comfortably. The curse will work better if you have more energy."

Viv stared at him, hard. "Are you kicking me off your land?"

Owen shook his head. "I don't want to have to do that, Viv. I don't want to see you deteriorate and die here. I also hate the idea of having to dig a big hole for you, because we've had three weeks of drought before tonight. That rain was over quick, and that clay is still hard as rock."

Viv sighed and stubbed out her cigarette. "I guess I'm coming with you."

———

Viv was in worse shape than she let on. She walked slowly, refusing to take Owen's arm. She was unsteady. I would've thought she'd been drinking or doing drugs in the shack, but I'd seen no empty bottles or drug paraphernalia.

"She needs medical attention," I told Owen when we got to my rental car. I bundled Viv into the passenger seat and closed the door. "I'll take her to the hospital to get checked out."

"Then what?"

"I'll see that she gets to a safe house, someplace where the Kings of Warsaw Creek can't find her."

"You promise?" Owen said.

"I swear." I meant it. Even if I had to take her home.

But the hospital was first. The ER took her right away.

I sat with Viv behind a curtain in the ER. She was hooked up to an IV and seemed to be dozing. Tonight was probably her first night in a bed in a while.

I flipped through the TV channels as she slept. I clicked off advertisements for the sheriff's reelection campaign, and ultimately wound up on the local news. The newscast showed an aerial view of a retaining pond outside of an apartment complex. The parking lot surrounding it was swarmed with sheriff's vehicles and the coroner's van.

"*. . . Local police aren't sharing the identity of the elderly man, but witnesses say he was found floating in the pond.*"

Viv awoke and chortled, her fingers knit together over her sternum.

"*He was reportedly walking his dog and vanished. His wife called the police, who found him in the retention pond off Meadoway Boulevard . . .*"

I gripped the arm of my chair. I wanted nothing more than to jump into the car and drive to the scene. I looked to Viv in her hospital bed, a brilliant, crazy smile covering her face.

"What are you grinning about?" I grumbled.

"You. You're my alibi for that death."

I peeled my lips back over my teeth, not sure if I was snarling or smiling.

I retreated to the hallway to get some coffee from the nurses' station and to text Monica to run down the girls' whereabouts.

The nurses surrounding me knew Nick, and they knew me. They gave me sympathetic smiles, but they didn't speak to me. They probably couldn't. Not with Nick being under investigation for passing info to me. I didn't push.

But Viv's ER doctor came to the station and spoke with me. I noticed that he was speaking in view of a camera, and with witnesses.

"Viv's dehydrated and has a fever, and her white cell count is up—really up. Her red cell count is abysmally low," the doctor said. "I told her this, and she gave me permission to speak with you." He was covering his HIPAA ass, clearly.

"So . . . she's got a bad infection? Like mono or something?"

"The numbers are higher than that. I'm thinking lymphoma or leukemia, but that's outside of my bailiwick."

Fuck. I blinked. "What happens next?"

"We sent her CTs and labs to the university hospital in the city. They'll be in touch to schedule an appointment and figure out what's going on."

"From what I understand, she fell ill rather suddenly."

"It can happen that way in acute cases. She needs to rest."

I nodded. "Do you think . . ."

I trailed off, hearing a woman's scream from down the hall. I spun, ran down the hall, and flung back the curtain around Viv's bed.

It was empty.

A nurse with a bloody nose shouted into the phone intercom, "Code gray on floor two . . ."

Fuck.

"Which way did they go?" I demanded.

He pointed to the left. "Two guys, and a woman in a hospital gown—toward the elevator."

I sprinted down the corridor, skidding up against the elevator, then turned down the stairs. I thundered down them, taking steps two at a time. Ahead of me, the door to the outside swung open and the alarm went off.

Two guys were running toward the parking lot, one with a motionless woman flung over his shoulder, trailing severed IV tubes. What the hell were they hoping to accomplish by abducting Viv?

"Freeze! Police!" I shouted.

But I was unarmed. I had no power, and they ignored me.

I still ran after them, my injured leg shrieking in pain. The two men piled into an SUV at the curb of the emergency area. The SUV swept off, leaving me panting on the sidewalk.

Fuck.

Fuck.

I had promised Viv and Owen I would keep her safe.

I had failed spectacularly.

Again.

———

"Do you know where they might be going?"

I sat in Monica's car while Gibby rooted in the back seat for snacks. She'd advised me to get the fuck away from the scene, so I'd retreated to a gas station a quarter mile down the road. I'd waited next to the ice machine until she'd pulled up and waved me in.

"I have some guesses." I pinched the bridge of my nose. "The Sumner house? The Hag Stone? The church?"

Monica drummed the steering wheel with her fingers. "I sent Detwiler and a couple other deputies down to sweep the Hag Stone. They haven't seen any activity, but I asked them to keep watch. I fed them a line about teens causing trouble for the Fourth of July weekend."

I didn't like lying to Detwiler, but I didn't think we had much choice. "Smart."

"Here's the video I got from the hospital." She opened her email and showed me videos of the getaway car. I could get only a partial plate. A still image showed two men in the hallway, one carrying an unconscious Viv over his shoulder. The men were dressed in jeans and T-shirts and had masks on. They didn't look like Lister or Sumner—one guy was too thin to be either, and the other was too short. And neither of my suspects had a tattoo of a poorly drawn snake on the inside of his arm.

"I don't know who these guys are. I'll check to see if that tattoo rings any bells in the jail database, but it's a pretty common tattoo."

I frowned.

"What are you thinking?"

"I'm thinking these are tweakers hired by the Kings. Or . . ." I stared at the snake tattoo. "Maybe witches." I felt okay about speculating with Monica about flesh-and-blood people who thought they were witches, though I kept my thoughts about the Rusalka hidden. We were accustomed to dealing with crazies, and I didn't want to be one of them in her eyes.

"I mean, half the guys at the local biker bar have ink like it." Monica frowned. "We've got a fuck ton of potential suspects, but no real leads. If we serve warrants on Lister and Sumner, they might never lead us to Viv."

"What about that drowning on the news? If there's a connection to Lister and Sumner there, maybe some evidence will—"

"The guy who drowned was Quentin Sims's uncle," Monica said quietly. "There are signs of violence."

"What about the girls?"

"Leah and Rebecca were accounted for. I have alibis so far for three of the other six—something about a bake sale. It's possible that the three I haven't been in touch with drowned the dude. Or they might say they were having a slumber party." She spread her hands. "They back each other up, just like the Kings of Warsaw Creek did back in the day."

"This isn't going to stop until all the Kings and all the Kings' men are dead." I stared at the clock on the dash. It was almost July fourth.

"Might not be such a bad thing." Monica's eyes were narrowed, and she was crunching some hard candy. "Seems to be wiping out church leadership. Not that I said that out loud."

"But where are Sumner and Lister?"

"I've had Vice cruising by their houses. Nothing yet."

Monica's phone dinged, and she scanned her texts. Her eyebrows lost their perfect shape and twitched. "Just heard back on Fred Jasper's alibi for when the kids nearly drowned and the cousins got killed."

"Yeah? He said he was directing traffic at the Flower Festival."

Monica frowned. "The festival organizer says he self-reported his overtime. Nobody actually had eyes on him the whole time."

My brows drew together. "You think Fred—"

"This isn't proof that he wasn't where he said he was. But it puts Fred on the table as a suspect."

I exhaled. "Yeah. I guess it does."

"I'll see if we can find any witnesses."

"But it can't be Fred," I said. "That man in the retaining pond tonight . . . A dead guy can't commit murder." *Right?* My thoughts spun. I had Viv accounted for. Jasper was dead. That left the girls . . .

Monica chewed her gum thoughtfully. "He may have had nothing to do with any of this. Or he may not have been working alone. He had means, motive, and opportunity for some of these incidents."

I sank down in my seat. "You're gonna get in a helluva lot of trouble for looping me in, you know."

Monica lifted a shoulder. "Maybe not as much as you'd think. You know that new radio system I've been so fucking leery of?"

"Yeah?"

"You notice I haven't been using it to contact you?"

I exhaled. "It's not secure."

"No. I wouldn't say anything on it that I wouldn't post on a billboard."

"This is why you're Wonder Woman," I said.

Monica nodded sagely. "Now get out of my car, Wonder Girl. I gotta go do an inventory of every meth head out on bond to try to find Viv. Go home. That's an order, or I will have you picked up and put in jail for your own protection. Understand?"

I nodded. I had fucked up by losing Viv, and Monica needed me out of the way if anything was gonna get done. It wasn't personal.

I took a bag of gummy bears away from Gibby, stepped out of the car with him, and stood by the ice machine once more as she pulled out of the lot.

At least Monica was covering her own ass.

But I had fucked up. Again.

And now I had to go admit it.

I shoveled the dog back into the rental car and called Owen Destin.

He picked up on the second ring. "Hello?"

I took a deep breath. "This is Anna Koray. I have to tell you . . . Viv was abducted from the hospital."

There was silence on the other end of the line.

"Who?" he asked at last.

"We don't know. Not yet. I'm so sorry, Owen—"

"I should've known better than to call the cops," he said quietly, then hung up the phone.

———

Heart heavy, I headed for home. There was one upside here. I didn't think Viv was my killer—she'd been in her hospital bed when the guy drowned in the retention pond. She hated the Kings, but that wasn't against the law. She was a victim, just like her sister. And someone wanted to silence her forever.

Likely, I would need to sit tight until Sumner or Lister led Monica to Viv. Then we could—

I stopped myself. I had no authority whatsoever in this situation. I was just a civilian. Anna. Not Lt. Koray.

I frowned. Night had fallen, and I was zinging down two-lane country roads toward home. Beside me, Gibby sat in his harness, buckled to the seat belt, sniffing the air. I heard an engine behind me, but I didn't see headlights in the rearview mirror.

Somebody behind me was running dark, and that was no good.

I rolled up the windows and stepped on the gas. If somebody meant me ill, they had another thing coming.

"Hold on, Gibby."

I rocketed over the hills, my stomach pitching into my throat. I killed my own lights, intending on not giving the jackass behind me an easy way to follow me.

I knew these roads like the back of my hand; there was no way some rich boy with his sports car was going to catch me . . .

A shadow crossed the road. In the moonlight, I saw a fox on the road. I slammed on the brakes, swerved . . .

. . . and a car hit my rear left quarter panel, shoving me off the road. Trees flashed past and metal squealed, until we landed in the ditch with a thud and the powdery puff of airbags.

"Gibby!" I gasped, punching down the airbag and reaching for him.

Gibby sat in his seat, whining. I ran my hands over his ribs and limbs. He seemed uninjured, and I breathed a sigh of relief.

I unhooked his harness and kicked open my door. I scanned the road. I was vulnerable here, in the middle of nowhere, but my best chance would be to retreat to the forest if they came here on foot.

The pursuing car had stopped on the road. I heard a car door open. They were going to come after me and finish me off.

I saw a figure climbing down an embankment, gun in hand. If I squinted, it sure looked like Rod's brother, Timmy.

I grabbed Gibby's harness, and we retreated into the woods. Timmy wouldn't be able to track us. I just had to bide my time.

I heard some half-hearted thrashing around in the brush, but Timmy seemed to have forgotten to bring a flashlight. He gave up after a short time, to my relief.

I waited until I heard a slamming car door and the receding rev of an engine.

I let my heartbeat settle, then called for a tow truck. We returned to the scene of the accident and circled the vehicle, inspecting it for damage.

Looked like I'd broken a wheel, crumpled a front fender, and lost a taillight and a headlight. Plus some dents. And I was sure that there was invisible damage.

Fuck.

I had a sneaking suspicion that the insurance company was gonna consider it totaled. Good thing I'd been paranoid enough at the car rental counter to buy all the extra insurance.

Gibby peed on a flat tire.

"Yeah, I think it's dead, too, Gibby."

———

I didn't get home until after midnight. I had Patrol carefully document the accident, and it took some doing to haul my poor rental out of the ditch.

Deputy Detwiler had come out to take my statement. "Are you okay, El-Tee?" he asked, frowning. At least he didn't look upon me with pity or ask me about my suspension.

"I'm okay, Detwiler." I told him that it might be fruitful to compare paint scrapings from whoever hit me to cars on the Lister lot. Detwiler didn't have much authority, but he'd try his best to make sure that the right thing was done.

Poor kid. Believing in the right thing was hard these days. I wasn't sure I even knew what the right thing was anymore.

The tow driver dropped me off at the end of my drive, so Gibby and I walked home in the dark. The moon was high overhead, nearly full, and tree frogs sang all around us.

I was tired. Really fucking tired. I was sore, and tired of the old boys' club. Somebody had tried to hurt me, and, worse, they'd tried to hurt my dog. Maybe Nick was right, and I needed to find something else to do for a living, before this bullshit caught up with me. Maybe I should resign before this investigation landed me in jail. They wanted me out of the way; I could oblige. Maybe if I got out of their way, they wouldn't charge me with anything.

The porch light was on, and Nick was sitting on the porch steps, drinking a beer.

"Hey," I said limply.

"Rough day?"

"You have no idea." I sat down beside him. Nick stood to turn off the porch light, which was attracting bugs, and Gibby plunked down at my feet, on the bottom step. The humid shadow of the forest sang around us, cicadas and crickets and tree frogs. In the distance, a solitary bullfrog looking for love twanged. My blood pressure dropped, and my heartbeat aligned with the pulse of the forest.

"There's dinner to reheat in the fridge," he said, coming to sit with us.

"I'm sorry." I leaned against his shoulder.

"How did you get here?" He scanned the driveway, seeing no car.

"Kindly tow truck driver."

"What happened to the rental car?"

"Got run off the road. The car's no more."

"You all right?"

I nodded, and he handed me a beer. I shouldn't be drinking on antibiotics, but apparently I sounded that defeated.

My gaze roved the yard. There was a blanket spread out on the grass, and a telescope was set up. *Aww.* He'd planned a picnic dinner, and I'd gone and fucked all that up. Like pretty much everything I touched.

He said, mildly, "I got us a new toy. We can supposedly see Saturn tonight, and I thought that would be cool."

I perked up. "Show me."

It turned out that Nick had acquired a very fancy telescope that sensed light and steered itself. One just had to punch in the location of a point in the sky, and it automatically oriented itself to that point. I laughed when he showed me Saturn. It looked exactly like the pictures in elementary school textbooks, so artificial and glowy, only upside down.

We pointed the telescope at the moon, examining the craters and rills. We poked around the Pleiades for a bit, and I realized how much I'd missed this . . . the childlike wonder of nature all around me—that, and seeing Nick smile.

I stepped back from the telescope to give Nick his turn. Gibby leaned against me, and I realized he had something on his collar.

My heart thundered as I knelt to remove it. It was a velvet jewelry box, tied to Gibby's collar with a ribbon. Nick must have slipped it on when I was distracted by the telescope.

Nick sat on the picnic blanket, feigning innocence.

I opened the box. It contained a ring, a solitaire diamond set flush in a platinum band. It was the ring he'd proposed to me with a year and a half ago, when I'd said no.

"I can't imagine having a relationship this honest with anyone else," Nick said. "I want us to be together for the rest of our lives, whatever it takes."

I stared at the ring, gleaming starlike in my hand. I could say no, and my world would be the same as it always had been—dangerous and solitary.

But if I said yes, I would be saying yes to closing this chapter and opening another, to something new and different. And I'd have the person who best understood me by my side.

I looked at him, holding Gibby, and Gibby's tail thumped on the ground.

There was a lump in my throat.

"I need . . . I need to think about it," I whispered.

"I understand." His face was still shining, hopeful. Hopeful that I'd come to the right decision. "Take the time you need."

I nodded.

I glanced toward the back garden. Two reflective fox eyes watched me pretend to be civilized.

27

TRACE EVIDENCE

I couldn't sleep, curled in Nick's arms, sandwiched between him and Gibby. All was quiet, perfectly still. I listened to the dog snore and felt Nick's breath tickle the back of my neck.

Things were changing. I could feel it. Perhaps all the havoc with this case was a sign from the universe for me to get the hell out of Dodge. We hadn't talked about it any further, about Nick moving to the city and me following him. I thought we had time. I thought for a moment about what would happen if we went beyond the city . . . What would happen if we moved west, to land where the sky stretched from horizon to horizon? What if we went to the ocean?

There was part of me that couldn't do that. At least not until I made peace with this place.

I slithered out from between Nick and Gibby, slipped on my shoes, and stepped noiselessly outside. I walked to the back garden, where the fox was waiting for me among the wilted lettuce and the sunburned tomatoes.

Sinoe watched me with shining eyes.

I wanted to tell her about how I'd fucked up with her mom, how I'd let things get so bad. How I had nothing left and I was sorry. So sorry.

But she was not here for that. She turned and trotted off to the forest.

I followed.

Fireflies hung low, gathering close to the ground. I followed the fox, sweeping through Virginia creeper and past black raspberries. I could feel my pulse, slow and steady; for a moment, I was thinking of nothing. Not of my failures or the future, just tracking with the fox.

Hunting.

Green washed over my vision like an aurora. I remembered hunting with my mom.

We slipped through the forest, following a light in the distance. Not fireflies this time, but headlights. Headlights shouldn't be this deep in the forest.

We crept up on the man who was our quarry. We'd been tracking his movements for weeks, the man and his Jeep filled with barrels of sickly sweet chemicals that killed everything they touched. We'd come to know his tire tracks, how they crossed the two-lane road into the forest at one of two access points. He always came on Monday and Wednesday nights, after midnight, when the moon approached the horizon.

There was no moon tonight. The forest was black and looming, thick and teeming with anger.

We crouched behind honeysuckle, watching as he rolled from the back of the Jeep big drums that hit the ground with a bang. He shoved one, two, three, four, five drums to the forest floor. One rolled within ten feet of our hiding place, but I remained frozen, watching. Mom was still and silent, her pupils dilated large and black like a cat's.

Now our quarry was busy rolling the drums to a spot a little distance from the Jeep.

My mom slipped to the driver's side of the Jeep. She grasped the keys and ripped them out of the ignition.

The headlights went dark, plunging us all in darkness.

———

I awoke from my trance in a little clearing. My heart beat steady and low, and I marveled at this new fragment of memory with both curiosity and dread. Pollution had been happening here for so long, decades. My mom had known.

But what had she done about it? I strained into the recesses of my mind, trying to conjure what had happened next.

I feared for the man with the Jeep. My mom wasn't a killer, like my father was. And she was a woman, no physical match in a fight with a young man.

But I was still afraid for him, afraid of my mom's wrath.

I sank down to my heels, sat on the ground and pressed my fists to my temples. Why couldn't I unlock that darkness at will? Why was it just beyond my reach? Was it truly so awful that I couldn't cope with it all at once?

Something laughed softly in the night. The fox. She'd caught a snake. She held it between her paws and gnawed at it. She'd already ripped off its head, and she was eating it the way a child might eat a Popsicle.

I didn't intervene. This was nature. The strong killed the weak; predator killed prey. I knew that was true in the marrow of my bones.

But where was I in all this? What kind of a predator was I, to be stripped of all my tools and cast out of the tribe? I had failed. My father would certainly be disappointed in me.

I lay down in the grass, feeling the earth pressing up against my back.

Part of me craved to be the kind of hunter he was, forever victorious, always getting his prey. Only I wanted to stay on the right side of the law, and get the criminals. I wanted to be the hunter defending the prey.

I'd failed. I hadn't inherited his ruthlessness. I wasn't breaking down Sumner's door and demanding answers. Instead, I'd let the law hamstring me and leave me bleeding in the ditch.

Sinoe, having consumed her meal, trotted up to me and looked down at my face. Her breath reeked of the metallic smell of blood and fresh reptile. Her eyes were black, dilated in the darkness to swallow themselves and swallow me.

The fox had lost. She had lost everything. But still she hunted.

And so would I.

———

I returned to the house.

The fox followed, and stretched out on the dog bed I'd put on the porch. She was domestic when she chose to be, and I could respect that. Perhaps she and Gibby would someday get along. Or perhaps she'd melt into the woods entirely one day, and no one would ever see her again.

I couldn't control her. And I had to remind myself that no one could control me.

———

When gray morning light seeped from beneath the curtains, I got dressed quietly to avoid waking Nick. I thought I would head into town to pick up Nick's favorite apple pastries from the donut shop. Gibby wiggled out of bed, eager to join me and have his breakfast.

I paused, looking at Nick's sleeping form in my bed. He'd be there for the rest of my life—if I let him.

I would just clean up this one case, I vowed. I would find Viv and put the Kings of Warsaw Creek behind bars. I would make a clean break. Justice for all, right? And fuck everybody else. It felt right to be with him. To follow.

But one last hunt, first.

I took Nick's car. His SUV had all the bells and whistles, and it must have automatically paired with my cell phone, because I got a call that came through his speakers right as I pulled out onto the road.

"It's Monica. I heard what happened last night. Are you and Gibby okay?"

"Yeah. We're okay. Luckily. Any news on Viv?"

"Nothing yet. I've been searching for Sumner and Lister on the down-low. Nobody's seen them, either. I'm checking the city's Flock cameras to see if any passive scanning picked up their license plates."

"Good idea." We didn't have that tech in our rural county, but the nearby city was experimenting with creating a web of interconnected public and private video cameras that would passively scan license plates. It wasn't uncommon for police cars to have that kind of tech installed, but involving local businesses was new.

"Also heard from Forensics. The blood found on the basement floor at the Sumner house matches the serotype for Dana Carson. Judge Chamberlain approved an arrest warrant for Sumner, at least. If we nab him, maybe he'll confess. I can only hope he'll implicate Lister if we reel him in."

"Are you ready for that?" I asked quietly. "They might come for you, too."

She exhaled into the phone. "There will be hell to pay for arresting him, sure, but Chief wants to see them in jail as badly as you and I do. So I'm gonna take that gamble."

"Good girl," I said.

"I'll keep you in the loop," she promised, and hung up.

I chewed my lip. I was afraid of those slimeballs going after Monica if she tried to arrest Sumner. Her career was one thing, but those assholes could do to her what they did to Jasper. And what they might be doing to Viv.

I considered that. They killed Jasper quickly, expediently. But they abducted Dana. Maybe in the same way they abducted Viv. Viv had been conscious when I left her, then suddenly not. Did they drug her? I doubted they used hospital drugs—that would have taken too much time. So they had to bring the drugs with them. I didn't think that meth would knock anyone out so quickly, but they might have access to other drugs.

Maybe Jasper hadn't been subjected to any weird ritualistic shit, but it was hard to know, given the flames at the scene. A lump rose in my throat. But Viv . . . I could see them doing to her what they'd done to her sister. And today was the Fourth of July, the anniversary of when Dana had disappeared. And given the amount of blood on the floor of the Sumner basement . . . she had to have died there. I knew it in my gut that they'd done some weird ritualistic shit to her and killed her, too.

When I got to the main street in town I could turn right, for donuts . . . or I could turn left and visit the coroner's office.

I was off the case. I could be charged with interfering with an official investigation if I went to the coroner's office.

But I already had it in my mind that I was going to resign. And I needed to see if there was something Dana left behind that could lead me to Viv.

I parked in the nearly empty parking lot behind the county coroner's office. Leaving the air on for Gibby, I locked up and headed inside. The secretary waved me through without looking up from her phone; evidently rumors of my suspension hadn't yet reached the coroner's office. I was betting my time on that was running out.

The coroner, Dr. Navarro, was waiting for me in the hall, tapping her toe on the green tile.

"You're keeping us busy, Detective Koray. I had to cancel my Alaskan cruise."

I winced. "Sorry. I really am."

"Don't be. I hate vacationing with the in-laws. Come on. I have some things to show you." She gestured for me to follow her to the morgue. I suited up in a Tyvek suit and followed her to the chilly examination room of the morgue.

I scanned the room, shoulders hunched. Jasper wouldn't be here. He was killed in another county. I didn't think I could handle seeing his ashes in a bag.

Dr. Navarro unzipped a body bag on a stainless steel slab. I presumed this was one of the Sims cousins, since the body was missing a head. The head was in a plastic bag tucked beneath an arm, a sunburned face with its mouth open.

"I just finished with this guy."

"Let me guess . . . cause of death is decapitation?"

"You'd think that, but they were actually drowned before any of that happened. I found water in their lungs."

"So the decapitation was postmortem?"

"Exactly. And given the angles of the cuts, the perp had to be in the water."

I frowned, recalling how they were found, on inflated inner tubes. "So the guys were chilling . . ." I headed to the body's empty neck. "And someone came up out of the water and drowned them . . ." I mimicked pushing down on the missing head, then slashed with my hand. "And then made off with the heads?"

"Yeah, exactly." Navarro stood back and nodded. "Your perpetrator was in the water."

"I don't get how one wouldn't be alerted to the other's death," I said. "You'd think that the second victim would try to fight back or escape."

"Well, I was able to compute BAC from the remaining blood in the bodies, and Amos was at .42 and Patrick was at .39."

"They might not have even been conscious," I realized.

"Exactly. And that, honestly, is the best-case scenario."

I hoped to hell that they'd slept through their murders, because if not . . . I shuddered, imagining how terrible it would be to drown in the dark, with no one to hear.

I exhaled. "Anything on the skeleton from the river? I heard you were able to ID the body."

"As a matter of fact, yes. And yes."

She turned away to approach a cart in the room's center, then pulled a plastic sheet away. Where the Lister cousin had looked fresh, this collection of bones looked very much like an archaeological display. Blackened bones were arranged in the fetal position. The skull was perched on top of a wobbly curve of vertebrae, with a tooth gleaming in the jaw. Dana's necklace was folded in a plastic evidence bag.

"Through dental records, we were able to positively identify these as the remains of Dana Carson," Dr. Navarro said.

I sighed. I knew this. But it was different to be told there was no hope that Dana was alive.

"How did she die?"

"This is weird. Very weird." Dr. Navarro pointed at the bones of the hands and feet. "I found evidence of trauma to the hands and feet, almost as if she was pinned down with something sharp. Some bones are missing, but I'm seeing shattered metacarpals and metatarsals, which is unlikely to be the result of predation; the marks that shattered them are too sharp and look like the result of a tool—"

"Like a railroad spike," I said quietly.

"Yes." She lifted her eyebrows. "Exactly like a railroad spike. It suggests to me some element of ritual murder, especially with the burning."

"So . . . she was burned alive?"

"I don't think so. I think the burning came after. I was able to recover part of a crushed hyoid bone, so I'm thinking it was the railroad spikes first, then strangulation. She died, or was rendered unconscious, and then the fire. I'm sure some sort of accelerant was used, though accelerants tend to burn off, and become hard to detect after this much time has passed," she said.

"Right. Human bodies really don't burn easily."

I stared down at the black bones. Such a horrible way to die.

"But here's the thing . . . We found extra bones."

My head jerked up. "Extra bones?"

"Yeah. I don't have any information on them yet, but there was another body burned here. She wasn't the first."

I exhaled.

This cemented the idea that the Kings of Warsaw Creek were involved in some very dark occult secrets. I made a mental note to text Monica to get a warrant for the railroad spikes in the Sumner home and the church, to check for blood residue, and also to check for other missing young women to compare DNA against.

I told the coroner about Jasper's suspicions, and about

Vapozene, the proprietary compound the plant was using. I told her I suspected it as an accelerant in the burning of his van.

"I can't back this up right now," I said, "but I have a hunch. Vapozene is supposed to persist at room temperature and not evaporate. Maybe, just maybe, there are traces still around."

"That's a long shot, but I'm willing to try to find them."

"May I touch the remains?" I asked, turning back to the bones. "And do you happen to have your UV light handy?"

"Yes and yes. Let's take a look."

She flipped the light switch, plunging us in darkness. The only light came from the frosted window in the door and a stripe of light underneath it.

The coroner clicked on a blue-tinged light and handed it to me. I swept it over the remains, and no telltale glow was revealed. "I guess we can confirm that Dana's remains weren't contaminated by the Vapozene in the river."

With gloved fingers, I approached her skull. The jaw was slack, and we peered inside the mouth. A very faint fluorescence glowed from a back tooth surrounded by a broken piece of orthodontic equipment.

"Her braces," Navarro breathed. "And she's got a cracked composite filling back there."

The coroner immediately grabbed a plastic bag and a pair of forceps. She reached into the mouth for the tooth. It released with a soft crunch, and the coroner hastily dropped the tooth into the plastic bag and sealed it away for analysis.

I swept the light over the necklace, but saw nothing. Dr. Navarro went after the pendant with pliers, pulling the pearl from the setting while I shone the light on it.

The pearl glowed faintly.

The coroner dropped it into another evidence bag.

"You know what else I'm thinking," she mused. "Benzene can be used as an anesthetic, to knock a victim unconscious."

I remembered the drugged state Viv appeared to be in while on camera at the hospital. "And there's a guy in town who has unlimited access to Vapozene."

28

TAKEN

I doubled back for the forgotten pastries, got fresh coffee, and headed back to the house. I'd make plans to meet up with Monica later, to share the new evidence with her. Maybe she could replicate what I'd done, get to Viv's house, and gain new samples from the debris to check for accelerants.

I pulled down the driveway, gravel crunching under the tires of the SUV.

My gaze fell on the front door of the house. It was standing open. The fox sat in the doorway, with an inscrutable expression on her face.

My breath hitched in my throat. Something was terribly, terribly wrong.

I erupted out of the car, with Gibby on my heels, and advanced soundlessly across the normally creaky porch. I lurched into the kitchen, and my heart plummeted to my feet.

A kitchen chair had been knocked over onto the floor. Papers were scattered on the counter.

"Nick?" I called softly.

No answer.

I moved deeper into the house. Gibby lunged past me, growling. The hair on his back stood upright. He ignored the fox, who refused to cross the threshold.

Signs of a struggle. The lamp on Nick's side of the bed was broken. His glasses were on the floor, under the bed.

He wasn't there. Wasn't in the bathroom, not in the closet.

I returned to the front door, observing that it had been kicked in. The lockset dangled from splintered wood.

Rage poured through me.

My phone rang. I picked it up, saying nothing, feeling my pulse beat a slow, deadly metronome in my temples.

"Anna?" It was Monica.

I didn't say anything.

"Anna? What's wrong? Are you okay?"

My voice came out as a hiss. "They took Nick."

———

I might not have had the authority of law anymore.

I might not have had my service gun.

But I was far from powerless.

I was my father's daughter. I had the blood of a fearsome killer seeping coldly through my veins.

And the Kings of Warsaw Creek were not going to survive this.

I dug around in the back of my closet for the shotgun I'd had for decades. I filled my pockets with shells and put the shotgun in a zippered blue case that once held a folding hammock stand. I looked like I was out to stake out a spot to watch the fireworks from the comfort of a hammock. I stuffed a flashlight, some bottled water, and a collapsible dog dish in the bag.

Monica arrived, and stood in the doorway of my house. "Jesus, Anna, I'm so sorry."

I incandesced with rage. Monica came to me and wrapped her arms around me. Gibby leaned against my leg. I felt their heartbeats close to mine, the same anger, the rage.

"I'm telling you that I'm going to find Nick and I'm going to kill those men," I whispered. I wanted to give her the choice to leave and disavow any knowledge of what I was going to do.

"I'm coming with you," Monica said. "We are going to find him."

I nodded.

We left the house, and I pulled the door closed behind me. It was useless, I knew. When I came back—if I came back—I wouldn't be surprised to find a raccoon in my bed and a deer standing in my living room, looking up at the buck head mounted on a plaque above my fireplace.

The wild could take it back. I didn't care.

We all needed to go get what was ours.

———

Monica and I rolled up on the Sumner house like a cloud shadow over the land.

There was a car in the driveway, Drema's blue SUV. I parked beside it, and Monica pulled in behind me. I was riding high on adrenaline, and I rocked up to the front door while Monica circled around to the back.

I rapped hard. "Police. Open up."

The door opened immediately, and Drema Sumner blinked at me.

"Is Jeff here?"

She shook her head. "No. He left about an hour ago."

She stepped aside and I went in, with my shotgun at my side.

"I thought you were steering clear of Jeff," I said.

"Mason's going to be released this afternoon. I'm packing up all our things." She gestured to suitcases on the floor.

"When did you get here?"

"Three. I was hoping Jeff would be gone, but . . ." She stared at the mess in the living room and wrinkled her nose.

Monica returned to the front door. "Nobody fled out the back," she confirmed.

"Did Jeff say anything when he left?"

"Not really. I went to Mason's playroom and started packing up his stuff."

"Was Jeff alone?"

"He was, until a cop came for him. Much to my delight." She couldn't suppress a smile.

"A cop?" My brow wrinkled.

"Yeah. I peeked down the hallway and kept my lips zipped. He said he was with the sheriff's office. Jeff pitched a tantrum, but the guy cuffed him and dragged him out. I sure as hell wasn't going to interfere."

"What did he look like?"

"Tall. Brown hair."

That could be anyone. But the skin on the nape of my neck prickled. I pulled up a picture of the interdepartmental softball team on my phone and showed it to Drema. "Was this him?"

"Yeah."

"Are you sure?"

"Totally."

I exhaled. I looked at Monica. "That's Fred Jasper."

"But . . . Fred is dead."

My hand slid up into my hairline. "Fuck. How did he survive that car accident?"

"Maybe . . . What if . . . what if he escaped somehow? What if that was the last straw . . . he finally snapped and went after the Kings?"

"What if . . . he finally snapped . . . and faked his own death?" Monica looked at me like I was batshit.

"I mean . . . he'd know how to do it," I insisted. "What if he did it so he could get his revenge and disappear into the night?"

"That sounds fabulous to me," Drema blurted.

I turned to Drema. "I'm going to have to ask you to leave, and leave these things here. This is an active crime scene, and you need to be someplace safe."

Drema nodded. "Of course, of course." She lifted her hands and backed out of the house.

Monica and I swept the house quickly. I took the upstairs, found no one, and descended to the first floor just in time to see Monica open the basement door from the kitchen. She took one step on the stairs, and then her shriek was obliterated by a deafening crash.

I lurched to the doorway and flipped on the light. "Monica!"

The top steps had caved in, the treads having been neatly cut away under the carpet. Beneath the stairs, Monica sprawled on a plywood board studded with railroad spikes.

Several facts converged on me at once.

Jeff knew we had been here.

He had booby-trapped the house.

And I had to get help for Monica.

I grasped the banister and scrambled awkwardly down to the floor, avoiding the mess Monica had fallen into. There was blood, a lot of it.

I stared down at Monica. She'd landed on several spikes; one was in her arm, one in her shoulder. Another railroad spike had pierced her thigh, and her leg was twisted under her at an unnatural angle.

She was pale and sweating. She should be swearing, but she wasn't. That was a bad sign.

"Hey, Monica, stay with me."

She rolled her eyes toward me. "I fucked up."

I grabbed her radio and called for help. Blood was spurting out like in a horror film. The spike in her thigh must've cut her femoral artery. She could bleed out in minutes.

Drema shouted at the doorway. "What happened? I heard screaming—"

"Don't come down here!" I shouted.

I turned back to Monica. She was starting to pass out.

She was certainly going to hate me for what I was going to do.

I ripped her leg off the spike. She screamed at me, cursing a hundred words I had never heard strung together. Blood splashed.

I ripped my belt out of its loops and fastened it around Monica's upper thigh. I wrenched it tight, with all my strength. At this point, she was going to lose either her leg or her life.

She cringed, gripping her leg. I held tight to the tourniquet.

"Stay here," I ordered.

Monica nodded. Her lips were turning blue.

"Sing with me," I said, desperately. I knew her favorite song, improbably, was "The Wreck of the *Edmund Fitzgerald*."

"The legend lives on from the Chippewa on down of the big lake they call Gitche Gumee . . ." I began, singing in my terrible voice.

Monica joined me. Her voice was dim, but she could still carry a tune.

The end of a bedsheet slapped me in the face. Drema peered down at me. "We've gotta get her out of there."

Still warbling about the woes of the *Edmund Fitzgerald*, I flung the end of the sheet back up to Drema, forming a sling.

I picked Monica up off the spikes, and her song wavered. None of the other wounds were life-threatening, but the sooner we could get her up, the sooner the squad could take her to the hospital.

"Have you got this?" I hissed to Drema.

She was braced with one foot on either side of the doorframe, with the ends of the sheet wrapped around her wrists.

"I do Pilates," she growled. "Lots and lots of Pilates."

I put Monica in the sling, supporting her from the bottom. I picked slippery footing among the spikes, pushing up as Drema pulled.

Drema was strong, far stronger than I expected. She pulled Monica up through the doorway and into the kitchen.

I climbed back up over the banister, my hands slick with blood.

"I'll flag down the squad," Drema said, scrambling to her feet and charging out the front door.

I yanked on Monica's tourniquet, and she nearly slugged me. She looked at me through slitted eyes. "You know what really sucks about this?"

"What?"

"That I'm gonna be too fucked up to wear that pink leather miniskirt I ordered."

———

The squad swept into the house, seized Monica, and swept back out of the house in moments. There were lights, sirens, and then silence.

"Is she gonna be okay?" Drema asked, wrapping her arms around herself.

"I don't know." My voice hitched. Monica was my mentor. My friend.

And without her, I would be totally alone.

Drema pressed her bloody hands to her face. "Jeff's a monster."

I inhaled, trying to break out of my mental paralysis. "You need to get somewhere safe, someplace where he can't get to you."

She nodded sharply. "I'll go to the hospital, protect Mason."

There was no use in trying to persuade her to do anything different. Sheriff's deputies would be coming, so I had to get out of there.

Drema shoved a suitcase at me. "There are clothes in here."

I stared at the hard-sided pink luggage.

"Go. Before they get here. Find him."

I flung the luggage into the back of Nick's SUV and peeled out of the driveway. In the distance, sirens echoed.

Gibby cried piteously at the fresh blood on my clothes.

"It's okay. It's okay. She's gonna be okay," I recited to him like a mantra. I meant it to be soothing, but I wasn't sure it was true. There wasn't any way I could be sure.

All I could do was try to find Nick before the Kings of Warsaw Creek managed to hurt him, too.

I drove down back roads until I found a spot to pull off near a pond. I pulled Drema's suitcase out. In it I found clothes for Mason, small shoes, a bag of cosmetics, and a couple of changes of clothes for Drema. I stripped out of my bloody clothes, and rinsed the blood off my arms and face in the pond.

I stared down at my reflection. I didn't see my own image there. I saw the Rusalka.

I wriggled into Drema's jeans and donned a very expensive-feeling black blouse, which clung to my skin like silk. I gazed at my reflection again. I still saw Rusalka, unblinking.

"Come on, Gibby," I said. "Let's go find your dad."

I got Jasper's address from good old Google and rolled up to his home. It was a small trailer on some pretty meadow acreage that was less than a mile from the Sumners' house if you cut through the marshland in the back. His car wasn't there, but I still knocked on the door. I peered through the windows, seeing that no one was home.

I couldn't imagine that Jasper was capable of hurting anyone.

But then again, I couldn't imagine that I was, either.

I tried the door. It was locked, but not with a particularly good lock. I plucked my driver's license out of my wallet and used it to press the tongue of the lock back into the door, and I was in within minutes.

Jasper wasn't living large. Not at all. I respected that; a lot of guys in law enforcement spent every last overtime dime they had on cars and big houses. Not Jasper. I poked through the kitchen cabinets. Everything was clean, and neat as a pin, but there wasn't any food there, except for a few cans of soup. There were a couch and a television in the living room. No computer.

The bedroom contained a double bed with simple coverings. The trailer felt like a temporary residence, with no real personality or, it seemed, intent to stay. His clothes were hung neatly in the closet.

On the dresser was a picture, and I paused. It was a picture of a boy and a girl in high school, in their prom clothes. It was of Dana and Jasper. Before it was a river pearl. I wondered if she'd given that to him.

I went outside, to the marsh. Part of me half expected to find Jasper's and Sumner's bodies floating there, but the water was peaceful, reflecting the sun and sky above. A lawn chair was set up on the bank, and there was a fishing pole stuck in the ground beside it. A breeze pushed dragonflies across the water's surface, creating bright spots of sun dazzle.

I blinked, and the dazzle churned. I saw the glitter of lights at a dance, young Jasper and Dana. They looked happy, like they had their whole lives ahead of them.

The vision faded, and I was staring at the glassy water once more.

A lump rose in my throat. He had really loved Dana. And he hadn't built a life at all after she was gone. He was just . . . existing. Not moving forward. Waiting. Waiting for what? For her attackers to be brought to justice?

And when they weren't . . . he'd gone to find justice himself.

Jasper and I understood each other.

———

I headed over to Mark Lister's house. If that son of a bitch was there, I was going to wring every last drop of knowledge out of him.

I pulled up before the Lister house and found Ross opening the back of a white minivan.

I emerged from the SUV, with Gibby close beside me. The young man grinned when he saw the dog.

"Hi! Is this a police dog?"

"Not really," I admitted. I forced myself to wear a congenial mask, the one I wore as Lt. Anna Koray doing community outreach. I forced my lips to curve upward benignly and my eyebrows to lift pleasantly, even while I ground my teeth and felt the stickiness of blood under my fingernails. Gibby went up to the kid and let him pet him, tail wagging. I looked at the kid closely. He was pale, and I saw bandages on his arms and legs.

"How are you feeling, Ross?"

He lifted a shoulder. "Still got a few weeks of steroids to take. A couple days ago, I saw some kind of specialist who gave me a bunch of new antibiotics. They make my pee change colors."

"I'm sorry."

A heavily pregnant woman climbed out of the driver's seat of the minivan and stared at me.

"Hi. Are you Ross's mom?" I asked.

"Yes. And you are . . . ?" She looked me up and down, skeptical.

"I'm Lt. Anna Koray, with the Bayern County Sheriff's Office." I said it automatically, even though I knew I was nothing.

"Oh. I thought Mark had finally met someone," she said sheepishly. "I'm Yvette."

"Nice to meet you." I glanced at Ross. "Hey, is your dad home?"

"No. He left earlier today. He called my mom to take me to Pennsylvania with her." Ross made a face.

"Do you know where he went?"

"Nah. He just got in the car and took off."

Yvette looked at her son. "Why don't you go get your stuff together, and I'll talk to Lt. Koray?"

"Sure," he said sullenly, and went into the house.

Yvette looked at me. "Why are the police here? Dare I ask what he did?"

"I can't say for now. But I think you need to make plans for Ross."

Her jaw hardened. "This is a really bad time."

"I know. But he's been through a lot. He needs to see a doctor about those scratches he got from when he almost drowned."

She rested her hand on her belly. "I'll take care of it. It's just . . . it's just gonna be hard to have a fifth mouth to feed."

I nodded. "Ross needs you right now."

She looked down the road. "Sounds like it."

I'd seen this a thousand times before, with parents of both sexes. A family splits up, and they rush to mash a new one together, with his kids, her kids, and the kids they decided to have together.

"You might also consider having him stay with friends to finish high school," I offered.

"Maybe." She frowned. "That would look pretty shitty, though, wouldn't it?"

"Doesn't matter what things look like. What matters is what's best for the kid. I would advise setting up some therapy for him regardless."

"Mark really screwed the pooch this time, didn't he?"

"Yeah. Yeah, he did." He just wouldn't know how much, not until I got his neck under my thumbs.

Ross returned from the house with a duffel bag and a backpack. He locked the front door, like a responsible kid.

"You got all your stuff, kiddo?" Yvette asked.

He grunted an affirmative and came out to the van, shoulders slumped in defeat. Gibby gave him a kiss on the back of the hand.

"Come on," Yvette said. "Let's get on the road. We should be able to get home in time for dinner."

He chucked his things into the back of the van, then got in and stared sullenly out the window as I gave my card to Yvette. I surreptitiously slipped one of my cards into Ross's bag. My personal cell phone number was scrawled on the back of each.

"If Mark contacts you, can you call me?"

"Will do."

I watched as they pulled out onto the road and headed east, toward Pennsylvania.

I told myself this was the best thing. He'd be far away from Bayern County and its wrathful Rusalka.

But I still felt sad for him. His parents sucked. I could empathize, with his dad being a killer and his mom off creating a new family.

I sure hoped he would be okay.

I stood and waved like a cheerful little cop.

When they were out of sight, I approached the house. I reached under the doormat for the key Ross had left behind, and let myself inside.

I swept through the house, searching for any sign of Nick or Viv, and evidence of any crimes. The worst thing I saw was something green rotting in the fridge. I wasn't gentle. I tossed the place like a burglar. Didn't find anything.

I descended to the basement and surveyed the gas pipes.

Mark's tools were well organized in a pretty red chest. I pulled the sleeve of my blouse down over my hand and picked up a pipe wrench. I loosened the fittings around the furnace pipe until I smelled gas.

I stared at the water heater. It was new, and it didn't have a pilot light, just an electronic ignition. It would spark at some point soon.

Letting the basement fill with gas, I left the house. I locked the front door behind me, climbed in the SUV, and pulled out of the driveway.

I was going to send a message to Lister. I was going to burn everything he had down to the ground for fucking with me, hurting Monica, and taking Nick.

By the time I pulled out to the main road, the water heater

must have cycled on, because a tremendous boom echoed behind me then. I looked in my rearview mirror at the orange fireball in the sky. My lips peeled back in a snarl. Gibby grinned at me from the passenger seat, his tongue lolling from his lips.

"Happy Fourth of July, asshole."

29

THE WALK-IN

Deep in my bones, I knew where the Kings of Warsaw Creek had to be going eventually, after dark, where no one could see them.

The Hag Stone.

I drove down twisting two-lane roads as rain began to pepper the windshield. As I got closer to the park, the rain thickened, coming down in sheets.

I turned on the radio. I expected the fireworks to be canceled at least.

"... the National Weather Service in Wilmington has declared a flash flood emergency for Bayern County. Residents are advised to seek high ground and avoid driving through standing water. The Copperhead River is expected to crest at nine feet. Anyone attending any outdoor celebrations along the river is asked to evacuate ..."

"Well, at least that's something in our favor," I said to Gibby. "No one's going to be out to see any of this."

I crawled the car up the access road to the park. The road had been washed out by rain, and the car swam against the current. I finally made the decision to put it in the ditch. It didn't matter. Nobody was getting out of this.

Gibby's ears were sharply alert. "Stay close, buddy," I told him. I regretted bringing him. But Nick was his dad, and there was no leaving him behind.

I stepped out into about six inches of running water. That much was enough to knock a person off their feet if they weren't careful, especially in the gathering darkness.

I didn't turn on a light. I didn't need a light to see. Gibby jogged next to me, and we entered the rain-spangled darkness of that cursed place. Or maybe it was sacred somehow, since Dana had died here. It felt like both.

Mud sucked at my shoes as we moved, and the rain rattled from the sky through the trees. I pumped my shotgun slowly in time with a thunderclap, so no one would hear. We descended into the ravine.

There were tracks in the mud ahead of me, men's and a woman's, it looked like—at least four different tread patterns.

I crept slowly to the bottom of the ravine, rain making my clothes leaden. A flashlight gleamed ahead of me, casting shifting silhouettes on the rocky shore beneath the Hag Stone's profile. One man held a gun on another, while two figures were on their knees. Another was prone. I crouched behind a honeysuckle to get the lay of the land.

I squinted, trying to determine who was who. I was able to make out Nick. Blood was running down his temple, and his eye was swollen shut. He was kneeling on the ground, next to a prone female form that I assumed was Viv. She was covered in a black tarp or blanket. Maybe a black cloak.

Gibby strained forward, and I had to wind my fingers in his

collar to keep him from racing toward his dad. My heart thundered to see Nick still alive.

Around the figures was a circle of something black washing away. Could be black salt or soil, or maybe blood. Candles in glass jars guttered around them like dim stars, some flickering out.

Lister was kneeling outside of the circle. He was wearing a black robe with a hood, his hands raised. He was looking at the gunman, at Fred Jasper.

My heart swelled to see him alive. But not like this. Jasper aimed the gun at Jeff Sumner, who was two steps ahead of him, with his hands cuffed at his belly. I suspected Jasper had used Sumner to flush Lister out.

"You can't do this," Sumner was saying. "You can't."

"Why not? You did this to Dana," Jasper answered coolly. "You did this to Viv, too."

"But that was—"

"Different? No, no it wasn't."

I straightened up and approached them with the shotgun raised. "Fred, stop."

Jasper didn't flinch, just kept his gun aimed at Jeff. "You can't stop me, Koray. This needs to happen."

"That's not up to you or me to decide, Fred." Rain pounded down on my scalp.

Beside me, Gibby growled. I put my leg in front of him to discourage him from lunging. I wasn't sure who he'd go after.

"Are Nick and Viv . . . ?"

Jasper gestured for me to come closer, through curtains of rain. I slowly got in front of Nick. Gibby stood at his side.

"Are you okay?" I hissed at Nick.

"Couple of bruised ribs, but I'm okay," he wheezed. "I was next . . ."

"Can you walk?"

He climbed to his feet. His hands were bound behind his back with a zip tie. I reached into my pocket for a knife, opened it with my teeth, and cut the zip tie with my left hand. I kept the shotgun at my shoulder.

I turned to Jasper. "You don't want to hurt him, Fred. Nick's a doctor. He's a good man. He saves lives. He loves dogs and planting our garden. He collects baseball caps from minor league teams and reads Roman history . . ." I let myself babble. It was important that Jasper see him as a person.

"And . . . and I love him," I finished. "He's the best person I've ever known."

Jasper stared at me, his face unreadable.

Gibby whined. Beneath rolls of thunder, I thought I heard singing.

"He can go," Jasper said at last.

I muttered to Nick: "Take Gibby and go to the high ground, okay?"

"I'm not leaving you," he said stubbornly.

"I need you to get Gibby away. This water is too high for him . . . he could drown. I'll be along in a bit," I whispered, as convincingly as I could. Truth be told, I didn't want him to see what I was going to do next. Because it was going to be something my father would approve of.

"I can't leave you," he insisted.

"Nick, please."

He reached out and kissed me, his lips cold in the rain. Nick and Gibby slowly retreated up the trail.

I turned my attention back to the scene before me.

Just yards from where Dana had been killed, Viv lay on the bank. I could tell she wasn't breathing. She was curled in on herself, as if she occupied an invisible egg. Her throat was bruised. Her hands, tangled under her chin, were pierced by railroad spikes, and more spikes prickled from her feet. Blood trickled into the sandy soil. I was too late.

"What the hell did you do?" I turned on Lister, wrath boiling in my throat.

Lister looked up at me. He choked on his snot before answering. "Jeff and Quentin and I . . . when we were in high school . . . we killed a girl. It wasn't my idea, I swear! And now . . . again . . ."

"Tell me," I hissed.

"It was Dana Carson! It was Dana Carson!" he burbled.

"Why?" I demanded.

Snot bubbled in his nose, and it was like a dam broke when he started babbling. "When we were kids, we messed around with the occult. At first, it was just fucking around with a Ouija board in Jeff's parents' basement. Stupid shit. Lots of drinking."

"Go on."

"So . . . this one time, when Jeff's parents were away, we tried to do a ritual at the creek behind Jeff's house. We'd been reading about the Order of the Golden Dawn, and we tried some shit."

"What kind of shit?"

He grimaced. "We found some stuff in Jeff's basement—black candles, and shit written in old books. Jeff said he could channel spirits. It was . . . I guess it was good, creepy fun at first, but I think we summoned something. Something . . . Jeff called it the Forest King."

I stopped breathing. "What did it look like?"

"Like . . . like a shadow with antlers."

My grip on the shotgun trembled. This couldn't be. It couldn't be my father's Forest God, Veles, could it?

"I thought I was drinking too much. Fuck me, I definitely was."

Lister's words came out in a panicked rush, and I let them wash over me. "We were all sort of fucked up then, you know? Jeff's dad had declared bankruptcy. Quentin was moving away. My parents were divorcing. Our worlds were coming to an end. Maybe that's why we were willing to believe in crazy supernatural shit, and that if we made an offering . . . so the Forest King would do our bidding."

"So you . . . sacrificed Dana?" My voice sounded remote, hollow.

"Shut up, Mark!" Sumner shouted, and Jasper kicked Sumner in the back of the knee, knocking him to the dirt.

Lister babbled. "Jeff . . . Jeff said we could make a sacrifice, and everything would turn out all right. We found Dana Carson on the Fourth of July. She was by herself, and we didn't think that anybody would . . . would miss her. Especially not twenty-five years later."

"She was a person. She mattered." I kicked him in the ribs. He grimaced and clutched his side. "How did you do it?"

He wheezed. "*Urk* . . . Jeff . . . he drugged her with a chemical, and we took her to his house. We did a ritual then. We needed blood . . . We drew blood from her hands and feet with railroad spikes. Quentin read from one of the books while Jeff choked her. We thought she was dead. Jeff said we should burn her body—deep in the woods, so the King of the Forest would see.

"We put her in Quentin's car, took her to the river. We drove past the fireworks, to here. This place was magic."

I stood over Lister, listening. In the distance, thunder rolled. Water had pushed the candles in jars away, and they floated into the swelling river.

"But Dana woke up when we took her out of the trunk, and we freaked the fuck out. She was half-awake, crying, wheezing . . . Jeff's dad . . . he kept some chemicals in the basement, and we took those. Jeff dumped her in the grass on that island in the river. He told me to throw the chemical on her. And he told me to set her on fire.

"I did it. I fucking did it. I threw a match on her. It was . . . horrific. She went up in a blue flash, screaming, and then lay down in the grass. When the fire burned out, I knew she was dead.

"I didn't tell a soul. But I told Jeff and Quentin I wanted no part of any of this shit again."

I exhaled. "Then what happened?"

"Things got better. Jeff's dad's company got a last-minute investor. Quentin didn't get sent to boarding school, and my parents didn't get a divorce. We had all of those things. Everything we ever wanted, and more.

"I thought this all was in the past, but weird shit started happening. We sort of figured out that Viv had cursed us, that she'd summoned something, just like we had years before. But whatever's here . . . it wants more blood. It wants our blood."

"I'm stopping the curse!" Sumner shouted. "Giving the Forest King another was the only way!"

"According to who?" I shouted.

"The spirits. I hear them . . ." He looked up into the trees, his eyes rolling white. Jesus, he was hearing voices. "The spirits are all around us. He's here, now . . . watching."

I didn't turn around. I did not want to see if the Forest God was here, haunting this place. I thought he was gone. I thought . . .

"You're going to pay for what you've done." Jasper's voice was cold and even.

Sumner turned his manic glare on me. "Shoot him. I'll give you whatever you want . . . money, power . . . I can make it happen. You and your boyfriend can go free. I swear."

"You've been helping out the meth heads with some Vapozene,

to cook up some meth? Using them to do your dirty work? They took Viv. And dumped some more chemicals in the river."

"The costs of industrial-waste disposal are fucking astronomical. I'm operating on the edge of bankruptcy. I had to cut costs somewhere."

"You fucker." Rain dripped down my chin. "And Viv cursed you. She thought she raised the Rusalka."

"Viv cursed us all. She woke something up. The only way to kill the curse was to give another offering." He was batshit mad, crazier than Viv. Maybe even crazier than me.

"And Nick?"

"Finding your boyfriend was an accident. We wanted to give you to the Forest King. But, y'know . . . the more the merrier."

"The spirits told you this?" I demanded.

"This place is full of them." Sumner laughed, spreading his arms out. "They're fucking everywhere. Can't you feel it? All that power . . ."

"I'm gonna kill you. All of you." Jasper said it without inflection, cold as a fish.

I turned on Jasper. "That guy's a babbling idiot, but you . . . did you kill those people?"

Rain swept down in sheets, and Jasper had to shout to be heard above it. "Go home, Koray."

"Fred, did you kill those people?" Rain hammered my scalp and arms.

He refused to answer me. "Koray, you're a good cop. You don't need to be a part of this."

"I can't let you do this, Fred." I said it listlessly, though. I was supposed to say it, right?

"I'm supposed to be dead," he said quietly. "We can all disappear into the night."

These fuckers deserved it, didn't they? I looked down at the water washing over Viv. They'd almost killed Nick. They killed the Carson sisters. They were complicit in the abuse of those girls. Nick's career and mine were dead; I wasn't a good cop anymore.

Jasper gestured to the water. "Sumner, Lister. Both of you, into the river."

He marched them into the water. Sumner was cackling, and Lister made a grab for Jasper's gun. But Jasper shot him in the arm, and he howled.

"Get in the water," Jasper said.

I turned my gun on Jasper. "Fred, stop it." But I only whispered. I don't think he heard me.

The Kings of Warsaw Creek were knee-deep in water.

That song—the song of thunder rolled over me, through me. I let go of my thin protestations. *Fuck that*. Fuck what I was supposed to be doing, all the rules I was required to follow. I wasn't a cop anymore. That authority had been stripped from me. I came to this place, this haunted, sacred place, not as a cop. Not as Nick's fiancée. Not as my father's daughter. But as myself, something dark and terrible, and powerful beyond all the identities given to me by men.

I was. Alone . . . I *was*.

Water swirled around my knees, and the Rusalka whispered in my ear, "Give in."

"What are you?" I asked.

"I have always been here. I wore Dana's skin for a time. I would wear yours if you'd let me."

She whispered to me of the forest, of this land I belonged to. I was what I had always known, deep in my dark dreams in the middle of the night, when my breath caught in my throat. I was an elemental power of my own, and I decided what I would do. I was beyond the judgment of these men.

But they were not beyond my judgment.

I cast the shotgun into the water. I had no need of it. There was nothing stopping what was coming next, a wall of floodwater, full of debris, bearing down on us. Roaring water swept down over the island, obliterating Dana's grave.

I inhaled, and the Rusalka stepped into my skin as easily as if she stepped into a dress. Water washed around my waist and swallowed the men before me. I was buoyant, not touching the earth. I splayed my hands in the current, approaching the men. The floodwater caught me, roaring, pulling me down and under.

A gunshot rang out in the water. Someone screamed.

I laughed, with Rusalka's voice.

I was suspended in the maelstrom. It was silent here, beneath the water's surface; I could hear only my own heartbeat. Sliding around in the current like an eel, I dodged the branches of an uprooted tree. There was no fighting it; there was only surrendering to the black water sweeping down. At that moment, it was a greater force than all of us.

I was not afraid. Rusalka had made me almost boneless, twisting my body in the current, around tree branches, past the debris of a wrecked boat. Rocks scraped my cheek. My fingers curled into claws slashing into the dark, where the water was unexpectedly warm. I was a passenger in this, her element.

Sumner was clinging to a piece of flotsam. He saw me.

Face twisted in rage, he lifted a gun in his cuffed hands. Dimly, I realized he must have taken Jasper's gun from him.

He fired.

I reached out to embrace him. I dragged him down, down into

the depths, feeling his pulse under my fingers wrapped around his neck. I thrilled in feeling his muted scream, the vibration of bubbles, the thumping of blood in his throat. I thrilled in feeling him still as water flooded into his lungs, making him heavy as stone.

———

A green flash washed over me. I remembered my mom and me, coming up against that polluter in the forest all those years ago.

I stared at the interloper. He was in his twenties, thin and stringy, his hands blackened with grease. My mom stood before him with a handgun, and his fingers twitched as he lifted them.

"What should we do with him?" Mom asked me. "Should we let him go?"

I looked at the oil slick staining the ground. A little milk snake slithered out of the puddle, gasping.

That infuriated me. I plucked the snake from puddle and tried to clean it off with my shirt.

"No." I said it with the haughty authority of royalty passing sentence upon a peasant. I was queen of these woods, after all. "He deserves to die."

Mom peeled her lips back and smiled at that man.

She gestured toward the chemicals with the muzzle of the gun. "Drink it," she ordered.

He blinked. "Are you crazy? I can't drink that."

She pulled the hammer back with an ominous click. "Drink. It."

He shook his head. His weight rocked back and forth, from his heels to the balls of his feet, as if he was thinking about rushing my mom.

The gun's muzzle flashed white, and I jumped at the clap of thunder. The man cowered on the ground before my mom.

"No more warning shots," she said. "Drink up."

The man crawled toward a barrel, pouring sweet-smelling liquid into the ground. He cupped his hands to capture the poison and took a drink. He gagged.

"Drink," my mom ordered. "Drink it all."

He didn't even come close. He drank until he retched, vomiting it up, and then Mom made him drink more poison. He begged her to let him go, but she was unmoved. She made him drink until he passed out.

I watched, fascinated. I knew what she was doing was right; my dad wouldn't have permitted anyone to defile his beloved forest. But I was fascinated by my own power, that I could visit this punishment upon this vile person. I felt a bone-deep sense of satisfaction in that.

When the man had passed out, my mom dragged him to the river and shoved him in. Face down, he floated down the river.

In the distance, the Hag Stone looked on, her profile sharp against the sky.

"She likes blood," Mom said, as she'd said when I'd sat with my bleeding feet in the sand.

The Hag watched silently as the man's body floated to her, for her to devour.

I was my mother's daughter.

———

I floated for a time, in the black between Rusalka and myself, in the water's roar.

Eventually, she let me go. I had a sense of being pulled to shore, of the murmuring of women.

I felt solid ground on my back. Consciousness was fuzzy, and I knew I had to get help. Water shimmered before me, looking a lot like the fluorescence of pollution under a UV light. In the distance, I saw burning. The river . . . the river was on fire. I could see the red and feel the heat from here.

"Hold still," a voice said.

Tree branches swayed above me. I was being carried to higher ground by many sets of hands. I had the same feeling I'd had when I played Light as a Feather, Stiff as a Board at a slumber party as a kid, unsteady and weightless at the same time.

"Stay still," a female voice said. "You've got a head injury."

I reached behind my head, and my fingertips came away with hot blood. "How did you find me?"

"We heard the singing."

That sounded like an entirely reasonable response.

"I'm so sorry about Viv. I was too late." I turned my head to look upstream. "She was at the oxbow . . . with the men."

"The island's gone. All of it," another female voice said.

"Jasper? He was here. Sumner and Lister, too . . ."

"They're all gone."

I squinted at the river. The roaring power I'd felt in my head and my lungs was gone. I stared down at my hands, pale and ordinary and bloody. "So is Rusalka."

I sank into darkness.

30

PAWNS AND KINGS

Bits and pieces of consciousness slipped in and out of my grasp. I felt Gibby's fur winding in my hands, saw Nick's face above mine. I heard sirens and saw the nausea-inducing flash of lights. I had to close my eyes to that brightness.

At some point, Nick and I were separated. I floated in a white room where I was urged to stay awake. It took a long time for my head to clear, and I asked for Nick.

He came to my bedside, looking very hungover. He held my hand. "They said you've got a bad concussion. But they'll release you to me."

"Is Gibby okay?"

"He's fine."

"How are you?" I asked, pushing hair from his eyes.

"I'm okay," he said. "Just bumps and bruises."

"What about Monica?" I asked quietly. I held my breath.

"They flew her to the university hospital for vascular surgery. She survived surgery. She's going to live."

I didn't ask for details. Not now. For now, it was enough for me to know that Monica was going to live.

A worry mark creased his brow. "What happened there, at the Hag Stone, after we left?"

"I went for a swim," I said. My body was covered with a plethora of scratches and bruises. I had a concussion—debris must have struck me in the head at some point. My head ached in time with my pulse. I wanted to believe that the feeling of being one with the Rusalka had been just that—a head injury.

But I wasn't sure.

Nick exhaled. He didn't ask further questions. Maybe he didn't want to know.

No cops came after me at the hospital, and they weren't waiting for us in the parking lot. Nick, Gibby, and I went home after spending the night in the hospital's blinding fluorescent light. Nick turned on the news, which was showing footage from the worst flood in the county in a hundred years. Copperhead Valley Solvents had flooded, and the Copperhead River was burning in lurid red flames. The National Guard had been called out. Dozens of houses had been destroyed, and more than twenty people were missing. Curiously, the Greenwood Kingdom Church caught fire before being plunged into floodwater. The newscasters speculated about whether the fire was caused by lightning or purposefully set.

I fell into bed and slept immediately.

I dreamed of the riverside, of bodies bobbing in the water. And I saw Jasper wading into deep water toward Dana. She opened her arms to him, and they disappeared beneath the black water.

An iridescent blue glaze of pollution gathered on the water's surface, but I knew it couldn't touch them in the blackness below the waves.

———

I awoke in my own bed, feeling unusually at peace. Gibby lay across my stomach. He was awake, his doggie eyebrows twitching with worry.

"You're such a good boy," I told him, patting his side. "Thank you."

I got dressed slowly. I stared at my calf. It didn't hurt like it did before—there was a different kind of pain. This felt like a surface, clean pain, not a bone-deep throbbing hurt. I peeled the bandage back and looked at the wound. It was red, not green. Maybe the antibiotics had finally kicked in. Or maybe the Rusalka was satisfied.

Maybe.

I didn't know if Viv and the girls had summoned a spirit that took Dana's face, or if Viv had practiced some kind of necromancy that brought Dana herself back for revenge. With Viv gone, I would probably never know if Rusalka had always been there, expressing her power through various women. And what about Viv? Would she take on the role of Rusalka now?

I had felt Rusalka. I felt her, and I felt me, and I felt the intersection of us. We were both killers. I had to admit, at last, that I was one. When I looked at the awards on my mantel, it was like looking at an alternate reality. While Rusalka hadn't stayed, she'd awakened something in me that I hadn't felt for a long time, not since I was a little girl running through the woods.

Freedom.

I went out to the front porch. The fox was there, in the midst of the ruined garden. I offered her a piece of bacon. She smiled at me, took it gently, gulped it down, and slipped off into the woods.

Nick had made breakfast: scrambled eggs, bacon, and waffles. We ate in silence, until I broke it.

"I want to see Monica," I said, though I knew I wouldn't be allowed to drive.

"I'll take you," Nick assured me. "My friend at the hospital in the city says she's awake, off and on."

I nodded, crumbling my bacon in my fingers. "There's a distinct possibility that I'm going to get criminally charged with some serious shit." I promised him long ago that I wouldn't lie to him. I meant it.

Nick drank his orange juice. "I figured. If you go to prison, I'll wait for you."

"Seriously?"

"Or, I dunno. We could just run away." He shrugged. "You have experience in creating new identities."

"I don't want you to fuck up your life for me."

"My life's already plenty fucked up, thank you very much. But I'd prefer that it were fucked up with you."

"Even if we have to go long-distance, with me in a prison cell?" I was only half kidding.

"Even if." He leaned forward and kissed my temple. "You're stuck with me, babe."

"Will you take care of the dog?"

"Of course. Don't be ridiculous. He's our child. And I'll get the best lawyers money can buy. I swear."

It was a lighthearted conversation, but we both knew what was at stake. His profession was still on the line. Mine was toast. If we could avoid criminal charges and getting sued, maybe we could still have something.

"Seriously, I don't want to go to prison," I told him slowly.

He reached across the table to hold my hand. "I know."

I saw complete devotion in his face. And not just because I'd saved his life. Maybe, though, saving his life was an evening of the scales. My father had taken his mother's life away from him, and I restored something for him. I wanted to set him free, so he could have something of a life of his own.

But I wanted him. And I would rather run. I took a deep breath. "What if—"

A knock sounded at the door, and my heart lurched into my throat.

"Do you want me to answer that?" he asked.

I paused. My eyes darted to the front door, then to the back door. I could run into the forest, run and not be found. My bare toes flexed on the linoleum.

If I ran like the fox, though . . . I wasn't sure Nick would be able to follow. His hand still held mine fast on the table. But I could shrug it off and run . . .

I looked into his eyes. "Okay."

Nick opened the door, and I saw Chief standing on the porch. Nick looked to me.

"Come in," I said. "How's Monica?"

"Hanging in there. I just came back from the hospital."

The three of us sat down at the kitchen table.

Chief cleared his throat. "I need to talk to you."

"Do I need a lawyer?"

"Hear me out." He put his hands on the scarred table. "There have been some changes in the sheriff's office."

"Oh?"

"Sheriff Wilson was found to be in contact with Jeff Sumner and his buddies, to aid and abet felony crimes. I charged him with conspiracy to commit murder. Judge Chamberlain signed his arrest warrant."

I sat back in my chair. "Whoa."

"Evidence shows the sheriff had ongoing communication with

Jeff Sumner and his cronies about privileged information regarding your investigation. Our shiny new radio system records everything, and Sheriff got used to using private Bluetooth to talk to his friends. Those records show he knew about Viv Carson's abduction, and I'm betting he knew more than that. I suspect he was fully aware of the extent of the chemical leaks in the river, and was exerting pressure to prevent Sumner's prosecution."

"But why?" I asked. "Why would Sheriff Wilson help the Kings of Warsaw Creek?"

"Campaign donations, I'm guessing. An audit has suggested these guys and their businesses and the church gave huge amounts of money to his campaign, in excess of campaign finance laws. And the trail of that money seems to end in meth manufacture and distribution. But that's going to be a matter for the state AG to unravel."

"How long have you been . . . investigating him?" This was not the sort of case that erupted overnight.

"A while. He just chose to trip himself up a lot faster than I expected. I figured I had at least until the election in November, but . . ." He spread his hands.

Damn. I had new respect for my boss. I couldn't imagine the sheriff taking this coup lying down. "Aren't you worried he'll amass a network and get even?"

Chief hesitated. "Well, the sheriff was found dead this morning."

"What?"

"He was at a Fourth of July party, hanging out on his boat in the river. The boat ran aground in the storm and capsized. He was found drowned not far from the boat. Everyone else seems okay."

"Oh my God." I rubbed my forehead. Rusalka. She cleaned house before she came to the showdown at the Hag Stone. *Fuck.*

"What this means for you is that I, as acting sheriff, want you to return to work on Monday. There's a lot of paperwork to be filed."

"I . . . but I figured . . ."

He winked. "I'm sheriff. Don't defy my authority."

He left, and I sat, stunned, at the kitchen table for nearly an hour. So much that I was unaware of had happened behind the scenes.

I wondered what would happen when they learned what had happened to Sumner and Lister, when they found their bodies. Because they would. And someone might come looking for me.

Nick quietly cleared the dishes, kissed me on the forehead, and left me to brood.

Fuck. There were so many machinations going on around me. Maybe I should've felt used, but . . . I didn't. Somehow, it seemed like the good guys won this time.

Somehow, but not really.

———

I waited in Monica's hospital room for her to wake up that afternoon. She was in and out of consciousness, occasionally mumbling verses from "The Wreck of the *Edmund Fitzgerald*."

She'd been able to keep her leg, but it was in a ring brace contraption, with screws drilled into it from many different angles. It would be a long time before she walked again, if she ever did.

I noticed something as I watched over her during those days in the hospital. She had a small tattoo on her left shoulder, a tattoo of a snake devouring its own tail.

I did not ask her about it.

After trips to the hospital, I limped out to the creek, listening for music. I didn't hear any, though I went back to the creek every day after that until the end of summer. I listened, and I scanned the creek with a UV light. A dim glow in the water gradually dwindled, and I saw nothing after a few weeks.

There were no drownings in the time after the flood. None.

Jasper's body was never discovered. Neither was Viv's. It was as if the river swallowed them whole. The highway patrol investigated Jasper's van accident and determined that the van had been run off the road, at approximately sixty-five miles an hour, by a vehicle with a very specific tire tread pattern. A vehicle with such a tread pattern, a damaged SUV, was found at Lister's dealership. The remains of Jasper's van bore Vapozene residue.

Lister and Sumner were found, dead, in the trees at Sandpiper Run when the river finally receded. Their bodies were heavily damaged, and the coroner ruled their causes of death to be accidental drownings.

Viv and Dana's mother passed away peacefully at the mental institution on the night of July fourth. A river pearl was found clutched in her fist.

Some of the river pearls recovered during the investigations were found to have Dana's prints on them. It was speculated that those pearls had been originally gathered by Dana, kept by Jasper, and then planted at the crime scenes. But Forensics wasn't convinced that Dana's prints could have persisted so long on the pearls, and the pearls remained a mystery in an evidence locker.

Still, Jasper was assumed to be at the root of the drownings. A collection of knives was found with his scuba gear in the trunk of his car. They tested positive for the blood of the Lister cousins.

I had a hard time believing Jasper had killed those people. Jasper had seemed so even, placid. Maybe he felt he couldn't get at the Kings any other way. It didn't explain Sims's death, and I found no trace of Jasper in the Sumners' pond, either. But that didn't mean he hadn't hung out at the bottom of it, waiting for his chance. He had tanks and a rebreather, which would've given him hours of air. His trailer was less than a mile from the Sumner house, and he could have traversed the wetlands to get there. No one knew of his whereabouts when Sumner's uncle died, either. Maybe he'd stalked these people, watched them for years, and his patience finally ran out.

Since Sumner's wife's testimony was part of the official record, people assumed Fred Jasper had sought revenge on the Kings of Warsaw Creek for Dana's death. He'd snapped on the twenty-fifth anniversary, abducted Sumner, and then lured Lister into the water, where he murdered them both. This assumption was backed up by records of a call made from Sumner's cell phone to Lister that night.

An all-points bulletin had been put out for Jasper and Viv. It was assumed that Jasper escaped. Viv must have run off with Jasper in some weird romantic trauma bond.

———

Nick and I were discussing our future, slowly, the shape it might take.

"We have time," he'd said.

I found him working in the garden one morning, trying to fix it with new plants. His mother's memorial had been swept clean and decorated with chrysanthemums. I had slipped his ring on and come to dig with him in the dirt. He took my dirty hand and kissed it.

"We have time," I said. "Do you want to spend it with me?"

"Always."

I offered him a platinum ring, and he let me put it on his finger.

And we did have time. I faced no charges as a result of my actions. I filed a very watered-down and redacted report of my actions in investigating Dana's death, and it stood.

My immediate boss, acting chief of the Detective Bureau Monica Wozniak, approved it without comment. She remained on bed rest for weeks after receiving her injuries, but then she had come to work, on crutches. She was thinner and paler, but rage spots burned in her cheeks. And I knew she was back.

One might think the families of the deceased would file suit against the sheriff's office. But the evidence from Sumner's house and Sims's car was too much for them to overcome—the Kings of Warsaw Creek had killed Dana. The law firm of Cortland, Cortland, and Cortland was silent when it was explained that the assets of criminals could be seized for victim restitution.

Copperhead Valley Solvents had experienced a catastrophic flood as well as the church. The flood damaged the containment facilities and caused a total shutdown of the plant, as well as an uncontrolled release of Vapozene, which caught fire on a segment of the river. EPA had become involved in the cleanup, and they found evidence of a history of dumping. The plant was shuttered. Some locals bemoaned the loss of jobs, while others were relieved that the company's pollution would cease. EPA was putting together a plan to mitigate environmental damage and research the effects of the pollutants on people, animals, and plants in the area. There was particular concern that exposure could cause acute leukemia in some individuals—the same kind of illness Viv might've had. I worried about exposure for Nick, Gibby, and myself, but there was nothing to do about that but to be watchful and wait.

Nick returned to the hospital from administrative leave, with the investigation dropped. Turned out that his supervisor, Dr. Floyd, who was leading the charge for his dismissal, had been on the boat with the sheriff on the Fourth of July. Dr. Floyd suddenly left town for Arizona, declaring that he wanted nothing to do with rivers ever again.

I wanted to forget much of what happened the night of the flood. Lister's house burning down was considered a freak accident, but I wasn't entirely certain that someone in Chief's network wasn't covering for me. I had to admit that the cops and fire department had their hands full from that night, and there weren't enough resources to offer much scrutiny. Still . . .

Rod Matthews rolled over on his brother and the rest of the meth heads. They fessed up to doing Sumner's bidding. Rod ducked charges and moved to Florida to start a used-car lot.

The church had been destroyed, and with the head of it cut off, it withered and died. The families who attended the church dispersed to other churches, or surrendered their faith entirely. At a local park one summer afternoon, I saw Leah, wearing shorts and a tank top, in the company of other girls and boys. None of them wore rings. Leah's foster parents were seeking adoption.

I wondered about the girls. I wondered if they had something to do with the church's burning down. I didn't ask them if they did. I just kept quiet and observed from afar.

Sometimes I missed what I'd felt when the Rusalka stepped inside me. I'd felt her unfettered rage, her forcefulness, her power. I wondered if that was what it felt like to be my father. I wondered if I'd ever feel that way again, if I could return to it if I wanted to. Or maybe I wanted that part of myself to sleep.

Drema and Mason moved away, to Illinois, to be with her parents. Mason made a full recovery and asserted that he had no further memories of his near drowning, which was probably for the best. He'd regained his voice, and was reportedly silent only when he slept now. I checked up on Drema on social media and found her photography being shown in a gallery. Her work was fascinating: black-and-white photos of nude women posed like ancient works of art. Her Venus, climbing out of a seashell, was a woman with head lifted, staring down onlookers on the shore. A trio of women linked arms to represent Hecate, the three-faced goddess of witchcraft, gazing out into the night. And another woman gave the impression of the famous Minoan snake goddess, bare breasted and holding a snake in each hand.

Was Drema a witch? Was Monica? How many of the church girls were involved with witchcraft?

I didn't know. I just knew that someone pulled me out of the river, out of Rusalka's embrace. I wished I could thank them, whoever they were.

My heart ached for Ross, now fatherless. And hell, I'd burned down his house. He called me once, to tell me he was coming back to Bayern County to stay with friends while finishing out his senior year. I was glad to hear from him, but guilt washed over me when I heard his voice. I could've saved his father. I could've changed the direction of Ross's entire life.

Maybe that was the difference between me as an adult and me as a child. My child self felt no guilt for directing the polluter's death. But I felt guilt for it now.

The idea that I was responsible for the death of a man when I was a little girl bothered me. I wanted to leave it alone, to believe it was a hallucination, or maybe some memory of the Rusalka that had gotten tangled with mine.

Maybe that was what differentiated me from both my father and my mother: the guilt.

The coroner's office determined that the bones found with Dana's on the oxbow island belonged to a male subject, likely in his early twenties. The body had been heavily predated, and the set of bones was incomplete. Cause of death was unknown. Anthropologists at the local university had attempted to do a reconstruction based on the skull measurements.

I looked at the resulting clay face. It was thin lipped and angular, like the man I remembered.

I couldn't look away.

Deep in my soul, I knew I was responsible for his death.

I'd been a killer since the beginning.

I told Nick. I told Nick about that killing and about the Rusalka. Maybe I told him because I wanted to drive him away, because I felt the need to be punished. He just listened, holding my hand.

"You had a head injury," he said quietly, and I couldn't refute that. It was certainly more plausible than believing I had become a supernatural creature.

"But I remember that man in the woods, the one I ordered my mom to kill." My voice was low, fragile.

"You were a child," he said. "You couldn't have known your mom would do that."

"But I'm responsible."

"No. You're not."

I disagreed. But we tended to come at things from opposing angles. He did everything he could to preserve life. I was . . . not like that. I was something different. And I still wasn't sure what I'd become.

―――

The last green flash washed over my mind's eye in the last week of summer, when the sun had turned south again and the days were beginning to shorten perceptibly. The water drizzling from our taps was cool and clean once more, smelling of nothing.

My dad returned without warning. Mom and I came in from hanging laundry, to find him sitting on the couch in the living room, unmoving.

"Dad!"

I flung myself at him, overjoyed. He smelled like wood smoke and flowers. I didn't ask where he'd been. I was just glad he was back.

"How's my favorite daughter?" He chuckled, ruffling my hair.

Mom slipped away from the room, as if she'd never been there. And I felt that absence, that hole. She retreated into herself once more, becoming cold and silent as a stone.

In the days that came, I told Dad about the poison. In my desire to impress him, I even told him what had become of the polluter, what I had done. Pride beamed on his face.

"You mustn't tell anyone," he told me, resting his hand on my shoulder.

"Why not?" My brow wrinkled.

He crouched before me in the kitchen. "Because you must not ever say anything that gets our family into trouble, all right? What happens in the family stays in the family."

I agreed.

I glanced up at the kitchen witch figurine that hung over the sink. It had been there ever since I could remember. The witch's beady black glass eyes followed me, always watching me, no matter where I stood in the room.

My mom had slipped away, though. She'd become distant with the return of my dad. It was as if Dad and she were part of a binary star system; only one could approach at a time.

I missed her. I felt that I was not only my father's daughter, but also hers.

———

I drove down to my mother's house and left a note in her mailbox.

I didn't know if she'd meet me. I didn't know what I expected.

I couldn't confront my father. I had to be at peace with that. I had to know that all my love for him could never have changed him, could never have brought him to the light. I could never have stopped his killing. I could never know what he thought about all of those deaths. He was dead, and there was no coming back from that.

But I could confront my mother.

She was dangerous, so I took my sidearm with me, hidden under my jacket. She had a lot to lose by talking to me. She could lose everything—the life and family she'd built.

And so could I.

I waited at the Hag Stone at dusk, staring at the spot in the river where there had once been an island, now drowned and swept away down the river. There were only a few snags of cedar stumps there now. The geese had fled, and the place was barren.

I heard footsteps approaching. My mother was not like my father; she couldn't move soundlessly in the woods. I thought about ambushing her here, hunting her. But I didn't. I just waited.

She picked her way through the leaf debris to stand beside me. She was much older than in my dreams, but her posture was still straight. She folded her arms in front of her and stared out at the river with me.

"What did you want?" she asked curtly.

I swallowed. "I remembered some things about my past."

Her eye twitched. "What things?"

My heart hammered, but I forced myself to spit it out. "I remembered that summer when the water was poisoned. When you and I . . . when we were together. It was like we were mother and daughter."

She nodded, her fingers tight as talons on her elbows. "I remember."

"What changed?" I asked. "Why were we so far apart?"

Her shoulder hitched. "Your father and I . . . we were at war. I tried to keep it from you, at first. I saw how you were becoming his daughter, in all ways. He called you his heir, the heir to his forest." She shook her head.

"But . . . the first time . . . when a man died, I was with you."

She stared out, over the water, at the island that didn't exist anymore. "Are you going to arrest me?"

I wasn't sure. I just knew that guilt lay cold beneath my ribs. "His name was Darrell Castner. He was a maintenance man at Copperhead Valley Solvents."

Her mouth hardened. "It doesn't matter. He killed my child. Your sister."

I exhaled. "Why take me along for that?"

"Because . . . I wanted you to be able to defend yourself. And I wanted you to know who you really were."

"Who am I?"

"You're your father's daughter. And you're also my daughter." She looked at me for the first time then, and her eyes glittered like flint.

"But why take that away from me? Why have my memory taken away?" My voice quavered. This was the question I'd always wanted to ask her.

I realized I was looking down at her. At some point, she'd shrunk and become a couple inches smaller than me, and that startled me. "Because I wanted you to be who you wanted to be, independent of the both of us."

She turned and began to walk away, calling over her shoulder, "Don't waste that life, Elena."

I let her go, standing there until it got dark and the fireflies rose. Arresting her would expose both of us, and I had no desire to do that. Justice mattered, maybe. But maybe I should just let the dead lie. Not be like Fred Jasper, who lived only a twilight life, in search of justice.

I wasn't sure who I was: the hunter's daughter or the witch's daughter or someone else entirely.

But, freed from both their shadows, I had the freedom to find out.

———

The wound on my calf faded afterward, turning the normal color of a bruise before finally receding to a white, frost-shaped pattern that looked a bit like lightning. I was glad the Rusalka's touch had faded, but I was disturbed to have a permanent reminder of her on my body. I guess it was a reminder that she'd worn my skin, and I shouldn't forget.

I sat in the garden, feeling the ground solid below me as I harvested tomatoes and peppers and pulled weeds from the soil. The woods teemed around me. Fish had even begun to cluster prolifically in the creek, and I had hope that the river would recover from Sumner's pollution.

Sometimes I felt eyes on me in the woods. Sometimes I'd glimpse an antler, and my heart would clot in my throat. Sometimes the eyes were those of a stag, moving serenely on deer trails. Other times they were Sinoe's, spying on me through the Virginia creeper. She'd approach when I offered her food, and she'd take it delicately from my hand, but always refuse to come inside. Still, she enjoyed sleeping on my porch.

I wondered at the influence of the forest on the Kings of Warsaw Creek. They dabbled in the occult as teens . . . but had they managed to connect with my father's Forest God? Where did they get the idea that they could force him to do their bidding? And was what Sumner said about the place being full of spirits true?

I didn't know enough about magic to say. All I knew about the supernatural was what I felt, what I saw in dreams and in reflective surfaces, like Viv's scrying mirror. None of it seemed real in daylight.

My parents had shown me the terrifying magic of this place. I wondered about my connection to it. Was it because I was their daughter, and I shared their delusions? Or did I have a spiritual connection to the supernatural? I had so longed to separate myself from my father, to hide from his influence, to cast off everything that he'd given me as a gift of evil.

My mother taught me to kill. Maybe she was evil, too. Where my father's killings had been cold, distantly calculated, my mother had killed in rage, for her loss. I listened to the water, as she showed me how to do, and felt that ages-old desire for revenge. Maybe she was a witch in her own way, and I had inherited that sense from her.

But maybe some of what my parents showed me just *was*. Maybe we heard things nobody else could hear. But maybe there were others who could hear those things, too.

Maybe we all were under the thrall of Bayern County's spell. Maybe we were trapped here, in our way, never able to leave, never able to escape our pasts or the sins of our fathers.

I exhaled and stared at the ring on my finger.

Maybe I could leave it behind.

Maybe I could be who I needed to be at the moment, and right now, I needed to be Anna, the person who loved and was loved in spite of darkness.

ACKNOWLEDGMENTS

Thank you to Jen Monroe and Candice Coote for all your editorial awesomeness in bringing Anna's story to life. A book has a story of its own between the idea and the execution, and I was so glad to have you with me in the process. Thank you for bringing this story to readers!

Thanks to Caitlin Blasdell for all your support. I'm so grateful for your help and insight. I'm incredibly lucky to have you in my corner.

Thank you to Roxanne Rhoads of Bewitching Book Tours and Chris Bick of Pioneer Agency for all your wonderful promotion help.

Thank you to my writer pals—Marcella, Mikki, and Michelle. May all our projects grow wings!

Much appreciation to the Gang—Cathy, Mike, and Connor. I swear I'll get around to putting together that fondue party any weekend now.

And many thanks always to my dear Jason, who is always my first reader.